OLIVER

-------------- AND THE --------------

MISSING SCIENTIST

BEV CARR

NEXTFRIDAY

OLIVER & THE MISSING SCIENTIST, A NEXTFRIDAY
PUBICATION, IN PARTNERSHIP WITH LULU PRESS.

A few words of thanks for all of the help, encouragement and motivation I have received whilst writing this book.

Andy, my husband, who has encouraged me to share my stories with you and for always reminding me how important it is to follow my dreams.

My boys, Oliver, Henry & Edward; the motivation behind every single word that I write.

Keep up-to date

www.oliverandthemissingscientist.co.uk

Coming Soon

The Audio book is now in progress.

We hope to have this available on Audible soon.

Missing

Uncle Will's Ford Fiesta bumped up and down on the lane as it approached April Cottage. Oliver scanned the grounds, searching for his mum and dad.

April Cottage was his family home; a converted farmhouse on the side of a mountain commanding magnificent views of the Welsh valleys. From the outside it looked like any other cottage, but in reality it was far more than a little house on a mountain.

In fact, it concealed the entrance to a labyrinth.

The rain was pouring and it was getting late. The house looked gloomy and empty, mirroring Oliver's feelings perfectly.

Today was not meant to have happened like this. Oliver had been planning it in his mind for months. Only a few hours ago he had been sat in his classroom, looking out of the window and dreaming of his escape. Not only was today the end of term, it was also his last day at primary school. He enjoyed school, but after seven years there he was ready for his next adventure.

Right now, he should have been in the back of his dad's car, singing "Summer Holiday", just like every other last day of term. However, instead of his mum and dad showing up to whisk him away, he was now with his Uncle Will, wondering where his parents were.

At the end of school, every last one of his school friends had departed but Oliver was left sitting on the wall, waiting. To make matters worse, Mrs Jones, his now ex-head teacher, had found him and insisted he return inside while she made enquiries.

Eventually, Mrs Jones had asked Oliver's uncle to come and collect him. On their way from the school, they had picked up Oliver's little brother Henry from nursery and left him playing happily with Will's wife, Karen.

Now, as they drove nearer home, it was clear that nobody was at the cottage.

It was timeless. From the outside nothing had changed a great deal in a century; its grey stone walls, its heavy roof that bowed in the middle from the weight of the slates, and the enormous chimneys on either side that always smoked – only there was no smoke today. The garage doors were left open, as they usually were. His mum's car was parked on the drive and his dad's Land Rover was backed in, as it always was.

As Uncle Will's car drew nearer, Oliver could tell that the Land Rover was empty.

"They're not packed," said Oliver to his uncle, knowing well that if they had been ready to go on holiday for the summer, his dad's car would have been bursting with luggage.

Oliver knew he was supposed to be going away, but he had no idea where. That was the way it was in his house. There were never fixed plans, every day was an adventure, and surprises lurked around each corner. That was the way he liked it.

Uncle Will parked the car outside the front door. Oliver reached for the handle.

"Wait here!" said his uncle, placing a hand on Oliver's shoulder. "I'll go in!"

"Why?" asked Oliver, frustrated.

He knew why: his uncle was worried something had happened to Oliver's mum and dad, although he would never admit it. Oliver had heard him on the telephone earlier that afternoon, just before he had closed the kitchen door when he knew Oliver was listening. However, Oliver had managed to hear "suspicious", "worried", and "not sure what to do next".

Adults had this infuriating habit of treating Oliver like a small child, too young to know the truth. For some reason, it was acceptable behaviour to lie to children, under the guise of "protecting" them. This had happened twice today. At school, he had overheard the phone call behind the part-closed door of Mrs Jones' office. He made out "very unusual" and "what shall I tell Oliver?" – only to be told by Mrs Jones that nobody had answered the telephone and she would try again later.

"Wait here!" said Uncle Will, trying to sound brave. He put up his hood and darted through the rain towards the door. He usually had to duck his head to fit through a standard door frame. With his strong hairy arms and a furrowed brow he often reminded Oliver of an orang-utan. It was odd to see him being so nervous about an empty house.

Uncle Will was not complicated. What you saw was what you got: a genuine bloke with a presence, probably best understood in three simple words: *steak*, *rugby*, and *noise*. Oliver was vegetarian, useless at rugby, and at his happiest when left in peace and quiet.

Uncle Will tried the door, but it was locked tight. He turned to walk back to the car, but had not noticed Oliver slipping out and standing behind him. "What the!" he blurted. "I thought I told you to sit in the car."

"Yes, but you do need the key," said Oliver as he offered it to him.

Uncle Will turned it in the lock and no sooner had it clicked than the door was flung wide open, closely followed by Winston, the family's excitable golden retriever. Uncle Will almost jumped out of his shoes.

"You've certainly got the jitters tonight!" said Oliver, reaching in and turning on the outside light, curious that he could hear his dad's radio playing in the kitchen. Winston weaved around Uncle Will's legs, wagging his tail frantically as if he had been left alone all day.

"All right, butt!" said Uncle Will. He called everybody "butt" – it was short for "butty", his affectionate term for a friendly face. He remained at the front door.

Oliver slipped past his uncle, who was stroking Winston and talking to him like a long-lost friend. Oliver walked down the hall, following the sound of the radio playing in the kitchen.

"Mum!" he called. There was no reply.

"Dad!" he shouted. Still no reply.

It was not unusual for Oliver to walk into an empty house, but this time everything felt wrong.

The kitchen was empty. At first glance, all appeared normal; all except for broken shards of a mug in the middle of the kitchen floor. This was not *too* unusual as his dad, Henry, and Winston were all naturally clumsy and managed to break things regularly.

Uncle Will nervously appeared. Oliver could tell that the mug had done little to quell his uncle's growing anxiety.

"It's just a broken cup of tea, happens all the time around my dad," Oliver said in a relieved yet deflated voice.

"Yeah, but why didn't they clear it up?" The words were an escaped thought, and no sooner had he spoken than it was clear that Uncle Will regretted his outburst. After all, he was the grown-up, the one who was supposed to be offering reassurance.

The radio was playing "Another One Bites the Dust". Oliver switched it off then gazed around the room. The kitchen was central to the house, sweeping around into the dining room in one direction and the living room in the other. It was bright and airy, and blended seamlessly with the collage of colours outdoors. The whole house was comfortable and cosy, with piles of books and magazines on the coffee table, sweaters and trainers littering the sofa, and various toys of Henry's strewn all around.

But it did not feel cosy today.

"Lights full!" commanded Oliver. The lighting system woke up, illuminating all of the ground floor.

"That never works for me," said Uncle Will.

"Dad's not programmed it for your voice, that's why," said Oliver to satisfy his uncle.

"They're definitely not here, are they?" said Uncle Will, pacing around the kitchen.

"No," said Oliver, still scanning each room. He had further checks to make before he could be as convinced as his uncle.

There was nothing that made alarm bells ring. Everything seemed as it should have been, apart from a broken mug and a very odd feeling.

There were no notes, no clues, nothing to point in the direction of where his mum and dad could be. Oliver paced around each room before stopping in the kitchen and staring at the remains of the mug.

Out of the corner of his eye, he saw a dusting of yellow powder speckled on Winston's basket. He had no idea what it was, but knew instinctively that his father must have had something to do with it.

"Could they be upstairs?" Oliver asked his uncle, not imagining for a moment that they could be, but desperately needing to get rid of him for a few minutes.

"I'll go and have a look," said Uncle Will apprehensively as he walked back out into the hall. Winston followed him; he clearly did not want to be left alone again.

Oliver closed the kitchen door. He wasted no time in pulling down the kitchen terminal and keyboard from under a cupboard and entering his password. He was good with computers and understood them far better than people. They were predictable and logical, unlike most of the people he knew.

The screen was blank apart from a command prompt:

```
Kitchen#>
```

He typed:

```
Kitchen#>Mail
```

It was his dad's account that opened on the screen – the one he used for home, not work. The screen rolled with unopened mail messages. The scrolling stopped at the last opened e-mail, which had a timestamp of *10.05.*

Alarm bells rang in Oliver's head; this was now even more serious than he had first imagined. Something was wrong; his father always opened his e-mails as soon as they arrived.

He closed the terminal, reached across to the worktop, and took hold of his mobile. He dialled 999 and asked for the police.

"Police emergency desk," a friendly voice responded. "How can we assist?"

"My name is Oliver Harris and I want to report my parents missing."

"How old are you, Oliver?" the voice said softly.

"Eleven."

"When did you last see your parents?"

"My dad dropped me at school this morning, and my mum dropped my brother at nursery. We haven't seen them since."

"Is there a responsible adult with you?"

Oliver thought kindly about Uncle Will, then said, "No." He added, "I have a three-year-old brother," for a more dramatic effect.

"Are you both safe?"

"Yes, but it's getting late."

"What's your address?"

"It's April Cottage, Mountain Road, Ebbwvenny." He spoke clearly and calmly. "It's where I am now."

"We'll send a car around straight away. Stay at home and don't leave the house. Would you like me to stay on the phone until it arrives?"

"No, I'll watch for it," said Oliver. "Thank you."

He put down the phone and glanced at the door to the hallway, but his attention was drawn to the larder cupboard – the secret entrance to the labs. He had an instinctive urge to check them out.

The Secret Labyrinth

Buried deep in the hillside beneath April Cottage was an abandoned coal mine. Oliver's dad used it to conceal his network of top-secret laboratories. It was the perfect place for him to conduct his research with the seclusion and secrecy he needed. Many people said that the cottage was as pretty as a chocolate box, and in a way it was, although if that was true then the box had a secret compartment that contained hidden gems.

The laboratories' existence was such a huge secret that even Oliver, who had lived in April Cottage all his life, had known about them for only the past two years.

Time was against him. Uncle Will could return at any minute, and for him to see Oliver disappearing in the larder would be unforgivable. He was as clueless about what lay beneath the cottage as he was about most things in life. Uncle Will may have been trustworthy, but some secrets were just too big to tell anyone.

"Lights, Study!" commanded Oliver. A dim LED above the secret door lit up.

A loud *thud* came from the room above the kitchen, then a muffled curse. "I'm just getting some clothes for you," Uncle Will yelled from upstairs.

Oliver dreaded the thought of what might be selected on his behalf, but decided this was a good thing to keep his uncle busy. It would be worth challenging him on his choice a little later, if all was well.

Oliver hurried across to the far corner of the kitchen and swung open the larder door. Inside were cereal boxes, breadsticks, porridge oats, a range of tin cans, and more. He stretched to reach past a box of muesli that masked a button on a hinge.

He pressed the little circle and heard air escaping from the cupboard. He withdrew his hand swiftly as the shelves shot towards the floor, revealing a considerably more substantial door. It was not the sort anybody would expect to see in a kitchen; it had similarities to outer torpedo doors traditionally found on nuclear submarines. It was made from layered metal with huge reinforced hinges. Oliver stepped into the newly revealed doorway; the larder *whooshed* back up behind him.

Oliver placed his thumb on the recognition panel above one of the torpedo door's hinges.

"Full access granted," said a familiar simulated voice.

The door began to automatically unscrew itself. Oliver's dad often joked that if a hurricane happened across the valley, all that would remain of their little house would be the doorway that led to the underground labyrinth.

As the door swung open, a suspended glass walkway was revealed, hanging from steel ropes fixed to the rocky roof. The ceiling was littered with artificial domes of light and halogen lamps. Along the transparent path that stretched before him were two sets of suspended glass stairs and, at the far end, a spiral staircase. Underneath the glass walkway, three lab areas were filled with every kind of machine that a scientist could dream of.

The contrast could not have been greater; this hidden space that once housed a bleak, cold, dark, and damp coal mine was now home to an artificially bright, airy, and clinically sterile lab complex.

Oliver scanned the labs. Everything was in its place, and it was immediately obvious that his mum and dad were not there.

As much as Oliver wanted to investigate, he could not. Time was against him.

He rushed across the bridge and down the first set of glass stairs, into the security room, where answers could be lurking. The day's events from the house, labs, and grounds could be viewed on video feeds. Oliver most often used this room when he managed to lose something in the house – usually his mobile phone or his homework diary. They usually turned up in the most unexpected places. Often Henry was the one to be held responsible for putting things into hiding. Today Oliver was using the feeds for something far more serious.

It was infuriating to have the coolest house imaginable but be unable to tell any of his friends anything about it. However, he knew the reasons why this was not possible, and respected them.

His friends knew that his dad was a scientist, and that was cool. He told them how he was researching and lecturing at the university.

However, he was far more than an average scientist. Firstly, he was a doctor of physics and nanotechnology, biology, and computer science. His *real* work, the work that he never talked about outside of April Cottage, was research into the kind of science and technology that, he said, "makes the world a better place".

Whenever Oliver asked what that involved, he always received the same sort of reply: "What I do is vital in the fight against the corrupt use of science."

Even at eleven, and a bit of whizz at science, Oliver struggled to understand much of his father's research. He was not sure who his dad worked for, but knew he must be working for someone. It was never discussed and he trusted his father enough to never ask.

His father had once worked for the government, where he did not need his own facilities. From what Oliver understood, he had been employed by the Ministry of Defence, but left years ago.

Whenever Oliver questioned him about why he moved on, he would receive the same answer: "I left on principle!"

This was followed by a short lecture that always began, "Sometimes, however difficult it may seem, you have to do the right thing. You have to do what you believe in and even if the answer seems impossible, don't give up – try even harder!"

Oliver remembered those years as being a difficult time for his dad; however, he recognised that after his father had made the decision to leave, he became a much happier person.

The room consisted of ten main servers, six screens for showing video feeds, and a further two control monitors.

Oliver sat down at the keyboard and punched in:

`bedroom3 feed`

Uncle Will appeared in Henry's room, sizing up various outfits and stuffing them into a carrier bag.

A second punch on the keyboard brought up the grounds. A small blue light was visible in the distance; probably the police coming to rescue him.

He typed:

`access/archive/17/07/`

The message returned:

`Feeds present`

He typed:

`kitchen: 08.30`

The main monitor flashed and an image of the kitchen appeared. Oliver's mum was putting his sandwich into his lunch box. A warm glow made him smile as he knew what happened next. She placed it on one end of the breakfast bar and slid it across to Oliver, who grabbed it just before it would have toppled off the edge and land in Winston's breakfast bowl.

He watched himself grabbing a piece of toast and stuffing it into his mouth in one go before his mum kissed him on the top of his head and sang, "I know something you don't know," teasing him about the forthcoming summer trip. To this, he gave a half-sarcastic smile, the best he could manage with a whole piece of toast in his mouth.

"Love you, Oliver!" his mum shouted as he ran out of the door, tripping over the half-dismantled train set and other toys that littered the ground floor and leaving a trail of crumbs behind him.

Seeing his mum on the camera was difficult. He had had such an emotional day, he did not want to watch her on a screen; he wanted to be with her and ask what was going on.

A lump rose in his throat. However, there was no time for sentiment. He checked the screen for the grounds – the blue light was getting closer.

Oliver punched at the keyboard:

`fast forward x 20.`

He watched his mum clear away the breakfast dishes and wipe Henry's face, then the two of them left. The kitchen remained empty until 9:30, when his mum returned from taking Henry to nursery.

His dad appeared next to her at the breakfast bar. They were hugging their mugs of tea and looking quite excited. His mum was showing his dad a list.

Oliver assumed it would be one of his mum's lists of jobs. This was quite normal. She had a thing about them – everybody got lists from her, especially Oliver. Even Henry, who could not read, would be given lists containing pictures.

The screen flickered and went blank.

"Strange!" said Oliver. His voice sounded loud in the silent security room. He typed:

```
reset
```

A message appeared:

```
SERVER ERROR
```

He tried resetting the program again, but the terminal showed the same message. He tried again and again.

```
SERVER ERROR
```

This was ridiculous. He knew the servers were backed up twice and it was virtually impossible for all the cameras to fail. He typed:

```
route

system log 19/7/
```

The screen flickered and responded:

```
Power failure 10:12. Power restored 10:14. Security
functioning 10:16.
```

Oliver scratched his head. If the main power supply failed, inverter batteries would run for 45 minutes. After that, the sluice gate on the lake near the house would open and the water turbine would power the generator for a further 24 hours, and even longer if it were raining.

Losing power for two whole minutes was absurd. It did not add up.

Amid the darkness filling one monitor, the flashing blue light was now almost at the house.

Oliver checked that it was safe to emerge into the kitchen unseen. Uncle Will appeared on the screen, walking down the stairs. His arms were laden with plastic bags bulging with clothes, plus dressing gowns, teddy bears, and Oliver's Wii. Auntie Karen would not allow her husband one of his own, so he seized every opportunity to play with Oliver's.

Uncle Will stumbled out of the front door in semi-darkness, arms full of clothes and computer games and obviously intent on loading his boot. He was blinded by the headlights and flashing blue above the police car.

Manipulating the camera controls, Oliver zoomed in to the car. Peering at the close-up image on the monitor, he could make out the occupants' names and numbers: the car was driven by a young man named PC Sharp, and beside him was the experienced-looking WPC Hughes.

The microphone fixed to the camera heard PC Sharp bring the car to a screeching halt, blocking the exit to the driveway. He picked up his radio and said: "SWV-23 to Control, over."

Oliver adjusted the volume of the computer to hear the response.

"Go ahead, 23."

"House of the abandoned children has an IC-one male removing property, over."

"Roger that, 23. Sending backup, over."

PC Sharp jumped out and reached for his truncheon, drawing it slightly. WPC Hughes began walking towards Uncle Will, who tried to focus on the two figures amid the lights.

"Are you the proprietor of the house, sir?" asked WPC Hughes.

"Who? Me? But . . . No! I'm just . . ."

Watching from the security room, Oliver thought it was as if his uncle suddenly saw himself and realised just how he looked, carrying bundles of goods out of a darkened house and hastily piling them into his car.

"I'll just put these in the boot," he said, flustered, and dropped Henry's bear into a puddle. He threw the bags into his car and collected the sodden bear. Winston appeared in the doorway, saw the commotion, and retreated into the house.

"Stay exactly where you are!" said WPC Hughes.

"Put your arms in the air!" PC Sharp shouted.

14

Oliver saw his uncle looking fretful in the car's lights, holding a wet teddy and raising his arms as water trickled onto his head. Oliver couldn't help himself smiling and found himself saying out loud, "Superb."

It was time to make a retreat. Oliver typed:

sleep

The screens went blank. He emerged into the kitchen and the door to the lab locked behind him.

He darted into the hall, and ran straight into PC Sharp.

"You must be Oliver," the officer said, trying to sound friendly.

Oliver just nodded.

"Where is your little brother?"

"He's at *his* house!" said Oliver, pointing directly at his uncle.

PC Sharp immediately arrived at Oliver's intended conclusion. "Oliver!" he bellowed. "Stay where you are!"

WPC Hughes began questioning Uncle Will. "So you say that you're his uncle?"

"I *am* his uncle!" he replied. "I'm William Edwards."

Oliver remained quiet.

"So where are Oliver's parents?" asked WPC Hughes.

"I have no idea!"

"We will need to see some identification, sir," said PC Sharp, fully drawing his truncheon.

"Butt, it's the truth," Uncle Will pleaded. "I haven't brought any identification – I only live in Llewelyn Close."

PC Sharp added abruptly, "Where's the little one?"

"At my house." Uncle Will tried to sound reassuring. "He's with his auntie."

While PC Sharp fired questions at Uncle Will, his colleague radioed for a check on Uncle Will's car to confirm his identity.

Before long, she interrupted the questioning by approaching with a set of handcuffs.

"You don't appear to be Karen Bennett, the car's owner, sir," she said.

"A stolen car, or a stolen identity!" said PC Sharp. "That technique has been used by many a hardened criminal attempting to evade capture. The next thing he'll say is that it's his wife's car!"

"But it *is* my wife's car!" exclaimed Uncle Will. "Karen Bennett was her name before we got married. We've had the car for years." He was babbling now. "Why are you questioning me? I haven't done anything wrong. I'm a law-abiding citizen."

Uncle Will looked as though he was about to cry. "I've already been on the phone to the police today, telling you how my sister and her husband have gone missing. Phone the station and you can ask them yourselves! They told me that there is nothing that can be done for 24 hours, and not to worry too much, then they went on to try and give me Social Services' phone number to get the boys looked after! There are some crossed wires somewhere!"

He said looking disapprovingly at Oliver, who realised for the first time that Uncle Will had taken the whole situation so seriously that he had alerted the police. He began to feel guilty; maybe that was who his uncle had been talking to in his kitchen with the door closed.

"You tell a good story, sir," said WPC Hughes, raising the handcuffs with a *clunk*. "If we just take you down to the station, we can see if it all adds up."

"Everybody *stop!*" Oliver yelled. "He *is* my uncle, but my mum and dad are not here. Something has happened to them!"

His uncle had been punished enough. Oliver could not just stand around and allow the supposed grown-ups to waste any more time and energy. They were missing the point completely.

"Can somebody please help me find my mum and dad?" he pleaded.

Uncle Will was clearly relieved by Oliver's statement and keen to turn the situation around. He put the sodden teddy bear into the boot of the car and invited the officers into the house.

"Come and look at this," he said as he led them into the kitchen.

Suitcases

"Lights full!" Oliver shouted, and the house lit up immediately like a Christmas tree.

PC Sharp gasped. "Quite impressive."

Uncle Will led everyone back into the kitchen. "We found this broken cup," he gestured, as he leaned down to pick it up.

"Stop!" yelled PC Sharp. "That could be evidence."

He headed out to his car for an evidence bag.

WPC Hughes took out her notebook and a pen and asked Oliver, "What are your parents' names?"

"My dad's name is Paul, I mean Paul Harris, and my mum's Megan Harris. I know they were here at 10:05."

"How can you be so sure of the time? Weren't you at school?"

"Yes, but I've checked my dad's e-mails. The last e-mail that he opened was at 10:05. He always opens his mail the moment it arrives."

A new blue light seemed to spread throughout the house, and the sound of tyres on gravel could be heard.

"That will be backup," said WPC Hughes.

Her colleague was already outside, and he briefed the backup team as they arrived before he re-entered the kitchen.

He said: "I've sent the other officers to look around the grounds to see if they can find anything unusual."

"Don't you think it's unusual that my parents aren't here?" asked Oliver.

"All right, anything *else* unusual."

WPC Hughes continued asking Uncle Will questions about Paul and Megan's date of birth. Uncle Will hesitated. Oliver guessed he did not know for certain. He never was good at remembering such things. Oliver answered for him, feeling like he was the responsible adult.

"What do they do?" the officer asked.

Oliver paused before replying. "Er . . . Mum looks after us lot, and Dad works at the university and does research."

The police became engaged in a discussion as to whether they should pick up the fragments of the broken mug, or leave them on the floor for CID.

For Oliver, the reality of the situation was starting to dawn. He did not know what to do, what to say, or what to think.

He looked over at his uncle for some support, but Uncle Will appeared dumbfounded and rooted to the ground.

Oliver was determined not to let his parents down, and if that meant being flexible with the truth and unable to divulge certain information about his father and his work, then he would say nothing. His father had trusted him with the secret, so Oliver was not going to betray him when he probably needed help most.

The moment was interrupted by two bright flashlights outside the front door, and the sound of police radios entering the kitchen.

"Did you notice anything suspicious?" asked PC Sharp.

"No!" answered one of the policemen. "Only, there were two suitcases packed and left in the garage just behind the Land Rover."

"That's not suspicious," said Oliver. "We are meant to be going on holiday today."

The officer continued, "One has the name *Oliver Harris* on it, the other *Henry Harris*."

"The one's mine, the other's my brother's," replied Oliver.

"We'll secure the garage," said one of the officers. "There isn't much else we can do in the dark."

"Before you lock it," said Uncle Will, "I may as well take the suitcases with me. Would you mind putting them in the boot of my car?"

The police officer glared at Uncle Will. Oliver supposed carrying suitcases was not really in his job description, but as Uncle Will had asked him to, he felt obliged. He nodded reluctantly, then picked up his radio in response to another call and left.

It must have been after nine and it was dark and damp, but the rain had stopped. Goodbyes were said, and the police seemed content with the knowledge that Oliver was in the care of his uncle.

They told Uncle Will that Oliver's mum and dad would not be officially missing until tomorrow morning. If there was still no sign of them, Oliver and his uncle should go down to the police station to file a missing persons report.

As the officers drove away, Oliver felt dreadful.

"Right, butt," said Uncle Will, sighing. He stood at the front door with Oliver, looking exhausted and a little bullied by the events of the past hour. "Let's get going. Henry will need his pyjamas and his teddy bear."

"Suppose we should," said Oliver reluctantly.

He did not want to leave April Cottage, or face the possibility that his parents were not just late or side-tracked, but had really disappeared and might be away all night.

At home, he felt closer to his parents; he did not want to go back to his uncle's house. He could do nothing from there. If he was at home, he could sneak back to the labs and check out what else happened at 10:12.

He thought about his little brother and how he would be waiting for him, depending on him. He thought about his mum and dad and it dawned on him that the only person they could rely upon now was him.

He was not sure how to find them, but he was sure that he was not going to let them down.

As they were ready to leave, Oliver told the house, "Lights off!" He stepped outside the door, which Uncle Will attempted to close behind them.

"Hey!" said Oliver. "What about Winston? He can't stay on his own all night."

"Oh!" Uncle Will had obviously not had time to give Winston a second thought. "I suppose that he'd better come with us too."

He reopened the door and was almost knocked down by a very anxious Winston. Uncle Will was quite fond of the dog, but did not have one of his own because Auntie Karen did not like them. Oliver knew she had some sort of phobia. Whenever she came to April Cottage, Winston was evicted from the house and sent into the garden.

"Do you think that we will be able to sneak him in without your auntie noticing?" asked Uncle Will sheepishly.

"No way!" said Oliver. "He'll be so excited to see everyone, and I expect he's starving."

"How about a cheese omelette?" smiled Uncle Will.

Oliver smirked. "Winston would probably prefer one of your famous sirloin steaks."

"Fat chance," said Uncle Will as they both headed back to Llewelyn Close.

Winston was the first out when Uncle Will stopped the car. He bounded down the driveway, through the wet grass and the vegetable patch, past the back door, and onto the kitchen floor, where he skidded to a halt at Auntie Karen's feet.

He greeted her with as much affection as he could muster, but this was not reciprocated, not even slightly.

"An extra guest for the evening!" announced Uncle Will as he followed Winston into the house. He carried both suitcases in his thick arms.

"I see!" snapped Auntie Karen. The look on her face spoke volumes. She backed away from Winston, unable to find any words of greeting but instead only a grimace.

She was, however, able to manage a frantic gesture to Uncle Will that Oliver could clearly translate as *you deal with it!*

Auntie Karen was mum to Ethan and Daisy, Oliver's little cousins. She was also a large lady who was probably half as round as she was tall. Her stern face was distinctly framed by a shiny, black, perfectly groomed hairstyle that formed two severe points meeting at her chin. She always wore bright red lipstick and had long, manicured nails painted blood red to match her lips.

Her heart was kind and sometimes it showed itself, but very often it had trouble escaping. To the outside world, she gave the impression that she was friendly and approachable. But when she was at home, the friendliness could change into a thick, cold frost. She worked part-time at the local job centre, and it was easy for Oliver to imagine her scolding people for not applying for enough jobs or having inadequate CVs.

Oliver was happy leaving Uncle Will to sort out Winston, because he was needed in the living room. Henry lay on the sofa, cuddling a cushion and looking very tired. He saw Oliver and managed a smile.

"Where's Mummy and Daddy?" he asked.

"They'll be back before we know it," said Oliver, unsure of what else to tell him.

Although Henry was Oliver's little brother, they were very different. Henry was three, and had wild, blond curls that made him look cute. Oliver did not think that he was particularly sweet; he was just annoyingly charming, in a way that enabled him to gaze at his victim with his big blue eyes and get away with just about anything. Oliver was eleven, and so no longer qualified to be considered cute. He had overgrown, mousey brown hair that flopped onto his forehead, impairing his vision. He thought of himself as not really tall, or short, or fat, or thin – he was just average.

Henry got away with pushing boundaries, and all too often Oliver was the victim. In fact, Henry was pretty mischievous and usually defiant. He liked noise, but not at night. Then the toddling super-villain would transform into an affectionate little boy who needed a cuddle and a story to go to sleep. It looked as if Oliver would need to sort that out tonight.

Auntie Karen led Oliver and Henry to the spare room in the attic. Uncle Will had put the suitcases at the bottom of the sofa bed, and the bags of clothes on top. He had managed to pack two pairs of pyjamas, one for each of them, so it was not necessary to go delving into the holiday suitcases for supplies just yet.

Oliver did not want to disturb the packing; he wanted to make sure the suitcases were ready for their holiday as soon as his parents came back.

The old pyjamas his uncle had found may have featured purple dinosaurs, and were six inches short on the legs, but he did not complain. He just kept his trousers on.

"I've brought you some milk," said Auntie Karen, leaning over to tuck Henry in and kiss him on his forehead.

Oliver was relieved that he had got away with just a tap on the head.

"Shout if there's anything else you need," she said. "You know where we are."

She switched off the lights and whispered, "Your mum and dad will be all right, you know. I'm sure there will be a perfectly logical explanation by the morning. Goodnight, boys."

Henry was very sleepy. Oliver cuddled him and told him the story of the three little pigs. He did not need a book because he had read that story so many times that he knew it word for word. Just as he reached the part where the wolf landed in the cooking pot, Winston jumped up onto the bed, smelling of sausages.

No sooner was Henry asleep than Oliver crept out of bed and tiptoed over to the attic's small window.

He opened the curtain and stared into the darkness, mesmerized by flickers of light as headlights flashed between the gates of the garden's high walls. Perhaps the next flash of light would stay and turn into the driveway and his dad would appear to take him home.

Several times, he held his breath when he heard an engine then saw a large black vehicle. Each time, it was not his dad's car at all, but instead a plain black van.

The lights were hypnotic, and his eyes grew heavier. Exhaustion had set in.

Oliver sat propped up awkwardly on a tiny slither of the bed, watching Henry and Winston sleep. Winston lay horizontally, preventing Oliver from lying down. He gently stroked him. Clutching his mobile in his hand, he checked again for messages, but there was nothing.

The light from the screen lit up the room just enough for him to notice a tinge on Winston's paws.

Remembering the yellow powder in the kitchen, Oliver reached for a tissue on the table next to the bed, then he wiped each paw carefully. He did not need Auntie Karen complaining about mess. Conscious of being a guest, he slipped the dirty tissue into his pocket.

Oliver closed his eyes and prepared for a very long night.

Missing Persons Report

The next morning, Henry woke early. As Oliver lay next to him, it was unquestionably his first task to make sure that his brother was awake too. Henry usually ensured this by clambering all over Oliver and forcefully opening his eyelids by grasping a bunch of eyelashes and lifting them as far as they would go before releasing them.

Luckily for Oliver, he was already awake. He had barely slept.

Oliver sat up and stretched. It was still early.

"Where's Mummy and Daddy?" Henry asked.

"Not far away," said Oliver, trying to sound convincing.

He reached for his mobile. No messages, no missed calls, and still no answer when he tried calling.

Winston lifted his head from the pillow and gave them both a slobbery greeting.

"I want to get up," said Henry.

"Only if you promise to creep," said Oliver. "We don't want to wake everyone else."

All three of them went quietly down the stairs. It did not appear that anyone else was awake, but as they walked through the living room Oliver overheard someone talking in the kitchen.

The door was partly closed, so he lingered outside. There was only one voice: Uncle Will was on the telephone.

"Shh!" Oliver told Henry, then grabbed Winston's collar, straining to hear.

"I'm not sure," Uncle Will said. There was a pause. "We are going to file a missing persons report this morning." Another pause, then, "Henry's fine. Not sure how Oliver is coping. He gave the police the impression last night that I was kidnapping him or something. He's old enough to know what's going on." An even longer pause. "Well, it's probably for the best if you do. Let me know the flight times."

Winston barged past Oliver, unable to keep still any longer.

As the door opened, Uncle Will greeted Oliver and his brother. "Anyone for a bacon sandwich?"

"Who were you talking to on the telephone?" said Oliver, expecting his uncle to lie.

"Nan. She'll be home on the next flight."

"She's coming home?"

Oliver knew that Nan had plans to spend the whole summer travelling. She had retired from work a few weeks ago, and was looking forward to a summer of reunions. She had had it mapped out: starting in France to visit an old school friend, then onto Holland, where she was now staying with Uncle John, her brother.

"Still no sign of your mum and dad," said Uncle Will, sounding troubled. "We'll wait until after breakfast and then go to the police station."

Winston was scratching at the door, so Uncle Will let him out into the garden. Henry wandered into the living room, and the next moment the blaring TV began to wake the rest of the house.

For Oliver, the next hour was unbearably chaotic. There was hustling, bustling, and tantrums over who was having which cereal from the variety pack, spilled glasses of milk, and, to top it all, Winston winding up Auntie Karen like a top.

It forced a smile onto Oliver's face when he watched her waving about a slice of toast, only to have it intercepted by Winston.

"Aaaarrgh!" she yelled, unable to control her frustration. She stood up too hastily from her seat, and as it toppled her arms swung. This began a chain reaction: a cereal box tipped over the table and fell onto a vase of flowers, which led to the jug of milk spilling everywhere, a very wet tablecloth, rivers of cascading liquids, and a air of tension so thick that not even a chain-saw could cut it.

"I think it's about time we took Winston for a walk," said Uncle Will.

"That is the most sensible thing you have said all day," said Auntie Karen through gritted teeth, as she frantically mopped up milk with tea towels.

Her outburst left Oliver feeling even more uncomfortable. Hastily, Uncle Will, Oliver, Henry and Winston retreated and made their way to the local police station.

It was a glorious day. The sun was shining and the sky was blue. It was the kind of morning that usually brought a smile to everyone's face, but not today.

They walked mostly in silence. Even Henry seemed subdued. The situation was surreal, as if Oliver was in a nightmare and at any moment was going to wake to his mum's voice telling him he was going to be late for school.

He pinched himself. It definitely hurt. That was not a good sign. The unavoidable truth was that he was walking towards the police station to report his parents missing.

Oliver tried his phone again. If one of his parents answered, Oliver and the others could turn around right there and go back home to meet up with them, where they would explain everything.

He pressed *Dad*, but it went straight to voicemail. His mum's phone did the same: "Hello, you've reached Megan Harris. I'm sorry I can't talk to you right now, but if you leave your name and number, I promise I'll get back to you soon."

Oliver had already left so many messages. Hearing his mum's voice brought a tear to his eyes. He looked towards the fields so Uncle Will could not see him crying.

As they entered the station, they were greeted by a man whose badge identified him as Station Officer Cross.

"Can I help you?" he asked.

"We're here to report my sister and her husband missing," said Uncle Will quietly.

"Have they been missing for longer than 24 hours?"

Uncle Will looked at his watch. "Just about."

"Take a seat. I'll get one of our officers to take a statement shortly."

The officer looked close to retirement age, if not past it. He was short and stocky, with a silver moustache and a very serious look on his face. He was sat at a desk, looking anxious and confused, typing slowly with one finger. Oliver could hear him occasionally mumbling under his breath: "Blasted targets."

Oliver and the others waited for a while but nobody appeared. Winston whined then climbed beneath the chairs. Then Henry started to whine, and climbed over the chairs. Uncle Will looked worried.

The telephone on the main desk kept ringing, and officers were coming and going.

Suddenly everything went quiet. Uncle Will looked around and asked, "Where's Henry?"

He was not in the waiting area. But from across the room came a very loud, very clear, "No!"

Station Officer Cross was holding both hands on his head, tugging at what was left of his grey hair. Henry was under the desk, grinning, with the plug from the computer in his hands.

"It's all gone!" said the officer. "Three shifts' work for the end-of-year targets."

"Didn't you save it?" asked Oliver.

"I'm really sorry!" said Uncle Will, not knowing what else to say.

Station Officer Cross did not answer, but simply stared.

Uncle Will decided it was probably best if Henry sat on his lap for a while. He would need to keep a closer eye on him. Winston sprawled on the tiled floor.

Oliver found it hard to think ahead. What would happen if his parents were not coming home? What if he was stuck at his uncle's house for days, or weeks?

Henry grizzled and fidgeted. Uncle Will looked agitated.

"We've been waiting nearly an hour," he told Oliver.

Oliver was aware of this already, but the alternative was worse: sitting in Llewelyn Close and doing absolutely nothing to find his mum and dad.

It was a hot day, so Oliver helped himself and Henry to water from a cooler in the waiting room. Hearing the sound of water, Winston bounded over and placed his front paws on the cooler, but it began to wobble.

Winston backed away and it toppled, emptying its contents over an open filing cabinet and splashing Station Officer Cross' desk.

At the very moment the water gushed, another officer arrived at reception, led by what appeared to be one of the force's working dogs. For no apparent reason, the Alsatian went berserk, pulling free of its lead and bounding in the direction of Oliver.

It barked ferociously and pounced on him. Two sharp paws landed on his shoulders, pinning him into his plastic chair and forcing it backwards.

The officer roared at the dog before forcibly pulling it away. Oliver was petrified.

"I'm really sorry about that, young man!" said the dog handler while gripping the animal firmly by the collar.

Uncle Will was attempting to hold Winston as he pulled and barked ferociously, trying to get between Oliver and the other dog.

"I'm f-fine!" Oliver stuttered, although he was shaking like a wet kitten.

"He's never done that before," said the officer. "Something must have upset him. You're not carrying any illegal substances, are you?"

Oliver shook his head, then emptied his pockets to show he had only a mobile phone, one pound and twenty pence, and a dirty tissue.

As Oliver held out the tissue, the dog once again went berserk, pulling the handler across the floor. The beast growled and snarled, standing so tall on his hind legs that the man could hardly restrain him.

"Would you mind if I took a look at that?" he asked.

"If you want," said Oliver awkwardly, handing over his mobile phone.

"And the rest."

Oliver danced around the Alsatian and passed across his money and tissue.

Immediately, the group were shown into an interview room and told to wait.

Soon a man in plain clothes entered the room. "I'm DCI Brady," he said. "I hear that you've been causing chaos in reception."

Oliver felt concerned.

"Don't be too worried," DCI Brady added hastily. "Station Officer Cross needed his morning livening up!"

The initial questions were fired at Uncle Will. Once all the formalities had been done, DCI Brady looked at Oliver and smiled encouragingly.

"Lots of people get reported missing," he said, "but most of them turn up within a day or two."

Oliver wanted to believe this to be true for his parents, but he knew it was not as simple as DCI Brady thought.

He wanted to say that his mum and dad were not just two more missing people: his dad had been working on a project in his hidden labs.

However, his father's words ricocheted around his head: "Under no circumstances should anyone outside of this family know about my work!"

Despite the fact that the situation was so serious, Oliver had made a promise and was not going to let his father down.

The moment was interrupted by a knock at the door. DCI Brady left briefly. When he returned, he looked far more concerned.

"Oliver," he said, "I need to know where you found that tissue."

"Uncle Will's house."

"How did the powder get onto the tissue?"

"It was on Winston's paws," said Oliver. "I wiped them last night. You haven't met my Auntie Karen, have you?"

Everyone in the room turned to look at Winston, who was lying in the corner, his paws wet from the ruckus in the reception.

"I doubt that there'll be much left on you now," said DCI Brady, "not since you've given yourself a bath."

Uncle Will gawped, looking even more confused than normal.

"That tissue," said the DCI, "was covered in military-grade explosive residue."

Oliver's jaw dropped. Uncle Will seemed to have reached the point of saturation; he could not absorb any more.

"That's why Chomper went mad," the DCI went on. "He's a sniffer dog, trained to detect explosives. There may well be more to your parents' disappearance than meets the eye."

"Does that mean that you are going to take this seriously and help me find them?" Oliver asked.

DCI Brady looked him in the eye. "Do you have any ideas where they may have gone?"

Oliver was never good at lying. It did not suit him. He took a deep breath and replied despondently, "I have no idea where they are."

"What about your house? My colleagues have told me there may have been a disturbance."

"I'm not sure about that," replied Oliver. "It was just a broken cup. Things like that are always happening at our house."

"I can believe that," added the DCI. He glanced towards the waiting room, where Station Officer Cross was on his hands and knees, holding dripping-wet files. "We may need another look around the house later."

Oliver felt uncomfortable about this, but he was sure that PC Sharp finding his way into the hidden labs was as likely as Uncle Will winning a Nobel Prize and Oliver being selected for the Welsh rugby squad.

"Have you contacted friends and relatives to ask if anyone else knows anything?" asked DCI Brady.

"Some," said Uncle Will.

"May I suggest that you continue to do that while we file the report? If there are still no signs of them, we will ask around. Maybe some of your neighbours will be able to shed some light. Somebody may have seen or heard something."

Uncle Will had to sign some papers before it was time to leave. They walked back to Llewelyn Close in no particular hurry.

When they arrived, Ethan and Daisy were watching TV in the lounge, so Henry joined them. Auntie Karen was still clearing up from breakfast.

Uncle Will told Oliver that he would start calling some of the family that he had not yet spoken to. He asked Oliver to think of some of his mum and dad's friends, so that he could ring them too.

Oliver did not go inside the house. Instead, he took Winston down to the bottom of the garden to the shade of the elm tree. He needed time to think.

Uncle Raj

Oliver sat with his back against the tree and Winston sprawled across his lap. He looked at his phone; no new messages, no missed calls. Again he tried to call his mum and dad, but it was the same message that sounded over and over.

He had no idea where his parents were. He desperately needed to talk to someone who could help. He opened his contacts, scrolled down, and stopped when he saw *Uncle Raj*.

Uncle Raj lived in London. He was not a relation as such, but he was Oliver and Henry's godfather, and also his dad's best friend. Whenever Oliver's dad had a problem, Uncle Raj was the first person he called. He was an incredibly busy man, spending lots of hours operating his construction company, but he still managed to make time for his friends and his family.

Oliver knew straight away that he would help. He pressed *Call*.

A cheery voice greeted him: "Hello, Oliver. Nice of you to call."

Uncle Raj was forever leaving messages for Oliver, and sending him texts, but only occasionally would Oliver get around to responding to them. Oliver disliked talking on the telephone, and much preferred conversations in person.

"Do you have any idea where Mum and Dad are?" he asked.

"Why? Don't you?"

"They didn't pick me up from school yesterday."

"But aren't you supposed to be on holiday?"

Oliver explained about the broken cup, the yellow powder, the police coming to the house, and how he had just been to file a missing persons report.

"Who's looking after you and Henry?"

"Uncle Will and Auntie Karen, and Winston's here too."

"I'm on my way!" said Uncle Raj. "I'll be there in about two hours."

"I thought you were in London," said Oliver. "That's three hours away."

"Yes. I'm bringing the Aston."

"Great!" Oliver leaned back against the tree and closed his eyes.

Uncle Raj was just like Oliver's dad in many ways. Oliver knew that he could not tell his uncle exactly what was going on, but he also knew he wanted him there and if anyone could help, it would be him.

The next hour dragged by. Uncle Will came out with apple juice, and a bowl of water for Winston.

"Are you all right out here?" he asked. "Why don't you come inside?"

"I think Winston feels more comfortable in the garden," Oliver said despondently.

Oliver wandered around the garden, stopping just outside the open kitchen window when he heard Uncle Will and Auntie Karen's raised voices. He hated arguments. He had forgotten that they were also planning a holiday, and he and Henry being there was a massive inconvenience.

If ever there was a disagreement or even a fight at school, you could guarantee that Oliver would be involved, but on neither side; he was the one in the middle. Today, he felt that because he was the cause of the argument, it would be best if he remained out of the way.

What was clear was that despite his parents being missing for just twenty-four hours, people were planning ahead. His auntie and uncle were making arrangements for the future for Oliver and Henry.

A lump the size of a tennis ball grew in his throat, and he could no longer hold back the tears. The size of the problem facing him, Henry, and Winston was starting to be all that he could think about.

It was not long before Oliver heard the distinctive rasp of the twin exhaust pipes from Uncle Raj's Aston Martin driving down the road. But he restrained any elation until he heard Uncle Raj turn off the ignition.

His godfather strode down the path towards Oliver and greeted him with, "Hello there, young man."

Oliver welcomed him with a big hug. Their "hellos" were usually a hair ruffle or a high five, but today Oliver was even more pleased to see him.

"Come on," suggested Uncle Raj, "let's go and see what Uncle Will has to say about all of this."

Before Oliver's uncle had time to get to his feet, he was met head-on by Winston, who was also very pleased to see a friendly face. He jumped onto Uncle Raj, who was wearing a particularly pristine pinstripe suit. He did not seem to mind, and when Winston started licking him behind his ears, he did not object to that too strongly either.

Not far behind Winston appeared Henry, who came running towards Uncle Raj wearing the biggest grin Oliver had seen for two days.

"I Just thought I would pop round to see what was going on," Uncle Raj announced as he tapped on the door and let himself in.

"What are you doing here, butt?" asked Uncle Will.

"I had a very troubled phone call from my godson."

Uncle Will smiled at Oliver. "I can't stop and chat," he said, grabbing his keys from the table. "I've got to go down to the airport to collect my mother."

"Is Nan home already?" Oliver asked, surprised.

Uncle Will nodded. "When I get back from the airport," he shouted to Uncle Raj as he left the room, "we'll have a beer!"

He dashed out of the door, almost falling over Winston on the way.

Auntie Karen directed "all children" and "that dog" into the garden to play. Nobody waited to be asked twice. Winston and his followers traipsed outside with tails between their legs.

"Would you like a cup of tea?" Auntie Karen asked Uncle Raj. Before he could reply, she added, "We're meant to be going to the South of France for my friend's wedding. Daisy is supposed to be bridesmaid, you know."

He replied breezily, "Let's just hope that they turn up before then, shall we?"

Auntie Karen's mood improved slightly as she grumbled and Uncle Raj listened. They stood in the doorway, watching over the children while she brought him up to date.

"So, what happens now?" he asked.

"The police are starting house-to-house enquiries."

"Have they gone to the press?" he asked, looking at his watch.

"I don't think so," she answered, not having considered that as an option.

Uncle Raj reached for one of his phones. He always carried three. One he used for work, one was for friends and family, and the other was his private phone, the number of which was known to only a few. This was the number that Oliver used.

He picked up his personal phone and dialled. "Hello, Yves," he said, "I need to call in a favour. What are the chances of getting a missing persons story printed for tomorrow?"

Uncle Raj spent the next half hour talking on the telephone.

Meanwhile, Oliver checked his own phone and waited for the next car to arrive, hoping it would be his mum and dad. He was pleased to have Uncle Raj around, but he needed to talk to him alone. That was unlikely at Uncle Will's house. He desperately hoped that Uncle Raj would take him out.

He wanted to go home.

The next car to arrive was Uncle Will's. Nan was sat in the passenger seat. Normally Oliver was incredibly close to his nan, usually meeting her every day, but he had not seen her for more than a month. Nan jumped out of the car as fast as her aching knees allowed and opened her arms when she saw Oliver heading towards her.

"Hello!" she smiled. "How are my boys?"

Oliver could not find any words. He bit his lip to hold back the tears and shook his head. She immediately understood and hugged him tightly. It was just what he needed.

As they headed inside, Auntie Karen announced, "Tea is in the dining room."

Oliver tried to follow.

However, his auntie blocked the door and said, "Go and check on your dog."

Oliver understood the undertone; it was code for *don't come into the dining room, we're talking* about *you, not to you.* He knew exactly what they would be talking about. He also knew that none of them had any idea about what could have happened to his mum and dad, and finding them was not down to them. It was down to him.

He made a graceful retreat into the garden, knowing that challenging his auntie was not worth his energy. He did not check on Winston, but instead waited for his auntie to move away, then tiptoed back into the house and stood quietly outside the room where the adults were sat.

The door was left ever so slightly ajar, and Oliver waited. Winston soon appeared from the garden, probably on the scent of biscuits. He barged past Oliver, opening the door wider as he entered. Oliver remained hidden outside, listening.

"Right!" said Uncle Raj. "I'll need some recent photographs, so that I can e-mail them over in time for print."

The conversation moved to the topic of Oliver and Henry.

"They should stay with me," said Nan.

"I'm sure that they'd like that very much!" added Auntie Karen without any hesitation.

"They would be most welcome to stay with me," said Uncle Raj. It was clear by the reaction he received that nobody had expected this.

"I'm sure that won't be necessary," said Nan. "It will be better for them to stay here so that they can be around their family."

"I *am* their family," Uncle Raj reminded everyone. "I'm the boys' godfather."

There was a very uncomfortable silence. "I always honour my commitments," he added.

Nobody spoke.

"There is something that we have neglected to consider," he went on. "Has anyone asked Oliver or Henry what they would like to do?"

Oliver saw this as the perfect opportunity to enter the dining room.

"Hello, Oliver!" said Uncle Raj. "We were just talking about you."

Oliver was pleased that someone was being honest with him. "I thought I'd come and find out if there was any more news."

Uncle Will just shook his head.

Oliver was relieved that he was not being asked to choose with whom he and Henry wanted to stay. Being faced with such a decision was unthinkable. All that he wanted was his parents back, and life as he once knew it.

"I need to borrow you, if that's OK," Uncle Raj asked Oliver. "I'd like you to e-mail a photograph of your mum and dad to a friend of mine, so we can put the story in the newspaper tomorrow."

Oliver nodded furiously. He knew instantly that that was the excuse he needed for his Uncle Raj to take him home.

"I'll need to go back to the house," he said.

"I'm ready when you are," said Uncle Raj, rising from his chair. "We can print off a list of your mum and dad's contacts, too. That should keep us busy for a few hours."

Oliver glanced into the lounge where Henry lay on the sofa watching television looking quite content. He was still at his wits' end with worry, but was made happier by the mere thought that he was with his Uncle Raj and soon he would be on his way home. He just wished that he could tell his uncle exactly what was on his mind.

His godfather gave a loud whistle, and Winston skidded to attention by his side.

Before opening the car door, Uncle Raj stopped, looked at Winston, and with great seriousness announced, "You can come, but there are some rules in my car that I insist upon. There will be absolutely no slobbering on the leather upholstery."

Winston pricked his ears and twisted his head in a gesture that must have been meant as a non-verbal agreement.

Oliver sat silently as they drove away. To be free of Llewelyn Close and on his way home felt good.

"Are you OK?" asked Uncle Raj.

Oliver nodded feebly.

"You don't look too good."

Oliver shrugged. His uncle did not have a magic wand to make his parents appear, and Oliver could not say what was really worrying him.

The relationship between Oliver and his uncle was simple; they enjoyed spending time together. They shared a mutual respect for each other that may have stemmed from one of their common interests: fast cars.

On the weekends they spent together, Sunday afternoons were never complete without catching the latest *Top Gear*, which was always followed by a fervent debate on horsepower, sleek designs, and which car they were going to buy next. Oliver could not share these discussions with his own dad – he was far more practical and his car preferences were decisions purely based on value, fuel consumption, carbon emissions, environmental impact, and the boot size, without a thought for shape, form, elegance, or speed. Much to Oliver's disgust, because of its environmental impact his dad's Land Rover had been converted to run on biofuel.

The only chance Oliver ever had to ride in a really cool car was when he travelled with Uncle Raj. He knew that when he grew up, he was going to drive an Aston Martin just as superb as his uncle's.

"There's never a dull moment in Will's house!" exclaimed Uncle Raj, breaking the silence and trying once again to engage Oliver in a conversation.

"Especially since Winston arrived," Oliver said looking down at his dog in the footwell. The retriever knew he was being talked about and he turned his head to one side, looked at Oliver, and showed his teeth in a rather peculiar smile.

"I don't suppose you get much peace," said Uncle Raj.

"Not really. I know it's awkward and Winston isn't welcome. I really hope that they don't send him to the kennels. He hates it there."

Uncle Raj nodded understandingly. "What about you? I don't think that they have plans to send you to the kennels, but maybe their plans are more geared towards sending you to stay with your nan. How do you feel about that?"

Oliver did not know how to answer.

"You could always come to London to stay with me." Uncle Raj paused, sensing Oliver's uneasiness. "I'll tell you what: think about it for a while."

Oliver was relieved he did not have to answer that exceedingly complicated question, and he did not want to give it too much thought. It was hard enough to consider the possibility of his parents not being home in time for dinner, let alone the next day or the day after that.

Someone Else

As soon as they arrived at April Cottage, Oliver leapt out of the car and headed for the front door. Before he had time to remove his key from his pocket, his uncle had got there first.

"You have a key?" Oliver asked, a little surprised.

"Your dad has one for my house too," Uncle Raj said. The door swung open. "Come on, there's a lot to do. Let's split up."

"I'll stay downstairs, you look upstairs," Oliver suggested.

He desperately needed his uncle out of the way for a little while. Sending Uncle Will upstairs the night before had given him just enough time to check out the labs.

"No," said Uncle Raj. "You can check upstairs. I want to have another look in the kitchen, where the disturbance was."

Oliver knew better than to argue; the last thing he wanted to do was draw any attention to the fact he needed to be alone to sneak downstairs.

"Keep an eye out for clues and an address book or something," said Uncle Raj as Winston followed him into the living room.

Oliver reluctantly traipsed upstairs, his mind somewhere between Plan A and Plan B.

He did not know what exactly he was looking for; nothing was different, the beds had not been slept in, and everything looked as it always did.

After wandering around each room, Oliver gave up searching for clues and returned downstairs with his mum's address book. Everything was exactly the same on the ground floor, too.

"I've found it!" he called out. There was no reply. "Uncle Raj!"

His godfather's absence was perfect for him. It was now or never.

Without wasting a second, Oliver headed for the kitchen. Winston lay in his basket, fast asleep.

Looking over his shoulder, Oliver threw open the larder door, reached for the button, and hastily stepped inside. Opportunity was with him, but time was not. Uncle Raj could appear at any moment.

With his heart beating like a pneumatic drill, he headed for the only place where he knew he might find answers.

Striding across the gantry, he descended hastily. A swarm of unanswered questions buzzed around his head, and the clock was ticking. With his mind two steps ahead of his body, he dived straight into the security room.

Slam! Halted by a painful thump, Oliver had collided with an object far larger than he was. His mouth opened and an involuntary sound escaped: *"Aaaarrgh!"*

In the moment that followed, his eyes refused to open, but something was clear. The sound of a breath and a feeling of the presence of another person was unmistakable. The large object was not a thing, but a someone.

It was only after hearing a familiar grunt that Oliver was brave enough to prise open one eye, just wide enough to see Uncle Raj standing boldly in front of him.

Oliver's jaw dropped. He attempted to speak, but no words came out.

"How do you suppose these labs got here in the first place?" asked Uncle Raj. He was smirking.

"A . . . ban . . . doned coal mine?" Oliver answered slowly. "My dad . . . built them."

"Your dad," said Uncle Raj smiling, "is talented at lots of things. But *building?*" he winked. "I gave him a helping hand."

Oliver could not respond.

"Before you were born," Uncle Raj explained, "I spent a long time at April Cottage helping your dad build these labs."

"Then how come Dad didn't tell me that you knew about them?"

"I suppose he had his reasons, or maybe the conversation never arose." Uncle Raj was still smiling. "I had a feeling I'd meet you down here."

Confused, but also strangely relieved, Oliver managed to smile back. Someone else knew about *his* secret! This meant that his uncle must know at least something about his father's work. The enormously heavy burden on Oliver's shoulders felt a little bit lighter; someone was there to help him carry it.

"We still have a lot to do," said Uncle Raj.

"I know."

"I'm not very good at using this security system that your dad designed. You have to program it. It's not my field."

"I did it already, but I didn't find anything useful."

"I thought that you may have done, but how about we take another look, check if you missed something?"

Oliver began turning on the monitors.

"Right," said Uncle Raj, "let's start by looking at what happened the morning they disappeared."

Oliver recounted what he had already discovered.

"OK." Uncle Raj sounded eager. "Let's look at what else was happening during the half hour before they went missing, and after that time, not just in the labs but around the rest of the house. Let's look at the power readings for the house and compare them with the footage we are playing back."

"I can do that," said Oliver. He set off with a burst of activity on the terminal keyboard.

One by one the feeds appeared.

The first monitor blinked and showed the labs, a quarter of the screen for each room. The second had footage of the garages. The third monitor was divided between the kitchen, living room, and dining room. The fourth covered the garden, the road to the house, and any approaching vehicles.

The screens continued to light up, showing each and every part of the house. The upstairs rooms were split across the fifth monitor. The sixth had the halls and the view of the entrance to the lab complex from the kitchen.

"That system's really quite remarkable," Uncle Raj sighed.

"Dad thought it was useless, said it was only good for finding things."

"Well, let's see what it helps us find."

Oliver nodded distractedly, trying hard to focus on every detail on the screens but sceptical that he would discover anything new.

"What time is this?" asked Uncle Raj, scanning one of the feeds.

"Nine-fifteen," said Oliver, pointing to the clock on the main monitor. "OK, here we go!"

The server monitor came to life with a graph illustrating the amount of power April Cottage was using versus what was being supplied by the cottage's turbines.

Oliver's dad was so painstakingly aware of every watt of energy they used that the wind turbines generated more than enough power to fuel the house, the labs, and probably the entire village. The surplus was sold back to the national grid. At the end of each month energy companies sent cheques to April Cottage instead of bills.

The mains electricity on the side of a Welsh valley was reliably unreliable; thunderstorms, and downed lines due to high winds, freak hail storms, or reversing tractors, were far from uncommon. Backup energy was vital. The power needed monitoring so closely because of the highly sensitive nature of some of the work in the labs. If the electricity was to fail, or even surge, it could destroy months or years of research.

Oliver screwed up his face in disbelief. The power available from the generator, sluice gate, and wind turbine was zero. The backup was not there.

"That's wrong," he said, pointing at the screen.

"Let's look at that later," said Uncle Raj.

Oliver's eyes moved to the fourth monitor. It showed his mum in the garage, strapping Henry into the back seat of her car before driving off. "Look!"

"What?" asked Uncle Raj.

Oliver pointed at the screen: not far from the entrance to the drive, a black van was parked on the road. It was not remarkable or distinct in any way. There were not even any markings on it. It was just a black van.

The only thing that made the van noteworthy was the way it drove off in the same direction as Oliver's mum, just seconds after she left to take Henry to nursery.

"Did you see that?" said Oliver.

They both stared at the footage. Behind the van was another one, as unremarkable as the first.

"Now that's suspicious," said Uncle Raj. "Can you save that file?"

"I can do far more than that." The screens went back in time, to the point where the first van was most visible.

"Watch this," said Oliver confidently. He clicked a key, and the van's rear quarter appeared, clear enough to see the make and model. The number plate was still blurred.

"Hmm." Oliver scowled as he looked at the picture. He was not a perfectionist but disliked being defeated by technology. "Hang on a minute, there must be a way around this."

Uncle Raj pulled up a seat.

"That's it!" Oliver said, tapping away furiously. "I can try using image recognition software."

This was something that he often played with for fun. He marvelled at being able to take an everyday object and look at it from a different perspective entirely. By looking at molecular structures and using an electron microscope to see formations of atomic nuclei and, with the right tools, even quarks, anything was possible. He knew his way around atomic maps; it was fundamental to his understanding of science.

He said, "My dad says that if scientists can't describe and recognise things that they think they know today, then there is no hope for progress and future discoveries."

"They sound like the words of a wise man."

"As wise as they come."

"You're far more like your dad than I thought," said Uncle Raj.

Oliver swelled with pride. He only hoped that his dad would agree. "This software," he said as he typed, "was designed to recognise objects that we relate to, stuff like numbers, letters, and icons."

As he hit the *Enter* key, a timer icon appeared and the servers behind them came to life. "Dad keeps the real-world objects on the servers in this room. He ran out of space in the physics lab."

"Doesn't he store it all in the cloud?"

"No way! Dad says if he's capable of hacking cloud-based storage systems, then someone else will be too."

"I was never any good with IT," said Uncle Raj. "I can *install* you a world-class IT infrastructure, just as long as I don't have to connect anything to it."

The server pinged, and a text document opened on the screen.

Objects found 22,675

Objects correlated to text 18

Text identified

TRANSIT Ford

RDV WM09

Oliver hit another key. The laser printer sprang into life and produced a copy of the van details.

"Wow!" said Uncle Raj.

Oliver was pleased with the result but still had to play it cool. "I'll try and get the second van."

A few more strikes, then another picture appeared. It was a blur. "Not quite so easy."

"Why don't you try to change the angle of the camera, and bring it into focus?" suggested Uncle Raj.

"Because," answered Oliver, "this footage was taken yesterday. So unless you have a way to travel back in time . . ."

Uncle Raj looked embarrassed. "So, what shall we do now?"

"We can enhance it with scrub software," Oliver said. He knew that his uncle meant well. He went on, "It's a clever piece of code that takes the TV picture, digitises it, then chops it into thousands of smaller photographs."

Uncle Raj raised an eyebrow.

"It then runs loads of mathematical processes on the data in an attempt to remove the fuzz before putting it all back together again."

"Urgh! And again in English?"

"It de-fuzzes!" said Oliver, pointing at a corner of the screen where a section of the image appeared cleaner and sharper.

"Amazing!" exclaimed Uncle Raj.

On the monitor in front of them was a clear picture of a Ford Transit van, facing them head-on, parked on the lane just outside the drive. The number plate read *RDG WM09*.

"Both of those vans are from the same company," Uncle Raj said out loud.

"How do you know that?"

"The number plates are almost sequential."

"Look!" Oliver pointed at the screen. "Look inside the van!"

Despite the darkened glass, he could see silhouettes of two figures, large and still.

Oliver's glare remained firm. The next few minutes showed movement on another screen. His dad's Land Rover returned. Now watching both screens, he noticed a black van close behind it.

He felt helpless, knowing that what he was watching had already happened and there was nothing he could do to change it. The Land Rover disappeared out of shot as the process was repeated and the third van's number plate was recorded: *RDP WM09*.

Oliver saw his dad reverse into the garage, get out, and disappear from the camera's view, then reappear as he walked through the front door. He seemed oblivious to the fact that he was being followed. Not once did he look over his shoulder. He blurred from room to room, screen to screen, before entering the hidden door and stopping in the nanotechnology lab. He sat at the terminal and quickly became absorbed. Without lifting his head, he typed furiously for ten whole minutes.

"Look," said Uncle Raj.

"Look at what?" asked Oliver, pausing the video stream.

"The power usage! It's . . . It's . . . shooting up!" Uncle Raj pointed at the graph they could see on the server. "What's your dad working on?"

"Something new, for sure. He's close to one of his eureka moments. He said something about 'tying up a few ends', 'putting things into place'. He's been working on this project for ages."

Uncle Raj's eyebrows rose simultaneously.

"It's something big," said Oliver. "You can tell when Dad is onto something big: he gets so distracted and engrossed in what he's doing, he loses track of the 'real world' completely. It can be quite funny. Yesterday he put salt on his cornflakes, and a few days ago he gave me Winston's breakfast and gave Winston my dinner money!"

Uncle Raj smiled.

Oliver looked up at the monitor. His dad had finished typing and was heading out of the lab. His eyes were drawn to the power usage graph – it was still climbing.

"What's he up to?" asked Oliver. "I'll need to look at the history file on that server to find out."

His focus was drawn to the monitor showing the lane outside. His mum's car was returning home. "I don't believe this!" he said angrily.

He watched helplessly as her car swerved around a black van before driving up to the house. She got out and walked straight to the front door and then into the kitchen.

Oliver wanted to yell at her: "Turn around" or "Look behind you". He knew it was futile.

His mum and dad met in the kitchen almost at the same time, and his dad put the kettle on. The cameras inside the house only recorded images, so the couple's filmed conversation was silent. The time on the clock read *10:10*.

"Somebody is getting out of the van," said Uncle Raj. "There are lots of them, heading this way."

Oliver stared at the monitor. There were two – no, five, then *nine* men, marching towards his front door. Oliver could only watch as an army of black-suited men with dark glasses drew nearer. He had no idea of what would happen next.

Each advancing figure walked with purpose. A suited mob was descending on April Cottage.

Two further figures emerged from the back of the black van parked closest to the house. These were different: they wore white overalls that were hooded so only their faces could be seen. The sort of clothing Oliver had only ever seen on television programmes featuring forensic scientists.

His blood boiled as he realised that something unthinkable could have happened to his parents.

With military precision, the army advanced. Oliver's attention was drawn by activity on the main monitor. The graph illustrating the amount of power being consumed at the house was going berserk. It had gone off the scale, and the gauge showing the amount of power available had plummeted.

"The inverters should kick in any time now," said Oliver. "This is so mad!"

He frantically scratched at his head, desperately trying to make sense of something that made no sense at all. Uncle Raj scratched his head too, even more confused than Oliver.

"So the power failed," said Oliver. "Why didn't the backup generator kick in?" He pointed at the screen. "Look, all the servers have reset!"

On every screen, the security system was dead. Each screen flickered. Oliver felt sick and had to force himself to keep watching.

How could he see something terrible happen to his parents? What good would it do?

Just as he felt that he could stand it no more, the power monitor reset; the energy level plummeted to zero and the screens flashed before going blank.

"Play it again!" said Uncle Raj.

"Play what?"

"The last few minutes."

"There's nothing to see!"

"Humour me," said Uncle Raj. "Only this time, bring the picture of the front door onto the main screen."

Oliver did as suggested and caught a glimpse of something, someone that he had missed before. Stepping up to his front door was a man whose image made Oliver shudder.

In the unfocused picture of the security camera, the figure was tall and wide. The blur made the features unclear, but the man's demeanour could not have been more distinct: determined, mean, and relentless. His fists were clenched, and he looked angry.

The eyes were hidden by dark glasses framed by one fat, furry, caterpillar-like eyebrow that went from one side of his face to the other with no gap for his broad, stunted nose. An angry scar ran from his right eye to his lip. A mobile phone was attached to his ear, and he was speaking.

The cameras outside were capable of recording audio, so Oliver adjusted the volume to maximum. They listened as muffled but unmistakable words were spoken: "Yes, sir!"

One by one, the monitors blinked, returning to life, displaying a still and quiet April Cottage. There were no strangers, no movements, no parents. Just an empty house. It was as if nothing had happened, as if Oliver had completely imagined the last few minutes.

"There!" said Oliver pointing to the screen displaying the road just outside the house. The backs of two men stepping into a solitary black van could be made out, just before the vehicle sped off.

"Where are Mum and Dad? Where are they?" shouted Oliver, holding the top of his head with both his arms. "They can't just vanish!"

"I could take a guess," said Uncle Raj.

Oliver was not naive. He could take a guess too. It was just that he did not want to.

"Winston!" yelled Oliver. Winston had appeared on the screen, emerging fearfully from behind the sofa in the lounge.

"Some guard dog!" said Uncle Raj, shaking his head.

"It was hardly his fault," said Oliver. "He was outnumbered, and wouldn't have had a chance!"

Trying hard to focus, he added, "The time stamp says 10:17. Security was only out for a couple of minutes."

"Long enough." Uncle Raj sighed.

"Do you think they've been kidnapped?"

"They may have gone with them of their own accord. Whoever they were, they knew all about the security system."

"But how could they?" said Oliver. "They can't have known anything about when the power would surge. They can't have known that Dad was in the labs, let alone what he was doing there."

"They obviously knew a lot more than we thought possible."

"Yes," said Oliver despairingly. "But what they don't know is that now we are on to them."

"But who are 'they'?"

"That's what we need to find out."

"We'll find them," said Uncle Raj. "Come on, let's check out the labs. There may be answers hidden there."

The Labs

"Right," said Uncle Raj, "you'd better start explaining what all these rooms are used for. It has been an awful long time since I've been down here."

Oliver had never shown anyone around the labs before, so to be able to give someone a tour felt peculiar. They crossed the glass gantry and arrived in the room opposite.

"This one's Dad's workshop," he explained. The large room was lined with rows of workbenches laden with heavy machines, each one spotlessly clean.

Oliver paused, thinking about explaining each of the machines, but stopped. That could take months, and there was so much to get through. He struggled to know where to start. "Dad hasn't spent much time in here recently. Shall we move on?"

Uncle Raj nodded.

They headed back to the gantry and a panel in the wall.

Oliver said, "It's from here that all of the environments are monitored. It ensures that the temperature, air pressures, background radiation, and electromagnetic fields remain constant. It also has the controls for the power management system."

He paused and sighed despondently. "I don't know what I'm looking for."

"We'll know when we see it."

"Let's go and check out the lower labs," said Oliver, jumping down the spiral staircase three glass steps at a time.

Whenever he entered this area it became so easy to forget that he was actually in a farm cottage in Wales. It was clean, white, airy, and clinical. The workspace was separated into three distinct areas, each very different and built to perform specific tasks.

Straight ahead was the largest section, taking up half the total area. This was the particle physics lab. It was full of testing and measurement equipment. The room was filled with a dull whirring sound from the particle accelerator; Oliver always though it sounded like a washing machine.

He introduced his godfather to the electron microscope, the cloud chamber, and particle accelerators, but he did not bother explaining them in any detail.

"This is where Dad looks at everything below the atomic level," he said. "You know how everyday objects are made from atoms? Well, the atoms are mostly space with minute pieces of matter in them."

"Right," said Uncle Raj nervously. "But how can you see what's going on inside an atom?"

"That's the easy bit, that's what the electron microscope is for." He pointed to a large metal cylinder on a desk.

"Is that just a microscope on steroids?"

"Basically."

Uncle Raj craned his neck and peered down the tube.

Oliver smirked. "You can't see them from there. They're far too small to be seen by a human eye."

"How small are they?"

Oliver looked thoughtful. "You've been to Wembley Stadium, haven't you?"

"Yes." Uncle Raj looked as if he was wondering what on earth watching Spurs could possibly have to do with atoms.

"Imagine a pea. It's quite small, isn't it? If the atom was the size of a stadium, then the nucleus, the part that is made from something solid, would be the size of a pea. All the rest of the atom is just a space around it where the electrons flow."

Uncle Raj nodded uncomfortably, then pointed towards the largest of the machines. "What's that for?"

Oliver explained, patiently. "The pipe," he began, pointing to the metal cylinder that joined the bulk of the machine to the wall, "goes deep into the old mine shaft. It's actually about a quarter of mile long. Particles are accelerated through it really quickly, close to the speed of light. They're then stored here."

He tapped a metal canister that looked like a huge drinks can. Uncle Raj smiled nervously.

"Don't worry," said Oliver, sensing his unease. "Think of it as a tool. Just like builders need tools, so do scientists."

This did not seem to help. Uncle Raj looked more confused than ever. "But what's it *for?*"

Oliver tried again. "Assume it's something to do with Einstein's theory of relativity . . . and Dad agreeing with him."

"Is that what uses all the power?"

"It certainly uses some of it to create an electromagnetic field and the strength of that field is 600 megavolts per metre to accelerate the particles."

"Where do they go when they reach the end?"

Oliver smiled. "That's where it gets really interesting."

He did not have the heart to tell his uncle that he probably would not understand. He tried to explain anyway.

"The particles are accelerated into this cylindrical machine, where electromagnetic fields keep them spinning around and around on the outer edge of the internal cylinder wall, thirty-two million times per second . . . or thereabouts."

Oliver pointed to the large steel canister with two access hatches almost tall enough to walk through. The chamber was draped with countless wires leading into the ceiling and connected to a network of metal pipes, each one steaming with a thin vapour.

"There's something coming out!" said Uncle Raj.

"That's just water vapour condensing around the liquid nitrogen pipes. The electromagnets need to be kept at minus 180 degrees."

Opposite where the particle accelerator entered the cylinder were two control panels, one for each access hatch.

"Dad does really complex stuff in here," said Oliver.

Uncle Raj scratched his head.

"It's quite cool really. Dad has found a way to control the particle assembly at the atomic level."

He said it in a matter-of-fact tone, almost as if it was the sort of thing that everyone did.

Now Uncle Raj looked blank.

Oliver was intuitive enough to know that his explanation needed to start at the very beginning. "Before you start building a house, you need accurate measurements . . . Right?"

"Right."

"What measurements do you use?"

"Metres, centimetres, and millimetres . . . Right?"

"Right!" said Oliver, smiling. "Scientists need scales too to look at atoms and things even smaller. They can't use millimetres so they use nanometres."

"Like a millimetre, only smaller?"

"It's one million times smaller than a millimetre," said Oliver. "What's the tiniest thing that you know?"

"A hair?" Uncle Raj offered.

"A human hair would probably measure about . . . 80,000 nanometres wide. A blood cell, now, that's smaller — it would measure 7,000 nanometres wide. In one nanometre, you could line up five atoms, end to end; ten if you use small ones."

Uncle Raj looked perplexed.

"Dad has spent loads of time in here recently," said Oliver to change the subject.

"What has he been working on?"

Oliver took a deep breath before answering awkwardly. "It's . . . complicated."

"I'm not thick!" Uncle Raj sounded bruised. "I do have a university degree in civil engineering, you know."

"And an excellent civil engineer you are too!" said Oliver, smiling, trying really hard not to sound too condescending. "Stop me if I lose you."

Uncle Raj perched himself against a wall with his arms folded, and listened attentively.

"This experiment my dad was performing was about relativity," said Oliver. "He was trying to create the conditions from another experiment so he could repeat it with his own special twist to see if something was possible. You know about Einstein's theory of relativity, yes?"

"E equals M C squared, but please don't ask me to explain what that means."

Oliver got up, pulled up a lab chair, and directed his uncle to sit down. "Look at your watch, and don't move . . . not even a millimetre."

Uncle Raj immediately began to fidget.

"*Don't move*," insisted Oliver. "When I say go, sit perfectly still and count ten seconds. Go!"

Despite the odd request, Uncle Raj sat and counted.

"Stop!" said Oliver. "How far did you move in ten seconds?"

"I didn't move at all. You told me to sit down and keep still."

"So, do you agree that from our perspective of space and time, you didn't move for a whole ten seconds?"

"Definitely!" said Uncle Raj. "Can I move now though?"

Oliver shrugged. "Now, I want you to imagine that there is a man on the other side of the universe with a great big telescope that has technology powerful enough to see right across the entire universe in an instant."

"OK," said Uncle Raj, shuffling nervously.

"Imagine that his telescope is capable of seeing right through our mountain and into our lab."

Uncle Raj nodded again. He was beginning to look like one of those nodding dogs that people often put on the dashboards of their cars.

"Let's call him Igor." Oliver thought that humanising the explanation might help.

"Igor?"

"It's just a name and a concept. Try and stick with it for now."

"If I must." Uncle Raj looked even more doubtful.

"Now, let's think about how you might look relative to him. He'd argue that you're sat in a chair travelling at 1,038 miles per hour, as the Earth turns. In reality, it's a little slower than that because we're not on the equator, but just run with it.

"Your chair and everything else on Earth is moving around the Sun in a different direction, at about 67,000 miles per hour.

"Plus, if Igor is across the Milky Way, he may suggest that our solar system is moving about another 250,000 miles per hour.

"If he were a scientific man, he could further argue that the entire universe is still expanding."

While Oliver was talking he had sketched some basic drawings on his dad's whiteboard. "Get it?"

"We're moving through space . . ." Uncle Raj began.

"That's right," said Oliver, "but not just space, we're also moving through time."

"But what's this got to do with what your dad has been working on?"

"Hold on, we need to grasp a few more basic principles first."

Uncle Raj gave a nervous smile.

"Dad has been trying to copy an experiment done decades ago that proved the theory of relativity."

"I get that bit, but what does it actually do?" Uncle Raj sounded frustrated.

"Basically, it accelerates particles to the speed of light."

"Why?"

"As they accelerate to the speed of light, time slows down the decay of particles so it appears to us that they decay slower. Time has become relative."

"Right."

"When the experimenters counted the number of times the particles travelled around the accelerator at the speed of light, there was an expected distance that they would travel before they decayed; a simple mathematical calculation. Dad's tracking the particles, and it's got something to do with how fast they travel, and how the speed of light affects how long they exist."

The look on his uncle's face confirmed that no more details were necessary.

"Shall we move on?" said Oliver.

Uncle Raj looked as if he was in pain. "Tell me again. Has this sort of stuff been done before?"

"There are particle accelerators in all sorts of labs," said Oliver. "Only, Dad has been tweaking the process for years. I don't know if there is a machine like this anywhere else in the world."

Uncle Raj sighed heavily. "I don't know if I understand it, but I think I'm starting to get it."

He got up off the chair, walked around the lab, sat back down, and opened his mouth to speak. But no sound came out.

"Are you all right?" asked Oliver.

Uncle Raj did not respond. He got up again and paced the room several times before stopping and saying, "Just how many experiments is your dad currently working on?"

"I have no idea." Oliver sighed.

"Take a guess."

Oliver began pointing his index finger at each fingertip on his left hand, then he raised each finger on his right hand, then looked down at his toes.

"All right!" said Uncle Raj. "I get it. There's something happening in these labs that someone wants to know about."

"They may already know." Oliver wandered out of the particle physics lab and into the electronics lab.

This was where he felt most at home. The whole lab was untidy, littered with circuit boards, wires, and robotics on every workbench. Computers, power supplies, and oscilloscopes filled each surface and the walls were lined with hundreds of tiny Perspex drawers full of brightly coloured electronic components. Each bench had some partly constructed project on it.

"This is my space," Oliver told his uncle. He jumped on the stool and rattled on a keyboard. A mechanical hand made from what looked like a metal alloy and full of intricate parts was on the bench closest to him. It was connected via a tangle of wires to an old computer with the side panel removed. The hand opened in slow motion.

"That's cool," said Uncle Raj.

Oliver jumped down and led his uncle out of the electronics lab and up to the door of the last room. Unlike the other labs, it was entirely sealed and had an airtight door.

"This is the biotech lab," said Oliver. "I never go inside."

"Why not?"

"Because of the brain." Oliver held his nose and opened the door briefly before slamming it shut again. A putrid smell escaped.

"What?" said Uncle Raj, gagging. "Who's was it?"

"I don't know! A chimp or a gorilla maybe. Dad calls it George."

"I thought your dad was a vegetarian!" said Uncle Raj, trying not to regurgitate his lunch.

"Maybe it was a gorilla with a donor card."

Uncle Raj appeared to have seen enough. "They'll be sending out a search party to find us if we don't go back soon."

"Why?" asked Oliver. "They haven't sent one out for Mum and Dad yet."

"Good point."

Content in the knowledge that the labs had been undisturbed, they returned to the house. In the kitchen, Winston was exactly where they had left him. He was lounging in his basket, pleased to be home, chewing his bone.

The First Black Van

"We really should get that photograph sent," Uncle Raj reminded Oliver.

Oliver logged onto the terminal in the kitchen and accessed the family's file of photographs. The most recent shots were from a camping trip in June. The new tent had needed testing, so the journey went ahead despite the forecast of storms.

Oliver looked at the picture he had taken of his mum and dad wrestling with the poles while the tent's outer skin was inside out. That made him smile. He found another shot of them standing outside the tent, warming their hands on mugs of tea. That seemed like the perfect picture.

"Are we ready?" asked Uncle Raj.

Oliver did not answer straight away. He was not looking forward to going back to Uncle Will's house. Eventually, he asked, "Will you stay?"

"For a short time. Have you got your mum's address book?"

Oliver had forgotten all about it. "Nope!"

He returned to the kitchen to collect it, and roused Winston. "Here, boy! I expect that Auntie Karen is missing you!"

At the very mention of his nemesis, Winston marched with his tail between his legs all the way to the car.

As they headed down the road, Oliver instinctively looked back at the house through his wing mirror.

He caught a glimpse of something black parked on the lane just around the corner. He looked again, hardly daring to turn around, and realised that what he actually saw was a black Transit van.

"They're back!" he yelled.

As they pressed on, the van moved too.

"They're following us!" said Oliver frantically.

"That's what they think!" said Uncle Raj through gritted teeth. "Have you got your seatbelt on?"

Oliver nodded.

Uncle Raj pushed the accelerator to the floor. The car sped down the dirt track, leaving a cloud of dust behind them.

The van emerged through the cloud. Uncle Raj gripped the wheel tightly; Oliver held onto Winston's ears, a little like handlebars.

Uncle Raj turned left at the bottom of the lane, and then right across the bridge. The van did likewise.

Oliver could not bring himself to look ahead, and his eyes were fixed on the wing mirror. The black van was still behind them, close on their tail.

They continued over the ford and then turned left again. Oliver's stomach felt as if it had lifted up into his chest, like the time he was strapped into the roller coaster at Alton Towers. This was different: there was no track.

"Why are they following us?" he shouted above the roar of the engine.

"That is what we need to find out!" said Uncle Raj as he changed gear on a sharp bend.

He drove faster still. The country lanes blurred as he continued to accelerate.

"What should we do?" shouted Oliver desperately.

"Lose them!"

Oliver felt sick. He wanted to close his eyes, but he also wanted to watch. What would happen if the van caught them?

Uncle Raj drove even faster down the lane, left at the bottom, and onto the main road. Oliver could see that the van was slightly further away, but still following. They were now near the town and would have to slow down.

They were approaching a roundabout, and Uncle Raj did not slow at all. Oliver closed his eyes and held his breath. Brakes screeched, horns tooted, and then . . . As he glanced into the mirror, he saw the black van swerve, then stop, as a car in front of it slammed on its brakes, blocking it from exiting the roundabout.

"Keep going!" shouted Oliver. "We may have lost them!"

"For now," said Uncle Raj, whose voice was trembling. "I think that we should probably keep this to ourselves, not telling Uncle Will – or the police."

Oliver nodded. He was not as sure as his uncle about not telling the police, but decided to trust his decision. They would certainly ask lots of awkward questions.

The Aston Martin skirted around the town and they composed themselves before they headed on to Llewelyn Close.

"What does your uncle know about your dad's work?" Uncle Raj asked Oliver.

"Just that he works on research projects for the university."

"And that's all?"

"It's all anyone knows. Nobody really asks."

"I'm not sure if I'm happy leaving you here in Wales, seeing what I've seen today."

"Do you think that they'll be back?" asked Oliver uneasily.

"That's just it; I don't know. I doubt I'll be able to persuade your nan or Will to allow me to take you back today, but you must do something for me."

"What?"

"Be on your guard at all times, and whatever you do, don't go out on your own."

Oliver sat quietly for the remainder of the journey, deep in thought and still holding on tightly to Winston's ears.

On returning to Uncle Will's house, they found all the adults sat around the table as they had been when they had left, discussing Oliver and Henry.

"It has been decided!" announced Auntie Karen. "It's best if you spend some time at Nan's house, until your mum and dad get back."

Oliver looked up at Uncle Raj, checking that he had his support before he spoke. His godfather gave him an encouraging nod. "That's fine," said Oliver. "Can Uncle Raj stay too?"

Nan hesitated before she answered. "Uncle Raj is a very busy man. I'm sure he has things to do in London."

"I'll tell you what," said Uncle Raj. "I'll settle you in tonight, and then if your mum and dad don't show their faces soon, I'll come and get you and take you and Henry to London. I can't fit you all in the car this time."

He turned to Uncle Will, Auntie Karen, and Nan. "Is that OK with you?"

"Let's hope that there will be no need to take them," said Nan.

At this point, Henry noticed that Oliver, Uncle Raj, and Winston had returned. He was pleased to see them, and gave each of them a hug.

"Better get your bags packed," said Uncle Will.

"We didn't unpack," said Oliver.

It was a beautiful summer evening. The sky was a pale shade of crimson and the silhouettes of the valleys could be seen in the distance. Despite this, Oliver felt uneasy; the reality of the past two days was beginning to dawn. He was mentally exhausted, and even thinking was beginning to hurt.

For the short journey to Nan's, he stared out of Uncle Will's car window, knowing that his parents had to be somewhere, but knowing too that it was down to him to find them. He could not help frequently glancing at the rear-view mirror, just to make sure they were not being followed by anyone other than Uncle Raj.

Nan lived in the same town as Oliver and Uncle Will, in Stanmore Place. It was a typical Valleys road, where everyone knew each other's name, each other's shoe size, and what they had for tea on Saturday. It was on the main road and so there was always the sound of traffic, day and night. Although it was a large house, Nan's was cosy and comfortable. It had, however, been empty for weeks; there was a mountain of post on the doormat to greet them. Even though everything was familiar, it lacked its usual welcome. It was cold and empty, and there was no smell of freshly baked banana loaf.

For the next hour, the house was full of activity. Uncle Will and Uncle Raj helped Nan to bring in suitcases and make up beds for the night. There were not many occasions where Oliver was left alone with Uncle Raj, but they did manage to grab a moment's peace just before he left.

Uncle Raj spoke softly to avoid being overheard. "Don't worry, we will find them. Just because I'm going back to London for a few days doesn't mean that I'm not still looking, or that I won't be able to help you. There is already an awful lot for us both to think about. I'll call you tomorrow, and the next day, and we'll make plans for you to come soon if your mum and dad haven't shown up."

"But what should I do if I see another black van?"

"Avoid it!" Uncle Raj paused, then asked, "You've got a camera, haven't you?"

"On my phone."

"Make sure that you keep it with you at all times and, if you can, take a photograph of anything suspicious. Send it to me and call me straight away."

"We will find them, won't we?"

"We won't stop looking until we do!"

Oliver gave him a smile and a nod. As he did, Nan appeared in the hall, handing Uncle Raj a packet of custard cream biscuits.

"They're for the journey," she said, sliding the packet into his hand. "I couldn't make you any sandwiches because I haven't got any bread or anything to put in them."

It was just Nan's way. It could never be said that she did not look after her visitors. It was one of those unsaid traditions that no guest ever left the house with an empty stomach. Uncle Raj understood this tradition and so accepted gracefully.

"Text me when you get back," said Oliver.

"Everything will work out, just you wait and see," said Uncle Raj as he stepped into his car.

"It has to," Oliver muttered under his breath.

All night, he tossed and turned, but could not stop his head from spinning. It ached from thinking so much, attempting to make sense of the events of the past few days. He also needed to keep checking on Henry. It was up to him to look after his little brother now.

His unsettled night was spent sat on the edge of the bed, listening outside his brother's bedroom door, and peering out through the window into the darkness to be sure that no black vans were looming. It was almost dawn before Oliver eventually closed his eyes.

The moment he woke, he rushed downstairs and asked, "Any news?"

"Not yet," answered Nan. "But no news is good news, eh?"

Oliver threw himself on the sofa next to Henry and was staring blankly at the TV when Indiana Jones' theme tune came from his mobile. He grabbed it, daring to hope that he would soon hear the voice of his mum or dad.

It was neither. Instead, it was Storm, his best friend from school.

"Hello," Oliver said sadly.

"Hi, Oliver," said Storm. Her voice was friendly and concerned. "I've just read the newspaper. That's awful about your mum and dad."

"Really?" Oliver had forgotten all about the press.

"It's in the *Sunday Times*."

"I should probably should have a look then."

"I had no idea."

"I know how that feels!"

"If you need a chat, I'm here until August." Oliver knew that Storm was planning a trip to Florida with her family. He could not forget, as she went on and on about it.

"Thanks," he answered solemnly.

"Are you OK?"

"Not really. I don't know what I'm feeling."

"Well, you know where I am. Who's looking after you now?"

"My nan."

"Text me," said Storm.

"Later," replied Oliver. It was nice to hear a friendly voice.

Storm was one of his oldest friends. Not a girlfriend, but a good friend who just happened to be a girl. They were in the same class, and the same patrol in the Scouts. Oliver and Storm got on really well. They had very little in common, but always had a laugh together. Storm was the type of person who managed to turn a boring everyday situation into something more chaotic and definitely more fun. Most of her mates referred to her as mad, and Oliver agreed. Being short for her age, she seemed to make up for her undersized frame with her oversized mouth. That was one of the things Oliver liked about her: she believed in being frank. Oliver thought it was an admirable quality. None of this namby-pambying, not answering a question with a straight answer, or beating around the bush and worrying who she might offend.

"I think we should go and get a newspaper," Oliver told Nan.

Under normal circumstances, Oliver would have walked to the newsagent to collect one, but not today. They all went in Nan's car. Oliver kept his eyes fixed on the rear-view mirrors.

It was not until they were all back at Nan's house that Oliver was brave enough to look at the paper. There was no mention of his parents on the front page, which surprised him. Their disappearance certainly felt like a front-page headline to him. He turned the page; nothing. However, when he landed on page five, he was greeted by a huge smile from his mum and dad. Beneath the headline *Valley's vanishing victims!* the story read:

A Welsh couple, Dr Paul Harris (42) and Megan Harris (32) have disappeared mysteriously in the South Wales Valleys. Dr Harris, a research scientist for the Heads of the Valley University, and Mrs Harris, a housewife, have vanished without explanation. They were planning to take a family holiday on the day of their disappearance, Friday, 17 July, but have not been seen since Friday morning. They are devoted parents to their two boys, Oliver (nine) and Henry (three).

Oliver looked up from the article in disgust. "Nine!" he said. "Nine!"

He got back down to reading the rest.

The children are now in the care of their grandmother, a Mrs Edwards (65) of Stanmore Place, Ebbwvenny. The family were due to fly out from Heathrow

Airport late on Friday evening, but failed to check in. Friends and neighbours are said to be out of their minds with worry.

Raj Patil, a close family friend, said: "It's so out of character. I know for sure that they would never leave their boys like this, so if somebody somewhere has any information at all, please contact Ebbwvenny Police."

Oliver stopped reading and took a breath. He glanced at his nan and said, "It makes it sound real."

"Somebody may read it and know where they are." Nan was trying to look reassuring.

"Do you think that Mum and Dad will read it?"

"Possibly," said Nan as she squeezed Oliver's hand. "Game of chess?"

Oliver did not want to play chess. What he needed to do was to go back home and search the labs more thoroughly.

"Can we go back to April Cottage?" he asked.

"We'll see later," said Nan.

We'll see was one of the adult responses that Oliver most detested. It was the sort of answer that so many gave when the proper answer was clearly *No chance!* but they were too weak to admit it. Instead they would just fob children off to temporarily shut them up, and then let them down later on.

The Press

"Knight takes bishop," said Oliver. "And that's you in check," he added as Winston started to bark.

"Shh!" said Nan.

"Lie down!" said Oliver insistently. But Winston only whimpered and whined; something was bothering him.

Oliver got up from the table and walked over to the window. He stopped and stared, hardly believing what he saw.

"Blimey!" Cars and vans branded with television logos were parked on the roadside. A crowd of people had gathered just outside the garden where reporters were setting up tripods with video cameras pointing towards the front door.

Oliver stepped back. "It's crawling with TV people!"

Nan rushed to the window and frantically tugged at the curtains until they closed. As she did so, the doorbell rang.

"Shall we answer it?" Oliver asked nervously.

"No!" snapped Nan, who was now walking around and around in circles.

"What should we do then?"

"Call the police!" said Nan, grabbing hold of the telephone.

"Wait!" said Oliver, but she had already begun dialling. "Don't call! It could be a good thing after all."

He understood how it was supposed to work; these journalists were here to tell people about his parents. The more who knew that they were missing, the greater the chances of finding them. He picked up his own phone, dialled Uncle Raj, and explained.

"Stay inside," his godfather replied. "Don't answer the door, and let me deal with it."

Winston began to tug at the curtains. Oliver grabbed his collar, held him tightly, and calmed him down.

Nobody dared stand near the window for a few minutes. Oliver disappeared upstairs to close the curtains in the bedroom, but his curiosity got the better of him. He angled the dressing-table mirror so that it pointed directly out of the window and he could see what was going on.

There were now even more people, even a few familiar faces. Neighbours from the street had gathered and were talking to the press; it looked like they were giving interviews. Oliver scowled. What could they possibly know about his parents being missing? Keeping well out of view, he hid behind the floral curtains and closed them.

When he returned downstairs, Nan had Henry by the hand and Winston on his lead and was heading for the back door.

"Your Uncle Raj phoned Uncle Will to arrange for someone to collect you," she told Oliver.

Uncle Will arrived within minutes, not at the back door but at the front. It was his job to create the decoy so that Nan, Oliver, Henry, and Winston could leave unnoticed through the back.

Uncle Will's car screeched to a halt right outside Nan's front garden. Bravely, he stepped out. Eyes, ears, and cameras were all focused on him. He began to speak . . .

At that exact moment, Auntie Karen's car arrived at the back of the house. Everyone jumped in and made their escape to Llewelyn Close.

Once they arrived, Oliver sat waiting for his uncle's return. It was half an hour before he came back, looking haggard and stressed.

He did not go into the house, but instead Oliver saw him headed for his shed.

He emerged with a hammer, a block of wood, and a pot of nails, and barricaded the gate.

"They won't be bothering us any more today," he announced as he walked back inside. "I've put them off the scent."

"What?" Oliver asked.

"The paparazzi. After I left Stanmore Place, they started following me. I felt like a celebrity being stalked!" He grinned. "I went on a detour, over the mountain and back through the town."

"Why would you do that?" asked Auntie Karen.

"To lose them, of course! I didn't want them following me here."

"*Did* you lose them?" asked Oliver.

"All apart from one black van," said Uncle Will, "but as I drove through the town, they got stuck behind a bus, and I went roaring off. Oh, it felt really good – I've never been in a car chase before."

Oliver did not hear the rest of the speech after *black van*. He went cold.

"Are you all right?" Uncle Will asked him.

"Yeah!" he said, trembling.

"Don't worry. My driving was awesome. They were left hanging high and dry!"

"What did you tell the press?" Oliver managed to ask.

"Raj e-mailed me a statement to read out. Pretty good job, as I think I'd got stage fright, stood in front of all those cameras!"

On remembering the cameras, Uncle Will walked over to the mirror above the fire in the dining room and studied his reflection, nodding to himself in approval.

"Here it is!" He handed Oliver a copy of the statement to read:

I would like to thank you for your time and concerns for Megan and Paul Harris. There have been no more developments and we are still completely baffled by the disappearance of my sister and brother-in-law. It is a difficult time for the whole family, and so we would request that the press leaves the family in peace, so the children can have some form of normality in their lives until the return of their parents. I would like to thank you once again for your interest, and ask you to respect the wishes of the family.

Oliver nodded wearily.

Auntie Karen huffed and puffed a bit before leaving the room. Oliver felt inclined to follow her and somehow apologise. It was clear that she had plans for the day that had not included hijacks, car chases, dogs, and even more children.

Oliver hesitated, then looked around, trying to find the right words. However, his attention was drawn to the kitchen.

The smell of a roast was filling the room. Oliver saw a large piece of meat in the oven, with a big bone sticking out of it. So, instead of finding what he had planned to say, Oliver used a different set of words that ran off the end of his tongue like an avalanche.

"Was that somebody's leg?" he asked.

"Yes!" his auntie said. "It used to be Larry the lamb's, but now it's our lunch!"

Oliver nodded. Moral debates with Auntie Karen were not something that anyone should enter into lightly.

"That reminds me," she said, "you'll be wanting something else, won't you?"

Oliver nodded, then watched as she rummaged at the back of one of her cupboards before discovering a faded packet mix that looked older the house. The box read *Nut Roast*.

"This looks nice for a vegetarian!" she said, smiling.

"Yum!" said Oliver. Every definition of *nice* seemed to imply that it would taste good, while every taste bud on Oliver's tongue tingled in pain in anticipation of something so bland and uninspired.

Nan began loading tureens and dishes full of vegetables and potatoes onto the dining table. Auntie Karen handed Oliver the plate containing the lamb's leg. Oliver carried it carefully, thinking that it must have been quite a large animal to have such a big leg. He placed it as far away from his seat as possible; he did not want to look at it all through dinner.

"Everybody inside and wash your hands," said Auntie Karen happily.

There was an influx of people into the house, all in anticipation of Sunday lunch.

"Whaaaa!" came from the downstairs cloakroom. Daisy cried, "Henry used my princess towel to dry his hands!"

Auntie Karen went immediately to deal with the incident.

Amid the hustle and bustle, Winston had also heard the dinner cry and assumed that the invitation was for everyone. He was first to arrive and thought it only fitting that he was entitled to first helpings. His attention was drawn to something that smelt like the closest thing to doggy heaven he could imagine: the leg of lamb.

Luckily for Winston, Oliver had placed it close to the edge of the table. With his mouth open wide, saliva dripping from the end of his tongue in anticipation, Winston grasped the bone firmly between his teeth. It weighed more than he had expected, so it dropped to the floor, splattering fat and grease everywhere. This encouraged him to take a firmer grip on the bone as he dragged it towards the front door, not wanting to share it. He was ready to make a getaway.

"No!" Auntie Karen yelled hysterically as she returned and discovered what was happening. "No! No! No! No!"

"What on earth are you shouting about?" asked Uncle Will, coming from the kitchen with a jug of gravy and a carving knife.

"No! No! No! No! No!" cried Auntie Karen, getting louder with each word. She pointed frantically in the direction of Winston and the front door, through which he had just disappeared.

"Well, I guess Winston's going to be one happy dog this afternoon," said Uncle Will as he spotted him dragging the lamb down the front step.

Once Auntie Karen was calm, everyone sat down to enjoy nut roast and vegetables. Even though Oliver knew it looked like cardboard and tasted like sawdust, he pretended to really enjoy it.

When Auntie Karen was able to say something other than *no*, Oliver took great delight in telling her how delicious it was. He added that she should enjoy her slice very much, based on the fact that it contained a lot fewer calories than the leg of lamb. Everyone thought that this was funny, except for poor Auntie Karen, who was deeply traumatised.

Winston had put himself in the shady spot under the elm tree, where he contentedly stayed for the rest of the afternoon, sleeping off his feast.

The day dragged into evening. After dinner, nobody dared to venture further than the garden and risk exposing themselves to the press.

Oliver found himself alone in the lounge with Uncle Will. "Where will we stay tonight?" he asked.

"It should be fine for you to go back home to Nan's house. I'll drive up alone a little later just to check that nobody's hanging around."

"Thanks." Oliver was relieved that he would not have to face another night at Llewelyn Close, and grateful about not facing the press.

He was glad to be alone with Uncle Will. He had something on his mind. Something that he knew was one of the main causes of Auntie Karen's stress: his uncle's forthcoming holiday plans for France.

"I've been thinking," said Oliver hesitantly. "I know that you're not so keen on going away, but I think that you should go anyway."

He did not want his uncle to miss his holiday on his account. In fact, it would be quite a relief for him to go. His uncle was followed by a black van earlier that day; Oliver saw no reason why he should hang around.

Uncle Will shook his head, looking concerned. "I couldn't leave you now. You need me here!"

He paused, then said, "We" – he put a lot of emphasis on the word – "need to find your mum and dad."

"We are not doing a lot of looking for them though, are we?" said Oliver.

"Maybe we need to leave that job for the experts!"

Oliver knew full well that if it was down to the "experts" to find them, his parents might never return home.

Oliver's uncle looked at him. "You are growing up very quickly." He smiled. "I'll have a think. There may just be a compromise."

Uncle Will reached over to grab the TV remote control. "Shall we try and catch the highlights of the rugby?"

Oliver nodded. He wholeheartedly supported Wales for the Six Nations, but would go to any means necessary to avoid playing it himself. He never really saw the point of standing around on a rugby pitch in the rain and snow, waiting for someone to swipe his legs from underneath him, as they so often did, then spending hours recovering in the medical room.

Uncle Will, on the other hand, was a rugby fanatic. He used to enjoy playing it, but had to retire due to lots of irreversible injuries. He supported the local rugby team, the Ironmen, and Oliver was quite aware that there was an important home game today. On no account would Uncle Will miss a single match, but today he was otherwise occupied rescuing Oliver from Nan's house, keeping watch for the press, and spending a family day at home.

The least Oliver could do was allow him to watch the highlights and catch up on the final scores.

As the TV blinked on, Oliver was greeted by a familiar sight: the road in front of Stanmore Place. A journalist was summarising the situation: ". . . have disappeared suspiciously. Nobody has any idea of their whereabouts."

Next, the camera diverted towards the front door of the house, then Uncle Will appeared on screen.

Watching himself, Oliver's uncle yelled to the kitchen. "Karen! Karen! Come and see this. I'm on the news!"

Both Nan and Auntie Karen rushed in to see the image of him looking nervously at the camera and reading out the statement. On screen, Uncle Will seemed petrified. At the end, he gave a kind of shimmy and ducked behind the wall as the camera turned to the crowds.

The footage went back to the journalist who had begun analysing the statement, and reiterating Uncle Will's request for anyone who may have any information that could help to find Oliver's parents.

Oliver suddenly thought: maybe he was breaking the law. He was withholding information from the police. Did that make him a criminal? He quickly put that to the back of his mind and decided that he would prefer to be a criminal than disloyal to his father.

The journalist ended with, "This is Penny Gossip, in Ebbwvenny, in the South Wales Valleys. Good evening."

The TV no longer showed Nan's house, but the rugby results.

"Good on you!" bellowed Uncle Will, raising his right hand in a fist pump as he saw the scores.

He then announced he was going to Stanmore Place to see if it was safe to return.

Once his uncle had left to get ready to go, Oliver stared at his phone. No messages. He thought about calling Uncle Raj, but decided to wait until he was alone. Instead, he sent him a text:

Did you see the news?

Within thirty seconds, a message beeped back:

Yes. Phone me when you're alone tonight. We need a chat.

This was the first positive news that Oliver had heard all day. He was convinced that he had to do something himself. He had an idea.

"Nan," he said, "would you mind if I phoned Storm and asked her to come over tomorrow?"

"That would be lovely," she said, looking pleasantly surprised.

"It should help you take your mind off things," said Auntie Karen condescendingly.

Oliver smiled back, but he thought, *As if anything could take my mind off "things"!* He went out into the hall to call Storm, aware of his two eavesdroppers nearby.

"Hi, you," Storm responded to his greeting.

"Yeah, I . . . I thought that I may take you up on that offer to come and keep me company tomorrow."

"All right then, course I can. What time and where?"

"About ten, at my Nan's house. Do you know where it is?"

"I've been before," she reminded him. "Shall I bring anything?"

"Just yourself. See you then."

Oliver's plans for tomorrow were taking shape. He was not sure what they yet were, but he was determined not to waste another day sat on his backside while his parents were counting on him.

"All clear on the Western Front!" announced Uncle Will as he returned to the room. "Are you ready?"

"It's time for Henry and Oliver to go!" shouted Auntie Karen to the rest of the household. Oliver detected a tone of elation.

"What have you been doing?" asked Auntie Karen as three smiling but muddy faces appeared from the garden. "You're all filthy!"

"Where's Winston?" asked Uncle Will. The dog appeared behind Henry, the muddiest of all. The front half of his body was covered in a thick brown layer of mud. It made him look no longer like a golden retriever, but more of a chocolate Labrador.

"Look at the state of you!" said Nan crossly.

Auntie Karen did not say anything, but only gripped the back of the kitchen chair so tightly that it made a cracking noise.

"Outside!" shouted Uncle Will to Winston.

Everyone followed, including Auntie Karen, who immediately said, "My! My! My! My!" Each word became more breathless and desperate, but louder nonetheless. "My . . . beautiful lawn!"

They were greeted by the sight of a mound of earth almost as tall as Henry. There was a hole next to the mound as deep as the earth was high. This was the final straw. Auntie Karen loved her lawn so much she even trimmed the edges with her nail scissors.

"We helped Winston," said Daisy proudly.

"He needed to bury his treasure!" Henry explained.

Oliver left, passing the hole in the garden. At the bottom was Winston's greatest possession: the lamb bone. When Auntie Karen saw it, she was reminded of her lost dinner and how, in one day, Winston had managed to ruin her feast and her prize lawn.

She scowled, then pulled a sort of pained face at the lawn, alternating expressions until Uncle Will announced, "Time to go!"

Winston was first to the car; even he knew that it was time to leave.

"He doesn't normally have bones," Oliver apologised to Uncle Will on the way home.

"Don't worry," said Uncle Will, who hated gardening anyway. "It's nothing that can't be fixed."

Uncle Will settled everyone into Nan's house. He even helped to bath Winston. It was as if he was delaying his retreat home. There were no journalists outside any more, just the odd neighbour who would walk past the house a little slower than usual and glance inside.

The evening was much calmer. It had been an eventful day and Oliver was exhausted, although he was no closer to finding his parents than he had been the day before. He seized the moment to call Uncle Raj.

"Hello there," his godfather greeted him. "I wondered when you would call."

"First real chance I've had."

He explained about the events of his wasted day: the press, the lamb bone, and the buried treasure. Uncle Raj immediately saw the funny side, and could not help but chuckle.

"I wouldn't write the entire day off yet," he said. "You may have been tied up, but I have been doing some homework of my own."

"What?" Oliver asked anxiously.

"Let's just say that some things are starting to unfold. I'll be back in Wales in a couple of days and we can talk properly. I think that we need to spend some more time at your house. I want to bring you to London too."

Oliver agreed and arranged to phone Uncle Raj the following evening, unless he needed to speak to him in the meantime.

Exhausted, Oliver lay on his bed with his headphones on and fell asleep.

Oliver and Storm Investigate

"It's still there!" Oliver whispered to Storm as he peered through Nan's upstairs window. In the lay-by opposite them was a black Transit van.

Despite the fact that the number plate was different to those he had identified on the video feed, it was too much of a coincidence to ignore. The glare of the sun on the darkened windscreen made it almost impossible to tell if anyone was inside.

If Oliver had one friend that he could trust categorically, that friend was Storm. It had only been three days since he had last seen her, but so much had happened that it felt like an eternity. She knew no more than anyone else about the disappearance of Oliver's parents, but as he needed her help, he would have to tell her something, starting with the black vans. Everything else would be on a need-to-know basis.

He lowered his voice even further. "You know that my parents have vanished?"

"Yes." Storm sounded sympathetic and curious.

"It's more complicated than everyone else thinks," said Oliver, pausing and carefully considering each word before he spoke. "There may be a reason why they've disappeared, something that nobody else, not even the police, knows about." Oliver paused again. "Not even Nan or Uncle Will. Nobody knows, except for me and Uncle Raj."

He had Storm's full attention.

"They haven't just gone off somewhere. It has some connection with my dad and his work." He took a deep breath. "They've been . . . kidnapped!"

Storm stared at Oliver, as if he was winding her up. She waited for a punchline, but none came.

"You have to tell the police!" she demanded.

"You don't know all of the facts. Believe me, if I could tell the police, I would've done it already. I need you to say nothing." He paused, then added, "I know how difficult it is for a motormouth to say nothing!"

Storm instantly hit Oliver over the head with the nearest book.

"I wouldn't have told you this," he said, "but I need your help."

He explained about the car chase, and how Uncle Will had been followed.

"If you're going to find them, we need to find out whose van it is," said Storm, raising an eyebrow.

"I know that, but I don't know how to."

"Aren't there police records or something?" she suggested.

"Hmm . . ." pondered Oliver, knowing very well that there were, but that he and Storm had no chance of accessing this information. "How about we follow the van?"

"Like when did you get a driving licence?" asked Storm. "Not to mention a car."

"That's not what I mean. What if we could track the van?"

"How? We're all out of high-tech spy gadgets! Plus, we don't know that *that* van has anything to do with the black vans that followed you."

"It's far too much of a coincidence not to be. It may be a little devious, but we could track the van if we use the SIM card from my phone. Set up a profile allowing the buzz application to provide a current location. That way, when the phone moves, we'll get to know about it."

Storm nodded in agreement while frowning in bewilderment.

"Nan has a couple of old phones in the dresser," said Oliver.

"She'll never let you take them though."

"It's for a good cause," said Oliver, "and besides, she won't even notice."

He headed downstairs to retrieve one. Inside one of the drawers was a selection of old mobiles, including one he recognised as his mum's old smartphone.

Nan was distracted as she and Henry were elbow-deep in pastry in the kitchen, making apple pie for tea. Oliver slipped the phone in his pocket and returned upstairs.

"Got one," he said as he pressed *On*. It bleeped, and the screen lit up for a second then went dead.

"A dead phone," said Storm.

"No! A tracking device."

She did not share his enthusiasm.

"We can charge it and set it up, then install the app. We stick it under the van, then track it on another phone. We'll know wherever that van is."

"OK, let me understand this," said Storm. "We just say hello and ask whoever's in the van if they would mind us placing a tracking device in their engine, and we risk being kidnapped ourselves in the process? Perfect!"

Oliver grimaced. "That's why I need your help."

"When I asked on the phone if there was anything I could do, you took it literally, didn't you?"

"Yep!"

"Urgh!"

"So are you in?"

Storm forced an uncomfortable smile.

Oliver knew that he was asking a great deal of her. He also knew that they needed a plan.

It took the remainder of the day to come up with anything plausible. They both had lots of suggestions about methods of distraction; some were simple, some highly complex. Every time Oliver came up with an idea that involved Storm doing anything risky, she invariably tried to simplify it, change it, or rule it out completely.

When they had eventually settled on a plan, they needed to gather the additional equipment and supplies to make it happen.

"Aren't you forgetting something?" asked Storm.

"Nope, think we have it all sorted."

"Not quite: the mobile is still flat."

"Good thinking, Sherlock. I should rig up a backup system to make sure that the battery lasts for a few days at least."

Oliver went in search of a phone charger. Nan had several, and did not seem to mind that Oliver was rummaging through her drawers. He removed batteries from three unused phones, and used scissors to dissect an old power supply. With this, some tape, and a small amount of tinfoil, he rigged up a super-long-life backup battery.

"Is that meant to look inconspicuous?" asked Storm. "Because if it is, you've failed: it looks more like a time bomb."

"Nobody is going to see it – it's going to be hidden under a van."

While the batteries charged, they went over the plan for the fifth time; each time had even more details than the last.

"It sounds simple enough," said Oliver. "What could go wrong?"

"I can't think of one single reason . . . I can think of a *zillion*, just off the top of my head!"

"Can I borrow your phone for a moment?" asked Oliver. "I'll need to tell my Uncle Raj that he won't be able to call me on my mobile anymore."

"Can't you use the landline?"

"I don't want my nan to know I've dissected my phone. She'd want to know why."

"All right. But don't use all my credit."

"Promise, I'll be quick."

Oliver briefly explained to his uncle, who said, "Thanks for letting me know. Watch this space and remember what I said."

The conversation ended.

"I've never met your uncle," said Storm. "What's he like?"

"Complicated!" Oliver handed back the phone. "Have you noticed something?"

Storm looked where he was pointing: the parking bay opposite the house. "What?"

"The van. It's gone!"

"So it has."

"I didn't see that go. I didn't see anyone getting in either."

"Creeps!" said Storm. "That means that we can't go ahead with our plan. I've been saved!"

"No." Oliver scratched his head. "It could come back, and if it doesn't, you'll have to come back tomorrow."

Storm looked thoughtful. "Can't do tomorrow."

"What?" said Oliver anxiously. He was crestfallen, and was about to try to convince her how much he needed her help when she smiled.

"Of course I will, you daft banana," she said, smiling. "You are so easy to wind up!"

"I knew you wouldn't let me down." Oliver smiled back.

The doorbell rang and the distinct melodic tune of a thoroughbred Valleys accent travelled up the stairs. Storm's mum had arrived to take her home.

They both made their way downstairs. Chatting with Nan in the hallway was a short lady, not much taller than Storm, and that was something as Storm was the shortest girl in year six. "Are you ready to go home?" she asked.

"Can Storm come back tomorrow?" Oliver asked.

"I'm not sure if that's a very good idea at all, given the 'situation'."

"They've been no trouble, really they haven't," said Nan smiling. "They've been good as gold all day, playing cards . . . and doing something with tinfoil."

She shrugged.

"How about Oliver comes to our house instead?" Mrs Minton asked Nan.

"Would you like that, Oliver?" asked Nan. "Or maybe, if it's too much for you at the moment, you'd be happier staying here."

Oliver needed Storm's help, and going to her house could prove worthwhile. They could always sneak back and keep watch to check if the van returned. Their scheme could still go ahead. "It's fine," he said. "I'll go."

Arrangements were made for Oliver to arrive at Storm's house the following morning at ten o'clock.

"Thanks for coming over!" Oliver waved them goodbye, happy in the knowledge that he had a plan for the following day.

The evening seemed to drag on forever. Oliver played fetch with Winston, and snakes and ladders with Henry. While Nan tucked his little brother into bed, Oliver stared out of the window, suspicious of every black vehicle that drove past.

"I phoned the police this afternoon," Nan told Oliver as she returned downstairs. "They said that one of your neighbours remembers seeing a van outside your house on Friday morning."

"Really?"

"They also said they would call around tomorrow for a chat."

The telephone rang, interrupting them. It was Uncle Will. Oliver strained to hear what he said, but only heard his nan's responses.

"Will and Karen have decided to go to France after all," said Nan after she had hung up. "Just for the wedding – going on Wednesday and returning on Sunday."

"Good! I told them to go. It's not like they are doing much here to find Mum and Dad. Auntie Karen really needs a holiday."

There was a loud knock at the door. Oliver was so startled, he flinched.

"Who is that calling this late?" Nan scowled.

"I'll go!" said Oliver, feeling that he should not allow his nan to answer it. He could make out the silhouette of a substantial dark figure through the distorted glass panel of the front door.

Taking a deep breath, Oliver bravely opened the door just enough to peer around the edge. A man dressed in black from head to toe stood before him.

"Oliver Harris?" said a deep loud voice.

Oliver nodded, immediately regretting admitting it was him. He gripped the door handle tightly for anchorage.

"Sign here!" the man instructed, handing Oliver a small tablet and a stylus.

Oliver followed his instructions, and opened the door wide enough to sign his name and get a better look. The light from the house was enough to see that the stranger wore a black leather jacket and trousers, and huge boots with dozens of silver buckles. He handed over a small box before turning swiftly around and leaving.

All that Oliver could do was to watch as he climbed onto a motorbike. Its headlight lit up the road, then there was an explosive bang and the roar of an engine. He drove away into the night on the most awesome bike that Oliver had ever seen in his life. It could only have been a Harley-Davidson.

Stood motionless in the doorway, his mouth open wide, Oliver stared into the darkness.

"Who was it?" asked Nan.

"I have no idea," replied Oliver, "but he's got a Harley-Davidson!"

This did not impress Nan. "What's in that box?"

Having completely forgotten about it, Oliver examined the package as they returned inside. "Oh, this? I don't know."

A label on it said *Oliver Harris*, and his nan's address was clearly marked.

Oliver opened it. A note inside read:

I didn't like to think of you being without one. I thought I'd get one couriered to you this evening. It's a different model, but I hope you like it. If you have any problems, give me a call later. Uncle Raj.

Under the note was a brand new phone. Oliver smiled as he held a Z-sphere, the greatest mobile ever invented.

"There's nothing wrong with the phone you've already got," said Nan.

"There is, because I sort of broke it."

"You should've told me. I've got some spares in the drawer."

Oliver shrugged.

"You had better phone your uncle to say thank you."

"I will."

Oliver waited until Nan was out of the way until he made the call. Uncle Raj's number had been pre-programmed, and his face popped up on the screen.

"Cool!" said Oliver. It was good to be able to see his godfather and to talk to him.

"It's not a toy," said Uncle Raj. "It's so that you can record anything remotely suspicious, and we can keep in touch."

Oliver explained his plan for the following day.

"That's not what we agreed," said Uncle Raj. "You are not meant to put yourself in any danger and go out alone."

"But I can't just do nothing! Could you?"

Uncle Raj sighed. "I suppose not. Just be careful and let me know how you get on. I'm not sure I approve."

"I won't be on my own. I'll be with Storm."

"Storm? Will she make a good bodyguard?"

"Better than a Rottweiler!" Oliver smiled.

"Just make sure that you're on your guard at all times, and stay one step ahead . . . and good luck. I'll come and get you the day after tomorrow and bring you back to London."

Oliver thanked his uncle for his new phone before saying goodnight.

He went to bed happier that tomorrow, things would start to happen.

Let's Get Going

A blob of drool landed on Oliver's left ear. He opened his eyes to see Winston hovering over him.

"Pancakes!" Nan shouted from downstairs.

Oliver had woken feeling positive. He knew that today was going to be a good day, and if his mum and dad were not home by tomorrow, then he was going to London. Devouring his breakfast and gathering up all that he needed, he left for Storm's house.

It was in the same town, but on the far end of the valley. Despite Oliver insisting that he could walk, it was far enough for Nan to insist that they drive. Oliver kept watch as they drove through town, dreading a black van following them and wondering what would happen if they were chased with his nan behind the wheel.

Although he worried about seeing a black Transit, he knew that finding such a vehicle was essential for the plan to work.

"What d'you two want to do today?" asked Mrs Minton melodically. She smiled pitifully at Oliver. "How's about we start with some board games?"

"No thanks, Mum," said Storm.

Mrs Minton took the hint and soon left them alone.

Storm and Oliver sat at the kitchen table. "We weren't followed," he said. "There wasn't a van there last night either."

"What do you think we should do?" asked Storm.

"We should wait, then head back to either my nan's, or my house, but not let anyone know where we're going."

Storm looked worried. "Let's go through the plan again."

Oliver groaned. "You know it inside out!"

"I just want to make sure. Maybe I'm hoping you've changed your mind."

"Why would I do that?"

"Because you saw sense?"

"Don't know anybody by that name!" said Oliver, smirking. "Let's just get on with it."

He jumped to his feet.

Storm poked her head around the door into the living room to speak to her mum. "Can we go outside?"

"If you want," she replied. "It *is* a beautiful day."

"Can Oliver borrow Liam's bike?" Storm asked.

This was part of the new plan, and Mrs Minton had to agree. Liam was Storm's older brother. He was fourteen, and away at summer camp.

"You must promise to look after it!"

As they headed towards the park, Oliver said, "Plan A, part one . . . Tick!"

"I feel like a piece of bait dangling from a fishing rod, waiting for something big and nasty to take a bite!" said Storm. She had to catch up with Oliver, who was not waiting for her to change her mind.

"You squirm a bit like a worm!" he said, smiling.

The trip to the park was their decoy. That was not where they needed to be, but as Mrs Minton had waved them off, it was the direction that they needed to head first. They lingered at the end of the road, and waited just long enough to be sure that she had gone back inside. As they were waiting, Storm came up with a few dozen excuses about why their plan was doomed to failure.

"How can you be so sure that we'll see a van today?" she asked.

"There was one there yesterday, wasn't there?"

Storm frowned.

The safest route back to Stanmore Place was to avoid the main road and take the mountain path. They would need to bypass Storm's house to get onto it. Vigilant as they left the park and veered towards Storm's house, something made Oliver pause.

Parked at the end of the lane, on the corner of the street, was an unmarked black Transit van.

"Same plan, different place!" Oliver whispered to Storm as they stopped before they could be seen by anybody in the house or van.

"But how do you know it's the same black van?" asked Storm.

"Because it has the same number plate. How about you stop making excuses, and we just get on with it? Ready?"

"Am I allowed to say no?" she whispered, her face a pale shade of grey. "Can we swap jobs?"

"You know why we can't do that. They'll recognise me. They've been watching my house for goodness knows how long. But you . . . They don't know that you have anything to do with me."

"They do now! Why are they parked on my street?"

"They must have followed my nan's car here this morning. Just cycle past." Oliver tried to sound encouraging. "Check if there is anyone in the van."

Mrs Evans, Storm's next-door neighbour, was in her garden doing a spot of weeding.

"Good morning," she shouted cheerily.

"Oh, hi!" said Storm without turning, not wanting to take her eyes off the van for a moment.

She cycled quickly around the block. On her return she gasped to Oliver, "Two of them . . . Both men, I think . . . Can't see much . . . Windows are black."

"Perfect! On the count of three, you know exactly what to do. We've been over this a hundred times. What could go wrong?"

"Do you really want me to answer that now?"

"I'll get in position!"

Oliver reached into his bag to remove the tracking device, a roll of tape, and scissors. He fixed the tape into position. Storm grabbed the miniature ketchup sachet they had brought and fastened her cycle helmet. As planned, she headed off and Oliver waited.

Storm had to arrive at the van first; she was the decoy. Oliver remained hidden to keep a watchful eye on her. Despite reassuring Storm that nothing could possibly go wrong, he knew all too well the dangers that they were both facing head-on.

He reflected on his friendship. Despite the fact that he had practically used emotional blackmail to coerce Storm into helping him, she could have said no.

Crouched behind a garden wall, Oliver waited for the exact moment when the pathway was clear.

He spotted his friend. She was heading straight for the van, exactly how they had planned. She was going quickly. In fact, she was going *very* quickly . . .

As she approached the van, she sped up even more. Then, with a thunderous crash, her bike collided nose-first with the front of the vehicle.

Immediately, Storm fell to the ground, her bike in a heap next to her. Oliver watched as she fumbled with the sachet of ketchup, squirting it down one side of her face.

She groaned. It sounded terrible. Despite knowing that this was all part of the plan, Oliver could not help wondering if that groan was an act of drama, or pain. However, this was how it was meant to happen, and Storm *was* an extremely accomplished moaner.

The distraction provoked the exact reaction that they had hoped for. Both the driver and passenger jumped out of the van to see if Storm was all right.

The two men who stood peering over Storm looked as out of place as two ballet dancers at a rugby match. Local van drivers usually wore overalls and baseball caps; these men wore smart black suits and dark sunglasses.

Oliver took out his phone, pointed the camera at them, and clicked. The image was fuzzy, and he was angry. Were these the same men he had seen at April Cottage? He could not allow himself to become distracted; he had to focus on what he needed to do.

The men's departure from their vehicle was Oliver's cue to move. He left the bike hidden and ran to the back of the van, then, without hesitation, dived underneath and attached the bug firmly to the chassis behind a rear wheel. It was snug and tight, and almost completely out of sight. Oliver's part of the job had been completed. He now had to hide before he was spotted.

The commotion at the front of the van continued. Moaning could still be heard from the ground, and Mrs Evans had run out from her garden, waving her hedge trimmers.

Storm lay on the road, her face covered in tomato ketchup. "Don't just stand there," she cried frantically. "Call an ambulance!"

"You stupid men!" yelled Mrs Evans. "What have you done?"

Oliver supposed she could not have noticed that the van had been parked, so had obviously assumed that Storm had been run over. It was an easy mistake to make; very few accidents involve bicycles crashing head-on into parked vehicles.

In no uncertain terms Mrs Evans told the men that if anything bad had happened to Storm, they would be locked up for a long time because of their idiotic driving. She claimed to have seen everything that had happened.

By this time, a few other neighbours had gathered, wondering what the fuss was about. One had gone to get Mrs Minton.

Eventually, Storm stopped moaning and Oliver saw her mum appear. Mrs Minton looked petrified at the sight of Storm lying on the road, with her bike next to her, her face covered in red. She went to her daughter's side and fell to her knees, cradling Storm on her lap.

Storm knew that it was time to tone it down. She opened her eyes, sat up and put her hand on her head.

"Hi, Mum!" she said as her mother squeezed her tightly. "What time's lunch?"

Her mum mopped her stained head with the sleeve of her cardigan. Storm looked a little better without the ketchup.

The next few minutes saw the ambulance arrive and Storm try hard to convince everyone that she was feeling much better. She had a hard time persuading the paramedics that she did not need to go to hospital, so she even resorted to doing a handstand in the middle of the road.

All the while, Oliver's eyes remained fixed on the two men, who appeared more and more agitated.

After the paramedics had conducted a thorough head examination, they appeared far less concerned. Oliver saw one of them wipe Storm's brow before sniffing the swab suspiciously. Finally, Mrs Minton promised to take Storm to be checked over by her local doctor, and the ambulance left.

Oliver left his bike and hid behind a conifer in a neighbour's garden that offered a better vantage point. The two men did not seem bothered by the tyre-sized dent in the van and were clearly not going to hang about a moment longer than necessary.

Oliver needed more pictures to show Uncle Raj, so he pointed, zoomed, and clicked at the man returning to the passenger seat.

Despite the dark glasses, he saw a face that he recognised: the beard, the joined eyebrows, and the scar. It was without a doubt the same man he had seen on the security camera outside his house on the day his parents disappeared.

Oliver would have known if he had seen the driver before; he was taller and much heftier than the other man. His dark hair was greasy, as if it had been painted onto his head, and it curled at his neck.

The van left.

It was time for Oliver to join the scene of the crash. Storm needed rescuing.

"What's happened?" he called.

Mrs Minton was still on her knees, sat in a heap on the roadside.

"You may well ask!" she said.

"Are you all right?" Oliver tried to ask with concern. He was a useless actor, but thought he sounded genuine.

Storm explained how she had been a little careless and bumped into a parked van.

Oliver tried to sound surprised. "Oooo, so very . . . Storm."

Storm's mum insisted that they go straight to the doctor's surgery. It would be ages until Oliver and Storm could be alone and able to talk.

Mrs Minton kept asking Storm if there was anything that she needed to talk about, and why did she have ketchup in her hair.

Storm tried very hard to explain that she was just carrying the ketchup when she fell off her bike, and it must have burst open.

Oliver was not sure if Mrs Minton bought the excuse, but she did run out of questions eventually. The doctor seemed curious about the smell of tomatoes but happy enough with Storm, especially as the vehicle was parked and she was wearing a cycle helmet.

When at last they got back to Storm's house, it was the first time they had been alone since the plan began.

"Bravo!" Oliver clapped his hands and gave Storm an encouraging and extremely grateful smile. "You did it! You deserve an Oscar for that performance."

"An Oscar? I deserve a medal the size of a dustbin lid!"

"Thank you."

"You can thank me for the rest of your life. You are forever in my debt."

"Your wish is my command."

"You can start by showing me that new phone of yours," said Storm. "That is so cool. When did you get that?"

Oliver explained about the man with the Harley-Davidson the night before. Storm was happy to accept the phone as compensation for the next few hours.

As Storm explored the handset, it vibrated and beeped. Oliver looked at the screen; it displayed a set of GPS co-ordinates. He pressed a few buttons, and a map appeared.

"The van is outside my house!" he announced angrily. Their plan had worked, but knowing the vehicle's whereabouts made him feel sick.

Storm was under doctor's orders to spend the afternoon recovering, and under close surveillance by Mrs Minton. There was no way they would be allowed out again to investigate, unless Oliver went alone, and that was probably not the best idea.

Knowing that those men were so close to April Cottage, maybe even inside, made one thing clear: there was no way that he could do nothing.

Oliver called Uncle Raj and explained.

"You champion!" said his godfather. "Best thing to do, right now, is to call the police, tell them that while you were out on your bike you saw a van lingering outside your house."

Oliver did exactly as instructed, and within half an hour his phone beeped again. The van had moved, heading west. The police must have driven by and scared the men.

When Nan arrived early that evening to take him home, Oliver was feeling far more optimistic. The updates continued to arrive, but with each one the men were further away.

Before he left, he thanked Storm once again.

She shrugged. "What are friends for?"

"That's right. It's in your job description."

"And in yours is a lifetime supply of paybacks. You owe me big time!"

She was still smiling. Oliver smiled back, and knew deep down that she was right.

"So," asked Storm, "will you keep me informed while you're in London, if you discover anything?"

"You bet. I expect you to be like the Welsh Guards while I'm away. You are the only person in the whole of Wales who has any idea of what's going on. I need you to keep your eyes peeled and your ears to the ground."

"Call me Miss Marple."

"I'd prefer to call you Storm!"

"Just call me when you're back from London."

Oliver thanked Mrs Minton for inviting him. She still appeared unusually pale.

As Nan and Henry had brought Winston with them for his evening walk, the journey home was a long one on foot. It was filled with all sorts of questions about Storm's collision with the van.

As they returned to Stanmore Place, there were no black vans outside, but instead a police car. PC Sharp and WPC Hughes were waiting.

They did not have any new questions to ask, but just repeated the same ones over and over again. However, they did reassure Oliver that after his phone call that afternoon, everything was secure at April Cottage and there was no van to be seen. Oliver thought this was the first time the police had done anything that could be considered helpful.

Every thirty minutes, the phone beeped and showed the vehicle's co-ordinates. They remained the same. According to Google Maps, it was somewhere in the middle of an industrial estate in Chepstow, about thirty-five miles away.

Every time the phone beeped, Oliver recorded the van's position. By midnight, the noise became annoying. He supposed the van was probably parked up for the night. Or had the tracking device fallen off, or been removed?

The Video Message

"We're going to London!" sang Henry excitedly as he bounded in through Oliver's bedroom door, not stopping until both his knees landed firmly on his big brother's ribcage.

Remembering the tracking device, Oliver grabbed his phone; twenty unopened messages. He opened each one: they all showed identical co-ordinates. The van had not moved.

As Oliver arrived downstairs, Nan was plating up his favourite breakfast: cheese and mushroom omelette, baked beans, and hot buttered toast.

"Good timing!" said Nan, "And good morning. Did you sleep well?"

"I did until Henry arrived!" Oliver poked out his tongue mischievously at his little brother. Henry smiled at him angelically from across the table.

There was a loud knock at the door. Henry was first to his feet, and Oliver followed closely behind. Neither of them were disappointed to see Uncle Raj.

"Are you guys ready?" he asked.

"Let's go!" said Oliver.

Henry clung tightly onto his uncle's leg, unwilling to let go.

"I think that we should say hello to your grandmother first," Uncle Raj suggested.

They all marched into the kitchen, Henry still attached to his godfather.

A quick cup of tea, a slice of toast, and an obligatory catch-up saw them almost ready to go. Uncle Raj chewed commendably on his second breakfast.

"Make sure that these boys behave themselves," said Nan nervously, not comfortable with them leaving her care, and particularly with them going all the way across the border to London. "I'll come and collect them straight away if they feel homesick."

Oliver went to collect his bag and picked up his phone from the bedside table. Instead of heading downstairs, he paused and stared at the screen. What if his parents returned home when he was in London? The house would be empty, and no one would be waiting for them. How would they know where he was? He had even changed his mobile number, so how could they contact him? He could not leave Wales without at least trying to phone them again.

He dialled his dad's number. The call went straight to answerphone.

"Hi, Dad," he said, his voice forlorn. "We're going away for a couple of days . . . to stay with Uncle Raj. We're looking for you, and . . ." He tried to find the right words. "I miss you! Please come home!"

He headed downstairs.

"You can't possibly drive all the way to London without a packed lunch," said Nan as she forcibly handed Uncle Raj a bulging carrier bag. She was not prepared to allow her guests to leave for such a long journey without eight cheese sandwiches, a Victoria sponge, some homemade shortbread, four packets of crisps, three bananas, two apples, two oranges, four cartons of juice, and a flask of tea.

When they eventually made it out, Uncle Raj gave a loud whistle. Winston barged through the hallway and heeled to attention at his side.

"You're taking Winston too?" asked Nan, sounding surprised.

"The three of them come as a team," said Uncle Raj. "I wouldn't dream of parting them. However, there is one condition . . ."

He looking sternly at Winston and waved his finger.

"He knows!" Oliver smiled. "No drooling on the upholstery!"

"Got it in one," said Uncle Raj.

Travelling in a Range Rover did not have the same kudos or appeal as the Aston Martin, but Oliver was willing to endure it. He felt relieved to be getting away from Ebbwvenny, although before he left there was something that he really wanted to do.

"Are you thinking what I'm thinking?" Uncle Raj asked Oliver as he drove away from Stanmore Place.

"If you're thinking about going to April Cottage first, then yes!"

Uncle Raj nodded and turned to Henry. "Shall we go home and choose some of your favourite DVDs to take with us to London? And that really big red fire engine?"

"Yippee!" shouted Henry.

As the car approached the cottage, Oliver looked out of the window. The house looked the same as ever, but felt different. It was not *home*, not without his mum and dad.

Despite its emptiness, the sun still beamed through the windows, creating warmth and a welcoming glow. Winston meandered from room to room, Henry dived straight into the toy box in the lounge in search of his fire engine, and Oliver stood in the kitchen talking to Uncle Raj.

"The police have been back," said Oliver, surprised.

The broken mug no longer lay on the kitchen floor. Even Winston's bed, which once lay at the end of the breakfast bar, was no longer there.

He walked towards the larder, but Uncle Raj stood in front of the cupboard door and said, "Perhaps I should go down first to check that everything is secure. Then you go."

Oliver did not argue as he knew that they could not both go; somebody would have to look after Henry. Winston jumped onto the sofa, evidently pleased to be back home.

It was a strange, uncomfortable feeling knowing that Uncle Raj was roaming freely in the labs among his dad's best-kept secrets. Oliver kept his eye on the larder door.

Minutes later the door swung open and Uncle Raj appeared. "It looks secure, exactly as we left it. There's nothing else I can do right now, but you could go and switch on the computers and have a probe around."

Oliver was pleased to be back in the labs; there were so many things that he wanted to check. Unsure of where to start, he felt drawn towards the particle physics lab, the room where he last saw his dad at work.

He turned on the computer. Logging on was not a problem; he had used the system so many times before. Oliver rattled away at the keyboard.

A familiar screen appeared, showing masses of files, each name as random and indistinct as the previous one.

Oliver opened a recent file. Spreadsheets expanded and a long list of numbers, symbols, and letters appeared. Oliver was sure that these made perfect sense to his dad, but to him they meant nothing.

Scratching his head with both hands, making his hair stick up even more than usual, he tried very hard to understand.

"But why did the power fail?" he asked himself aloud.

As nobody answered, he shook his head. "The file that recorded keystrokes would be broken."

He began pacing the room.

"When the system reboots, a new file should have been created in the place of the broken one."

Oliver nodded, agreeing with himself, and then went on pacing.

"The file needs fixing so it can be viewed!"

He stopped pacing, threw his arms in the air, and shouted, 'That's it! I need to repair the file, so I can figure out what Dad was doing just before the power failed."

Then there was silence except for the sound of a keyboard rattling.

He typed:

History0092.txt

There were more than 100 broken files on the server, all current files that were open when the power failed.

Oliver groaned. Not knowing what he was looking for did not make finding it any easier. Each and every file he opened looked the same. The easiest thing in the world would be to give up, to decide that it was too difficult, but he knew that was not an option.

Oliver looked closer at each file name. There were numbers on the end and logic told him that the highest would be the most recent file. It was a message. He clicked, and it opened:

Dear Oliver,

I knew that you would find this. I had every faith that I could count on your help. I had hoped that you wouldn't need to, but as you have, something has gone wrong. If I'm not mistaken, you've reached the point where you're beginning to work out what has happened to me. I feel that I need to provide you with a helping hand. I can't be sure of what events have occurred for you to find this message, but I have an idea about some people who might wish to interfere with my work and may well cause me issues.

As you already know, what I'm working on is extremely sensitive and secret. I'm afraid that the police will not be able to help you. I need you to reassure Mum, tell her that everything will be fine. Give her and your little brother lots of hugs. Mum knows a little more than you do about my project, so show her this message and she will fill you in.

Firstly, you will need to access the following file:

\\biometric_research\old_files\archivefrom1977\PaulHarris.wmv

Oliver clicked on the file link. A window opened up with the media player, the amplifier attached to the server jumped to life, and the projector pointing at the whiteboard lit up.

An image appeared. It was old footage, a little grainy, but unmistakably an image of Oliver's dad, only a very young Oliver's dad: he looked about five, playing on a beach.

Oliver was confused. Why would his dad ask him to watch this? He glanced at the media player, which suggested the footage was eighteen minutes long. He had seen this clip once before, but he did not remember it lasting more than a minute or two.

Oliver was happy peering into a window of his father's past. He even smiled as he saw his dad jumping the waves and falling over.

The clip suddenly ground to a halt, the film strip became visible and the projector went blank. That was exactly how Oliver remembered it ending, but the screen flickered, filled with light and focused on a much older version of his father. He looked different; he wore a green military shirt and had a striking, bushy black moustache. Oliver remembered his dad's moustache; his memory was of pulling it. He calculated that this must have been eight or even nine years ago.

The film went on to show his father in a lab. It was somewhere that Oliver did not recognise. His dad was conducting an experiment with six powerful cathode rays not unlike the ones that he still used today. The beams were focused directly into the centre of a pot of molten metal. The experiment was set up on a bench in the centre of the room, contained within a large glass vacuum chamber about the size of a large fish tank. The whole system was being heated from underneath the vacuum by a flame that burned white.

His dad spoke. "The molten metal will be reshaped using the electron beams." He sounded nervous. "The beams are generated using digital signals to create localised structures within the molten metal."

He hesitated before adding, "This experiment is extremely dangerous, and we have not yet been able to control the speed of expansion."

Filming experiments was not rare. He did it all the time, but there was something about the way he spoke that told Oliver that he was not alone.

The view of the room switched to one of the lab bench, but now it was seen through a sheet of protective glass. As the camera swung around, the heads and shoulders of several other men could be seen, all watching the experiment. Some wore military uniforms draped in medals; others wore lab coats, but they all had the same sombre expression. The camera passed two men dressed in military green who stood close together.

There was something odd about them, something that made Oliver look more carefully. They stood side by side like clones, both with dark brown hair, thin, pointed chins, and piercing green eyes. They were identical, even down to the same signet ring on their left hands. Twins.

Oliver's father spoke again. "The molten liquid temperature appears to have stabilised."

His voice was shaking. Sweat was gathering on his forehead.

"Electron beam ready," he said softly. "Test constrained to flame strength at fifty-five per cent."

He stepped back and stood behind the glass screen. He pressed a few buttons on the computer terminal and said, "Initiate digital signature."

He looked reluctant, but then gave the command, "Apply beam."

The beam of electrons shot across the molten liquid. There was an unmistakable air of excitement from the onlookers. Some dared to move away from the screen, to try to lurch a little closer to see what was happening. Oliver noticed a man in uniform pacing up and down, straying beyond the security of the screen.

"Ve need more power!" He demanded, his accent foreign. Oliver assumed it was Russian or Eastern European.

"The power is not the limiting factor," Oliver's father answered defensively. "It's the rate at which the molecules form and build structures that is taking the time."

The camera refocused onto the molten liquid, which bubbled and burst again and again. Most incredibly, the hot liquid was changing shape. From out of the chaotic mixture a shape was rising, a form of cylinder, shining and smooth. The liquid metal was draining upwards as a pole grew from the pot.

Oliver watched in amazement. He had never seen anything like this before. His father had never even spoken about it. He was unable to take his eyes off the projector for a single moment.

"Ve need more power!" shouted the same man again. "Zis is ze last chance!"

He waved his arms and pointed forebodingly at Oliver's dad.

Another military figure, tall, with thick grey hair and wearing more medals than any other spoke. "Increase the power to ninety per cent!"

His voice was commanding, British and resolute.

"General Whimsy, I'm unable to guarantee that it would be safe to do that," Oliver's father replied anxiously. "I would strongly recommend against it!"

"I didn't get these stripes by playing safe, Harris! I command you to increase the power!"

Oliver's father shook his head, then a blur swerved past the camera and someone in a white lab coat took hold of the controls and turned the dial.

"Clear the room!" demanded Oliver's dad.

At that moment, the molten spike split into branches of solid metal, splitting again and again as the electron beam struggled to control the exponential expansion. Oliver saw a blur of movement heading towards the door, followed by a deafening explosion and a display of lights. What was once the molten rod was now an array of thousands of annealed steel bullets shooting uncontrollably in every direction.

The film went blank. There was a silence.

Oliver sat motionless, trying to comprehend what he had just seen and why his father was showing him this.

The screen flickered again then showed the room some time later. It had been almost completely wrecked: all the equipment had been destroyed and the walls and ceiling had dents deep into the concrete. It was still and empty, except for two red roses that lay among the rubble.

The picture changed from the film to a slideshow of still photographs of a grey marble tombstone with the inscription *In Memory of a Brave Man, General Alexander Whimsy.*

The picture faded away, showing the next. An image of another tombstone appeared with the inscription *Here Lies George Elwood, Died 17th Jan 2007.* The bottom of the stone read *Nothing Ventured, Nothing Gained, Just Lost Forever. In Loving Memory of a Father, a Son, and a Twin Brother.*

A cold chill ran down Oliver's spine. He was more confused than he had ever been. Why was this relevant? Why was this important?

The next image was a document. It read *Medical Discharge Notice*, followed by:

Patient Name: Vincent Quark

Reason for Discharge: Self-discharge, against doctors' orders.

Condition Status: Facial scar tissue beginning to heal. (Industrial accident.)

Oliver knew that some of the men that he had watched on that video had been injured, and some had probably been killed. The name Quark did not sound particularly Russian, so Oliver guessed that this was not the man who had commanded his dad to increase the power.

Oliver began to understand that his parents' disappearance may just be something even more complicated than he had imagined. His head ached, and he was unsure if he could take in any more. He closed his eyes.

As he did so, a familiar voice spoke to him. He saw his dad on the screen, sat at his desk.

"I understand that you must be feeling a little confused right now," his father said to the camera. "I know that it's a lot to take in. I would much prefer to have explained all of this to you in person, but I was sworn to secrecy. The fact that I'm not there now means that circumstances have changed, and now, you must know that something has gone wrong. I'm glad that you've found this message. A few things have happened recently that have put my research at risk."

Oliver's eyes widened and his head was spinning. His hands grasped the table in front of him, gripping on tight as the room seemed to turn.

His father continued, "I have made a somewhat significant breakthrough and because of this some scientists want to use my work. I have no intention of sharing it yet, as I believe that it could be used in a way that could bring harm. Some people may be prepared to do almost anything to get hold of my results; the value of such science is unquantifiable. Some of the people who have approached me have even posed as my friends, but it is possible they may well have been working for foreign powers."

He paused. "If some of my discoveries were to fall into these hands, it could be a matter of national security."

Oliver took a deep breath, trying to focus on his dad, who went on, "I'm not going to explain the experiment; it is far too complicated. I have documented very little of the process so it cannot be copied. The results and methods have been safely filed in my head so this information can never be stolen. I'm suspecting that it is for this reason that I am not there now."

Just as Oliver felt that he could take in no more information, his dad said, "There's just one more thing that you need to know: there are some people who you can trust, and there are others who you must never trust."

His hand shaking, Oliver reached for some paper and a pencil.

"You can always trust your mum," his dad explained. "She can help you fill in a few of the gaps. There's also an old friend of mine who you haven't met, Graeme O'Sullivan. He's trustworthy and has helped me out in the past. However, there are some people who I want you to know that you should be wary of. If I am not around, there may be people who try to get close to you, but take heed: stay clear. There are four people who I want you to do everything in your power to avoid."

Oliver's dad lowered his voice and spoke slowly and clearly. "Remember these names: Victor Borofski, Thomas Elwood, Vincent Quark, and Silas Tudor. Even though I have listed only a few, please keep in mind that my research is not to be discovered by anyone. The only trust you should give unequivocally is to your own instincts.

"So, Oliver, it's over to you, my son. I'm very sorry to have to ask you to help me, but I am afraid that I have no more answers for you. I need you to be strong, and always do what you believe to be the right thing. I have every confidence that your instincts will not fail you."

Oliver's dad bowed his head, the film stopped, and the screen went blank. Oliver waited for something else, but the timer displayed *18:00*. The message had ended.

Oliver left the labs after closing down each document, covering his tracks by placing blocks on his history files. He had to tell Uncle Raj. He closed every door behind him, leaving the labs safe and secure.

As he reached the porthole entrance that led back into the kitchen, a horrible hollow feeling engulfed him almost to suffocation. *Why hadn't Dad mentioned Uncle Raj?* Why had he not listed his name as someone Oliver could trust? After all, he had built the labs in the first place. To tell his uncle what his father had told him would be a betrayal – but otherwise, how could he possibly figure this out by himself?

Re-entering the kitchen gave him clarity, a penny-dropping moment. Snippets of conversation between his mum and dad only days before they disappeared were beginning to fit together.

The family holiday was never longer than three weeks, but this summer there were no plans to return until September. This year's holiday was not meant to have been a holiday at all.

It was an escape plan.

When Oliver entered the lounge, Uncle Raj and Henry were snuggled on the sofa watching *Chitty Chitty Bang Bang*. Winston lay wallowing in the sunshine.

"Any luck?" asked Uncle Raj.

Oliver bit down on his lip to stop the wrong words escaping. He took a deep breath and decided to go with his sixth sense, his instinct. His uncle had never given him any reason to doubt that trust and, after all, his father trusted him.

"I found a message from Dad," he said hesitantly. "He suspected that something like this could have happened."

"Did you?" Uncle Raj looked strangely unsurprised.

"He told me to ask Mum to fill me in on the details," replied Oliver. Henry was in the room and Oliver did not want him to hear anything to worry him. "I'll explain later."

The journey to London gave Oliver time to think. The words, the pictures, the message, all replayed over and over inside his head. Despite Uncle Raj being by his side, Oliver felt as though the burden was once again all his. Trusting his uncle now felt wrong. The way he reacted when Oliver told him about the message felt wrong.

Everything felt wrong.

Annoyed with himself for having suspicions about someone he had trusted all his life, Oliver was beginning to feel that he could rely on no one. He knew that Uncle Raj could never betray him; he was his godfather. Should he be suspicious of everyone except Graeme O'Sullivan?

His head span faster. Who on earth *was* Graeme O'Sullivan?

London

Beep . . . Beep . . . Beep . . .

Oliver's phone vibrated across the dashboard towards the open window. He grabbed it with both hands.

"It's the van!" he announced. "It's moving again!"

The co-ordinates confirmed that not only had it moved, it was heading east on the M4 – the same direction as them.

"I'm hungry," whined Henry as they left Wales behind and crossed the Severn Bridge.

"As it happens," said Uncle Raj, "your grandmother predicted this would be the case and has sent supplies."

They looked for an SSP, otherwise known by the Harris family as a "suitable stopping place". One was located just on the edge of a service station, next to the river.

Oliver got out of the car and stared at his phone. No news and no new messages.

"I thought that the battery had gone flat," he said nervously, "or the tape holding the tracker onto the van had fallen off. It is safe for us to stop right now, isn't it?"

Uncle Raj looked confident. "Of course it is. Are you going to help me with this blanket or what?"

He took a picnic rug from the boot.

"Was it free with the car?" Oliver asked while removing the plastic wrapper. He knew that his uncle was more a fan of the great indoors.

Uncle Raj was smiling, but as the others tucked into the picnic Oliver kept one eye on his phone and the other on every passing vehicle.

After an uncomfortable twenty minutes, his phone beeped. "They've gained on us."

"Let's get back on the road," said Uncle Raj.

The remainder of the journey seemed faster. Oliver did not take his eyes off the wing mirror, aware that something, someone, was tracking his every move. Every time a black vehicle approached, his stomach somersaulted.

There were so many things to worry about, he did not know which one to think about first: being trailed by kidnappers; making sense of what his dad had told him; figuring out who he could trust without betraying his father; and working out how on earth he was going to get his parents home.

Instead, Oliver tried to blank his mind, just for a few moments.

As they neared London, all of his suspicions were confirmed when his phone beeped with a new set of co-ordinates. "They've followed us here," he sighed.

"Who?" asked Henry.

He knew that he had said too much. Henry already had too much to cope with. "Nobody."

As they approached Merlin Drive, Oliver recognised the familiar landmarks that he had seen many times before. A row of large Georgian houses standing four floors tall with slim elegance and symmetry; neat panelled windows and doorways framed by stone steps and stately arches. At the end of the street, closest to the park was a most welcome sight: his uncle's house.

The car stopped outside number 107. Despite the fact that Uncle Raj lived alone, Auntie Manya, his sister, stood waiting at the front door to greet them.

"How lovely to see you!" she said, embracing them both and Winston too, almost suffocating them all in layers of sari. Auntie Manya was kind, sincere, and, above all, an amazing cook.

The smells of warmed spices came from inside the house. "I hope that you don't mind," she said, "but I decided that I would come and stay too. I have already moved my things into the spare room."

No sooner had they settled in than dinner was served: warm samosas, vegetable korma just the way Oliver liked it, and chapattis. They sat around the table, chatting away. For a brief moment, Oliver found himself smiling, until he remembered the real reason why he was there.

It was a warm, pleasant evening, and Oliver made to wander out into the garden.

"Wait a moment," said Uncle Raj as he beckoned Oliver back to the house and into his office. "Where's the van?"

"I'm not sure." Oliver looked at his phone. "Somewhere inside the M25. It hasn't moved since we got here."

"I'd like to keep an eye on those messages for a while."

Oliver hesitated as he handed his phone over. He did not feel able to say no; strictly speaking, it *was* his uncle's phone.

"You will keep checking, won't you?" he asked.

"You bet!" said Uncle Raj. "You look as if you could do with an hour off."

Oliver nodded, then lingered, wondering if it was the right time to have that chat. They were alone, for the first time all day.

"I suppose—" Oliver began, but before he had finished his first sentence his uncle's phone rang.

"Hot chocolate and cookies!" shouted Auntie Manya. "There's some for you too, Winston."

Oliver wandered into the lounge, where Henry lay sleepily on the sofa under a blanket, watching cartoons. Oliver felt exhausted and snuggled in next to him.

"Oliver!" said Uncle Raj, peering out of the office.

Sleepily tucking Henry back in, Oliver went to see what Uncle Raj wanted. He had already decided what he would say; he had had plenty of time to think. He did not have to tell his uncle everything. He could tell him only what he needed to know, stuff that Oliver felt he could help with. He knew that he needed someone to help.

Sat behind a mountain of paperwork, Uncle Raj pulled up a chair for him and asked, "What was in the message?"

Taking a deep breath, Oliver began, "Dad knew that somebody was onto him. Someone wanted the results from one of his experiments."

Uncle Raj was listening carefully.

"He suspected that someone was prepared to take any risk to find the answers, so that's why we were all going away."

Oliver was comfortable with what he had said. In fact, he was not telling a single lie, just withholding some truths.

"Which experiment?" his godfather asked.

"He didn't say," answered Oliver. "He just asked me if I would help him."

Uncle Raj nodded.

"He didn't tell me what to do, he just said that he needed help."

Uncle Raj could see Oliver's anguish. "That's what you're already doing."

"I hope so."

"So tell me exactly what he said."

Oliver thought carefully before he answered. "He didn't mention anything about the men that came to the house, nor the black vans. He said that he suspected that something like this could happen, and also that he had made some sort of breakthrough."

"*What* breakthrough?" asked Uncle Raj, sitting bolt upright.

"He didn't tell me." Oliver felt he had said enough.

"I want to know more about this breakthrough."

"That's all that I know," Oliver said sadly, feeling uncomfortable.

"It confirms what we suspected." Uncle Raj loosened his collar. "Did he give you any ideas about who it could be?"

"No."

"Can I see the message? Did you print it?"

"No. I deleted it as soon as I read it." Although this was not true, it seemed like the right thing to say.

"Let's find out more."

Oliver nodded and looked at his phone on the desk. "Where is the van now?"

"It's in a car park in Kensington. It has been there all evening."

"So what should we do?"

"You get yourself a good night sleep. Tomorrow, if it's still there, we'll go and check it out. Auntie Manya will look after Henry and Winston."

Oliver nodded nervously. They went on to talk about what he and Storm had discovered, and looked through the pictures on the phone.

"What did you find out about the vans?" Oliver asked.

"I have called in a few favours with someone I know," he explained. "They're from a hire company, based in Clapham. My friend wasn't able to tell me who they have been rented to, but what he gave me was the registered address of the hire company. We can pay them a visit, and see if they can tell us something."

Oliver forced a smile.

"First things first," said Uncle Raj. "The tracker has been on the van since Tuesday. We don't know how much battery is left, so the priority is following the lead of the van. I've a good feeling about tomorrow."

Oliver picked up his phone. "Can I take it?"

"Don't let it stop you having a good night sleep. Put it on silent."

Oliver went straight to bed. He was exhausted, confused, but also optimistic that tomorrow was a brand new day.

L'escargot

Despite the fact that Oliver went to sleep fully clothed, dreaming about black vans erupting into colossal molten explosions, he slept all night.

The moment he woke, he reached for his phone. It was not there. He tiptoed out of his room, making sure that he did not wake Henry, and crept downstairs.

Nobody else was awake apart from Uncle Raj, who was sat in the lounge with his laptop on his knees and Oliver's phone by his side. Winston was sprawled on the sofa.

"You've got it!" said Oliver.

"I didn't want it keeping you awake," said Uncle Raj. "You're up early. Breakfast?"

"Later." He was far too eager to stop for something to eat. "Where's the van?"

"It hasn't moved all night."

"If it's still sending messages then the battery must still be alive. Let's go!"

Oliver crept eagerly – Uncle Raj a little less so – out of the house.

Uncle Raj showed Oliver two sets of keys: one for the Aston, one for the Range Rover. He held out both hands.

"Do you really need to ask?" said Oliver, smiling.

They both climbed into the Aston.

"We may need to make a quick getaway," Oliver suggested while fastening his seatbelt.

Uncle Raj nodded as Oliver entered the co-ordinates into the satnav.

London was as busy as ever, so it took a while to get to their destination. When the satnav announced that they had reached it, Oliver recognised a hotel he had seen on TV and in his mum's glossy magazines. Hotel Dubois was one of the poshest hotels in the city, with porters waiting at the entrance to greet limousines.

"Is that where the van is?" Oliver asked.

"Looks that way. Let's park up."

"We need to be inconspicuous. How on earth can we sneak in unnoticed?"

"I thought that you were resourceful!" Uncle Raj sighed. "I've got an idea."

He swerved into a side road and veered left, seemingly knowing exactly where they were heading.

"We'll use the trade entrance," he said as they drove into a dark tunnel leading down to an underground car park.

Oliver's stomach did a double flip. Parked in a row were three black Transit vans with familiar number plates. Even though this is what they had come looking for, seeing three together was chilling.

Uncle Raj reversed into a space a few metres from the vans. They made their way on foot across the car park.

"Are you OK?" Uncle Raj asked.

Oliver nodded nervously, but he was feeling dizzy.

"Don't look at the vans," Uncle Raj whispered. "We are bound to be on CCTV, and being watched. Act completely normal."

Oliver was not sure he could when his stomach felt like a whirlpool, his legs had turned to jelly, and his head gyrated like a tornado.

"Remember," said Uncle Raj, "we are just guests. Don't tell anyone your real name."

They walked past the vans and towards a lift.

"Which floor?" asked Oliver as his fingers lingered over the buttons.

"Ground."

As they stepped out of the lift, they found themselves stood in a grand hotel lobby. Lavish drapes, chandeliers, oil paintings, and antique furniture adorned every inch of space.

The room teemed with people coming and going, staff darting across the lobby with enormous brass luggage trolleys. Oliver felt as though a dozen eyes were glaring at him. From the looks he was getting from the staff on the reception desk, it was clear that he was in no way inconspicuous; he was a child, so by definition he stood out just by being there.

Uncle Raj quickly led Oliver through the grand entrance hall and towards a restaurant. They were directed to a small table in the far corner of the restaurant.

"I've got an idea," Oliver whispered to Uncle Raj. "You know that we mustn't give anyone our real names?"

"Yes . . ." Uncle Raj sounded nervous.

"How about we throw them off the plot completely and pretend we're German or French?"

"Can you speak German?"

"Er, no . . ."

"French?"

"A little bit."

By *a little* he meant *a teeny-weeny itsy-bitsy minuscule bit*. He had started to learn it in year six at school, and had used it on a trip to France at Christmas, successfully ordering an apple juice.

"I don't think that's a great idea," said Uncle Raj. "My French isn't great."

"Quick!" said Oliver. "Here comes the waiter."

"Allo," said the waiter, who sounded Russian. "Vot can I get vaw yaw, sir?" he asked Uncle Raj, ignoring Oliver completely.

Uncle Raj opened his mouth to speak, but Oliver spoke first.

"*Je voudrais un café au lait.*" He did not actually like coffee, but he could not remember the French for apple juice. The waiter appeared rather irritated, and asked again. Uncle Raj looked hot and flustered.

Oliver feared that he may even have been about to answer in English, so he answered for him. "*Il voudrais, un tasse de thè, s'il vous plait.*"

Uncle Raj looked as if he would much prefer a brandy to a cup of tea, but Oliver did not know the French word for brandy. Anyway, his uncle was driving.

The waiter tried again, irritably. "Daw yaw spayk aynglish?"

Oliver glared at his uncle, forbidding him to give up their disguise and expose their identities. If they backed away now, they would draw even more attention to themselves and would certainly look suspicious. Oliver had started something and he was committed. Instead, he just smiled uncomfortably at the waiter. Annoyed, the man tapped his pen on his notebook and his shiny black shoe on the floor.

There was an awkward silence. Neither Oliver nor Uncle Raj knew what to say. The waiter smiled thinly, turned on his heels, and left.

"Right," said Oliver, "Hotel Dubois." He got out his mobile and found the hotel's website. There were pictures of the inside of the lobby, some of the elaborate penthouse suites, and even one of the restaurant.

"Can I see that?" asked Uncle Raj. He followed a link that took him to a page showing the building's history and a photograph of the proprietor. "It's owned by a Russian billionaire called Ubinon Folovich."

The name meant nothing to Oliver. The photograph was of a stout, wealthy-looking man, whose cheeks ballooned from his round face. Uncle Raj used the phone to search for more.

Oliver looked around the room, unable to settle his eyes on any one thing; he was far too nervous. He was uncomfortable knowing that there was some sort of connection between this hotel and his parents disappearing. Was it possible that his parents were here?

From where he sat, he had a view across the lobby. A stream of people were arriving and leaving. He watched, wondering if the next face he saw would be one he recognised.

The waiter returned, but this time he brought with him a colleague. "Awer Frreench vaytair vill tayke yoor awder, sir!"

This was not going well.

"*Bonjour monsieur, bienvenue à Dubois Hotel. Si je comprends bien mon collègue que vous êtes tous deux français. Que puis-je faire pour vous aujourd'hui?*"

Oliver had lost the conversation after *Bonjour monsieur*. Uncle Raj twitched nervously. The waiter waited patiently for a response. Uncle Raj stepped in and uttered something that sounded a bit like *milk and tea*.

"*Aujourd'hui, notre plat speciality que nous servons pour le petit déjeuner est servi les escargots avec une huile à l'ail.*"

Oliver had no idea what the waiter had just said. By the look on his uncle's face, neither did he. There was an awkward silence. Oliver felt responsible and said the first thing that came into his head. What could possibly go wrong if he answered, very simply, *yes?*

"*Oui monsieur.*"

Uncle Raj nodded. The waiter smiled and left.

"That worked," said Oliver proudly. The drinks arrived shortly after, and Oliver thanked the waiter. "*Merci beaucoup.*"

The restaurant was quiet, with only a few tables occupied at the opposite end of the room, but Oliver felt uncomfortable. Despite being ignored by most of the hotel staff, he still felt like someone was watching him.

"So what do we do now?" he asked.

"Keep a low profile and keep watch."

The French waiter neared the table with two large silver platters.

Oliver did not know that they had ordered food, but they must have done. The waiter whisked off both the platters' covers and revealed their identical breakfasts.

De-shelled and dressed for breakfast on each plate were slippery, oozing, slightly charred, slimy snails greased with oil. Horrified, Oliver tried not to react. Despite his more mature and cultured palate, even Uncle Raj looked just as revolted.

"Don't get me wrong," said Uncle Raj as soon as the waiter left, "some of my closest friends are French." He stopped, gulped, then continued, "But if there's one thing that puts me off the entire culture, it's their prehistoric, boorish ability to contemplate eating molluscs!"

If Oliver had not been faced with the same plate, he would have found this funny, but he was in no mood for laughing. He looked down at the rout of snails in front of him and thought he saw one move. He could not bear to even touch one, let alone chew or swallow one.

"Do people eat these for pleasure?" asked Uncle Raj, grimacing while sliding a snail across his plate with a fork. "We can't bring any attention to ourselves. We can't make a scene. There's nothing else for it, we'll have to eat them!"

"This is going to be one 'slow' breakfast."

"Have you brought a bag?" Uncle Raj asked.

"No!"

"Then how about you put them in your pocket?"

"Urgh!" said Oliver in disgust. "Put them in your own pocket! You can have the slime and grease drip down your legs!"

"OK. Not such a good idea."

This was all too much for Oliver, who had turned a slight shade of green and was feeling queasy.

"I can't!" He shook his head.

"Just pretend."

"But I'm a vegetarian!"

"Think of them as a vegetable," said Uncle Raj. "They're hardly in the same category as a cow or a pig."

Oliver watched as Uncle Raj speared a small, slimy snail with his fork as something oozed out of its side. Very reluctantly, he moved it towards his mouth. His eyes watered, and he looked pained and anguished.

Oliver needed to find another way. He had an idea. Fussing around with his cutlery, he deliberately dropped a spoon on the floor. Uncle Raj reached down to get it, and Oliver seized the opportunity to place three snails from his own plate onto his uncle's.

Uncle Raj swallowed, and gagged discreetly. He slid a long, thin snail across his plate. "I'm sure these are multiplying."

Oliver smirked sympathetically, and said, "We need a new plan."

Uncle Raj picked up his phone and opened Google Translate. He caught the attention of the French waiter, who returned to the table.

"*Les escargots goût moisi!*" said Uncle Raj.

With that, the waiter looked horrified, swiped both of their plates from under them, and stormed into the kitchen.

Oliver was not sure what he had said, but did not really care. What was important was he no longer had to eat snails.

Uncle Raj got out his wallet, put some notes on the table, and without waiting for the bill suggested to Oliver that they leave.

As they stood, an angry chef came towards them from the kitchen with a look of fury. What was even scarier was the way he frantically waved a frying pan, ranting something about *insulté*. From the little French that Oliver understood, it was not a good sign.

They made straight for the lifts, managing to get back to the car park without any frying-pan-related injuries.

The black vans had not moved, and Oliver even noticed that the one closest to Uncle Raj's car had a bicycle tyre-sized dent in the middle of the bumper.

Oliver was tempted to check the tracking device but could not risk bringing any attention to its whereabouts. They made their getaway.

"That was so close," said Oliver.

"You're not joking!"

"By the way, what did you tell that waiter?"

"Only that the snails tasted mouldy."

"That figures."

Uncle Raj drove them away without looking back. Oliver kept his eyes glued to the mirror, checking that nobody was following them.

"That was a wasted trip," said Oliver. "We may now know where the vans are, but how do we find out what they've got to do with Mum and Dad?"

"It wasn't a wasted trip at all. We now know that there's a connection with the hotel, and Ubinon Folovich owns it."

"But what does that mean?"

"He's an ex-minister for the Russian government, and there's rumour that he has links with the mafia. I'd say someone probably best avoided."

Oliver grimaced. Things were going from bad to worse. "Where next?"

"To the van hire company."

After another slow drive across London, they neared a garage. The sign above it read, *London Van Hire.*

"Let me do the talking," insisted Uncle Raj. "Stay in the car."

Oliver watched Uncle Raj as he made his way to the little Portakabin office. It appeared that nobody was inside, as he then continued to wander into the yard, which was lined with dozens of black and white Transit vans parked in rows.

"You all right, mate?" Oliver heard a man ask his godfather. He was wearing a sweatshirt emblazoned with the company logo, and he had a thick East End accent.

"I saw one of your vans this morning," Uncle Raj told him, "and I'm sure I recognised the driver, an old friend of mine who I haven't seen for years." He smiled. "Do you think you could have a look and check his contact details?"

"I don't know about that. That's more than my job's worth."

"You'd be doing me a huge favour."

"Sorry mate, no can do. Confidentiality and all that."

Uncle Raj continued to try to convince him. At one point, Oliver saw him even take out his wallet, but he did not appear to be having much luck.

Oliver got out of the car and wandered off, looking around the vans in the yard. He spotted a younger lad, dressed in overalls, hosing a white van and looking fed up.

"That van looks filthy!" said Oliver.

"The state people bring hire vans back in, it's disgusting!" said the lad. "I've spent half the morning trying to get chewing gum off the passenger seat in this one."

"I don't suppose you know who hired a load of vans from you recently, registration numbers began in RDV and another with RDG?"

"Yeah," said the cleaner. "They're still out. Some bloke . . . Foreign name, I think. All booked online. He's got five vans, all top spec."

"How long has he booked them for?"

"Not sure. They went out sometime last week. Hope when they come back they're cleaner than this one!"

Oliver laughed. "It wasn't Ubinon Folovich, was it?"

"Never heard of him. It was Ivanov or something like that."

Oliver saw Uncle Raj heading back towards his car, and asked the cleaner, "Do you do repairs here, too?"

"We don't touch the engines, but sometimes we do paint or bodywork."

"Good. There's a tyre dent in the front of one of those Transits."

The lad in the boiler suit looked confused.

"Catch you later," said Oliver. "And thanks."

When he got back into the car, Uncle Raj said, "That could've gone better."

"I thought it went OK."

Oliver explained what he had discovered.

"Fantastic!" his godfather replied.

It was late afternoon by the time they returned to Merlin Drive. Other than Uncle Raj's snail they had not eaten a thing all day, and neither of them could have considered eating either, until they smelt Auntie Manya's cooking as they walked through the door.

Charlie

Friday was all about finding answers. Uncle Raj had gone to work, so Oliver tucked himself away in the study. He sat at the desk, using his uncle's laptop to search the internet for anything about Russian hotel owners in London.

It felt as though he was searching for a black cat in a coal mine. The easiest way would have been to search on social media, but Oliver knew that looking up people held risks; it was easy to see who has viewed your profile, and that would have been a really bad idea. This was why Oliver did not have social media accounts himself.

He settled for Google, wading through dozens and dozens of newspaper articles and periodicals. It was exhausting as most of what he read made no sense to him at all. He had no idea how the FTSE worked or what accredited investors really did.

He googled each of the names of the men he was not to trust. He found very little on any of them, except Victor Borofski. He was a decorated Russian General who had died of natural causes three weeks ago, he was seventy-three. Dead end.

Each time Oliver opened a page, he placed blocks on it, so not even his uncle could check what he was looking at. This made him feel awful as Uncle Raj was being so kind, but Oliver could take no chances.

Five vans, the man had said. Three parked at the hotel, one of those with a tracker . . . and two more. He walked across to the window and peered out. There were no black vans in sight. To his amazement, the battery on the tracker device was still sending signals confirming that the vehicle was still in the hotel car park.

Oliver was still deep in printouts and notes when Uncle Raj returned from work and asked, "A productive day?"

"Not really, just some stuff about Folovich. He's a busy guy who does a whole lot more than hotels. I've looked him up on the Companies House website, which tells you who owns companies in the UK. He's on loads of registers, seems to have his fingers in a lot of pies. I can't find any specifics on the companies though; no websites, no advertising, no social media, and they're not even listed in the phone directories."

Uncle Raj sat down as Oliver said, "There's this one article from the University of Yorkshire that is interesting."

Oliver searched through the papers on the desk and handed a printout to his uncle. "It's five years old but it says that he was a hero for funding a postgraduate research project. Apparently he gave them millions of pounds. Generous."

"The physics department?"

Oliver nodded. The door flung open and Henry came bounding into the room, followed by Winston.

"Can we go to the *zooo*?" pleaded Henry. "I want to see the baby elephant, *pleeeease!*"

He gazed at Uncle Raj with his big blue eyes.

"Next time you come," said Uncle Raj.

"But I really, really, *really* love baby elephants, very, very much!" declared Henry as he climbed up to sit on Uncle Raj's knee.

"I'm sure you do!"

"Please, please, please can we go?" His bottom lip changed to a pout and it started to quiver.

"Maybe for an hour . . . tomorrow." Uncle Raj had been defeated by a three-year-old. He turned to Oliver. "You're coming too."

Normally, Oliver would have been fine with this, but right now going to the zoo felt wrong. Trips out were treats, days to relax, days to be with the family. He was not in London for a holiday; in fact, he no longer wanted to be in London at all . . . He wanted to go home. The return to Wales was planned for Tuesday, but that was far too long for him to wait.

The evening was spent with films, watching traffic drive past Merlin Drive, and eating pizza. Oliver's phone continued to beep every thirty minutes – by early evening, the van was on the move again.

Oliver followed its path as it headed deeper into London, until the inevitable happened: the messages stopped arriving.

The following morning, Uncle Raj, Auntie Manya, Henry, and Oliver all left for the zoo, travelling by train. Despite feeling sorry for himself, Oliver was even sorrier for his little brother, who was so confused by what was going on. He spent some time with him, even helping him to pack extra sandwiches for the baby elephant.

At the zoo, it was decided that they would split up and regroup in time for lunch. Henry did not hang around; he headed directly for the elephant. Auntie Manya went chasing after him.

"That leaves you and me," said Uncle Raj.

Oliver forced a smile. Today he felt as though he needed to be alone to think, to plan his return to Wales – sooner rather than later – without offending anyone. His thoughts were more geared towards how he could slip away from his uncle.

"Where first?" Uncle Raj asked.

Oliver did not care. "You choose."

They meandered around the zoo until they both stood mesmerized at the side of the penguin pool. The funny little creatures marched clumsily around the rocks. For a brief time, Oliver felt relaxed – today could have been just a normal day.

They made their way towards the lions. The plan to regroup on the green for lunch meant that they needed to head back. They walked through crowds of people. Most children looked happy with their parents, but Oliver felt as though nobody understood what he was feeling.

As they walked around a group of scouts, someone in the distance was calling.

"Mr Patil!" a man bellowed at them. Uncle Raj looked around, then instantly put his hand on Oliver's shoulder and guided him in the opposite direction.

"What's going on?" asked Oliver.

It was too late.

"Mr Patil!" The voice was closer. Oliver turned to see a tall man with long silver hair heading straight towards them. His hair reminded Oliver of Saruman the White in *The Lord of the Rings*.

"Mr Patil!" he said as he stopped right in front of Uncle Raj. "So nice to see you again."

He grabbed Uncle Raj's hand and shook it vigorously.

Uncle Raj looked most uncomfortable. This man clearly knew him well.

"Oh . . . Um . . . Hello!" Uncle Raj answered awkwardly.

"How the devil are you, old chap?" the stranger said while clapping Uncle Raj on the back. "Are you well?"

"Er, very well."

"Tell me, who is this young fellow?" The stranger winked at Oliver.

Uncle Raj did not answer, so Oliver filled the ensuing silence with, "I'm Oliver."

He smiled at the stranger, catching his eye for a little longer than he had intended. Oliver was caught in the glare. The stranger's eyes were cold and icy, and Oliver was first to look away.

"Not your godson?" The man smiled, and Oliver thought he looked devious. "I've heard much about you, Oliver."

Oliver had no idea of the man's identity, but he seemed to know who Oliver was. Uncle Raj seemed to be searching for the right words but failing to catch them.

"We really have to go now," Oliver said.

He had worked out that Uncle Raj was looking for an excuse to leave. He danced on the spot, crossing his legs and bouncing as if desperate for a wee.

The stranger looked at Oliver curiously. Oliver grabbed his godfather by the arm in an attempt to lead him away.

"Exciting times!" said the stranger. He tried once again to fix Oliver into his gaze.

Oliver did not make eye contact, and shouted, "Bye!"

He led Uncle Raj away, in the opposite direction to the green, and the toilets for that matter.

"Who was that?" Oliver asked when they were sure they were far enough away.

"Umm," said Uncle Raj. "I can't remember his name . . . He's just someone who I did some work for a few years ago."

It was blatantly obvious that his uncle knew this man far better than that. Oliver knew that he was being lied to. "So how did he know I was your godson, and what did he mean by 'exciting times'?"

"I often tell people about my godson," said Uncle Raj defensively, "and, quite frankly, some people are just plain weird."

Oliver agreed.

It was nice to see Henry smiling when they met up at lunch. He talked non-stop about Daphne the baby elephant, and how he desperately wanted to go back and watch her take a bath.

140

Auntie Manya sprawled on the grass, looking exhausted. It seemed only fair that Uncle Raj volunteer to take over looking after Henry. This might also have been because he wanted to avoid questions from Oliver. They hardly spoke to each other over lunch.

Everyone wanted to see the penguins. Oliver wanted to be alone. He headed off in the direction of the orang-utans.

By early afternoon, the zoo was even busier. Oliver found a quiet spot on a bench watching the orang-utans. How could he get back to Wales sooner? It would be so easy to just walk out of the zoo. Nobody would stop him. However, that could be pretty stupid if no one knew where he was, and it meant abandoning Henry.

As the world hurried by, Oliver was surrounded by a haze of doubt and mistrust. He thought about Uncle Raj.

Could he have already been in Wales when Oliver called? He did arrive sooner than he should have done, and he had a key to the house and access to the labs. Why did he not want to report the black van to the police after they had been chased? Who was the man with silver hair? Oliver hated feeling this way about Uncle Raj; he was his father's closest friend, and his godfather.

Oliver's head felt heavy, and his eyes blurred. The loud voices of the crowds and passers-by were muffled.

A glint of silver blurred past. Oliver turned his head as an old lady walked by.

He thought about the message from his dad, and the list of names of people who he should and should not trust. He also remembered the words *some people have even posed as my friends.*

Confused, angry, and hurt, Oliver stared at the orang-utans. They were called Frieda and Fraser. Their lives seemed straightforward, just like Oliver's life once was. Until a complication came in the shape of a single banana, poked through the cage by a little girl while her parents were not looking.

They both grabbed for it at the same time. Fraser got to it first, but Frieda had her hand on it too. Neither wanted to let go. The banana slid from Fraser's clutches and was snatched away. Fraser showed his teeth in a sad, defeated smile.

Fraser reminded Oliver of someone. He looked Fraser in the eye and the beast stared back; he was used to being watched. There was something uncannily familiar about him. Breaking the stare, Oliver glanced at Frieda. She looked familiar too. Oliver smiled inwardly; Frieda and Fraser had given him an idea, and perhaps the perfect solution.

Uncle Will and Auntie Karen were in France. Today they were at the wedding, and tomorrow they were returning to Wales. They would practically have to bypass London on their way. That was it; they could collect him.

Oliver decided to call them later. He was thoughtful like that. He knew his uncle well enough to predict that if someone at the wedding would have forgotten to put their phone on silent, it would be him.

He left the orang-utans, grateful for their unknowing help, and began to wander around the zoo. He was not really watching the animals, but instead paying more attention to the crowds, looking particularly for anyone with silver hair. An honest conversation with the stranger could prove useful. However, there was no sign of him anywhere.

Eventually, Oliver met up with the others just before it was time to return home. It was a relief to see Henry appearing with an exhausted-looking Uncle Raj in tow.

It was a long walk back to the station, and the heat of the sun weighed heavy. Henry lagged behind, struggling to keep up; his little legs had walked miles. Oliver had spent very little time with him since they had arrived in London. He dropped back to ask him all about Daphne.

"Daphne is nice," his brother said, "but the meerkats are better."

Oliver smiled, grabbed Henry's hand, and pulled him along. "I think that you've worn Uncle Raj out!"

Henry chuckled.

"I hope that you were a good boy, and looked after him."

Henry nodded thoughtfully, then added, "I only lost him one time."

Oliver squeezed Henry's hand tighter. He trusted his uncle with his little brother, but anything could have happened if Henry had managed to wander off for a while. He bit his tongue; no harm was done, Henry was safe, and they were all heading back.

"Daphne's legs got tired," Henry told Oliver.

"Like yours?" asked Oliver, smiling.

Henry nodded. "She went to sleep and we saw penguins, giraffes, meerkats . . ."

"Shall I carry that big bag for you?"

Henry shook his head. "I'm a big boy."

Oliver did not question that. He was very proud of how his brother was coping.

When they got back, Oliver flopped on the sofa. Winston was especially excited. He welcomed everyone back with even more excitement and curiosity than normal, and bounded from room to room.

As he ran in the direction of the kitchen, Auntie Manya screamed.

Oliver jumped to his feet. The scream was immediately followed by a bark, and then a peculiar high-pitched whistle.

Oliver went to investigate. Auntie Manya was stood frozen in the kitchen, holding Henry's backpack with the zip slightly open. Something black that resembled a nose poked through the opening.

In an instant, it was clear that it definitely *was* a nose. What followed through the gap was a pair of eyes with striking black rims, two little ears tipped with black, two little paws, and a long silver body, and then the rest of a terrified-looking meerkat slipped out of the backpack. It stood upright, almost a foot tall on the kitchen table.

"Aaaarrgh!" screamed Auntie Manya as she leapt onto the kitchen chair.

"Aaaarrgh!" screamed Uncle Raj as he jumped onto the chair next to her.

"Aaaarrgh!" screamed Oliver, as it seemed like the only appropriate thing to say in the circumstances.

"Woof!" barked Winston excitedly.

The meerkat leapt down from the table and ran into the lounge, where Henry was watching TV. Winston chased him, barking and knocking over everything he passed.

Henry smiled proudly. "Do you like him?" he asked. "He wanted to come with me from the zoo."

"What?" exclaimed Uncle Raj.

"Can we keep him?" asked Henry timidly.

The meerkat was now attempting to burrow between the cushions on Uncle Raj's sofa. Winston was ecstatic with the company of his new guest, who clearly loved playing chase as much as he did. He ran around and around, his tail wagging so fast that it looked as if it could come unhinged and fly off into the air.

Oliver grabbed Winston by the collar and dragged him outside into the garden.

"Catch it!" yelled Uncle Raj.

The race was on: four people against one meerkat. It darted behind the sofa, to the chair, across the fireplace, and back into the kitchen, where Auntie Manya still stood on the chair. She gave it the same greeting as the last time.

The meerkat continued darting around the kitchen, knocking over a ceramic pot, which made a horrendous crash and frightened the animal into retreating into the hall, where it hid behind a heavy wooden trunk. Uncle Raj stood ready to pounce with a towel in his hand.

Using a golf umbrella, Uncle Raj attempted to persuade the meerkat out from hiding. He leapt across the hall and pounced, but missed completely. He groaned as he lay face-down on the rug.

The excitement continued in Merlin Drive as people darted, crashes sounded, and screams continued.

"What do we do?" Uncle Raj pleaded with Auntie Manya as he encouraged her down from the chair.

"How should I know?" she answered crossly.

"You've got children."

"Children?" she snapped. "What does that have to do with meerkats?"

Uncle Raj rummaged in the cupboard under the stairs and came out carrying a fishing net. The meerkat ran past him, heading upstairs; everyone ran after it.

The animal was too fast and nobody was sure which room it had gone into. Manya remained at the top of the stairs while everyone else was given a room to search. Even Henry was helping.

Uncle Raj came out onto the landing after searching his room. He was shaking his head. "I don't think it's in there, but I can't be sure."

Oliver had checked the room where he was sleeping, and had decided that it was not in there either. Each room was searched, then a sudden whistling sound came from across the landing.

The meerkat stood tall on his back legs, probably warning all the other meerkats in its clan that danger was lurking. It then ran for it, right between Auntie Manya's legs.

"Catch it!" screamed Oliver.

His auntie threw down a blanket, which landed on it.

"Don't let him go!" yelled Uncle Raj.

"That's easy enough for you to say!" she cried. "He might have rabies!"

The meerkat scratched and snarled until Auntie Manya could no longer hold it. The creature continued down the stairs and out through the cat flap on the back door, where Winston was ready to play chase in the garden.

The meerkat ran around and around, taking refuge in bushes and shrubs. They now needed a plan B; plan A had failed. If it escaped from the garden it would surely be impossible to find.

It might not even make it across the road, and as for the foxes . . . They knew it was time to bring in the experts.

"We'll have to phone the zoo," said Uncle Raj.

"Agreed," said Oliver, who had just crawled out from behind a rose bush.

The appropriate calls were made, and soon the garden was full of zookeepers in green uniforms. They carried nets and cages.

The experts were far better at catching meerkats than Oliver and his family were. They had brought worms, ant larvae, crickets, and grasshoppers, and Oliver even spotted a dead mouse in one of the keepers' hands.

The meerkat eventually gave in and was caught next to the willow tree, eating the ant larvae. It was not long before it was secured in a plastic case and placed into one of the vans.

After the vehicle left, Oliver returned inside and watched through the window as the commotion continued. Some zoo officials remained. The enquiry as to how a meerkat had been stolen had begun.

Uncle Raj explained what had happened. Eventually, it was agreed that it was not a deliberate theft, and Henry was far too young to understand the consequences of his actions. The blame was with the child's guardians. The officials from the zoo decided that it would be in everyone's best interest not to call the call the police. Uncle Raj was encouraged to make a large donation to the zoo as a gesture of goodwill.

The road outside was blocked because of all the disruption. Cars and vans were forced to turn around.

Oliver thought that in the distance he could see the rear of a black Transit van as it drove away. He went to find Henry.

It was late by the time everyone had left, and Oliver wanted to take his little brother to bed. Henry was more confused than ever.

Oliver tucked him in.

"I really wanted to call him Charlie," said Henry sleepily.

"You do understand that taking things is naughty and that animals aren't possessions but creatures that need special care?"

"I didn't really take him," explained Henry. "He wanted to share my snacks. I showed him what was in my bag and then he climbed in."

"Where was Uncle Raj when this happened?" asked Oliver.

"I don't know; it was when I lost him." He looked sad. "I found him talking to a man."

"Which man?"

"The wizard man," Henry whispered sleepily.

"Wizard?" asked Oliver.

Henry yawned.

"Did the wizard have silver hair?"

Henry nodded, then nodded off mumbling something about Daphne and Charlie. He was fast asleep.

Oliver tiptoed out of the room. Before joining the others, he snuck into the garden; he had his new plan to deploy. He took a deep breath, composed himself, and took out his mobile. He was ready to make the call.

"Hello," came a familiar voice.

"Hi, Uncle Will," said Oliver feebly.

"Hiya, butt, how are you?"

"Not so good!" This was it: time for dramatics. A loud sob, followed by a big sniff.

"Is everything OK?"

Oliver changed his voice from a pathetic whisper to a throaty, high-pitched squeak. "No!"

"Whatever's the matter?"

"I want to go home!" *Sniff . . . Sob . . . Sniff!*

Uncle Will immediately suggested that tomorrow morning he could drive through London and collect him to take him back to Wales.

Oliver agreed. Not only had his plan worked, but Uncle Will had even thought it was his own idea. He now needed to make one more call.

"Hi, Storm."

"Hello, you," she replied. "Any news?"

"A bit. I'll explain more when I see you. How are you fixed for the day after tomorrow?"

Storm paused. "Can't! I have to study for a blood test."

"Tell your mum that you are coming to my nan's house, and I'll tell my nan that I'm coming to yours."

"Then where are we going?" asked Storm nervously.

"April Cottage. I'll call you tomorrow."

This plan was just falling into place. Oliver now needed to explain to Uncle Raj.

He made no objections, and even looked relieved.

Oliver bade goodnight to his aunt and uncle and went to bed, but not before checking the road outside. When he was happy that there were no stray black vans, he climbed into bed, knowing that he absolutely needed a good night's sleep and his wits about him for tomorrow.

Working Late

"Are you sure that you don't want to stay?" Uncle Raj asked Oliver over breakfast.

"I'm sure," answered Oliver, still mindful of the fact that he might offend his uncle by leaving early.

"I'm really glad that we came," he added diplomatically, "but it doesn't feel right being in London. What if Mum and Dad came home and we weren't there?"

Uncle Raj gave one of those understanding nods. "Just call me if you need anything."

Henry was also sat at the breakfast table. He automatically assumed that his uncle's offer included him too.

"I need new batteries in my fire engine," he said.

"Consider them changed," Uncle Raj chuckled, returning to the table with a packet of double-As and a screwdriver. "You'd better go and get it."

Oliver returned upstairs to finish his packing. Suddenly, he caught a glimpse of something through the window. Parked on the opposite side of the road, barely metres away from him, was an unmarked black Transit van.

Stepping back from the window, he hid behind the curtain. The van's windows were darkened, so it was hard to tell if anyone was inside. The number plate was different from those he had seen, but that meant nothing as he knew the numbers for only three of the vehicles.

Despite there being thousands of reasons why a black van could find itself parked on Merlin Drive, Oliver kept watch. With his eyes fixed to the vehicle, his mind raced. Had it been there all night? For a reason he could not explain, Oliver could not stop thinking about the man at the zoo.

Oliver thought about Henry in the garden. He leapt down the stairs three at a time and shot into the garden to check that his little brother was safe. He was knee-deep in the herbs, digging up worms, but Oliver did not want to leave him alone.

The sound of gravel crunching and a familiar hum of several Welsh voices talking at the same time confirmed that Oliver's ticket home had arrived.

The back door swung open and out came Daisy and Ethan. They were followed by Uncle Will and Auntie Karen.

"How was the wedding?" asked Oliver.

"Very nice, thank you," said Uncle Will.

"How was it?" asked Uncle Raj as he followed them into the garden.

"Rushed!" Auntie Karen answered curtly.

Uncle Will quickly diverted the conversation before it developed into a full-blown rant. "Thank you for looking after the boys."

Henry told Uncle Will all about Daphne the baby elephant, and Oliver told him all about Charlie. Auntie Karen's face was a picture. First, Uncle Will smirked, and then he laughed out loud. He clearly thought the story of the meerkat was made up by the boys, until Uncle Raj corroborated it. Uncle Will laughed until his sides hurt.

"You are staying for lunch?" asked Auntie Manya once he had calmed down.

"Thanks, but we still have long journeys ahead of us." Uncle Will turned to look at Auntie Karen. "Some longer than others."

"What?" asked Auntie Karen.

"Maths has never been my strong point," said Uncle Will, "but there are six of us heading to Wales, and only five seats in my car."

"Oh!" said Auntie Karen, who was useless at driving.

"I'll drop you at the train station, and pick you up in Wales when the train arrives," said Uncle Will calmly.

Auntie Karen grunted. Her bottom lip pouted and her nostrils flared; not unlike those of a moose, Oliver thought. "So I'm expected to find my own way back?"

"It's either you or one of the children," replied Uncle Will. Oliver thought he must have been feeling very brave at that moment.

Oliver looked at his Auntie Karen, and thought about Frieda the orang-utan. He then looked across at Uncle Will, and Fraser came to mind.

Oliver was a little confused: it was obvious that six people would not all fit in the car, and Uncle Will must have realised that before he set off. Perhaps he was simply too scared to have mentioned it to Karen until now.

Uncle Will drove Auntie Karen to the station, and soon the others were getting ready to leave.

"She'll get over it!" Uncle Will told Oliver, who was fixing Henry's seat belt. "It may take a while, but one day she will get over it."

The black van was still there as they drove past. Oliver stared at it suspiciously, trying to convince himself that not every such vehicle in London was following him.

The journey home was interesting. Henry, Daisy, Ethan, and Winston whinged most of the way, so there seemed little chance of any quiet contemplation.

"Are you all right?" Uncle Will asked Oliver, who sat next to him in the front.

"I suppose. Are *you* all right?"

Uncle Will nodded. He was also a little quiet. Oliver put this down to the fact that he had been sat beside Auntie Karen since the early hours of the morning, and he was happy to allow his uncle some peace.

On his return, Oliver's main priority was getting back to April Cottage. He had already planned to return home on Monday with Storm, but first he needed some time there alone. After racking his brain for one 167 miles, all he could come up with was sneaking out when his nan had gone to bed. It was risky, but there was no other way without raising suspicion.

Uncle Will safely delivered Oliver and Henry to Stanmore Place. There was even time for tea before he had to embark on the perilous quest of collecting Auntie Karen.

"I'd better get off!" said Uncle Will eventually. "The train should be arriving soon."

Oliver looked sad, but this was part of his plan.

"Is there anything you need before I get your auntie and we head back?" his uncle asked. "I could drop by April Cottage – just for a minute, mind you."

"You could check if Mum and Dad are home," said Oliver. "And, bring my bike. I'm meeting Storm in the morning."

Uncle Will agreed. Even without a bike rack, he managed to fit the bike into his car.

"Wish me luck," he said to Oliver as he drove off again, two children and one dog lighter than when he arrived.

"Break a leg!" Oliver responded, knowing full well his uncle would probably need more than luck to get through the rest of the evening with Auntie T-Rex.

Once the boys had settled in, Nan said, "So tell me all about your little trip to London."

"It was good," said Oliver simply.

"Uncle Will told me that you were upset."

"Not really, just . . ."

"It's all right, you're back now."

"What have the police said?" Oliver asked, to change the subject.

"I'm afraid there's very little news. They'll work it out though. It sounds like they are going to step up their enquiries. Don't worry your head about it."

Oliver nodded for the benefit of his grandmother. She looked upset too.

"It's been quite a busy day all round," said Nan, yawning loudly.

"We should all have an early night," he suggested.

Nan felt Oliver's forehead, checking for signs of fever. Satisfied, she said, "That sounds like a very good idea. What shall we do with you tomorrow?"

"Storm has asked me if I want to go to her house."

"Why don't you ask her to come here?"

"Because . . ." Oliver thought quickly. "Storm has an Xbox, a PlayStation, and a Wii. Anyway, it was her mum's idea."

At bedtime, Oliver waited for hours until the house was still. It was just after eleven. He had to be sure that his nan did not hear him leave, or his plan would fail. Tiptoeing out of his darkened room, he checked her bedroom door. It was slightly ajar.

He stood silently outside it for a minute or two, straining his eyes to see if she was awake. When he was sure she was not, he crept downstairs. Through the window, a dim street light showed that there were no vans parked in the lay-by.

154

Oliver was careful to only stand on the edge of each stair, with his back pressing firmly against the wall. Downstairs was in darkness. Feeling his way to the back door, he was careful not to fall over Winston, who made no attempt to follow as he was clearly far too tired.

The night was dark, as the moon was new. Oliver felt for his bike, glancing left and right to check that it was safe to move. He had been told by his Uncle Raj not to go out alone, but since his visit to London, his godfather's instructions felt less important. He cycled as fast as he could.

Once he left the main streets and reached the mountain road, the street lights disappeared completely. His dynamo bike light was barely bright enough to allow him to see a metre ahead.

He had never cycled like this before. Desperately attempting to convince himself that his fear of the dark was stupid, and that the hedges were not threatening and were the same ones he passed on his way to school, he felt incredibly nervous. However, there was something important that he needed to do.

Abandoning his bike behind a tree, Oliver headed into the cottage without turning on the lights and thereby bringing any attention to the fact that he was home alone.

Feeling his way through the hall and into the kitchen was easy. He headed straight for the labs.

Opening the larder, he instinctively looked over his shoulder. It was pointless; he could not see beyond the end of his nose, let alone if there was someone else lurking, but he sensed it was OK. He pressed the access button and the shelves disappeared. Placing his thumb on the recognition pad, he was met by a blinding array of halogen lights.

He woke the security monitors, each of which showed a grey image of every room of the house. Using the main monitor to access the system, he began typing. His dad's history files popped up again. Still the numbers, the random letter patterns, the complicated equations, made no sense. There was only one way of checking the files; he began to open them, one at a time. It was going to be a long night.

There was nothing distinctive about any of them, nothing that was shouting out at him and giving him the answers he was looking for.

He opened the file named *VB17_01_01*. It gave him a different response to the others: a box appeared on the screen.

PASSWORD REQUIRED

This was bizarre. His dad's files were not password-protected, he never saved anything into the cloud, and he always used his own servers. They sat in the labs, which were themselves hidden underground, protected by an outer torpedo door, fingerprint entry, and the added security that only four people in the world knew about them.

Oliver tried entering the obvious passwords: *Paul, Megan, Oliver, Henry*, and even *Winston*. None worked. He followed these with *cup-of-tea, mug-of-tea, knickerbocker glory, supercalifragilisticexpialidocious*. With time ticking on, he tried every password that he could think of, but each time the same message appeared:

PASSWORD INCORRECT

The sad truth was, and Oliver knew it, the probability of him guessing a correct password without even knowing if it involved numbers or digits, or a combination of both, would be almost impossible. He would have to return to this file later.

The clock read *00:30*. His thoughts wandered back to his nan's house, and he hoped that she would not find out that he was missing. He was starting to feel really tired, but could not risk falling asleep in the labs. He had to make sure that he was back and tucked up in bed before she woke.

Oliver yawned and stretched. He had an idea: adults drink coffee to keep them awake; he had seen it on television. The smell of it had never appealed to him, and the thought of drinking an entire cup, *urgh!*

He decided to treat it like medicine. He took a large spoon and dipped it into the instant coffee jar that his dad kept on the desk. He gulped, opened his mouth, held his nose and . . . *urgh!* Finding his mum and dad was playing havoc with his taste buds.

Instead of continuing, Oliver sat back at the desk with a pen and paper in his hand. With his mouth stinging with bitterness, he made a list of all the people that had been in the room with his dad back in January 2007, at the time of the ill-fated explosion.

Firstly, he wrote: *Victor Borofski; senior military Russian, demanded power to full. General Alexander Whimsy; dead (headstone). George Elwood; dead.*

According to his headstone, Elwood had a twin brother. Remembering the two clone-like men from the video, Oliver decided that the Thomas Elwood his father mentioned had to be George's twin.

Oliver wrote *Thomas Elwood*. Next to Thomas's name he added *the one not to trust.*

He knew five people had been present with his dad. He had to find out the identity of the other one.

Oliver re-ran the video message, forwarding it to the part before the explosion. He looked carefully at the screen and froze the image right where the camera swung past the unidentified man. He wore a lab coat; the others wore uniforms. Oliver recognised his broad eyebrows instantly. He was the man on the doorstep of April Cottage and in the van that Storm had crashed into. However, one thing about him was different.

"He doesn't have a scar!" Oliver blurted out loud.

That was it. He had pinned down every face in the video. All of the names matched up, except this man. From the list of those not to trust, there still remained two names that he could not connect: Vincent Quark and Silas Tudor.

He now had a face and two names. He had to find out who these people were.

Silas Tudor proved difficult to find online. There were no references to anybody with that name born in the past 200 years.

Oliver gave up, and instead looked for *Vincent Quark*. Once again, he arrived at a dead end. He yawned and stretched. The clock read *01:31*.

Finally, he stumbled across an article in a business journal that mentioned a Vincent Quark. There was a picture of a Russian businessman. Oliver studied the photograph: there was something vaguely familiar about him. The caption underneath read *Ubinon Folovich*. This was the face he had seen on the website at Hotel Dubois.

Oliver's head throbbed, and his eyes were getting heavier. He read the article:

A British research laboratory due to close because of government spending cuts has been rescued by the Russian entrepreneur and venture capitalist Ubinon Folovich. The sizable donation was made out to a trust set up by the facilities manager, Thomas Elwood. Dr Vincent Quark, a scientist at the Atomic Research Facility in Yorkshire, said: "It would be such a shame for the facility to close as our future is in science. Thanks to Mr Folovich's investment, thirty jobs have been secured . . ."

The article went on, but Oliver had read enough. The words were blurring into one another.

It was time to go back to Nan's. He needed some sleep, as tomorrow was going to be even busier than today.

"Supspicious"

The cycle back was just as eerie as the journey home, only slightly faster as it was all downhill.

Creeping silently in through the back door, Oliver sloped into the darkness of the kitchen, managing once again to step over Winston.

As he reached the top of the stairs, Nan called, "Oliver, is that you?"

Oliver dived into his room and said, "Yes." He tried to sound sleepy. "I was just fetching a drink."

"Straight back to sleep," said Nan. "It's the middle of the night."

Oliver yawned loudly. "OK." He slipped into bed and closed his eyes.

He was woken by a loud bang at the door. It felt as if it was the middle of the night, but when he opened his eyes enough to focus on the clock, it read *08:33*.

He could hear a man whose voice he did not recognise talking to Nan.

Jumping out of bed, he ran to the front bedroom to look out of the window. There were no black vans, and the parking bay was empty. Oliver dressed quickly and headed downstairs.

The visitor was already sat at the kitchen table, and Nan was pouring tea. "Who's he?" asked Oliver sharply.

"This gentleman," she said, scowling at Oliver, "has come from CID to step up the investigation to help find your parents."

The man was tall, and probably about as old as Oliver's dad. He had dark brown hair and was wearing a crumpled grey suit. In a broad Irish accent, he said, "Detective Chief Inspector Graeme O'Sullivan." He stood up and reached to shake Oliver's hand.

Graeme O'Sullivan . . . Graeme O'Sullivan . . . Graeme O'Sullivan . . . the words ricocheted around Oliver's head. Was this the man that his dad had told him about?

"Ouch!" yelled Oliver as Nan prodded him in the ribs.

"Say hello!" she demanded.

"I'm sorry. How do you do?" Oliver's reached out his hand to the DCI. "I'm Oliver."

"I know," replied the DCI. He nodded and winked. "I've been appointed to head the investigation, and right now we don't have nearly enough answers."

Oliver nodded. How would he find out if this was the man? How could he be sure?

The awkward introduction was interrupted by the sound of the front door opening. Uncle Will walked in, sat at the table, and helped himself to tea.

"You need a family liaison officer," the DCI explained. "That is usually a case worker, but if you have no objections I have asked to take on that role."

"Why?" Oliver asked.

Both Nan and Uncle Will glared at him, but he thought it was a fair question, and he needed to know.

"I'm glad that you asked," DCI O'Sullivan replied. "I'd like to help because I believe that your father would want me to."

"Do you know my dad?"

The DCI smiled. "We've helped each other out in the past—"

160

"But isn't that against police rules," said Oliver, interrupting, "if you already know the people involved?"

Uncle Will and Nan looked mortified.

"I do apologise – Oliver has been terribly upset," said Nan, sounding very embarrassed.

"Understandably so," said DCI O'Sullivan. "Maybe Oliver and I could have a little chat sometime."

Oliver had proof that his dad knew the DCI, but parting with his trust was something that he was not prepared to do freely.

The DCI explained over and over what they already knew, and asked the same questions that the other police officers had already asked.

Oliver may have been sat in the room, but his mind was elsewhere. He looked at the clock: it was *09:55*. He had arranged to be at his house in five minutes to meet up with Storm. Tired, hungry, and now late, he stood up.

"Can I go?" he asked. "I promised Storm that I would be at her house by ten o'clock."

DCI O'Sullivan also stood. "If you can think of anything that may or may not seem important, or if you just need to talk, you can phone me anytime."

He passed Oliver a business card containing his phone number.

"Do you want a lift," said Uncle Will to Oliver.

"Thanks, but I've got my bike."

"Be careful," Nan instructed him. "Put your helmet on!"

Oliver was a bit late by the time he got to April Cottage and there was no sign of Storm. He put his hand in his pocket to collect his phone and call her, but realised he had left it on the breakfast table. He would have to go back.

He was astride his bike when he heard an angry cry from behind the conifers at the side of the garage: "Oy, you!"

Oliver smiled. One arm and one leg emerged from the greenery, followed by the rest of a fiery-looking Storm.

"First, you're late!" she exclaimed. "Then you decide to abandon me."

"Hi, Storm," said Oliver.

"You'd better have a very good excuse."

"An excellent one."

"Well, start explaining!"

"You first. Why were you hugging the Christmas trees?"

"Isn't it obvious?"

"Nope," said Oliver.

"There are two reasons actually, if you must know." She sounded quite matter-of-fact. "Firstly, I didn't want anyone to see me stood alone, outside your house, for obvious reasons. Secondly, and justifiably, you said you'd be here at ten, and you are late.

"Because you are late, I wanted to punish you and make you think that I wasn't here. I was planning to jump out and surprise you, if you must know, but my plans changed when I caught my jacket on a branch and somehow managed to get myself attached to it—"

"Storm," Oliver interrupted her in the middle of her rant.

"Plus—"

"Storm!" Oliver tried again. "Thank you for coming." There was a moment of silence. "I knew that you wouldn't let me down."

"You're welcome," she replied calmly. She had stopped.

He thought it was funny, the way in which she could switch her moods so easily. She was similar to Auntie Karen, only on a far less severe scale.

"So, what have I missed?" she asked.

"Plenty."

They hid out of sight of the road and Oliver recapped the events that had occurred since he last saw Storm. It took a while. There was the incident at the hotel, the van hire company, the man at the zoo, Oliver's suspicions about his Uncle Raj, and his message from his dad. He told her the names of the men he could not trust: Silas Tudor, Vincent Quark, Thomas Elwood and the recently deceased Victor Borofski.

Oliver did not tell Storm anything about the labs; nor did he mention any other details that were in the message. He said only that his dad had suspected that something bad might happen.

There were several gasps, many sighs, and even an outburst of giggles when he happened to mention the incident after the zoo. Now Storm was up to date.

"First things first," said Oliver once he had finished. "I've forgotten my phone. I'll have to go back and get it."

"Really?" asked Storm. "You're not leaving me here on my own. I'm coming with you."

"Fine. And another thing, a DCI has turned up this morning. He claims that his name is Graeme O'Sullivan."

"*The* Graeme O'Sullivan? The one you said your dad mentioned?" asked Storm.

"Who knows? But I'm not prepared to trust him without some sort of proof. I don't know how, but I need to get some."

Storm recovered her bike from the trees and they both cycled back to Stanmore Place.

"I won't be a minute," said Oliver as they arrived at Nan's back gate. "Stay here!"

He did not want any delays or any questions. He just wanted his phone and to leave again.

Nan, Uncle Will, and DCI O'Sullivan were still sat at the table, talking.

"Back so soon!" said Nan.

"Not really back," said Oliver. "More passing through and on my way out again, as soon as I've got my phone."

He scoured the table for it.

"Is this what you're looking for?" asked the DCI as he pushed aside the pot of marmalade in front of him, and handed a phone to Oliver.

"Er, thanks." He left through the back door before anyone could stop him.

"I've got it!" he said to Storm, who had wandered into the garden and was sat on the wall. "Let's go!"

"Hand me that," she said.

"Why?"

"I want to check Facebook."

"I haven't *got* Facebook."

"Doh! You mean that you are trying to find some goss on this bloke and you haven't used Facebook?"

"I haven't got an account. Don't you have to be thirteen?"

"You have to *say* you're thirteen. *I've* had one for ages." Storm pulled the phone from Oliver's hand. "I've got something to show you."

She pressed several buttons, downloaded Facebook, and entered it using her own logon details. She began typing names into the search bar.

"What are you doing?" asked Oliver.

"Remind me, who are you not meant to trust?"

"Silas Tudor -" Oliver began.

Within moments, Storm handed Oliver the phone. It showed a profile picture of somebody that he recognised immediately. It was the man at the zoo.

"I don't believe it!" he gasped. "I knew that I shouldn't trust that guy!"

While this conversation had been going on, neither of them had noticed Henry come out into the garden.

As he suddenly climbed onto the wall behind them, looking at the picture on Oliver's phone, Storm said, "Hi, Henry."

"He's supspicious man!" Henry pouted.

"Go away," said Oliver to his little brother. He needed to focus.

"Don't like naughty man! I won't go away!" said Henry fiercely.

"Say it again," Storm asked Henry. "That was so sweet."

Henry looked puzzled.

"What did you say about the naughty man?" Storm asked.

"He's supspicious!" He smiled angelically.

"Awwww, that's so sweet. He can't say 'suspicious'."

"What are you going on about?" Oliver asked his little brother.

"Daddy's friend."

Oliver looked at Henry with great interest and instantly stopped being irritated. He asked, "Do you know him?"

"Yes!" insisted Henry. "He found Uncle Raj at the zoo."

"But why is he Daddy's friend?"

Henry shrugged.

"Did he come and see Daddy?"

Henry nodded.

"At our house?"

Henry nodded again. "He's naughty because he shouted at Daddy."

"Really?" Oliver now gave Henry his full attention. "Are you sure it wasn't somebody else who looked like him?" Oliver held out his phone to show Henry the picture again.

Henry shook his head.

"Do you know what his name is?" Oliver asked.

Henry frowned. "Daddy said he was suspicious man!"

Oliver's mind was reeling as he pedalled back to April Cottage in silence, Storm in tow.

The Biggest Secret

Stowing their bikes behind the trees, Oliver and Storm went inside. They headed for the kitchen, where Oliver pulled down the computer monitor.

"Facebook!" he announced.

"Shall I set you up with an account?" asked Storm.

Oliver shook his head. "Can we use yours instead?"

He passed the keyboard to Storm, and she logged in.

"Nice picture," he said, smirking at a selfie of his best mate with a cheesy pout.

"Shut it! At least I've got an account. Do you want my help or not?"

Oliver was quiet.

"Silas Tudor," said Storm as his face appeared on the screen.

The face Oliver saw was undoubtedly that of the man at the zoo. "What does it tell us about him?"

Storm tapped away at the keyboard. "He doesn't really use the account. There are no personal details. He's a bit of a saddo for sure, a Billy-no-mates."

"How do you know that?"

"Because, he's only got one friend." Storm sniggered.

"Who?"

She tapped away, and instantly both their jaws dropped as a different face appeared on the screen.

"It's him," said Storm. "Monobrow Man."

The last time Storm had seen this man, he leant over her as she lay covered in ketchup in the middle of the road. Despite the fact that her eyes were mostly closed, she did get a glimpse of him, and had no doubt that this picture was of him.

"I don't believe it!" Oliver was trembling. This was the last man still unnamed from the footage in the lab.

He glared at the image of a man with dark eyes, piercing like a snake's, that were framed by a thick single eyebrow. The most distinct feature of all was a long, angry scar running from the base of his right eye to his lip.

"Vincent Quark!" said Oliver.

"Two out of three," said Storm proudly. "What did you say the other bloke was called? EndWood?"

"Elwood." Oliver replied. "Thomas Elwood."

Storm entered his name into the search bar. "He doesn't have a Facebook account. Sad."

Now, more than ever, Oliver wanted to get back into the labs and find more information. He would have to do the right thing. He looked at Storm.

"What?" she asked.

Oliver took a deep breath. "What's the most important secret you've ever kept?"

Storm looked curious. Oliver was about to take an enormous risk. It went against everything he had ever been told by his dad, other than to trust in his own instincts.

Storm thought hard. "I once knew that my brother was getting a bike for his birthday because I saw it in the garage."

Oliver shook his head. "Bigger!"

"I know that my dad once dropped my mother's toothbrush down the toilet when he was cleaning the bathroom, and just rinsed it off, and didn't tell her."

"That's disgusting!" Oliver gagged. "No, even bigger!"

Storm thought for a moment then said, "I'm afraid of the dark. Oh, and I wet my bed once when I was on holiday in Spain last year."

"Really?" said Oliver, smiling.

Storm glared. "Why did I just tell you that?"

She was turning a dark shade of pink.

"OK . . ." Oliver paused. "I'm about to tell you something that I have never told another living soul, and I also promised my father I would never tell."

Storm was silent.

"You know that my dad is a scientist?"

"Yes. He lectures at the university, doesn't he?"

"No," said Oliver. "Well, he does, but only now and again."

"So, what *does* he do?"

"He's a research scientist working on an experiment that is very controversial." Oliver stopped to think very carefully about his next sentence. "My father has invented something huge. Actually, something so big that I think that someone has been trying to steal it. That's the reason why my mum and dad aren't here."

Storm's eyes widened and her jaw plunged. The kitchen fell silent.

"And there's something else," said Oliver. "The labs where he works." He pointed to the ground. "They're downstairs."

There, he'd said it. There was no going back.

"What?" asked Storm. "Downstairs?"

"Do you promise you will never, ever tell anyone about what we do next?"

"Cross my heart and hope to die."

"Then I've got something to show you."

Oliver led Storm to the larder and opened the door.

"Is this a joke?" she said.

Oliver moved the cereal box and pressed the button. "Stand back."

Storm watched in awe as the shelves dropped down and revealed the torpedo door.

As the large steel entrance swung open, Storm followed Oliver onto the gangway. The door closed behind them.

Her eyes were as wide as saucers. However, not even shock was enough to impede her silence for very long. "What the . . ."

"Welcome to my dad's secret labs."

Storm gazed at her surroundings in astonishment.

Oliver's eyes scanned each part of the labs, checking that everything was in place.

"I can't believe that I have never noticed this hiding behind your cornflakes cupboard," said Storm, her voice quaking.

"It's easy to miss. You're not meant to notice it. I lived here for eight years before I knew about it."

"Didn't you think it a bit odd that every time your dad reached for the cornflakes, he disappeared?"

"He never disappeared in front of me, stupid!"

"Too awesome," said Storm dreamily.

"You do realise how big a secret this is, don't you?"

"I don't think that anybody would believe me if I *did* tell them."

"You're probably right. Do you want a tour?"

"Do I ever!"

Oliver led Storm down the larger spiral staircase, which stopped in the centre of the enormous complex.

"It's a lot to take in," he warned, preparing Storm for even more surprises.

"Pinch me!" she said.

"OK." It was rare to have permission to inflict pain on his friend.

"Ow!"

"You *told* me to pinch you."

"But I thought I was dreaming."

"No, you're not dreaming. Welcome to my world."

Storm smiled uncomfortably.

Oliver began the tour of the labs, stopping only briefly in each section to highlight the main functions. It was important that he did not overload Storm with technicalities. Today was not about touring the labs, or introducing particle physics. It was about finding answers.

"My dad . . ." Oliver hesitated and took a deep breath. "My dad used to work for the British government, but when he left, he began working here."

"What was it you said he was working on?"

"I didn't."

"I *am* dreaming," Storm sighed as they left the particle physics lab.

"Then if you're dreaming," replied Oliver, "I'm having exactly the same dream as you are, only mine's a nightmare."

Storm smiled sympathetically. She looked lost, standing in the middle of the labs with a mesmerised grin on her face. She needed directing into the security room, where Oliver placed her on a stool then switched on the monitors.

"This is where I need your help," he explained. He felt it necessary to return to the purpose of them being there. He snapped his fingers, as if trying to bring Storm out of the trance. "It's really important that we use every minute possible."

"I'll do whatever I can." She paused. "No more bike crashes though."

"I need to break through a barrier in the system that has been password-protected by my dad."

"I can't code-crack files. I can barely remember my own passwords. You're so much better at that sort of thing than I am."

"But you're so much better at researching and stuff," said Oliver. "I was going to ask you to find everything you can about Vincent Quark and Silas Tudor. I think that these two should be our priority. They certainly seem to know who I am."

"I thought you said that you did that on Friday at your Uncle Raj's house and that you did some looking last night."

"Yeah, but I spent hours looking and didn't get anywhere. You, on the other hand, spent ten minutes this morning and already you have found out loads."

Storm looked pleased to have received such a compliment.

Oliver pointed towards the screen in front of her. "I need addresses, places where they work, phone numbers, newspaper articles, and anything else that you can find."

"Oliver," said Storm nervously. "You can't deal with this on your own. You have to get some help."

"I'm not on my own. I've *got* someone to help me." He smiled at his best friend.

Storm looked terrified, but directed her attention to the keyboard. Oliver set to work on the main computer. He had already begun trying to bypass the password. He continued to open documents until there was only one remaining that had not been opened and checked.

Oliver understood the science behind passwords and how the encryption worked, and he was aware that, given the correct tools, passwords could be breakable. All he needed was the correct bandwidth and the correct piece of software. He turned his attention to searching the systems for a file that would help him. He knew that his dad would have one somewhere.

After they had spent an hour staring at their screens in silence, Storm asked, "How are you getting on?"

"Not great. I've tried running a codebreaking piece of software, but if it was that easy, then Dad probably wouldn't have bothered protecting it in the first place. What about you?"

"Well, nothing much on Mr Supspicious—"

"Wait a minute. What did you say?"

"What?"

"His name, what did you call him?"

"Who?"

"It's Silas Tudor you mean, isn't it?" said Oliver frantically.

"Yeah, 'Mr Supspicious' is what Henry called him."

"Mr Supspicious!" said Oliver. He typed *SUSPICIOUS*.

There was a pause.

"How mad is that?" said Oliver. "I don't believe it. Henry knew the password!"

"What's in the file?" asked Storm as she abandoned her research in favour of Oliver's and a document opened on the screen.

"How bizarre," said Oliver, baffled. The monitor displayed an internet job advert. He read it aloud: *"Highly talented, world-class atomic engineers and physicists required to work at innovative lab complex. Contact Dr V. Quark . . ."*

He fell silent.

"Don't stop reading," said Storm. "What else does it say?"

"North Yorkshire Scientific Research Laboratories, Puddingdale, North Yorkshire, YO71 9AF. Please send any interests by e-mail to . . ."

He sat bolt upright. "I don't believe it!"

"I don't get it."

"I think I do." He scratched his head vigorously. "What this means is . . . that we know where to find Vincent Quark. We now have an address, for his labs. *And* this means that we are going to Yorkshire."

"Hahaha!" laughed Storm nervously.

"Ha!" Oliver's own laugh sounded determined. He reached over to the filing cabinet and took out his dad's credit card.

"You're not joking, are you?" Storm's voice quivered.

"Absolutely not!"

Oliver, grinning, booked and printed the train tickets. Storm, meanwhile, was in charge of packing a rucksack with essential supplies for the journey.

He would hide the bags in his nan's shed and collect them in the morning. They were wasting no time at all.

Things You Do

Even before his alarm went off, Oliver was wide awake. He considered calling Uncle Raj and wondered whether he should tell him about his plan, just in case something went wrong. He also thought about the DCI; how could he be sure that he was trustworthy?

His thoughts turned to his little brother and his mum and dad. His head buzzed as if a swarm of bees had found their way inside while he was asleep. The day was going to be long and far too complicated to think of as a whole. Instead, to stop his head from exploding, he broke it down into thinkable-size chunks.

Step one: the easiest part, escaping from Nan's. Then step two: getting to Yorkshire. Step three was the complicated bit; what to do when he got to the labs. Step four: returning to Wales.

Oliver picked up his phone and DCI O'Sullivan's business card and put them in his pocket.

"Good morning," said Nan as she followed him downstairs. "Up with the lark, I see."

"I was awake. I couldn't sleep. I was going to meet Storm in the park this morning anyway."

"Again? Well I suppose it may help take your mind off things. There must be an awful lot going on in your head."

Oliver nodded. *If she knew only the half of it!*

Nan flung open the lounge curtains, and daylight flooded in. "It looks as if it's going to be a nice day for a day at the park," she said. "Put some suncream on before you go."

Oliver placed his hand over his mouth; a black Transit van was parked on the opposite side of the road.

"Are you all right?" Nan asked.

"I'm fine," said Oliver, stepping back from the window. The van had been showing up all week, so why had he not considered that this could have happened?

This was disastrous. If he was seen getting on a train to Yorkshire, he could be followed. Black van or no black van, he had to get to the station unnoticed by 8:30.

"That van's there again!" said Nan, still peering out of the window. "Maybe we should call the police."

"Why?"

"The police asked us to be vigilant and let them know if we see anything suspicious."

"There must be thousands of black vans in Wales. Loads of people drive them."

Nan watched it for a few minutes.

"They'll think we're paranoid if we report every black van we see," said Oliver. "If you're still worried later, maybe you could ask DCI O'Sullivan. Henry told me he's coming back today."

"You're right. I think that I will." Nan set off in the direction of the kitchen, leaving Oliver stood behind the curtain, peering through the window.

"Fancy some breakfast?" she called out.

"Yes, please!" said Oliver. He picked up his phone and texted Storm, hoping that she would have a suggestion about how he could get to the station without being followed:

DISASTER! There's a black van parked outside my nan's! How can I get out without being followed?

He hit *Send message* before entering the kitchen.

Nan handed Oliver a lunch bag. "I thought you might like to take a picnic."

"Thanks, Nan," said Oliver. The clock on the kitchen wall read *07:30*. Time was moving on.

His phone beeped with a message from Storm, written in her usual haphazard way:

Ordud taxi, 4get bike. Outside No.1 @8:10! Ware disguise!!!!!

Oliver read the message twice. The taxi bit was straightforward. The disguise bit, what was that all about? He texted her back:

What, like Superman?

A message came back:

2 obvius! Prtend 2 b a girl!

Oliver laughed out loud nervously. The idea was absurd, stupid, but it might just work.

"What's so funny?" asked Nan.

"You don't happen to have a wig in the house, do you?" he asked. He thought he had better justify the odd request. "A couple of my mates who are meeting at the park have this thing going on, sort of like an initiation into this new club we've started."

"It's not one of those cults, is it?" Nan asked suspiciously.

"No!" Oliver was quick to try and reassure her. "It's just for a laugh. Before we meet up this morning, everyone has to set a forfeit for the girls who don't turn up looking like boys and the boys who don't turn up looking like girls." The lies flowed one after the other.

"It just so happens," replied Nan, "that I have got one, but I'm not sure if it's your kind of thing."

"What is it?"

"It's part of a costume I wore to a world fancy dress party. I dressed as Austria . . ." She smiled awkwardly. "It has two blond plaits."

"Better than facing a forfeit."

Nan looked strangely at Oliver before going in search of the wig. While she was gone, a sleepy Henry wandered into the kitchen, wearing his pyjamas and cuddling his teddy bear.

"Morning, Henry," said Oliver, smiling as the memory of Uncle Will holding the same bear dripping above his head flooded back.

Henry smiled and yawned. "Can we play football today?"

"Tomorrow," said Oliver, feeling ever so guilty. "I promise."

"There you go," said Nan as she came back into the kitchen, carrying a wig with plaits tied either side with red ribbons.

Oliver tried it on and looked in the mirror. He looked like an eleven-year-old boy wearing a girl's wig. He also knew that the disguise would do the opposite of what he had intended and attract even more attention.

He could not believe he was indeed capable of asking his nan the next question, but the clock was ticking, and he was desperate, so he did.

"Do you have a dress to go with it?"

She gave him that odd look again, then said, "I'll be right back!"

Moments later, she was carrying an Austrian Tyrolean national dance costume with a flowing red skirt, frilly blouse, petticoat, and pretty lace apron. Oliver headed for the bathroom.

As he emerged, Henry and Nan laughed out loud.

"You look silly!" Henry giggled.

"Stay there!" said Nan. "I need to get my camera."

Oliver groaned. "Can I borrow that today?"

"I thought you had a camera on your new posh phone."

"I have," he said, "but yours is better. It's got a zoom lens."

"You'll look after it, won't you?"

Oliver smiled reassuringly as Winston approached, needing a quick sniff to check that it was actually Oliver underneath the layers.

It was eight o'clock. Oliver gathered up his things, remembering to take his normal clothes and stuffing them into his bag along with his lunch box.

"Are you sure you don't want a lift?" asked Nan.

"No, I'm meeting Storm on the way."

"It's terribly early to go to the park, don't you think?"

"Not really," he said. "That's sort of the initiation too. Whoever is the last to arrive will have to do a forfeit."

"I'm not sure I like the sound of any of this." Nan shook her head.

Oliver had moments to convince her. "It's a laugh, that's all."

The clock said *08:06*. Oliver glanced out of the window: the van was still there. A taxi drove past and stopped outside number one; it had to be the one that Storm had ordered. Grabbing his bag, he headed for the back door, shouting, "Bye!"

"Are you going by bike?" said Nan as he passed her.

"No," he said, trying to think of a reason why bikes could lead to forfeits.

"Are bikes banned too?"

"Ummmm . . ." said Oliver, this time not as quick with his response. "I think I've got a slow puncture."

Nan and Henry chuckled as he hurried past with his skirt flowing behind him.

He grabbed the rucksacks from the shed and peered through the back gate. Nan's house was in the middle of a row of terraces, with each garden separated by a picket fence or a privet hedge. Oliver did not want to be spotted on the road behind, so instead jumped the first fence to Mrs Cadwalader's garden, then the privet hedge to the Rowlands's house. As he jumped, his skirt parachuted and his plaits bobbed up and down. He really hoped that nobody was looking out of their windows. Stepping cautiously out of the gate at number two, avoiding having to climb their six-foot hedge of holly bushes, Oliver checked to see if the way was clear. He headed to the back gate of number one.

Oliver dived behind the greenhouse, avoiding being spotted by Mrs Williams. It would have been a difficult situation to explain. He had to make it look as if he was casually leaving the house and getting into a taxi.

The taxi driver hooted his horn. Mrs Williams looked out of her window. Oliver was forced to wave to her on his way past as he walked down the alley at the side of the house before appearing in the front garden and leaving through her front gate.

Diving into the back of the taxi, Oliver closed the door and announced breathlessly, "Train station please."

The taxi driver, a sober-looking man in a flat cap and anorak, turned his head to look Oliver up and down. "Taxi for Oliver?" he asked, sounding confused.

"Yes!" Oliver grinned nervously. "I'm Oliver and I need to catch a train."

"You get to see all sorts of things in this job."

Oliver glanced at the driver's rear-view mirror. The van was still there.

He considered changing his clothes in the back seat, but thought better of it. He could not unfasten his seatbelt and risk the driver throwing him out. He would have to wait. He would change at the station. By some stroke of luck or insanity, the plan had worked. It was ridiculously brilliant, although he did feel like a right plonker.

Oliver hoped that when he got to the station, Storm would already be there. There was a chance that she might have decided to bail out, and Oliver thought nobody could blame her if she did, even if he would be forced to go alone.

When the taxi arrived, Oliver was relieved to see Storm waiting on a bench next to the taxi rank. He paid the driver, grabbed the bags, and dived out. Storm laughed so hard she fell off the edge of the bench. When she eventually managed to stop, she sniggered, "What *do* you look like?"

"A complete wally!" replied Oliver. "It *was* your idea in the first place. And besides, all of my other girl's clothes were in the wash."

Storm snorted, trying to talk while still laughing.

"It worked, didn't it?" said Oliver. "I wasn't followed."

An old lady walked past, dragging her trolley bag and looking peculiarly at Oliver.

"We've got four minutes before the train leaves," Storm reminded him. "You had better change into something a little more inconspicuous. You have brought something else, haven't you?"

"Of course I have," said Oliver, ducking behind the nearest tree, creating a blur of red skirts and petticoats.

When he reappeared, he looked almost normal.

"What about the wig?" asked Storm.

He grabbed hold of one plait and pulled. The wig landed on the ground.

"We'd better run!" said Storm.

Oliver shoved the costume into the bag and they headed for platform three, arriving at the same moment as their train.

The Journey North

"What did you tell your mum?" asked Oliver as he placed his rucksack under his seat.

"She wanted to know when I'd be back, and why I wouldn't be there for lunch." Storm sighed as she fell back into the window seat. "I don't think that she trusts me anymore."

"I can't imagine why." Oliver smiled guiltily.

According to the timetable, they would arrive in Yorkshire by lunchtime. That would give them only a few hours to make their investigations before catching a train back at three o'clock. That would get them home by seven.

"Tickets, please," came a voice from the back of the carriage. Oliver reached for his rucksack.

Both Oliver and Storm sat quietly, waiting for something to go wrong.

"Tickets, please!" came the voice again. This time, the ticket inspector was standing right next to them.

Oliver handed his over, and the inspector looked at it. "It says two children."

"That's right," said Oliver.

"Are you two travelling alone?"

Oliver considered lying and claiming that his mum was in the next carriage, but thought better of it; he could be found out far too easily.

"Yes," he answered. "We are being met by my grandmother. My mum spoke to the guard at the station, and he said that it would be all right."

"Is that so?" asked the inspector suspiciously. He clipped the ticket, frowned, and handed it back.

"Phew, that was close," said Storm once he had gone. "I thought that he was going to send us back."

"Looks like we should have booked an adult ticket, too," said Oliver as an afterthought. "Never mind. We'll know for next time."

"Next time!" scolded Storm. "You reckon there will be a next time? You have to be kidding. I'm in danger of being grounded for the rest of my life if my mum finds out I've been to Yorkshire today. She thinks we're painting a fence in your nan's back garden."

Oliver shrugged. "Today we are going to find my mum and dad."

"I hope it's all going to be worth it. Have you brought the address?"

"Yes." He showed her.

"Have you worked out how far it is from the station?" Storm asked.

"Better than that. I've got my new phone. It's got GPS. When we get closer, we can put the address of the labs into it, and we can work out which station we need to get off at."

"It all sounds so simple."

"It is."

"I still can't believe that we are doing this," said Storm. "It's crazier than coconuts!"

"Crazy maybe, but it's even crazier if we don't go."

"Ever fancy a career in solving crime?" asked Storm, sounding a little more relaxed.

"No way! A professor of physics."

"I should've known you would say that, Dr Oliver."

"I've spoken to the guard on the train," said the ticket inspector suddenly. He had reappeared and was peering over them, looking concerned. Oliver dreaded what he was going to say next. "He hasn't spoken to your mum."

Oliver grimaced.

"It must have been someone else she spoke to," the man went on, "but the rule is, when children travel alone, they need to be met by an officer at the station to ensure they are collected safely by their guardian."

"Oh!" said Oliver. "My mum said that someone would keep an eye on us."

He was feeling quite relieved, as that conversation could have gone far worse.

"That someone seems to be . . . me," said the inspector, clearly not very happy about it. "At which station are you getting off? I need to arrange for an officer to meet you."

Oliver thought quickly. He knew that they would have to get off the train before the officer expected them to. He answered, "Knaresborough."

That was the last stop on the line. The last thing they needed was to be held safely at the station, waiting for their grandmother to appear. They could be waiting for a very long time.

Throughout the journey, the inspector kept a regular check on them.

"What does he think that we are going to do?" Storm asked Oliver after he disappeared for the fourth time.

"Vandalise the armrests? Or maybe someone could kidnap us."

"That's not funny!" Storm scowled. "So, what do we do once we get off?"

"Find my mum and dad."

They both stared out of the window at the fields and trees. It was a relief to not have to keep checking a rear-view mirror, looking for black vans.

When it seemed they had been travelling for hours, Oliver began fiddling with his phone.

"What are you doing?" asked Storm. "You should save the battery."

"Checking the GPS." Oliver scratched his head. He looked worried.

"What now?"

"It's slightly complicated."

"How slight?"

"Slightly large," said Oliver nervously.

"Just tell me."

"We've got three hours, right?"

"Right . . ."

"The nearest station to this postcode is . . . twenty-five miles away."

"We'll have to head straight back."

"No way!" Oliver was immovable.

"What then? Twenty-five miles. That's nearly as far as a . . . as a . . . London Marathon." Storm's voice was rising.

"Shh! It's OK, I think I've got an idea."

"Just tell me what it is. I'm getting really stressed now."

"I'll only tell you if you promise not to thump me." Oliver held his upper arm in readiness.

Storm's nostrils began to flare.

"We get off the train closer to the labs," said Oliver.

"How?" Storm sounded frantic.

"When we get really close, we stop the train using the emergency cord, and make a run for it."

"What's plan B?"

"There isn't one."

"We could get a taxi from the nearest station," she suggested hopefully.

"How much money have you brought with you?"

"I've emptied my money box. I've got about fifteen pounds. What about you?"

"I brought twenty pounds out of my birthday money, but it cost four for the taxi here. Will we have enough to get back, too?"

"I don't know," she frowned. "What if we take the bus?"

"Too risky. We've no idea which buses run close to the labs in Puddingdale or how often they run. We really don't have enough time."

Storm fell silent, but only for a moment. "So how does this emergency cord work?"

"Above all the exits is a cord. You have to break the glass, and then pull it, then the train stops."

"But can't you get fined loads of money for doing that?"

"Only if you get caught."

"Have you done this before?" asked Storm. "You seem to know exactly what to do."

"Of course not. I've just looked at the leaflet." He pointed to the list of emergency procedures in the seat in front of him.

"So we break the glass above the door, pull the cord, and the train stops. Then what?"

"We get off!" Oliver tried to be blasé.

"But what if the doors are locked?" Storm was sounding more uncomfortable by the second.

Oliver had already considered this. "We open the window. It's big enough to climb out."

Storm looked pained.

"Don't worry." Oliver did his best to sound reassuring. "We've got about half an hour before we need to get off. There's plenty of time to eat our sandwiches."

He took a brown paper bag from his rucksack, and Storm watched as he tucked into his cheese and pickle roll. He stopped mid-bite and spoke with his mouth full. "You haven't brought any, have you?"

Storm just shook her head. "I've got some tins."

Oliver handed Storm the second roll in the paper bag. "It could be a long time until tea."

Storm took the roll eagerly.

"They look nice!" came the now-familiar voice of the ticket inspector.

"We shouldn't really eat too much because my grandma is making us lunch when we get there," Oliver told him. The lies were stacking up like delicate dominoes; one slip of the tongue and they could all come tumbling down.

"Forty minutes and we will be at the end of the line," the inspector announced. "When we get there, I'll give you a shout and hand you over to the officer."

He left to check tickets further down the carriage.

Storm and Oliver smiled and nodded, knowing full well that there would be no need for him to do that but they were not going to tell him.

Oliver checked his phone. "Ten minutes."

Storm looked anxious.

"Do you think that we should leave from different carriages?" Oliver suggested.

"Absolutely not!"

"You're probably right." Oliver checked up and down the aisle for the guard. "I think it's time. I'll go first, so it doesn't look too suspicious, and then you follow in a couple of minutes."

He picked up the rucksack and handed the other to Storm, then walked to the end of the carriage and waited. Luckily, the *Engaged* sign was on the lavatory, so to any passers-by it looked as if he was simply waiting to use the toilet.

The inspector walked past. Oliver smiled, and danced a little. The inspector smiled back at him then carried on checking more tickets. Storm waited for him to go through the far doors into the next carriage before joining Oliver.

"Not yet!" he said. "About three more miles."

At this point, the door to the lavatory swung open, and the sharp smell of a chemical toilet filled the air. An old man swaggered out. He looked as though he had been in there for quite some time.

"It's the inspector again!" said Storm, looking down the carriage. "He's coming this way!"

"Hide!" said Oliver, pushing her into the toilet cubicle.

They both squeezed in. Oliver's back was squished against the sink, his knees against the toilet. Storm and the rucksacks filled every other cubic centimetre of space, making movement impossible. Somehow, they managed to lock the door. Liquids swashed around their feet, and the stale, putrid smell of urine was nauseating.

"What do we do now?" Storm was squirming.

"Wait!" whispered Oliver.

"Please take your elbow out of my ear."

"Only if you take your shoulder out of my rib cage."

"Do you think the inspector will notice that we are not in our seats?" asked Storm anxiously.

"I hope not," whispered Oliver. The sound of air escaping could be heard right next to them. Someone was outside the door.

Knock. Knock. Knock. The door shook.

"Are you the youngster travelling unaccompanied?" asked the inspector.

Oliver had to answer. "Yes."

"Where's your sister?"

Oliver smirked, and Storm nudged her elbow further into his ear. "We both ate a dodgy sandwich and she had to find a toilet in a different carriage," he added. "The cheese was off."

Oliver hoped that that would be enough to get rid of him for a few vital minutes.

"Half an hour to Knaresborough," said the voice, followed by the sound of a door opening and closing.

"Right," said Oliver. "It's now or never." It took a little scrabbling to locate the door handle, but when they did it was a relief to breathe the fresher air as well as move their arms and legs.

Oliver took the torch out of his rucksack. "On the count of three," he said, "One . . . two . . . *three!*"

He whacked the torch on the glass above the door as hard as he could, then jumped to reach the cord, just managing to grab it by his fingertips.

Immediately, they heard the deafening sound of wheels screeching on the rails. The train decelerated rapidly as the brakes slammed on, throwing them both rebounding off the walls and into each other before landing on the floor in a heap.

Getting straight to their feet, they knew not a single moment could be wasted; it was time to leave.

Oliver tried the exit door. It was locked. He opened the window, waited a moment or two for the train to slow even further, and flung both the rucksacks out of the train. He gestured for Storm to climb out, but she hesitated.

"Go!" cried Oliver. "The train has almost stopped!"

Storm used Oliver's outstretched leg as a step and placed one leg out of the window. Then Oliver gave her a helping hand by pushing through the other one.

"Aaaarrgh!" she screamed. Luckily, the screeching of the brakes was enough to drown her out.

Oliver put his head through the window and, in a very unbecoming fashion, pushed himself through with his bottom in the air. He landed with a crash and an unintended forward roll that was repeated several times over as he cascaded down a steep embankment.

When he eventually stopped, with the help of a fallen tree, he looked around for Storm. She was sat on the embankment, next to the tree trunk, holding two rucksacks and her leg.

"Don't talk to me!" she said, looking disorientated and angry.

"Come on," said Oliver, grabbing one of the rucksacks. "We have to get away from here before anyone realises that was us."

"I said, don't talk to me." She glared at Oliver, who forced a smile as he had collected a few injuries of his own.

He began hobbling as quickly as he could down the hill. Storm followed until they reached the security of the dense wood, continuing east to get as far away from the railway track as possible.

"Can I talk to you now?" he asked breathlessly, checking over his shoulder.

"I suppose you'll have to. I cannot believe what you just made me do!"

"Do you think anyone saw us?"

"I hope not!"

Their run slowed to a fast walk with them both holding their sides and out of breath. They continued until they arrived at a main road. A sign pointed east: *Puddingdale, 2 miles.*

Oliver glanced at his phone. "According to this, we are about two miles away from the labs too. We can't walk along the road; we need to stay out of sight."

They crossed the road and rambled through woodland.

Oliver said, "My map says we need to head north-west."

"That's great, if you have a brain with a built-in compass."

"No need, the phone has one, and there's one in my bag."

"Akela would be proud of you," said Storm. She paused. "Then again, he probably wouldn't. I think he would most likely strip you of your patrol leader badge for lying to your nan, fraudulently using your mum's credit card, withholding information from the police, stopping a train illegally, and, to top it all, impersonating an Austrian Tyrolean dancer."

She began to laugh.

"If it's crimes against society we are talking about," said Oliver, "let me think what you would be found guilty of . . . Lying to your mum, causing damage to a parked vehicle, and, oh yes, falsifying a road accident and squirting tomato ketchup all over your head."

He started laughing too.

"And they were all totally your fault," she reminded him.

The woods were getting thicker and darker. They seemed to be in the middle of nowhere, but Oliver insisted that they were heading in the right direction.

"We are getting close now," he told Storm, who was struggling to keep up.

"*Please* can we stop for a rest soon?"

"You can have a three-hour sit-down on the train on the way back." Oliver stopped walking. "According to the phone, we're less than five hundred yards away."

"But we are in the middle of the woods!" said Storm.

They continued until they reached the edge of a clearing. Within view was a large sandstone building that just had to be North Yorkshire Scientific Research Laboratories.

The Woods

Oliver and Storm remained within the shadows of the trees, feeling both relieved to have arrived, yet terrified by actually being there. They stood barely twenty metres from Quark's labs.

Nestled in the woods, the imposing Georgian manor house was a perfect combination of nature and grandeur. It could not have looked any less like a lab complex. However, Oliver knew at first hand to never judge a book by its cover; April Cottage was the epitome of this.

"What now?" asked Storm as they stood staring at the building.

Oliver smiled nervously; he was not sure himself. "We wait."

Storm flung her rucksack onto the ground and then her bottom on top of it.

"What we shouldn't do," whispered Oliver, following Storm's lead and sitting down next to her, "is let anyone know that we are here. We have to keep our heads low."

"Do you honestly think that I would want us to draw attention to ourselves?" Storm snapped.

Oliver did not answer, and they both sat silently for a moment, Oliver desperately wondering what was the right thing to do. He looked longingly at the building. "My mum and dad may be in there."

"Don't get your hopes up. They may not be."

"We have to find out either way."

"Are we going in?" Storm asked, her voice shaking.

Oliver sighed. "Probably. I need to think, get my head straight; it's been a bonkers day."

"You can say that again," said Storm, lazing back on the rucksack and closing her eyes.

"Don't you dare go to sleep."

"Today has felt like a month already, and it's" – Storm looked at the time on her phone – "just gone two."

Oliver stood. "We need a better vantage point."

He collected his rucksack and signalled for Storm to follow.

Remaining behind the trees, they swept around the perimeter of the wood and stopped when they could see the front of the house, which had a courtyard and overgrown rose garden. A single gravel track led to it, and just beyond was a small car park.

"No black vans," whispered Storm.

"They're probably all in Wales."

"I do hope you're right."

"At least we can see if anyone arrives." Oliver peered around the trees. "Let's wait here."

"Wait for what?"

"We'll know when we see it."

Storm looked fed up. Oliver said very little, and neither knew what to do next.

They watched. Oliver struggled with the thought that his parents could be so close.

"Do you think that anyone is in there?" Storm asked. "I can't see anything through the windows."

"There will be; the boiler's on." Oliver pointed to the steaming pipe on the far end of the side wall. "Plus, there are three cars parked."

"Does anyone actually live there?"

"It's hard to tell. It may just be a lab."

Storm huffed a bit and puffed a bit, and kept checking her phone. "Truth or dare?" she suggested.

Oliver glowered at her.

Their wait continued. Nobody arrived and nobody left.

"We can't wait forever," said Storm. "We'll have to go soon."

"We can't go yet," said Oliver, frowning. "We haven't done anything."

"It's going to take even longer to get back. We need to walk to that town to get a bus to the station."

Oliver looked at his watch. "We've got an hour before we need to leave."

"*Half* an hour. We can't miss the train."

"I can't leave unless I take something back with me," said Oliver, standing again.

"Like your parents?"

"Something to show that O'Sullivan bloke, so I can be sure that he'll take us seriously." He began rummaging in his rucksack. "We need photographs. Some evidence. Some pictures of the inside of the labs."

He took out his nan's camera, pointed it towards the house, and starting clicking. "It's no good; I need to see what's going on inside. The zoom won't work from here."

"You can't go any closer."

Oliver sighed. He too knew it would be risky, but he had to do something.

"I'm really hungry," Storm groaned.

"Make a start on the food that you brought from my house."

Storm delved deep into the rucksack and handed Oliver a tin of beans and one of rice pudding.

"Tell me you've packed something else," he said.

Storm shrugged. "Plenty of tinned veg. You only said to pack some food."

Oliver sniffed and said, "I've eaten worse on scout camp."

"Oops! I've forgotten spoons."

Oliver groaned. "Just as long as you brought a tin opener, we can improvise."

Storm grimaced, and Oliver knew her unspoken answer.

She said, "We'll have to get something to eat in town before we get on the bus."

"Shh!" he said suddenly. "Look over there!"

He pointed towards the front of the house. Two men in lab coats had stepped outside the front of the building to smoke cigarettes.

"See," he added. "It's definitely the labs. We can't go yet."

Oliver took a photograph.

"Do you recognise either of them?" Storm whispered.

Oliver shook his head. "I wish I could hear what they were saying though."

"If we get any closer, they'll see us."

"The zoom on this camera is rubbish."

"Can you just imagine what would happen if we were to get caught?" asked Storm. "That would make us about as useful to your parents as this tin of carrots to a rabbit!" She glared, brandishing another tin from the rucksack.

Oliver could not disagree.

Storm had not finished. "We already have some proof that there is a lab complex: we have a photograph of scientists who work here. It's time to put your trust in DCI O'Sullivan."

Giving up was not Oliver's style, but neither was being stupid. The sad, sick feeling in the pit of his stomach told him to stay, although instinctively he knew that Storm was right.

"We could always come back," he whispered.

"We won't need to if you tell that DCI."

Storm grabbed her rucksack. Oliver sighed heavily and gave one long last glance at the house, hoping that something would happen. Nothing did.

He followed Storm back into the thick of the woods and soon the manor house was out of sight.

The sun beamed overhead, casting little rays of spotlights on the ground of the August woodland. The smell of wood, the wild flowers, and the freshness of the air were hypnotically soothing, although the children's attention was not on the woodland but instead on ensuring that they were walking in the right direction.

As they reached the main road, Oliver stopped. "We need to go back."

"Too right."

"I don't mean back home. I mean back to the labs."

"Are you out of your mind?" Storm scowled.

"Not really."

"*Really!* Come on, we've got a bus to catch." She continued walking. "We'll go back to April Cottage tonight."

Oliver followed reluctantly.

"I hope they've got a McDonalds in Puddingdale," said Storm, sounding optimistic.

"Who knows? I'd consider eating absolutely anything. I'm so hungry!"

"Anything? What about pig's ears?"

Oliver humoured her and answered yes to everything she suggested, ranging from boiled caterpillars to bogeys. Soon, the woods became thinner and houses came into view, dotted on either side of the road. They were nearing civilisation.

"Keep your eyes peeled for a bus stop," said Oliver.

"One is peeled for buses, the other for burgers."

The main road ran directly through the centre of the town. It was quiet. In fact, it was almost deserted. They walked past a post office, some quaint cottages, a petrol station, and a pub called Thistle Do, until they saw a sign that read *You are now leaving Puddingdale.*

"We've gone too far," said Oliver, turning around and heading back the way they came.

"What if there isn't a bus stop?"

"There must be. Every town has one."

Oliver took out his phone and tried Google Maps. They followed directions until they arrived at a solitary green post; it was the closest thing to a bus stop they could find.

"I have a bad feeling about this," said Storm nervously.

"It's fine," said Oliver, looking at the timetable on the post. "There's a bus arriving in twenty minutes."

"Fantastic. Let's get something to eat. I'm starving."

Oliver was reading the notice just below the timetable. "Not fantastic at all," he sighed. He read it aloud: "*All drivers have committed to unite in industrial strike action to support our rights as individuals to demand better working hours. Buses will resume on Wednesday. Please support us. We apologise to our passengers for any inconvenience caused.*"

Storm groaned. "Taxi?"

"We haven't got enough money." Oliver paced back and forth. The sun beat down, and his head was aching. "We need plan C."

"What's plan C?"

"I'm working on it!"

"I can't think straight. I'm *so* hungry."

Oliver was too. They headed back towards the shops. The post office had a *Closed* sign, and the only other shop was closed too. There was just one place to go.

"Where can we eat?" Storm moaned.

"Thistle Do."

"What'll do?"

"*Thistle Do.*" Oliver led Storm towards the pub.

"We can't go in there!" she cried.

"I thought that you were hungry?"

"Starving!"

"Come on then!"

Before Storm had time to voice any more objections, she was being led through the door. They were greeted by the combined smell of wet wood, damp carpets, beer, and chips; and by the attention of the barman.

"Do you serve food?" Oliver asked hesitantly.

"Food," said the barman, "aye! But children . . ." He shook his head.

"We don't want any beer," said Oliver defensively.

A voice of an old man came from behind a glass-screened booth, followed by his face. "What 'arm will it do?" He smiled at Oliver and Storm.

"Menu's on t'wall!" said the barman, pointing towards a table for them. They ordered, paid in advance, and waited for the food to arrive.

"What now?" asked Storm. "How are we going to get back to Wales?"

Oliver shrugged, which made Storm glower. "You'd better have a plan!"

Oliver did not, but there was no way he could tell Storm that.

The food arrived and not a single word was exchanged between Storm and Oliver for a good five minutes or more. There were stern glances from Storm, but no words.

Too Close for Comfort

Having eaten, they felt far more capable of making decisions.

"Plan C?" Storm asked as she pushed her plate aside.

"Plan C," said Oliver. He paused. "We get a taxi, give the driver all the money we have left, and hope that he will accept an IOU for the difference."

Storm looked unconvinced. "Plan D?"

"That's more complicated. You call your mum and tell her that you are staying over at my nan's house tonight. Tell her that I'm really upset; maybe suffering delayed shock or something. Then I call my nan and tell her that I'm staying at your house. Don't know why yet – I haven't got that far."

"But aren't you forgetting something?" asked Storm, frustrated.

Oliver shrugged.

"We still need to get back to Wales."

Oliver knew this, but returning to Wales was marginal to his master plan of returning to Quark's labs.

"Without sounding as if I'm stating the obvious," said Storm, "what if my mum or your nan says no?"

"We go with plan E."

"What's plan E?" Storm asked suspiciously.

"We could always hitch a lift back to Wales."

"No! Absolutely not! No way!"

"It's cheaper than a taxi."

"It's just stupid and downright dangerous. We could be abducted and murdered or left on the side of the road to die!"

"So you don't like the sound of plan E?"

Storm scowled angrily.

"You two finished yet?" shouted the barman.

"Almost," said Oliver, shovelling a forkful of chips into his mouth.

"What about plan F?" Oliver asked Storm.

"What are you asking me for?" Storm snapped.

"Because I came up with A, B, C, D, *and* E, so I thought that maybe you could have a go."

Storm's nostrils began to flare and her face reddened. "So it's taxi and train, or phone calls home to give us more time to get back."

"As much as I can't believe I'm saying this, I think that underpaying a taxi and running away may get us arrested. So it looks like phone calls home is the only real option that we have."

"Can we go now?" asked Storm. "That bloke keeps staring at us."

Oliver glanced over to the old man in the corner, who smiled at him.

They headed for the exit, thanking the barman on their way.

"You call first," Storm suggested, delaying the conversation with her mum for as long as possible.

Oliver opened the door to leave, but before stepping foot outside he stopped in his tracks. Stepping back, he grabbed hold of Storm, pushing her into the pub.

"Get off!" Storm shouted.

"*Shh*," whispered Oliver. "There's a black van!"

Storm quietened immediately and peered through the small glass window in the door. Across the road was a shiny, unmarked black Transit van with a familiar number plate.

"What shall we do now?" Storm stuttered.

"Stay calm."

"But . . . What . . . How . . ."

"D'you forget summit?" the barman said as they reversed deeper into the bar.

"Toilets?" Oliver asked.

The man pointed to the far corner of the room and a doorway. It led them down a staircase into the basement.

"Could things get any worse?" Storm was quivering.

"Forget phoning home. We've got a new priority: that black van!"

Storm nodded.

Oliver opened the door to the men's toilet, then closed it again and wandered into the ladies'.

"Come on!" he held the door for Storm to follow. "I have no idea how, but they followed us. If we leave through that front door, they've got us, but if we climb out" – Oliver pointed to the tiny window, almost at ceiling height, that looked barely bigger than a cat flap – "and leave by the back way, then we're in with a chance. We can make a run for it."

"Where?" Storm was trembling.

"As far away from the black van as possible!" Oliver stood on top of the toilet, gesturing for Storm to follow suit. For the second time in one day, he pushed her through a window.

"All clear," came the instruction from above. Next, Oliver handed her the rucksacks before climbing through.

"I think I get it," said Storm as Oliver emerged out of the window and onto a muddy verge behind the Thistle Do. "I think I know how they followed us here."

Storm helped Oliver to his feet. Behind them were fields, and a footpath.

"How?" he asked.

"The same way as you tracked the black van."

"What?"

"They're tracking your phone."

"How can you know that?"

"Think about it," said Storm as she excitedly connected the dots. "You've been using that thing for GPS all day. It would be easy for them to find us with that kind of information."

"I knew there was a reason why I brought you with me," he whispered.

Storm was already checking the alleyway on the corner. She started running, and said, "We'll have to ditch it!"

"Hang on!" said Oliver, running behind her along the footpath. "What about your phone?"

"They won't be tracking me."

"You used your account on Facebook to look up Silas Tudor, didn't you?"

Storm suddenly looked horrified. "They've tracked me?"

"We can't take any chances. We'll have to ditch them both."

The mere suggestion made her cringe. "My mum will kill me if I lose my phone."

"It's either your mum kills you or someone else does."

They kept running until they could see the garage they had spotted earlier.

Storm handed her phone to Oliver.

"I've got an idea!" he said. He ran until they emerged onto the garage's forecourt. "Go into the kiosk and buy something."

Storm frowned, but did exactly that. Oliver leaned casually against a lorry parked next to a petrol pump. Its side read *Yorkshire Transport Company (Reliable European Freight Haulage).*

Storm emerged carrying chocolate and a Coke, at the same time as a man carrying a coffee and a newspaper. Given the lack of other vehicles, Oliver assumed he was the lorry's driver, and smiled at him. "Hello," he said, attempting to sound friendly.

The driver looked at him suspiciously before returning the greeting. "Ay up!"

"Going far?" Oliver asked.

"What's it to you?"

"I just like lorries." Oliver smiled.

"Hamburg," the man answered.

"Perfect!"

"I don't take passengers . . . especially kids." The driver looked him up and down before he began to survey his lorry.

Oliver wondered if he was looking for damage, or maybe checking for potatoes in his exhaust pipe or a lack of air in his tyres.

"Quickly!" said Oliver to Storm as she stood on the forecourt. "We need to stay out of sight."

They retreated to an embankment behind the garage, as far away from the road as they could manage.

"What was all that about?" Storm asked as they watched the lorry drive away.

"You'll see. Now stay exactly where you are and wait."

Within minutes, the black Transit van sped past the garage in the same direction as the lorry.

"What?" Storm asked.

"It was your idea, really. All I did was convince whoever was driving that black van that we are heading out of Yorkshire and going south, probably on our way to Germany. Hamburg, perhaps."

"You planted the phones, didn't you?"

Just as Storm was about to congratulate Oliver on his ingenious idea, she stopped. "That's good news, but we're still in Yorkshire."

"But we're no longer being followed."

"*But* we're still two hundred and fifty miles from home. What are we supposed to do now?"

"We'll get the first bus to the train station in the morning."

Storm looked horrified.

"I'm sure that we passed a phone box on the road to Puddingdale," said Oliver. "We can call home from there. Tonight, we can go back to the labs."

They began another long journey, this time in the reverse direction.

Storm asked, "What if my mum flips when I ask her if I can stay at yours tonight? What if she says no?"

"She'll be fine!" Oliver could not worry about Storm's mum; he was more concerned about other things. They carried on in silence.

"We've been walking forever," wheezed Storm after a while. "Where's this phone box?"

"We're bound to pass it soon."

They walked in the shadows of the trees but kept the road in view and looked out for the phone box.

The walk back definitely felt longer than the walk to the town. Without their phones, neither of them knew what time it was, but the sky had changed from the colour of a pale mill pond into a darker shade that resembled the depth of the ocean.

They followed the contours of the road and walked on, taking no risks of being seen and remaining within the trees, the uneven ground tripping them with every step.

"We really need to head north-west," said Oliver. "We can't just keep going. We're bound to have passed the place where we cut through this morning."

"We could go back into town."

"If we do that, it'll take hours. Then we'll never find our way back to the labs; it'll be too dark."

"My nan and your mum are going to kill us if we don't find a phone," Storm snapped.

"They'll be annoyed tonight, but we can explain when we get back. If we tell them we were looking for my mum and dad, they'll get over it . . . eventually." Oliver knew he was attempting to convince both Storm and himself.

"I'm so not comfortable about this," said Storm. "We could always head back to the road, flag down a car and borrow a phone."

"Isn't that just as dangerous as hitchhiking?"

Storm frowned.

"It's not as if we are running away or anything," said Oliver angrily. "We're here to find my parents . . . and to protect my dad's work. It's worth far more than one night of worry."

Storm screwed up her face and pushed both her hands down forcefully in her hoodie pockets. Suddenly, a little worrying by her mum and Oliver's nan seemed almost justified.

They turned around and went in search of the path that they had taken earlier in the day, heading for the thick of the woods.

The familiar path was far less recognisable in the fading light. The woods demanded their full attention. Tired and anxious, Storm traipsed behind Oliver along the uneven ground, concentrating on not stumbling. They hardly spoke through fear of falling, concerned about distracting words tripping them along the way.

As they neared the old house, the lights guided them. Stopping in the very same place where they had stood a few hours before, they both dropped to the ground.

"My mum," said Storm, pulling her hoodie over her head, "is going to kill me!"

"Just tell her it was all my fault."

"I will!" Storm uttered something else under her breath that Oliver could not hear. He understood perfectly well, however. It was obvious just how vexed Storm was.

The night was still and silent, the only sound the breeze that rustled the leaves, creating a whispery echo. It was getting cold.

"This is the stuff that horror films are made of," said Storm, breaking the near-silence.

"*It was a cold, dark night . . .*" Oliver began.

"Oh, shut up!"

"You're the one who started it," Oliver reminded her.

"It's eerie enough just being here, let alone telling creepy stories."

It was too dark for Oliver to see Storm's face. "Are you tired?" he asked as she yawned loudly.

"Whatever gave you that idea?"

"Why don't we take it in turns to keep watch?"

"Watch? I can't even see my hand in front of my face," Storm muttered.

"You'll see if there are any car lights."

"You can take first shift," said Storm, leaning against an old oak tree.

"I was going to suggest that anyway. I'll wake you in an hour, shall I?"

Storm did not respond. Alone with just his thoughts, for Oliver the silence of the woods grew louder, and the guilt of not telling his nan heavier. He imagined her and Henry searching the park, looking for him.

"Are you sleeping?" Oliver asked.

"Yes!"

"Then how come you answered me?"

"Because I'd like to be sleeping, but my mum is going to kill me!"

Lights were approaching.

"Stay low!" Oliver whispered.

As they grew nearer and brighter, it became clearer that they belonged to a van. Gravel on the road crunched as it came to a halt outside the house's grand entrance. Oliver and Storm watched silently as its arrival prompted a reaction from within the building.

The large front door swung open, dispersing even more light onto the courtyard. A man wearing a white lab coat walked to the back doors of the van and opened them. Inside were several large boxes. The driver and passenger, both dressed in black, had got out and joined the man in the lab coat. They all began to unload boxes.

"Come on," Oliver whispered.

Reluctantly leaving their hiding place, Storm followed him out of the trees, remaining behind the shrubs that lined the driveway. Tiptoeing towards the light, they stopped just a road-width away from the van.

The sound of a twig cracking beneath Oliver's foot stopped them in their tracks.

They held their breath. Poised, ready to run . . . Nothing happened. Oliver guessed that the sound of the van's diesel engine had saved them.

Reaching out to Storm, he turned and placed both of his hands onto her shoulders. He whispered, "Get to the side of the house, stay tight to the wall. We can do this."

One step at a time, and keeping low, they crossed the drive and stood with their backs pressed against the wall. They were now close enough to hear voices, but too far away to make out any words.

"Let's go back," whispered Storm, grabbing hold of Oliver and sinking her nails into his forearm.

"Stay here! If I'm caught, go back into the woods, hide until first light, then phone DCI O'Sullivan. I'll say I'm alone."

He handed Storm the DCI's business card. She had no time to object; Oliver had already freed himself from her grasp and gone.

When he was as close as he dared go, he crouched beneath a shrub, curling his body up into a ball and concealing himself in the shadows. Branches became his cover, leaves and thorns scratching and tickling at his head. He listened hard.

"What held you up?" asked an authoritative voice.

Oliver winced as a thorn scratched the back of his neck.

"The kid didn't leave the house all day," came the reply.

"Is this the last of it?" asked another voice.

"For now. Has he told us anything useful yet?"

"He's only got until tomorrow!" another man replied. "If there's nothing new by then, we'll make our move."

Oliver heard a loud scraping noise, as if something heavy was being dragged out of the van and grated across the ground. He craned his neck and saw what looked like an electron microscope, just like his dad's, being lifted from the vehicle.

"Let's call it a night," said one of the men. "Quark's running out of patience."

"He'll have the kid by tomorrow, one way or another."

They continued talking, but to Oliver the space between him and the conversation may just have well been filled by the Atlantic Ocean. The voices became muffled and echoing, movements blurred, and even time seemed to stop.

He had heard enough. He had to retreat to tell DCI O'Sullivan. He would go as soon as the van left and the technician returned inside . . . but the van remained and the conversation went on. The swaying leaves of the branches were tickling his face.

"Van 'V' is on its way, gone back down tonight," said a deep voice. "Looks like he's on his way out of the country."

The van's door slammed, the lights dimmed, and footsteps crunched on the gravel as someone headed into the house. Oliver dared to look: the two men in black had turned around and were returning to the front of the van.

Oliver lurched forward to make a run for it, heading back towards Storm.

However, his rucksack slipped from his shoulder and landed on the ground with a thud.

"What was that?" said the deep voice. "Someone's there!"

The van's main beam shone brighter. Oliver grabbed his bag and ran back into the trees.

Footsteps and voices followed him. The deeper into the woods he ran, the darker it became. He held both hands in front of him, feeling for trees and branches as he went, running deeper and deeper into the darkness.

Pounding footsteps remained close behind, with each thud reverberating and filling the silent woods with the sound of a beating drum. His breathing was becoming loud and heavy.

Powered by fear, Oliver ran and ran, colliding with branches and trees, every collision bringing more attention to his whereabouts. He stopped, but the pounding of nearby footsteps continued to beat like a bass drum. The sound of his own wheezing breath was echoed by the heavy rasping of someone else's.

The silent woods were filled by a chilling orchestra of fear. His side ached, so he leaned against a tree. His whole body was trembling, and he held onto the tree with his arms and legs wrapped around the trunk to stop himself collapsing. Somehow, he found the strength to climb, to pull himself upwards.

Aware only that the space between himself and the ground was increasing, he had no idea of how high he had climbed. He waited.

"Who's there?" demanded the deep voice, echoing through the darkness.

Oliver clung on tighter, hoping, praying that he was high enough to be hidden by the branches. Two torches' lights were heading towards him. This was a hunt . . . and he was the fox.

Oliver thought about Storm. Where was she? Had she been caught? If she had, he was sure that even from deep in the woods he would have heard the scream. There was no way that she would have gone quietly.

Torches shone around him; the men were directly beneath him.

The silhouettes of two men passed underneath Oliver but did not stop. The drumming of their footsteps slowly drifted, their voices faded, and the darkness grew as the two orange dots became smaller and smaller.

Oliver now had to find his best friend.

"Storm," he whispered, walking back towards the manor house. He stopped every now and then to listen, checking that he was still alone. With his hands out in front, Oliver scoured the woods, knowing that he could not just leave without her.

He was deep in the woods without his phone, without GPS, and without Storm. The only compass he had in his possession was his own nose. He hoped that it would not let him down. Aware of the enormous risk he was taking, he decided to head back in the direction of the house. It was the only way he could get his bearings, and it was closer to where he had last seen Storm.

"Storm!" Oliver whispered again, louder, as he made his way through the silent woods with his arms outstretched.

"*Storm*," he called for a third time. When he felt as though he would have to give up and wait until dawn, to his amazement he heard a feeble voice in the distance: "I'm over here."

He followed the direction of the call. He would have recognised that voice anywhere.

"Help me out!" Storm pleaded. She sounded very close now.

Oliver looked around. "Where are you?"

"Down here!"

He looked down to see his best friend's head and torso protruding from a large hole in the ground. He reached out a hand towards her.

"Phew!" he said, heaving Storm by the arm back to her feet. "We need to get as far away from here as possible."

Storm was trembling like a frightened rabbit. She linked arms with Oliver and allowed him to lead.

"How do you know which direction we are walking?" asked Storm.

"I don't. I'm following my instincts."

"I've lost faith in your instincts." Storm's voice, like her body, was shaking.

"We know there's no phone between here and Puddingdale," said Oliver. "We need to get back into town to phone the DCI."

As they walked, he explained all that he had seen and heard.

Storm eventually stopped trembling, and began telling Oliver in great detail about how she had taken cover in a badger hole, how her mum was going to kill her, and how she had never been so scared and cold in her life.

They walked and walked in darkness until sunrise.

The Wrath

Exhausted, aching, and still looking over their shoulders, Oliver and Storm eventually emerged from the thick of the woods. The sound of a vehicle let them know that they had finally reached the road.

"How much further?" Storm moaned. "We've been walking forever!"

"How should I know?" Oliver yawned.

"I just hope that we've been walking in the right direction."

Oliver looked around. "If the sun rises in the east, then that definitely means . . . we're going the right direction . . . ish."

Storm dragged her feet as they followed the road, keeping out of sight by walking the unbeaten track.

Neither spoke much. They both had an awful lot to think about.

"I can't walk any further," Storm grumbled.

"You've got to!" Oliver insisted. "We need to get to a phone, call DCI O'Sullivan, then get the very first bus out of here. Eat some of that chocolate you bought in the garage yesterday, that'll keep you going."

Storm looked guilty.

"You've already eaten it, haven't you?"

"It was *so* cold in that badger hole."

"We can get some at that garage, and ask if we can use their phone."

They walked on and on, until Puddingdale came into view and, soon after, the garage.

"Breakfast!" Storm gasped. The motivation of chocolate gave them the final push they needed.

A garage attendant sat behind the counter, reading a daily newspaper.

"Do you have a phone?" Oliver asked him.

"There's a payphone out back," he answered without looking up.

Oliver joined Storm, who had arms laden with a haphazard selection of everything that looked edible. The attendant peered over the top of his paper, glowering at them suspiciously with sudden recognition in his eyes.

"It's OK," said Storm, "we *are* going to pay for them."

The attendant put down his newspaper and stepped from behind the counter, carrying a bunch of keys. He walked towards the door.

"Thank God you're all right," he said. "But you're gonna 'ave a lot of explaining to do!"

"Excuse me?" asked Storm.

"You *are* Oliver Harris and Storm Minton, are you not?"

Oliver and Storm both appeared bewildered.

The attendant proceeded to bolt the door and then place the bunch of keys into his pocket.

"Hey!" Oliver shouted. "You can't lock us in!"

He looked for another door as Storm began banging desperately at the window.

"Help us!" she yelled to the empty garage forecourt. "We've been kidnapped!"

"You will never get away with this!" Oliver yelled.

The man returned behind the counter and picked up the telephone. "Hello," he said into it, "police please."

There was a moment of silence. Oliver was confused. Why was their kidnapper calling the police?

"Look!" Storm quivered as she pointed at a pile of newspapers on the floor.

The headline read: *"Further victims vanish from South Wales Valleys!"* Underneath were two photographs: one of Storm, the other of Oliver.

Oliver read the first part of the story:

Police are asking the public for their help in finding two eleven-year-old children, Oliver Harris and Storm Minton. They have not been seen since leaving their homes in Ebbwvenny, South Wales, around 8am yesterday morning. A number of sightings have been reported, and it is suspected that they may have travelled north on a train to Yorkshire, although it is unclear at which station they got off. The disappearance is even more baffling as Oliver's parents, Paul and Megan Harris, were reported missing twelve days ago. Concern is rising for the safety of these children. Police have been baffled by both disappearances but are particularly worried about the danger the children could be facing. A ticket inspector from British Rail is reported to have last seen the children on board the train heading to Yorkshire. He said, "They were travelling alone, on their way to visit their grandmother. She was supposed to meet them at the final station." However, it appears that neither parents nor guardians know anything about this . . .

Oliver had read enough. He tried to listen to the attendant on the telephone but all he could hear was his racing heartbeat. He gripped the shelves in front of him to stop the world spinning.

"Oh bum!" said Storm. "Oliver!" she shouted. "*Oliver!* We've been reported missing. We are going to be in so much trouble!"

The attendant hung up and gave them what looked like a painful smile. Oliver guessed the police operator had told him to be nice to them both.

"I suppose that you're hungry then?" the man asked.

Hungry was probably the very last thing either of them felt right now, thought Oliver. Sick, that was more like it.

Within moments, sirens could be heard in the distance. Within minutes, flashing lights were right outside the glass box where they stood captive. The attendant unlocked the door.

"We've really gone and done it this time," Storm whispered, her voice quaking.

"Let me do the talking," said Oliver. "Remember, nobody but the DCI must know why we are really here."

"But we'll have to tell them something!"

"I want to talk to DCI O'Sullivan first. Let me talk to the police. I'll think of something."

"I cannot believe we've done this!"

There was no more time. Another police car arrived, then a police van, and soon two more cars. The forecourt was teeming with uniforms.

A number of bodies descended on the small garage shop. Each and every pair of eyes fixed on Oliver and Storm.

"Are you Oliver Harris?" one officer asked.

"Yes," replied Oliver, knowing all too well that he could not deny that. His school photograph was plastered over the front page of the newspapers.

"Are you Storm Minton?" the same officer asked.

Storm nodded awkwardly. Their fate was no longer in their control.

A strong hand was placed on Oliver's shoulder. "I think that we had better get you back home to Wales!" said its owner's stern but friendly voice. They were both being led out of the shop and into the back of a police car.

Oliver was surprised that the questions were few on the journey home. He assumed it was part of the police's method of interrogation: make the suspects sweat.

Sat between him and Storm was a policewoman. Oliver glanced across her to see how Storm was faring. Her face was grey. He felt really bad; it was not Storm's fault they were in this mess, but because of him she was going to have to face her mum's wrath.

The policeman in the passenger seat radioed to his controller that both Storm and Oliver were safe and well, and travelling back to Wales.

Relieved, but also dreading their return, Oliver attempted to hatch a plan. He knew what he needed to tell DCI O'Sullivan, but he had absolutely no idea what he was going to say to everyone else. If they could tell the truth, it would be so much simpler, but they both knew that was not an option.

There was plenty of time to ponder the conversation that Oliver had heard the night before. Today was the day "he" would "have the kid by". Was "the kid" him? Was it Henry? Oliver really needed to see his little brother.

Several hours of contemplation after leaving Puddingdale, the police car approached Ebbwvenny. They were not heading for the police station as Oliver had expected, but Stanmore Place.

"Aren't we going to the station?" he asked.

"I think it's way time you two went home," replied the policewoman who sat between them. "Your families are anxious to see you."

The car stopped outside Nan's house. Oliver's heart sank; he knew he needed to face the music, but he was unsure which tune would be playing. He had to persuade his legs to step out of the car and walk through the front door.

"They'll be waiting for you," one of the officers said encouragingly, attempting to speed up their exit.

With each step, the beat of *Darth Vader's Theme* from *Star Wars* drummed inside Oliver's head.

Storm lingered in the police car until the officer said, "You too! Your family are also here!"

Storm and Oliver went through the front door. There was silence as they walked down the hall, Storm pushing Oliver to the dining room.

A chain reaction began. All heads turned, chairs scraped, there was a blur of movement and colours, and the next thing Oliver knew, he was suffering a fate worse than death. He was being hugged and kissed by his nan, Auntie Karen, Uncle Will, Henry, Daisy, Ethan, Winston, and even one or two police officers he had never even seen before. Not kissed by the officers, but hugged and squished nonetheless. When he managed to raise his head ever so slightly, just enough to look over at Storm, he saw that she too seemed to be suffering the same fate. This was torture!

Then came the worst bit. After everyone had slobbered and squeezed, they all stepped back, leaving barely a square metre of space around the two of them.

The room fell silent. Then, with Oliver and Storm like frightened foxes watched over by a pack of dogs, standing their ground and waiting to take the first bite, waiting to pounce . . . it began.

"Where have you been?"

"Are you all right?"

"Did someone make you do it?"

"Why did you go?"

"Were you running away?"

"Were you punishing your family?"

Questions were being fired at them from every direction, but they had no answers and nowhere to hide.

Oliver looked around and saw Uncle Raj; PC Sharp; faces he did not recognise; Storm's mum, brother, grandmother, and grandfather; and a stranger with a video camera pointing straight at them. His eyes continued to search until he saw the one face that he was pleased to see: DCI O'Sullivan. How could he possibly talk to him alone?

There was another silence. It was Oliver and Storm's cue to speak.

Oliver looked to her for some divine inspiration. She looked at him in complete despair. He took a breath and opened his mouth.

But it was too late: the words had already started flowing from beside him.

"Sometimes," announced Storm, with a serious, sincere expression, "it is difficult to do the right thing."

This was so true, but as she said it her right hand raised and somehow found Oliver's left hand, which took Oliver so much by surprise that he allowed Storm to hold his hand.

She moved in closer to him and announced, "We just wanted to be together, and grown-ups don't understand."

It was at that moment that Oliver wanted to crawl up in a ball and die. He could not believe what he was actually hearing. This was not really happening; he must have been hallucinating . . . lack of sleep, stress, lack of food.

Then it got worse: "We decided that it would be best if we didn't tell anyone and just . . . *eloped!*"

That was the word that ricocheted around and around, again and again, not only to Oliver. Amazingly, for that second, it was as if he could also hear it bounce around like a ping-pong ball inside the heads of everyone in that room.

The silence that followed was stolen by a chorus of gasps. Uncle Will was the first to speak. "Is that all, butt? That's all right then. I thought it was something serious."

Oliver did not know where to look. Every time he glanced at someone, he seemed to cause their eyebrows to rise; it was as if Storm's announcement provoked a Mexican wave, but entirely for eyebrows. There were not two linear brows in the entire house. The eyebrow dance was followed by disapproving glances, a few sniggers and smirks, a look of utter dismay from Nan, and a very disapproving glare from Uncle Raj. He was fuming.

Just when Oliver believed that things could *not* get any worse, Storm opened her mouth again. "You see, in Wales and England it is illegal for us to get married, but we thought that if we crossed the border into Scotland and went to Gretna Green, then we'd be allowed. I saw it in a film."

Oliver's bottom jaw plummeted wide enough to fit a football. He glared at Storm, who was still holding his hand, and desperately begged her to stop with pleading eyes. She was making things *so* much worse. Not only had she dug a hole as large as a swimming pool, with every word she spoke it was increasing to the size of the Pacific Ocean.

"We only wanted to be together," she ran on, "but it started going wrong . . . when we got on the wrong train."

To Oliver, this was torturous. He would have preferred to endure the pain of having his toenails removed one by one, or even wearing an England rugby shirt on international day in Cardiff, than standing there while Storm humiliated him. The only thing holding him back from salvaging some dignity was the knowledge that by accepting the humiliation he was keeping his dad's secrets.

Luckily, Oliver knew it was all a complete sham and he also knew for a fact that Storm was not really deeply in love with him, but if a room full of gullible adults were prepared to accept this he was not going to argue with them.

The endless questions continued and continued and continued. He had to go along with the story; he had to pretend that he and Storm had eloped to Gretna Green. He spent the next few hours telling more lies than he had ever said in his entire life.

Eventually, Oliver could not stand it any longer. He removed his hand from Storm's grasp and left her with their audience. He walked into the kitchen, dropped onto the floor, and wilted in the corner.

He saw Henry standing over him, looking sad.

"Come here," Oliver said.

Henry sat on the floor next to him. "Can we play football now?"

Oliver smiled. He had forgotten all about his promise of a game. "Will you do me a big favour?"

"What?" Henry asked.

"Stay inside today."

"But Nanny said we can't play football inside." Henry frowned.

"I know," said Oliver, "but it's not safe to go outside."

"Why?"

Oliver did not have a reason that he could share with his brother. How could he tell him that he could be in danger?

Oliver stood and looked out of the window. "It's because . . ." He tried to think up a reason. A butterfly floated past and landed on the marigolds. "There are some poisonous butterflies escaped from the zoo" – this was sounding so silly – "and if they land on you, your skin will turn green."

"Urgh!" said Henry. "Will the zookeeper catch them, like Charlie?"

"They are out looking for them now. So how about we save our game of football until tomorrow?"

Henry thought for a moment. "OK," he replied sadly. "Is that why all the people are here? Are they hiding from the butterflies?"

Oliver nodded, then hugged Henry tightly. Looking back into the living room, he saw Storm still surrounded, seemingly enjoying the attention. He hated this; the lies, the deceit. He wanted to hide.

The police asked more and more questions until eventually they were satisfied that they had all the answers they needed. One by one, people began to leave. As DCI O'Sullivan said goodbye, Oliver followed him out into the hall. This was his first chance to speak to the officer. He asked, "Can we have a chat?"

"Anytime you want, son. I was hoping that I'd catch you alone."

The DCI gave a reassuring smile.

"What about now?" Oliver asked intently, careful to remain out of the others' earshot.

"Later," suggested the DCI. "I was going to suggest that we met later anyway. Meet me at the old rec in an hour. Don't tell anyone where you are going; your nan will never approve. She's not going to be happy letting you out of her sight for at least a year or two."

Before Oliver had chance to say anything else, Uncle Raj walked into the hall.

"Am I interrupting something?" he asked.

"Of course not," said DCI O'Sullivan, smiling, as he opened the door. "I was just leaving."

Oliver was angry that Uncle Raj had interrupted him.

"So," his godfather began, "I know that you didn't really try to elope to Gretna Green with Storm. Some people believe you, but I'm not one of them."

Oliver was not going to tell him anything that he did not have to. The journey back to Wales had given him time to think, to get his head straight, and one overwhelming thing that he could not explain was how his phone had been tracked. He knew that only the police could access phone records. Someone had needed to be close enough to plant a bug, and Oliver had never let his phone out of his sight. Except on one occasion: Uncle Raj had asked to look after it in London.

Oliver felt so let down he could not look his godfather in the eye. Uncle Raj had not only betrayed him but Dad too. "No," he answered. "We did not elope to Gretna Green." Anger gave him the strength to look his uncle in the eye and say, "But I really don't want to tell you anything else!"

"But Oliver—"

"Save your explanations for my dad! Because I will find him!"

Uncle Raj looked truly hurt. Oliver had no sympathy for him. The sad truth was, his godfather had let him down and now Oliver deeply regretted having ever trusted him.

"But Oliver," Uncle Raj tried to explain while putting a hand on his shoulder, "I know that you must be angry and confused—"

Oliver slipped out of his grasp, merely shaking his head in dismay and wasting no time to listen to any more excuses or lies before swiftly returning to the dining room. He now had a new priority: to get Storm's attention and arrange yet another breakout.

She was still playing centre stage, only now she was delivering lines from *Romeo and Juliet*. She had a captive audience: the journalist was lapping it up and the child psychologist who had recently arrived with Social Services was also making notes.

Mrs Minton was suffering silently. It was as if she had gone into a state of shock. She sat next to her daughter, clutching her hand, but Oliver had to get Storm's attention, unless he chose to meet the DCI alone.

He felt as though the evidence, the proof, would be better believed if he had Storm to back up his story. He needed her help to convince Graeme O'Sullivan that they really had seen a lab complex run by Vincent Quark, and that it was the place where his parents were most likely to be.

The immediate problem was extracting Storm from the house without anybody noticing. They were the star attraction of this gathering, and were both being watched very, very closely.

"Storm!" Oliver interrupted her mid-flow. "I need to talk to you."

"Of course, my darling," replied Storm, sounding blasé. For dramatic effect she added, "If you wouldn't mind excusing me, we just need a moment together."

Oliver tried to shrug off that thought, but played along.

"We could go into the garden," suggested Storm.

"Best idea you've had all day."

They traipsed through the back door and away from the circus. Several faces glared at them through the kitchen window.

"We need to get away from here, and soon," said Oliver.

"That isn't going to be easy."

"I need you to help me convince the DCI to check out Quark's labs. He's asked to meet me by the old rec in an hour."

"Why the rec?"

"I don't know," Oliver answered firmly. "I can't stand it here anymore. Are you with me or not?"

"But how?" asked Storm, waving to her mum through the kitchen window.

"We'll have to make a run for it."

"Let's meet back here in the garden at one o'clock."

Storm returned to the house and left Oliver alone with Winston. He had to take the risk of escaping. Besides, his day could not possibly get any worse.

The remainder of the hour passed in much the same way as it started: a lecture from Auntie Karen about responsibilities and other people's feelings, a couple of nudges from Uncle Will, hugs and frowns from Nan. Oliver did his best to avoid Uncle Raj, who was staying for some reason.

Then, as Oliver had promised, he and Storm met in the garden at one o'clock sharp.

It was, in fact, very good timing as Nan had just placed a mountain of sandwiches in the dining room that proved a helpful distraction. Without delay, Storm and Oliver opened the back gate and ran to the old rec.

As they ran, Oliver vigilantly checked for black Transit vans, but was comfortable that the police cars and reporters were enough of a deterrent.

The old rec was on the quiet side of the valley, close to a derelict industrial estate. Not many people used the park, ever since it had been replaced by the new sports fields next to the leisure centre. Oliver did not mind; he too wanted to meet somewhere quiet.

"Do you think he'll believe us?" puffed Storm as they neared the fields.

"I don't know," said Oliver thoughtfully, "but we will have to do everything that we can to convince him. He's now our only hope."

"Then we'll make sure that he *does* believe us," said Storm, looking around for the DCI. He was late, and nowhere to be seen. "Shall we try calling him?"

"With what?" Oliver smiled sarcastically at Storm.

"So what should we do?"

"We wait!" He made his way towards a park bench.

"Now where have I heard that before?"

Kidnapped

Despite the heat of the sun, there was a frosty atmosphere between Oliver and Storm on the bench. Storm's supposed bombshell had left Oliver feeling uncomfortable.

"So," Oliver asked, attempting to break the ice, "do you think that anyone has noticed we're not there yet?"

"Probably. Although it's hardly as if we've gone far this time, is it?"

The sun was bearing down, so Oliver led Storm towards the shade of a tree. She threw herself onto the grass. "It has been a *long* day!" she groaned.

"Too right!" said Oliver, lowering himself onto the ground, "it started . . . thirty hours ago, and it's only just gone one o'clock."

"I think I'll just close my eyes for a minute," said Storm sleepily.

"Not just yet," said Oliver, getting to his feet. A familiar figure had appeared from behind one of the factory units. He waved.

Storm clambered to her knees. "You're sure that this is the right thing to do?"

"It's the only option left."

DCI O'Sullivan approached on foot. There was no sign of a police car.

"What a glorious afternoon," he said, standing over Oliver and looking cagily at Storm. "You've brought your 'friend' with you."

"Yes," answered Oliver, sensing his disapproval. "I thought that it would be safer than coming alone after the week I've had."

"So . . . Who knows that you are here?" asked the DCI.

"Nobody!" replied Storm defensively.

"Let's walk." DCI O'Sullivan began moving away, and Storm and Oliver followed.

"So what did you want to tell me?" asked the chief inspector.

There was a silence as Oliver searched for the right words. Before he could answer, the DCI had more to say. "Running away like that." He shook his head. "What were you thinking of by eloping to Scotland?"

Oliver's voice had found a way out. "We didn't run away." It was a relief to be able to tell the truth instead of even more lies.

The DCI did not appear to be interested in any excuses. "You both put your families through a great deal of worry." He glared at Oliver. "Your poor grandmother was a nervous wreck!"

"It's not what it seems," said Oliver bravely.

"So what *was* it all about?"

Storm gave Oliver an encouraging nod, hoping that this time he could find the right words.

"Well," Oliver began, then he paused and asked, "How well do you know my dad?"

The DCI looked surprised. "Very well."

Oliver looked the DCI in the eye, wondering if he would dare lie to him.

"I've been helping your father out with his work," the policeman explained. "Do *you* know what he does?"

"I know about some of the things," Oliver answered honestly. "Why haven't I seen you before?" He had to be 100 percent sure that the DCI was *the* Graeme O'Sullivan whom his dad had told him to trust.

"I suppose it's because your father didn't want you to worry, knowing that the police were involved in his work."

Oliver was still unconvinced. "So why did he need the police to help him?"

"I would much prefer your father answered that question."

"So would I!"

"I can tell you that your father has been working on an experiment that is very, very sensitive." The DCI looked away.

"What experiment?"

"That, I am afraid, I cannot tell you."

"Just tell him!" Storm blurted as she grew increasingly impatient.

Oliver took a deep breath. "My father trusts you," he muttered.

The DCI smiled, almost in relief. "I think that he trusts me too."

"Can you help him?" Oliver asked.

"That's what I'm doing." The DCI smiled. "However, it would help if you told me where he is."

"*Me*, tell *you?*" Oliver snarled. "Isn't that your job, to find out where he is?"

"We are doing all that we can."

Oliver had heard that line so many times before. "No! I'm not asking for the police to help me; I'm not asking *DCI O'Sullivan* either. I am asking *you*, as my dad's friend, to help me find him, and my mum. Can you help me or not?"

This was going nowhere fast. If Oliver was ever going to get any help from this man, he had to tell him more. He took another long breath. "I know where they are."

"You know where your dad is? Where? Where *is* he?" His eyes were suddenly magnetic, catching Oliver's now uneasy glare.

Oliver looked away. He wasn't sure who he was telling his secret to; he wanted to tell his dad's friend, not the police.

"I am a friend of your dad's," the chief inspector said. "You can tell me where they are."

"They are in a town in Yorkshire called Puddingdale." There, he had said it. With those words, he gave his trust to this stranger.

"Why would they be in Puddingdale?" the DCI asked doubtfully. Oliver could see that he had a lot more convincing to do.

"Let me put it like this," he tried again. "I think that my dad knows about something really important that nobody else knows about."

Storm nodded to corroborate everything Oliver said.

"What does he know?" asked the DCI impatiently.

Storm, who was listening to Oliver's explanation, shook her head in desperation. "You are not making any sense!"

"I know that you're upset, Oliver," said the policeman, "and I know that your father is a clever chap, but what does that have to do with Puddingdale?" He was pacing in circles. "That's where the police picked you up. You went looking for them, didn't you?"

"You didn't really believe that we eloped, did you?" asked Oliver.

"Why Puddingdale?"

"That's not important. What is important is . . . they've been kidnapped, and are being held there."

"Kidnapped! What makes you think that they've been kidnapped?"

"A feeling . . . and something to do with the mafia . . . and a man called Vincent Quark." Oliver stopped himself from revealing more. Saying these words aloud sounded almost ridiculous.

"And you figured all this out on your own?"

Oliver knew that what he said *did* sound as if he could have been making it all up. He nodded nervously, and so did Storm.

"Where in Puddingdale?" asked the DCI.

Oliver filled him in with the details, describing the lab facilities, and what he had seen and heard in the woods the night before. It was a relief to feel that the DCI was beginning to believe him.

"Well, who'd have thought it?" said the DCI as he paced around and around. "Paul's son, and only eleven years old."

Oliver smiled nervously. Did he now have the reassurance and backing of one of his father's friends?

"A plan, a plan." The DCI was still pacing. He got out his mobile.

"You're not phoning this into the police, are you?" Oliver pleaded.

"No, of course not," said the DCI, but he continued to press buttons on his phone.

He did this for a few minutes. Oliver and Storm began pacing behind him until the DCI stopped.

"OK," he said. "I need you to follow me." He pointed, and they could see what looked like a distant warehouse.

"Where?" Storm asked.

"To do something that should have been done a while back," said the DCI.

"What?" she said.

"You ask far too many questions."

Storm looked quite put out. "That's only the second question I have asked since we met you!"

Oliver sniggered. Storm just grumbled a bit, but did as she was told.

They neared the building. It was an old lock-up and looked like an abandoned garage or bus depot.

"Wait here!" said the DCI. "I'll only be a moment."

He disappeared through a small door on the side of the building. Storm and Oliver loitered outside.

"Do you think that he really believes us?" Storm asked.

"Are you asking questions again?"

"What do you think he's doing?"

"I don't know," said Oliver, "but I do think he believes us."

Storm nodded. "Will anyone be worried about us yet?"

"Probably." Oliver imagined his nan's reaction when she looked out of the window to discover that they had gone again. "But I suppose as we've disappeared a few times recently, they are getting used to it."

"They probably understand that we needed time" – Storm smiled – "alone." She fluttered her eyelashes. "Together." She sniggered.

Before Oliver had chance to respond to Storm's sarcasm, someone was standing behind them.

Someone who turned light to dark, freedom to restraint, and a glorious afternoon into a horrific nightmare.

Terrified

Restrained and blinded by sacking that had been thrown over their heads, both Oliver and Storm fiercely fought to free themselves. They thrust their arms and legs in an attempt to throw off the cover that engulfed them and stank of oil.

"What is going on?" Oliver screamed as he fought to remove the sacking. Something was wrapping around his waist, pushing him and Storm tighter together. Standing back to back, they were being squeezed with a grip as unforgiving as a boa constrictor.

Wrapped in sacking and bound by rope, they were powerless to defend themselves. The rope pulled tighter around their middles, forcing them to gasp for breath. It continued to weave around them until it reached their legs. Then it was tugged, and they collapsed in a painful heap onto concrete.

Terrified, they screamed and shouted frantically for help as they writhed on the ground. They knew that they were far from the town and nobody would hear them . . . except DCI O'Sullivan.

"Shh!" yelled Oliver towards Storm. He needed to hear what has going on.

She was sobbing loudly, but he could make out the sound of footsteps, then a grating noise that might have been a garage door clattering open, then an engine.

"We're going to die!" Storm cried.

Oliver could not find any words. The darkness that shadowed his vision had also shadowed his hope. What could he possibly say to reassure Storm that everything would be all right when the truth was that he was just as petrified as she was? The reality was clear: their worst fears had come true, and they were facing kidnap.

"Help!" Oliver screamed. Nobody answered. He wriggled and kicked, but every movement felt heavy as he took Storm with him.

Powerless, Oliver listened as Storm sobbed and he felt her whole body tremble. There was no escape. The darkness engulfing both his movements and his hopes was filling him with a deep, heavy feeing of despair and terror. For the first time in his life, Oliver no longer recognised himself. He had failed his parents, himself, and now his best friend.

Above the sound of Storm's sobbing cries, he heard an engine coming near, then wheels crunching on gravel. A car door opened, and footsteps drew closer.

The sudden feeling of being hoisted, then grabbed around their middles, knocked the wind from their lungs. Oliver gasped for air with his face and mouth pressed against the sack. He breathed in dust and pungent fumes.

Gravel scraped against their bodies. Oliver's hip grated against the floor before the ground disappeared from beneath them . . . and then they were dropped. The back of Oliver's head hit a surface before rebounding and smashing painfully against Storm's.

Storm trembled uncontrollably, her breaths quick and shallow. Oliver kicked his legs furiously, but his every effort was futile, and each kick only added to the pain.

Storm's sobbing faded. They lay still and quiet, listening and waiting. They heard a car door, the revving of an engine, and then vibrations rumbling from beneath them.

They were no longer still. They were on the move.

"Let us go!" screamed Oliver as loud as he could. He kicked as hard as possible, his legs being the only parts of his body that he could move, and banged his feet on the hollow surface underneath them. Every movement that he made, Storm made too. Every tremble that Storm felt, Oliver felt as his own.

"Help!" he yelled furiously.

Storm whimpered, then she spoke, her voice quiet and shaky. "What's going to happen to us?"

"We're going" – Oliver spoke through gritted teeth as his legs found a solid vertical surface to push against – "to get out of here!"

The force of his kick sent them sliding across the hollow floor, stopping only when their heads hit another solid wall hard.

Storm screamed.

"Keep still in there!" yelled an angry voice with a distinct Irish accent. "You're going nowhere. And for God's sake, shut up!"

"You traitor!" Oliver seethed. He had been deceived. "You made me believe I could trust you!" he yelled through the sack muffling his voice. "That's what you did to my dad too!"

"And he was gullible enough to believe me too! Like father like son!" The DCI cackled.

The despair brought with it clarity; Oliver Harris was not going to give up without putting up the biggest fight of his life.

He lay still, listening: Storm whimpering, an engine rumbling and vehicles passing, the beep of horns, car doors opening and closing, and the roar of motorbikes. It was obvious where they were: driving through the town.

Oliver nudged Storm with his elbow. "We're in town," he whispered. "Someone will hear us if we shout! Make loads of noise!"

Storm only sobbed.

"On the count of three," Oliver told her, "we kick and scream as loud as we can! One, two, three!"

This time, they kicked their legs together, making a huge clatter as their legs hit the ground.

"Aaaarrgh!" screamed Oliver.

"Help!" croaked Storm.

They kicked until the pain was unbearable, and screamed and shouted until their throats were burning. However, the DCI turned on loud music, the *boom*, *boom*, *boom* of the bass making their efforts futile.

"Help us!" begged Storm against the din.

"Stop shouting," said Oliver. "We need to listen."

Storm continued to whimper and Oliver lay still. The vibrations were increasing; they were travelling at speed on a busy road. There were no sounds of cars stopping, or people talking, just the hum of engines.

"I want to go home," said Storm.

Oliver kicked so hard with both his legs that he used up every last ounce of energy left inside him. However, the ropes that bound them were tied so tightly that his efforts felt wasted. As the van sped up, and the sounds around them changed, they no longer wasted strength on calling for help; on a motorway, nobody would hear them scream.

The vehicle swayed from side to side, weaving through traffic; each time, Oliver and Storm slid across the ground before colliding with a surface, which delivered a painful blow.

"Where are you taking us?" Oliver yelled towards the driver. "You're meant to be the police! Why are you doing this?"

"Shut it!" said the DCI.

"Why aren't you helping us?" said Storm.

The volume of the music increased again.

"Let us go!" Oliver shouted. "You'll never get away with this!"

"That's where you're wrong!" jeered the DCI, shouting at the top of his voice to make himself heard. "Remind me: who knows you're here?"

Oliver knew the DCI had planned this. Why else would he have insisted on meeting in a secluded place? Why else did he insist that Oliver told nobody where he was going? The sad truth was, nobody would suspect anything other than Oliver and Storm had sloped off again. They had cried wolf before, so this time no one would even bother looking for them.

"You are supposed to be my father's friend!" cried Oliver, the words encased in hatred.

"I have no friends!" hissed the DCI.

The music blared. The inside of the vehicle grew hotter and hotter, making it feel like they were roasting in an oven. Their breathing was hampered, their sight was taken away, they had to rely on their remaining senses. The smell of petrol fumes and oil was overpowering, and the boom of the music and the roar of the engines deafening. Above all, the feeling that grasped them both was terror.

Storm moaned. Oliver tried to speak, but he could find neither the words nor the energy. How could he tell her that everything would be all right? He closed his eyes.

He saw his mum and dad; his mum kissing him goodbye on his way to school, and his dad smiling. His thoughts turned to Henry. Henry was back at his nan's house, and Oliver was not. It was up to him to protect his little brother. His parents were not able to, and now neither was he.

Exhausted, Oliver felt as if he was drifting in and out of consciousness. If he closed his eyes, he knew that he would sleep, but the fear that maybe he would never wake again was enough to keep him alert.

The vehicle was slowing down. They were no longer hurtling at speed, and the dull hum of the engine began to lose momentum.

They had stopped snaking in and out of traffic. The music had stopped too, and the sounds around them were different.

Oliver nudged Storm. She had not spoken a word, or even whimpered, for quite a while. He wriggled and jabbed her until she responded.

The combination of heat, near-suffocation, and fear might have made her pass out, but Oliver knew that if something was going to happen, if they had any chance of an escape, then he needed help. Storm's fingers moved, touching his arm, which Oliver read as a sign of support, a sign to show that they were in this together, a sign of camaraderie and hope.

The engine eventually stopped. Oliver attempted to listen for clues about where they were; there was a loud creak, a sudden jolt, and then the sound of someone getting out from the front of the vehicle. There were footsteps.

"We have to get out of these ropes," he whispered, "and make a run for it!"

Storm nodded, or at least Oliver assumed that she did by the jerk he felt as his head was dragged backwards and then forward again.

There was another creak, then a cool draught of fresh air. The rope tightened and they were moving; dragged by their feet, they slid across a hollow-sounding floor until it disappeared from under them. They landed with a thud. Oliver gasped with pain as his shoulder took the impact. The side of his face pressed hard on the ground, dust filled his mouth, and the grit from the earth scratched painfully against his cheek as they moved across it.

"Stop!" he yelled. "Let us go!"

Abruptly they stopped; there was the sound of a garage door screeching open, then footsteps walking away. There was nothing that they could do but wait. Wait for whatever DCI O'Sullivan had in store for them.

A grating sound of metal scraping along concrete almost deafened them; their whole bodies felt the vibrations. Something heavy was being dragged across the floor.

The DCI said, "Don't you try anything. You'll regret it if you do." His voice was callous.

Oliver feebly replied, "Just untie us."

"Please, *please* let us go," begged Storm. She was trembling uncontrollably.

"I promise we'll behave," said Oliver. He was lying, but he did not care. Breaking his word to this man meant nothing. He was prepared to say absolutely anything.

The rope tightened again, this time forcing Storm to gasp as it squeezed around their waists. They were moving, being dragged across the ground. They no longer lay in the blazing sun but on a cold, hard floor. The sound and vibrations of a garage door crashing down made them both shudder.

Footsteps drew closer then, to their relief, the rope began to loosen, first at their necks, then their shoulders, down as far as their waists. They were being untied.

Fighting Back

Oliver and Storm fought desperately to free themselves. Cold fresh air filled their lungs as the sacking covering their upper bodies fell to the ground. A shaft of blinding light stung their eyes, inhibiting their sight until both their kidnapper and their prison were revealed.

Bare concrete walls surrounded them. Oliver guessed they were inside a hollow shell of a derelict industrial building. The room was empty, except for a few rusting tools propped against the walls and a metal chest that was followed by a trail of scarred concrete across the floor. The damp air reinvigorated Oliver's senses, allowing him to think.

Not wanting to miss a single detail, he scanned the room. He had to know where they were and, more importantly, how could they escape? His eyes stopped searching when his glare was met by another: the DCI's. Towering over Storm and Oliver, he held the end of the rope.

"Where have you brought us?" Oliver asked, easing himself forward and attempting to sit up.

The DCI did not answer.

Storm lay still and silent. Oliver's eyes were drawn to the small gap underneath the shuttered door and the slit of light. He squinted through the haze and something came into focus: the wheels of a van.

"You're one of them!" Oliver seethed.

"No."

"Then you work for them!"

DCI O'Sullivan answered calmly. "Everything I do, I do for me."

"Why? Why did you do it?"

"Do what?"

"Kidnap my mum and dad!"

"I always get what I want, and I'm not going to let two little kids get in my way! You have no idea how much trouble you have caused." His voice was cold, coarse, and menacing.

He began pacing, his fists clenched. "What am I supposed to do with you two now?" He pulled hard at the end of the rope, making Oliver and Storm gasp with pain.

"Let us go!" said Oliver.

Storm attempted to sit up. "We won't tell anyone," she pleaded breathlessly.

"How can I possibly let you go?" asked the DCI. "I've seen what trouble you can cause."

"You'll have to sooner or later, you can't keep us here forever!" Oliver tried to look him straight in the eye, although his eyes felt as distant as Oliver and Storm were from home.

"Wrong," the policeman said. "You are so very wrong. *I'm* the one who decides what happens to you." He appeared agitated; his face was red, and he wiped sweat from his forehead with his sleeve.

"Please!" Oliver begged. "Please just let us go!"

The DCI stood over them menacingly. "I had it all worked out. One more day . . . That was all I needed, but you kids had to interfere." He stared at Oliver, his eyes piercing straight through him. "You are not going to mess this up. I have been waiting for this day for far too long."

The heightened atmosphere in the warehouse was suddenly halted by the cheerful sound of Nokia's standard ringtone. The

DCI took his phone from his pocket and looked at the screen. His brow furrowed. Oliver thought he looked worried.

"Sir," the policeman answered. There was silence. "No, everything is fine," he said, attempting to sound calm. "The police have returned the children to Wales."

Oliver considered screaming and shouting, but stayed silent. He did not know who was on the phone, and what could he gain by alerting his father's enemies that he and Storm were there, bound and helpless?

The call continued.

"What do we do now?" said Storm quietly as the DCI paced away from them to the far end of the warehouse.

"Can you move your feet?" Oliver whispered.

"A little bit."

The DCI marched past them, still on the phone. Oliver and Storm lay still.

"Try it a little bit, until you get good at it, then move them a big bit," said Oliver. He wriggled on the ground, but each movement was laboured due to the added weight of Storm. His arms reached beneath the sacking that had covered them, and he felt a knot.

"There's only one of him," said Oliver. "There are two of us." He picked at the knot that bound their ankles.

Storm groaned, but began desperately trying to wriggle free every time the DCI walked away.

Oliver pushed his feet down with all his might and allowed Storm's heels to repeatedly kick his ankles while she pulled her legs upwards.

"Keep going," Oliver whispered. "He's really worried!"

The DCI was pacing the circumference of the warehouse, his phone still attached to his ear. He seemed distracted, and his voice was raised.

"I can feel it loosening," said Oliver. "I think that we are in with a chance if only you can get one leg free. That should leave enough room to get our legs out." Oliver winced in pain from another dull blow to his ankle.

"We can make a run for it!" said Storm, pointing to the gap under the door, which looked almost big enough to them both to roll through.

The DCI saw them move and glared at them. They lay still.

"As soon as we're free, we tie him up." Oliver waited until their captor walked away, then he picked again at the knot. It slowly began to loosen. "I'll jump him from behind, wrap around his neck, and cling on. You'll have to work fast. You'll only have as long as it takes him to throw me off his back. Tie his legs first, bring him to the ground, and then we both work on the rest when he's down."

"What if it goes wrong?" asked Storm, accidentally kicking Oliver painfully on the shin.

"It can't get any worse."

By some stroke of luck, genius, or determination – or perhaps failure by the DCI to secure them properly – the rope was loosening, but not fast enough. Oliver saw that DCI O'Sullivan had finished his call and was heading straight for them.

"Who was it?" Oliver snarled at him. "Was it Quark?"

The DCI glowered.

"Why didn't you tell him about us?" Oliver said. He stared at the phone in the DCI's hands. If only he could get hold of it. If he could, he could phone . . . *who?* Not the police; they would never believe him. Nor could he phone his family. Through the haze of adversity came a sudden moment of clarity; Oliver knew that he had made a huge mistake.

He closed his eyes to focus, and remembered the DCI sitting comfortably at Nan's breakfast table, handing him his new phone. *He* was the one who planted the bug. Uncle Raj had only been trying to protect him.

A crushing feeling of guilt was quickly stifled by an agonizing blow landing on his shin. Storm had freed one of her feet.

This was it. The DCI had his back turned as he paced away from them. This was perhaps their only chance.

Storm's freed right foot had created enough space for her to remove the other. Buried by the sack, their feet still appeared bound when the DCI passed them. Oliver managed to free his legs.

They had to pick the right moment. They needed an advantage: the element of surprise.

"Now!" whispered Oliver, stumbling to his feet.

As the DCI turned around, Oliver leapt onto his back, wrapping his arms around his neck and gripping on with all of his might.

"You!" snarled the DCI as he twisted and turned in an attempt to shake him off.

Oliver clenched his arms tighter, anger powering his grip as he was overcome by rage he had never felt before. All the frustrations of the past few weeks were erupting like a volcano spewing its deadly lava.

The DCI fought back, leaning forward until Oliver hung upside down. He was furiously attempting to pull Oliver off, tearing his clothing. Oliver held on. Although he was thrown around like he was riding a rodeo bull, his grip was firm and his hands around the DCI's neck were making the policeman gag. Oliver wrapped his legs around the man's middle as Storm appeared with the rope.

Standing like a cowgirl, she threw the coiled rope with some accuracy and luck. The fight was on as it whipped behind the DCI's knees and she pulled it back, bringing him to the ground. As he fell, Oliver let go, just before the large metal chest broke their fall and delivered a severe blow to the DCI's head. He bounced off the chest before landing on the concrete floor with a thud. He lay still, his expression vacant.

"We've killed him!" cried Storm.

"Afraid not!" said Oliver.

The DCI slowly clambered to his knees before attempting to stand while delivering even more threats. His arms waved in an unsteady attempt to grab Storm and Oliver.

Oliver grabbed the rope; Storm continued weaving around the DCI. He staggered, confused, disorientated, and angry. He managed to grip Storm's arm, pulling her towards him, then grasped her with both hands.

Oliver pulled at the rope, bringing the DCI back to his knees. However, the policeman still held Storm firmly.

In panic, Oliver looked around. His eyes fell upon a spade propped against the wall. Without time to consider the consequences, he dropped the rope, reached for the spade, and raised it in the air, aiming for the DCI's head.

"Don't!" screamed Storm. "Don't do it!"

Oliver hesitated, the spade suspended in mid-air.

"You're better than him!" she cried urgently.

Oliver hurled the spade. His aim was random, not unlike his skills on the rugby pitch. It landed on the DCI's shin, causing him to yell out in pain and grasp his leg. Storm freed herself from his clutches as he clung to his leg with both hands. Storm grabbed the end of the rope and helped Oliver tie him up.

Oliver stood over the DCI. "How does it feel now?"

"Never underestimate eleven-year-olds!" Storm added smugly, rubbing her hands together.

Oliver stepped back, his back against the wall, and wondered what to do next. The DCI lay writhing on the ground, his legs and arms bound. Beside him on the floor was his mobile phone.

"Grab the phone!" Oliver shouted as he saw the DCI manage to stretch out a hand and press buttons.

As soon as Oliver spoke, the DCI threw it hard against the nearest concrete wall. A shattering sound echoed throughout the warehouse. Shards of glass, metal, and circuit boards bounced in every direction. There was silence.

Storm wound the rope further around the DCI. With her hands on her hips she said, "A taste of your very own nasty medicine!"

Oliver checked the ropes, ensuring that he was better secured than they had been.

"Why?" asked Oliver. "Why would you do such a thing?"

"You are a kid; you have no idea!"

"I know what is right and what is wrong, and what you are doing is so *very* wrong!"

Oliver's foot was on the DCI's shoulder blade, pressing down, inflicting pain. He wanted to make the DCI suffer as much as he had made Oliver and his parents suffer.

"Now what?" asked Storm, clapping her hands together to congratulate herself on a job well done.

Oliver eyes rose, and stopped to stare at an engine crane with a hook suspended by a metal chain, positioned above their heads.

"Hmm," said Storm. She checked the reef knot Oliver had tied before walking towards the wall where the clamp was secured. She began to lower the large, dangerous-looking hook down, down, down until it was low enough to attach onto the rope that bound the DCI and, for added strength and security, onto the belt holding his trousers.

"No!" snarled their prisoner, squirming on the floor. Oliver's foot found its way onto the DCI's back.

"Or what?" shouted Storm.

"You will regret this for a long time!" the DCI snarled.

"Not for as long as you will!" said Oliver. "Up!" he shouted as he removed his foot.

The chain rose and the DCI was lifted into the air. The hook gripped him firmly, forcing him to almost fold in half. His head fell level with his feet. Despite threats and violent twisting, he continued to rise, the contents of his pockets emptying onto the ground.

"I'd say he's not going anywhere for a while," said Storm as Oliver helped secure the chain. Their kidnapper hung three metres above the ground.

Elated, Storm leapt into the air, landing directly in front of Oliver. She swung her arms and hugged him. Apart from the pain Oliver felt from every touch, he also felt his face turning red; he was uncertain of how to react.

"You'll pay for this!" DCI O'Sullivan shouted.

Oliver had not finished. He looked around the warehouse until his eyes landed on a pitchfork propped up against a wall. He picked it up.

"Don't, please!" begged the DCI.

"I don't intend using it," said Oliver calmly, "I just thought that I'd leave it here for safekeeping." He leant the fork, prongs upwards, against the metal chest and directly underneath the DCI.

"I wouldn't wriggle too much," said Oliver. "It won't be a very soft landing."

"See you later!" shouted Storm. Oliver saw that she had noticed something among the coins that had fallen from the man's pockets. She bent down to pick it up.

"You won't need this anymore," she said. She picked up the DCI's police identification and put it in her pocket.

Oliver turned to leave. "While you're up there," he said as he glared at the DCI, "consider this a thank you from my dad."

Retrieving as many pieces of the mobile phone as they could, hoping that they would somehow be able to piece it back together, they left, squeezing under the opening of the shuttered door.

The relief they felt was short-lived. They were still lost, in the middle of nowhere, with no phone and no help. Also, time was against them.

They looked, left, right, behind, in front. There were trees, mountains, fields, and a road that looked as little-used as Oliver's thesaurus on his bookshelf. They had no idea in which direction to head.

"We've got to get to a phone," said Oliver. "I want to call Uncle Raj."

"But isn't he a traitor?"

"No. I got it wrong."

Storm frowned, but there was no time for a full explanation.

"Just trust me on this one," said Oliver. "We need to get this phone working." He began examining the broken parts, but in frustration he threw it onto the ground. "We need to let Uncle Raj know where my parents are before someone comes looking for the DCI."

Oliver scratched his head. "We're on the edge of a forest, right?"

Storm appeared distant and distracted.

"Which direction do you think we should go to find the nearest phone?" he asked despondently.

"*No* direction," replied Storm. She looked at the black van.

"Absolutely not! I'm not driving it. I *can't* drive. I'll end up killing us both!"

"No," said Storm, pointing enthusiastically at the van. "That's not what I mean."

Oliver looked again.

"You don't get it, do you?" Storm grabbed Oliver by the arm.

She led him to the front of the vehicle. She lifted her hand and ran a finger down a tyre-sized dent on the bumper.

"If this," said Storm, "is the van that I crashed into on my bike .. . then *this* is the van with your mum's old phone attached to the underside of the back wheel."

It was a jaw-dropping moment. Oliver's eyes widened as he looked at Storm. "Abso-bloody-lutely!"

"Did you just swear?"

"I think I did," said Oliver, "but never mind that." He darted around to the back of the van. "Let's check!"

He placed his hand in the exact spot where he had placed the tracker device. "Flipping heck! It's still there."

In less than a minute the tape was unfastened and in Oliver's hands was his mum's old phone.

"What about the battery?" Storm asked.

Oliver fell to his knees and began foraging on the ground for the battery from the DCI's now twice-destroyed telephone. He found it and examined it carefully.

"Does it still work?"

"There's only one way to find out," said Oliver, decided to bodge together a temporary battery circuit. Using bits of wires, connectors, and recycled pieces of masking tape, he soon held in his hand a working mobile.

"It's genius!" said Storm.

Luckily, Oliver remembered his uncle's number.

"Uncle Raj!" he said when his godfather answered. "I'm really sorry; I never should have doubted you."

"Just tell me where you are."

"I have no idea!" Oliver said pitifully.

"Whose phone are you using?" asked Uncle Raj.

"It's my mum's old phone, with my old SIM."

"What?"

"DCI O'Sullivan kidnapped us in the black van, the one with the phone attached."

There was a pause. "What's your GPS location?"

"Oh, yes!" Oliver had forgotten that in his hand was a device that had been used to track black vans. He reeled off the number.

"You're near Chepstow," said Uncle Raj. "In fact, you seem to be in the middle of nowhere, on the edge of the Forest of Dean."

"Sounds about right."

"Are you safe now?"

"Sort of. It's a long story!" Oliver drew breath. "I know where Mum and Dad are, and I need your help to get to them, and it has to be fast."

"Where's Graeme now?" asked Uncle Raj.

"You could say he's a bit tied up!"

"Well done! I will be with you as soon as I can."

"Don't be long!"

"Already on my way." From the other end of the phone came the sound of a car door opening and closing, then the revving of an engine.

"Hang up now," said Uncle Raj. "Stay exactly where you are, as long as it's safe to do so. Call me if anything changes."

"How long?" asked Oliver knowing his uncle would have already entered the co-ordinates into his satnav.

"Thirty-two minutes. Possibly even quicker!"

The phone went dead. Uncle Raj was on his way.

Storm collapsed in a heap. "What a day!"

Oliver joined her but in a separate heap. He eased himself down as his sore hip, shoulder, ankle, shin, and every other bone in his body ached.

North Again

Relieved to be able to spend a whole thirty-two minutes recuperating, they waited.

"Are you sure that you are not being too hasty?" Storm asked.

"That was the problem last time. I had no idea who that man was" – he pointed towards the warehouse – "but I trusted him over my godfather."

"You did what you thought was right."

"I know."

"I ache." Storm groaned.

"Me too," said Oliver, examining the bruises on his shoulder underneath his torn T-shirt.

"You look dreadful," said Storm. She pointed to the grazes on the side of his face.

"Thanks!" said Oliver. "I feel dreadful too." He looked regretful. "I could have killed him, you know."

"But you didn't. Don't feel sorry for him. He deserved everything he got, and more."

"Still . . ." He paused, thinking about what could have happened. "At that moment . . ." He shrugged off that thought. It was as if in that warehouse he hardly recognised himself.

"I know," said Storm, seeing his torment.

"Should we just leave him there?" asked Oliver, reflecting on what they had just done to a police officer.

"For a while. At least until we get to your parents."

Oliver agreed.

The time spent waiting for Uncle Raj passed quickly. In fact, for Oliver, the whole world seemed to move in a state of fast-forward. He was there, but he was not. His world was different: it was surreal and it moved at a different speed to reality. His body felt capable only of slow, laboured movements, while everything happening inside his head continued to accelerate.

From inside the warehouse, the occasional sound reminded them that they were not alone. But as long as they could not hear the sound of somebody being impaled, they remained where they were.

One sound, however, seized their interest: the distant yet distinct rasp of the twin exhaust pipes of an Aston Martin. Dragging themselves to their feet, they waited eagerly for Uncle Raj to arrive.

When his car stopped, Oliver was standing next to the driver's door. Uncle Raj got out, opened his arms, and embraced Oliver, then ruffled his hair.

"Ow!" Oliver grimaced.

"What the Dickens has happened to you two?"

"Could have been far worse," said Oliver, pointing at the building.

Uncle Raj approached the door and peered underneath.

"Raj!" shouted DCI O'Sullivan. "Look what those kids have done to me. Get me down from here!"

"I don't think so," said Uncle Raj. "You can simmer for a while longer."

He turned to Oliver and Storm with an approving nod. "Looks like you managed pretty well on your own." He ruffled both their hair. "What a team!"

"Mind the hair!" said Storm.

Uncle Raj smirked pitifully. "Believe me, it didn't make a difference." He did it again.

Oliver felt awful about doubting his uncle. He wanted to apologise, to explain, but when he smiled at him, he knew his godfather had already forgiven him.

"We need a plan," said Uncle Raj.

"Let's drive," suggested Oliver. "We'll talk on the way."

"Drive where?"

"North!"

Uncle Raj stepped into the car, and then Oliver and Storm paused at the passenger door.

"Oh!" said Oliver.

"Oh!" said Uncle Raj.

"Come on!" said Storm, being the optimist. "With the day we've had, a lack of space is not a problem." She pushed Oliver into the car, nudging him over towards Uncle Raj as far as humanly possible, and then squeezed into the passenger seat next to him.

"Cosy!" she said, wrapping the seat belt around the both of them.

Oliver's uneasiness must have shown. Uncle Raj gave him a wink and a nod before revving the engine and winding down the windows. He shouted "Adios!" for the benefit of the DCI.

As they cruised at speed down the narrow country lanes, Uncle Raj asked, "Where are Megan and Paul?"

"Puddingdale," said Oliver. He related the highlights of what his uncle had missed since he returned home from London.

"So your parents are being held . . . in a laboratory . . . in Yorkshire?" Uncle Raj sounded confused. "So is that why you both headed north?"

Oliver nodded.

"I knew all along that you weren't stupid enough to elope to Gretna Green."

"What if we had?" Storm pitched in defensively, nudging Oliver in the ribs with her elbow. He almost choked. She grinned.

It took the next few miles to explain what had happened the previous night when they staked out the labs, and why he was so convinced that his parents were being held there. Storm told Raj in great detail about how they had been captured by the DCI, smothered half to death, bound in ropes, dragged across the ground, thrown into a suffocating black van, and locked in the warehouse. She also explained how they managed to bind and hoist him.

Oliver interrupted Storm. "Henry!"

"Henry was fine when I left him," said Uncle Raj reassuringly, "but just to make sure . . ." He readied his phone, but Oliver could not imagine who he was calling.

"Helloooow!" came a familiar deep and friendly Welsh accent from the speaker on the dashboard.

"Will," said Uncle Raj. "I need you to do something for me."

"Name it, butt!"

"I need you to get Henry, put him in your car, and drive him to Puddingdale."

"What?"

"He could be in danger if he stays there. And, more importantly, don't say a word to anybody about where you are going, not even Karen."

"Puddingdale," said Uncle Will. "Is that somewhere in Ireland?"

"Not quite. It's north Yorkshire."

"But I can't just up and go. I'm needed here; Oliver and Storm have run off again."

"It's OK, they're both with me." Uncle Raj had forgotten that nobody else knew. "Tell Oliver's nan and Storm's mum that they're both safe, but they won't be home in time for tea. Call me when you're close."

"What?" asked Uncle Will again, struggling to digest the information at the rate it was being fed to him. "Right, butt!" he said at last.

The call ended.

"Why do you want them to go there?" Oliver asked. "And why tell Uncle Will?"

"Right now, we need people who we can trust," said Uncle Raj. "Can you think of anyone else that you could trust more with your little brother than Will?"

Oliver thought. "No, you're right, but—"

"But nothing! Henry will be safer away from Ebbwvenny, and if he's on the move, there's less chance of anyone taking him. We will ask Will to meet us somewhere safe. After all, when we find your mum and dad, won't they want to see him?"

It made sense. They reached the end of the lanes and then the sound of the engine changed as they joined the motorway.

"How do we make sure that we get your parents out of these labs?" asked Uncle Raj.

"I'm not sure," said Oliver.

They continued north, leaving the Forest of Dean far behind them.

Despite the fact that Oliver was squashed, feeling a bit like a sardine in a tin, he closed his eyes. The relief he felt was tremendous. His whole body ached from injuries and exhaustion, and his head hurt from lack of sleep.

"Why did you pretend that you didn't know Silas Tudor?" Oliver still needed to understand why his uncle had lied.

His godfather sighed deeply.

"Why did you tell me that you didn't know his name?"

They began to go faster. "Because when I saw Tudor at the zoo, I wanted to get as far away as possible from him. I didn't want him to see us both together. He didn't know who you were, and that's the way I wanted to keep it."

Oliver nodded. He could understand that, but he was not satisfied and knew there was something else.

"And yes," continued Uncle Raj, "I *did* know him. Because of your father. There was a time many years ago that he caused your dad a great deal of worry."

Oliver listened hard to every word.

"He once worked as a senior scientist for the British government at a facility in South Wales, leading a team investing in defences against chemical weapons."

Oliver's eyes widened.

"This was a long time ago. I'm not even sure if you were born. That was until he was discharged for ethical misconduct. I believe that he was charged with selling state secrets to the Russians." He hesitated. "Your father was one of the team who investigated this and oversaw the discharge, so that is why your father wouldn't have appreciated me introducing you to him.

"There were regular threats made to your dad, as Tudor feared that his reputation had been ruined. He made it quite clear that your father would regret what he had done. I met him on a few occasions while I was here in Wales, building the labs, but I haven't seen him for many, many years. I thought he had emigrated, tried to make a fresh start somewhere."

"Where did he go?" asked Oliver.

"The last I heard, he was in Russia."

Oliver nodded.

"Is that why you did not trust me?" his godfather asked.

"One of the reasons."

"But now? We need to get to Puddingdale and find your parents. Only I'm not sure what we need to do when we get there."

Storm, who had been listening intently, seized the opportunity. "I thought that it would be better if you knocked at the door while we stay in the car, and you could pretend that you have come to . . ." She paused to think. "I've got it!" she said, reaching into her pocket to retrieve the DCI's identification. "You could pretend that you're the police, and have come to recommend an upgrade in their security systems due to an increase in local burglaries."

Oliver and Uncle Raj shook their heads in unison. "That is a really bad idea," said Oliver.

"You have the DCI's warrant card?" asked Uncle Raj anxiously. "Get rid of it!"

"Why?" asked Storm.

"Because if anybody finds out that we've got hold of that, and the DCI is still missing, the police will not rest until we explain exactly how we got it."

"What shall I do with it?"

"Here," said Uncle Raj, passing her a travel wipe from the car door. "Wipe it for fingerprints."

He pressed a button and the passenger window opened, their speed creating a near-hurricane inside the car.

"What?" asked Storm, shouting at the top of her voice. "You mean . . ."

Oliver and Uncle Raj nodded.

"Right!" she answered, placing her hand out of the window, holding the card inside the wipe. She let it go and watched it fly away on the wing of the breeze.

"We can't take any chances," said Oliver, reaching over to close the window. "I do know that if the DCI gets out of his ropes without killing himself, then we may not be the first to arrive at the labs."

"We'll have to get there as fast as possible," said Storm.

"Fast we can do," said Uncle Raj, "but we are in a car, not an aeroplane, so we'll be another two hours."

The sun glared through the windscreen, as if reminding Oliver to look out and notice that the day was in fact glorious. His head ached and throbbed. He closed his eyes.

The Siege

"Wake up!" said Uncle Raj.

Oliver pushed Storm's head off his shoulder and wiped the dribble from his cheek. "Where are we?" he yawned.

"Almost in Puddingdale."

Storm opened her eyes.

"Don't drive to the house," said Oliver. "It would be better to leave the car somewhere and walk."

Uncle Raj nodded. "I've been thinking." He paused. "We definitely need some help."

"No!" said Oliver desperately.

"We can no longer do this alone. We don't have to tell the truth, but if we need to get close to the house, we should create a distraction even before we arrive."

"But how?"

"We make sure that we are not the only guests. We need the police, but they can't know it's us, and we can't tell them the real reason we want them there."

"If you want the police," Storm smiled, "I know how. It always works in the movies."

Oliver glowered.

"We phone the police anonymously and tell them that there are drugs in the building," said Storm.

Oliver grimaced, but she went on, "It will work, and anyway, isn't it about time we follow my instincts?"

"No!" said Oliver.

Uncle Raj intervened. "If you know that your mum and dad are inside these labs, and you already know the sort of people you are dealing with, it may just be our only chance."

Storm smiled in satisfaction.

"If we call the police," said Uncle Raj, "they won't suspect that you pair are involved. As far as they're concerned, they have just returned you to Ebbwvenny."

Oliver was not convinced.

"Armed police," said Uncle Raj. "How do you get a load of armed police to surround a building?" It was one of those escaped thoughts rather than a question that was directed at anyone in particular. He continued, "Police . . . Who knows about police?"

After pausing to think, he spoke to the car's hands-free system. "Dial. Ben Collins."

The car rang on speakerphone.

"Hi, Ben, have you got a minute?"

"As long as you like, Raj," came the reply through the speaker. "What's up?"

"How do I get a load of armed police to surround a building, quickly?"

"Report an armed incident, maybe a hostage situation. If there are firearms reported, they'll be there like a shot!"

"Thanks, Ben."

"Dare I ask why?"

"Probably best not to," said Uncle Raj. "We'll catch up soon." He hung up.

"Who's Ben Collins?" Oliver asked.

"A family friend, he just happens to work for Scotland Yard."

"But that's what I said," said Storm. "Drugs, guns, it's all the same thing."

"Then I think that it's a great idea," said Uncle Raj. "We need to make that anonymous call we were talking about."

Oliver shook his head despairingly. He really was not comfortable involving the police at all.

"When the police find your parents are being held in the labs," Uncle Raj explained, "they will have no idea why they are there, and I'm sure that nobody will want to tell them."

Outnumbered, and out of any better ideas, Oliver agreed. Involving the police was not ideal by a long shot, but time was short, stakes were high, and with just him, Storm, and Uncle Raj, the odds were stacked against them.

The road was familiar. It was the same route they had spent hours walking along on their way into Puddingdale.

"It's so much quicker when you're in a car," said Storm.

"Shall we make the call?" suggested Uncle Raj.

"Do you have an unregistered mobile with you?" asked Oliver, knowing that if anyone was likely to have a spare mobile lurking somewhere, then it would be him.

"Actually," replied Uncle Raj, "I don't."

"We could use the payphone at the garage," Storm offered.

"Well I don't think there are many other payphones around here," said Oliver.

"We need fuel," said Uncle Raj as he drove into the garage forecourt. "I'll fill it up, you can go on in and ask where the payphone is."

"It's around the back," said Storm, nervously sloping down into the seat.

"We can't go in there," said Oliver. "It's the garage that reported us to the police this morning. We'll be recognised for sure."

"You didn't tell me that," said Uncle Raj, who had already begun filling his car with fuel.

"You didn't ask," said Storm.

"Keep your heads down," said Uncle Raj.

They both descended further, their heads below the level of the window. Storm was in the footwell.

Uncle Raj tried to look casual as he returned to the car. He hastily drove around the back, out of view of the garage and in search of a payphone.

"Shall I make the call?" asked Storm, sliding back onto the seat.

"I think it should be you," said Oliver to Uncle Raj. "An adult's voice would be far more convincing."

"You'll have to disguise it though," warned Storm.

Uncle Raj grimaced.

It was decided that Storm and Oliver would be required to produce a loud bang for authentic sound effects. Storm looked around. Her eyes fell upon a rogue brick lying on the side of the road, just waiting for someone to pick it up.

"How about this?" she suggested, holding the brick in her right hand and raising it over her head, aiming it directly at Uncle Raj's bonnet.

"No!" screamed Oliver and Uncle Raj at the same time. Storm dropped the brick on the ground.

"Philistine!" shouted Oliver. "You can't do that!"

"It's time for desperate measures. There's nothing else to make a loud bang."

"That's not desperate," said Uncle Raj. "That's sacrilege!"

Oliver saw a metal bucket full of sand at the side of the garage. "Now that would work," he said, tipping the sand onto the ground and gathering up some small stones.

"Shall I scream?" asked Storm.

"No, you div!" said Oliver. "First, if you had been shot, you couldn't scream, you'd be dead, and second, the bloke in the garage would hear you."

Uncle Raj checked to see that everyone was ready. Oliver held the stones, Storm held the bucket, and he held the telephone.

He dialled 999. "I vould vike to revort an ostage!" he said in a confused South African/French accent. Oliver tried not to snigger. "Vere's a man viv a gun. He's got ostages!"

They must have been taking him seriously, thought Oliver, as the next thing he heard was Uncle Raj giving the address.

"You vant to know my name?" said Uncle Raj nervously.

He gave Oliver the nod, turned the phone away from his ear, and pointed it inside the bucket.

Bang went the first stone, and then *bang* went the second. Uncle Raj hung up.

Oliver and storm ran back into the car, ducking their heads as low as possible as the attendant from the garage appeared from around the corner and said, "What the heck is going on?"

Uncle Raj had hastily put one foot in the metal bucket. Now he began stumbling. He said, "You should be more careful where you put your buckets!"

The attendant rolled his eyes and returned to the kiosk.

"Keep your heads down," said Uncle Raj to the children as he jumped back into the driver's seat and set off along the road. "Which way?"

"I'll show you the place where we staked the house out yesterday," said Oliver. "Keep going for another mile and then pull over."

Uncle Raj stopped at the edge of an old farm track. The car was out of sight of the main road. They headed straight into the woods.

"I'm so glad that you're here this time," Storm told her chaperone as she attached herself to his arm.

"I'm glad too," said Uncle Raj nervously. "At least I think I am. You two . . . here all alone . . . at night." He shrugged the thought away.

Storm yelped as she stumbled on a root.

"Are you both OK?" Uncle Raj asked.

"I ache," moaned Storm.

"Me too," replied Oliver, "but I'm not moaning about it."

"You *are*."

"Only because you are."

They walked, and hobbled, and limped, and talked, preparing Uncle Raj for what to expect when they got there. Oliver was able to make sure that they were heading the quickest way, as he had his uncle's GPS to guide them.

"Shh!" said Uncle Raj as they were still in the thick of the woods. "*Quiet!*"

"What?" whispered Storm.

As they stopped, the sound of a distant siren could be heard. Then they realised it was actually several.

"They must have believed us!" said Oliver, picking up his pace. Their awkward walk became a scurry as they followed the sound of the sirens.

"Stop!" Oliver commanded as they neared the edge of the woods. They had arrived at the old Georgian manor house, seemingly just before any other guests. The sirens were growing louder.

"This doesn't look anything like a dodgy lab complex," whispered Uncle Raj as they peered through the trees. "Are you sure you've got this right?"

"What exactly does a dodgy lab complex look like?" asked Storm, jumping to Oliver's defence.

"We need a better place to keep watch," said Oliver.

They dropped back a little deeper into the woods as they made their way towards the far side of the house, the same place they watched from the night before.

"Look," said Storm nervously as she pointed towards the car park. There were four vehicles, one of them a black Transit van.

The sirens stopped. One, two, three police cars finished tearing along the lane and skidded to a halt strategically along the perimeter of the house. Within moments, police officers jumped from their vehicles and stood behind them, using them like shields.

"I'm not sure that this was a very good idea at all," said Oliver with his head in his hands. Armed police were pointing guns at the building.

"Perhaps we should go now," said Uncle Raj uncomfortably.

"No! We've come this far. I need to see them. I need to know that they are all right."

Uncle Raj looked petrified.

Another car arrived, then another, and another, until the forecourt swarmed with dozens of men and women wearing baseball caps and bulletproof vests and carrying rifles. Oliver thought there had to be a full SWAT team surrounding the house. He saw a man emerge from one of the vehicles with a speakerphone.

"It's just like the movies!" announced Storm excitedly.

Oliver scowled.

"This is so exciting." She grinned.

"I'm not happy about this," insisted Uncle Raj. "This is downright dangerous, and we should not be here."

Oliver frowned. "You can go if you want," he said, "but I'm not going anywhere."

"Nor am I!" added Storm.

Uncle Raj had no option. "There are rules that we need to stick to," he began sternly. "We are in so much danger. We must keep our distance and stick together!"

The negotiator stood out from behind a police car and through his speaker phone, bellowed: *"Come out with your hands up! You have been surrounded!"*

Go! Go! Go!

There was an eerie silence, much like the calm that precedes a raging storm. Even the air thickened, as if it too became weighted by tension.

"What will happen now?" Storm whispered.

"I don't know," said Uncle Raj. "Maybe they'll just wait until the hostage-takers make their demands."

"But they're not going to make any demands, are they?" said Oliver, already knowing the answer.

"But the police don't know that!" said Storm.

"Not yet, but how long will it take until they discover that the phone call was a hoax?"

"They will eventually," said Uncle Raj, "but they'll still have to go inside and check out the building."

The sound of the megaphone stopped them, each word booming into the air before crackling and fading deep into the woods. *"You are surrounded by armed police. There is no escape. State your demands!"*

The silence stretched as the tension intensified. The still air held each and every sound and movement, freezing them in a moment of time. There was no response.

"I'd love to be a fly on the wall inside the lab," Storm whispered.

"I'd prefer to be one of those armed police," said Oliver.

"Why don't they just go in?"

"It's not that simple," said Uncle Raj. "There's a protocol that has to happen in hostage situations."

"This *isn't* a hostage situation," Oliver reminded them both. "Nobody is about to make demands for anything. Everything they want is already inside." He sighed.

"Come on," said Storm, leading the way to a better vantage point. "We need to see everything."

Uncle Raj and Oliver followed, silently battling and trudging their way through the woods, every movement laboured and conspicuous.

They froze to the spot as the negotiator spoke again. "*You have been surrounded! Come out with your hands up!*"

"I think that it's stalemate," said Storm, deciding that neither player was able or willing to make the next move.

"No," said Oliver, "it's not stalemate until there are no moves left at all."

Still hidden in the trees, they stopped. The view of the house was clearer here.

"If they don't do something soon," said Oliver, "then I will!"

"And that would help, wouldn't it?" said Storm with her hands on her hips.

Oliver opened his mouth to speak, but Storm continued, "Last night you took a huge risk, but today you may not be quite so lucky. The whole place is swarming with police, and they will spot you. If that happens, they'll be onto your dad like a pack of beagles in a rabbit burrow. They will want to know everything. Your dad's secrets will be headline news in tomorrow's newspapers."

Oliver knew better than to argue. He saw Uncle Raj give Storm a wink.

To Oliver's relief, Storm diverted her assault to Uncle Raj. "That's off, isn't it?" she asked, looking at his mobile phone in his hand. "We wouldn't want it to ring now, would we?"

"Of course it's—"

"*Go! Go! Go!*" The negotiator's words suddenly ricocheted through the woods. Spellbound and powerless, all the trio could do was watch.

A loud *bang* brought their attention to the front door of the house as police burst through with a battering ram. Oliver could see officers dart in every direction, while other uniformed men and women stood guard at every corner, firearms aimed. The assault had begun.

One, two, three, four, five police officers charged in through the front door. One, two, three, four ropes came cascading down from the roof while police slid down them, stopping at upstairs windows and shattering the glass.

Oliver held his breath. The excitement and relief was shrouded by the sheer terror that things could so easily go wrong. Within minutes, his mum and dad could be found. They could walk right out of the house and onto the courtyard. But between now and then, they were inside the building, a building under attack.

Nobody dared to speak. Oliver held even tighter onto the tree trunk he was peering around. Storm held onto Oliver, and Uncle Raj held onto them both.

Shadows and silhouettes blurred past windows, both downstairs and up. Oliver wondered if any of those blurs were his parents. He closed his eyes and hoped with all of his heart that soon his life would be back to normal and his parents would be found safe and sound.

Within minutes, three men in lab coats, cuffed and guided by police officers, appeared at the front door. Oliver tried to figure out if he recognised any of them, but they were too far away. They were taken towards a van. Not a black van this time, but a white police van with yellow and blue stripes and a flashing blue light on the top.

One by one, three other men were directed out of the building, then boxes, machinery, computers, and brown paper evidence bags were removed.

"They really believed us," said Storm. "We are going to be in so much trouble when they find out our call was a hoax."

"Our call may have been a hoax," said Oliver, "but we do know that something must be wrong, or they wouldn't be taking all this stuff." He pointed to Uncle Raj's phone. "Can I borrow that?"

"What for?"

"Not sure yet."

Uncle Raj held out his phone, and Oliver took it.

"Don't follow me," he said as he began walking away. Before either of the other two had time to stop him, he was running towards the house. He had no intention of being spotted, but he had to find out if his parents were inside.

"Come back!" snarled Uncle Raj as he reached out to stop him.

Oliver kept going, remaining low, stopping right next to the police van on the courtyard, the one containing the men in lab coats. A single tree trunk no wider than Oliver was all that kept him from view. He was as close to these men as he had been the night before. The van's rear doors were open, and Oliver listened.

There were voices, but they were muffled. With his back pressed against the tree, he looked down at what was in his hand: a device that could go far closer than he could; a mobile phone. Oliver searched the apps and saw what he was looking for, the one with the red dot: *Record*. Lowering himself down, he placed the phone on the ground, and with a branch he slowly and carefully pushed it closer to the van. Then he buried it beneath some foliage and silently waited. Muffled voices, car doors, occasional shouts, sirens, and police radios were all he could hear.

Soon footsteps returned to the van. The door slammed and the vehicle was driven away. Using the branch, Oliver reversed the process to retrieve the phone. He sloped back to the security of the woods and the company of Storm and Uncle Raj.

"Idiot!" Storm scolded him. "You could have been so busted!"

"But I wasn't," said Oliver. "Listen!"

He brushed the mud off the phone and pressed *Play*. A deep voice spoke. " . . . *anything you do say may be given in evidence.*"

"What?" asked Storm.

"Shh!" said Oliver. "Listen!"

The same voice continued. "*Thomas Elwood, you're under arrest on suspicion of running an unlicensed operation, and being in possession of illegal firearms. You do not have to say anything but it may harm your defence if you do not mention when questioned something you later rely on in court. Anything you do say may be given in evidence.*"

"*The* Thomas Elwood?" Storm gasped.

Oliver frowned. He knew all too well that it had to be.

There was a shuffle, the sound of someone stepping out of the van, then a silence.

Three ears drew near the muddy speaker of Uncle Raj's phone, listening intensively.

Another voice spoke, although this one was barely louder than a whisper. "*Have they found the stun grenades?*"

"*Let's hope that's all they find!*" came a hushed reply.

Someone rasped, "*Nobody say anything to the police. If you so much as mention the boss's name, we'll all regret it!*"

The sound of footsteps followed, then the crashing of a van door closing and a revving of an engine.

There was a silence. Storm was first to break it: "Thomas Elwood!"

"The one and only," said Oliver. "Plus, we now know that these labs must be funded by Ubinon Folovich."

"What about Quark?" asked Storm.

Oliver shrugged.

"I always believed that stun grenades were military-issue only," said Uncle Raj.

"Isn't that what they found on Winston in your house?" Storm asked.

"That just confirms it doesn't it," said Oliver. "They're definitely in there."

"It does seem that way," said Storm. "Maybe you are right. So why haven't they found them?"

The sound of tapping and scraping came from Uncle Raj's phone.

"What's that?" he asked.

Oliver smiled. "That'll be me trying to get your phone back with a branch."

Uncle Raj rubbed the phone with his sleeve, inspecting it for damage. The recording ended.

More vehicles left, another lorry arrived, computers were carried out, and more and more equipment was taken away, then several vehicles began to leave. The courtyard in front of the house was almost clear. Oliver watched the front door, hoping that the next people to leave would be his parents.

The only vehicle left in the courtyard was one police van.

"I don't understand!" he said. "Why are they all leaving? Where are they going?"

"There can't be anything left to find," said Uncle Raj.

"That's wrong! Mum and Dad are still in there!"

Uncle Raj sighed. "I'm sorry," he said. "They can't be."

"Of course they are! You *know* they are!"

Uncle Raj placed a hand on Oliver's shoulder, which made Oliver cringe in pain.

The rhythmic banging of a hammer came from the direction of the front door.

"Look!" said Storm. "They're securing the house."

Only two men remained, both with tool boxes and wooden planks. They had hammered wood across broken windows to secure the building. Now they were sealing the front door. Soon, they too drove off.

"I think," said Uncle Raj, "it's a good time to leave."

"I know," said Oliver, "that it's time to investigate."

"What do you mean, 'investigate'?" Storm asked suspiciously. "We now know that the police have arrested the people who work there and that the building is empty."

"Wrong!" said Oliver. "The police think that the building is empty, but we know that it isn't."

"Do we?"

"Get with it! The police have checked my house for clues, but they didn't check all of it, did they?"

"But now it's all boarded up!" said Uncle Raj.

"Let's just have a closer look," said Oliver. "I need to do this."

Uncle Raj knew that Oliver needed reassurance, and he would never be happy until he had at least looked for himself. He nodded nervously. "We can look through the windows before we leave."

Oliver nodded back, although he knew he could not leave until he had checked out every nook and cranny that existed inside those labs.

"Over here!" called Oliver, who had headed straight for the front door. "Give me a hand."

Before anyone had time to persuade him otherwise, Oliver had parted his godfather from his keys and was using a one of them as a screwdriver in an attempt to remove the wooden plank fixed diagonally across the front door.

"We can't do that," Storm said to him as she approached. "That's illegal!"

"So is kidnap!"

Uncle Raj did not stop him, but said, "I'm not letting you go in there alone."

"Now you're encouraging him!" said Storm crossly.

"No," said Uncle Raj, "I'm saying that I am not happy letting Oliver go inside on his own."

"Then who's going to stay here with me?"

Uncle Raj grabbed hold of the plank of wood with Oliver and together they pulled.

"You could always come in with us," Oliver suggested.

Storm scowled at the same time as the huge front door swung open.

Face to Face

Oliver nervously stepped inside, Uncle Raj and Storm close behind. Standing in the entrance hall of North Yorkshire Scientific Research Laboratories, they looked around. A grand winding staircase led their eyes upwards towards a stained-glass dome that flooded the room with light, mystical patterns, and colours. The place felt old and in some ways untouched by time, as though they were stepping back 200 years.

"Cor blimey," said Storm. "This place is ancient!"

Oliver was not listening. He was far too preoccupied, and his eyes were scanning everywhere. "You go upstairs," he told Storm. He then pointed to the opening at the back of the entrance, where they could see a small servants' staircase going down. "And you check downstairs, Uncle Raj. I'll look here."

"I'm not going on my own," said Storm.

"It's a big house. If we all stay together it is going to take us three times as long to find them. You'll be fine. Just yell if you need us."

"Yell?" she answered. "I'll do more than yell!"

Oliver had no doubts at all that if Storm needed help, even in a house the size of this, he would know immediately.

Storm and Uncle Raj reluctantly followed orders. Oliver was alone in the hallway. He knew that there must be rooms, places, hidden doorways and passageways, that the police did not find; secret entrances behind bookcases and crevices behind oil paintings. He was not prepared to leave until no stone was left unturned and he had found who he was looking for.

Oliver walked through a large panelled doorway to the left of the staircase and entered a magnificent grand room that he supposed was probably once used as the drawing room. The walls were a deep red, elaborately edged with gold stencilling and tarnished from centuries of open fires. A large marble fireplace created a focal point for the room, which was framed with picture rails, decorative patterns on the ceiling, and dark oak panels. The irony of the magnificent room was stark; nothing in there looked as though it belonged. Each wall was lined with rows of tables cluttered with computers and tangled wires, with gaps where Oliver assumed computers once stood. Shiny silver boxes were dotted all around the room, each connected to more wires connected to more computers, and leading his gaze towards the far end of the room. There Oliver caught sight of something that he instantly knew and recognised: a small particle accelerator.

"I knew it!" he said. "I just knew it!"

He moved on, searching under rugs for access hatches, pulling every bell and cord, even searching behind the remaining oil paintings. He knew that there must be a hiding place, somewhere the police had failed to find.

Confident that he had not missed a single thing, Oliver retreated back through the entrance hall, past the stairs, and through the door on the right.

He was now in the library. Books lined three walls from floor to ceiling on dark mahogany shelves with ladders attached on rails. An enormous wooden table, surrounded by a jumble of non-matching dining chairs, was at the centre of the room. Oliver felt sure that this was by far the most likely room to find a secret passageway. He was going to have to touch, feel, and press random books, hoping that one would act as the catalyst and reveal the hidden doorway he hoped was there.

However, it looked like the police had already beaten him to it. A doorway, partially concealed by dusty, old volumes of

Encyclopaedia Britannica, stood in the furthermost corner of the room.

Cautiously prising the bookcase away from the wall, Oliver stepped inside. A dark room with a single oak desk was all that lay behind the bookcase. Drawers had been emptied and the contents removed. An inscription on the desk read, *Dr T Elwood.*

As Oliver stepped back to leave, he felt something under his foot. Looking down, he saw a ring. He picked it up. It was gold with an engraved signet, the pattern looked like a figure of eight between two overlapping circles.

He heard a sound: a floorboard creaking; somebody was in the entrance hall.

He pocketed the ring and headed back to the hallway. There was no way that Storm could possibly have searched every room thoroughly. She would have to check again.

Storm was not there. From behind the staircase, a man dressed in black appeared. Oliver froze. This man was no stranger; he was Vincent Quark.

Quark walked towards Oliver until they stood face to face.

Oliver did not scream. He *could not* scream. He had lost control of his voice and his legs too. His feet were frozen, his eyes were wide, his breathing was going faster and the hairs on the back of his neck stood on end.

Quark moved around to the front door. He stood with his back against it, blocking the exit. His snake eyes fixed onto Oliver's as if attempting to burn into his mind.

"You may think that what you're doing is clever," he said in a cruel, calculated, and coarse voice, "but you are nothing more than an interfering, meddling little boy!"

Oliver tried to step back on quivering legs. He could not retreat any further as his back was against the wall. He opened his mouth to speak, but no words came out.

"You do not know what trouble you have caused," said Quark, his voice barely louder than a whisper yet still evil and threatening.

Oliver shook his head, his eyes fixed on the scar on the man's face and the single eyebrow that stretched from one side to the other.

"This time you have really gone too far. I cannot let you go until you tell me everything that I need to know."

Despite Oliver's inability to articulate a sentence, he stuttered, stammered, and grimaced, and from somewhere inside him words escaped timidly. "You don't scare me." This was the biggest lie he had ever told. "You can't treat people like this and get away with it."

Oliver suddenly remembered that he was not alone but Quark might not know that. He was not about to tell him.

"How did you know I was here?" Oliver asked.

"You were spotted snooping around here last night, and I knew that you were the type to hang around, like a bad smell!"

Oliver shrugged.

"I know it was you who brought the police here. Now tell me, why you would do a silly thing like that?" Quark's glare was firm, but his eyes were angry.

"Why don't you ask them yourself?" Oliver snarled back.

"I don't need to ask the police anything because they don't have the answers. But you do!"

"You want *me* to give *you* answers?"

"No. I'm telling you my patience is running out. Tell me where your cowardly father is hiding. You are the only chance I have left, and you're not going anywhere until you tell me exactly where I can find Paul Harris."

The words went in but did not land. Instead they thrashed around like a salmon on the riverbank. This made no sense to Oliver. It could not be right. He knew that this man was at his house the day his parents were kidnapped; so how was it that he did not know where they were? Quark was as desperate as Oliver to find his dad.

Oliver felt as if the ground beneath him was crumbling. He had lost his grip. He no longer knew what he thought he knew. Everything he had believed had gone; with it, his hopes of ever finding his mum and dad. The realisation that his parents were not there was more than enough to bear, but Oliver had even more to worry about. He was trapped, alone with his dad's nemesis, Vincent Quark. For the second time in one day, he was facing kidnap.

Looking around, Oliver made for the front door, pushing Quark aside.

Quark lunged backwards, forcing the door closed with his back. "I've told you!" he roared. "You are going nowhere!"

Oliver steadied himself and was grabbed by the arm and pushed back. Quark glared and held a firm grip. Oliver began to tremble. He was petrified.

"You are going nowhere until you tell me where your father is!"

"I can do better than that. I can tell you where my godfather is." He screamed at the top of his voice, "*Uncle Raj!*"

Quark's eyes broke away as he caught sight of Uncle Raj appearing from the doorway at the back of the entrance hall. Oliver's godfather looked as shocked as Oliver himself, and despite the two men having never met before, no introductions were needed. He seemed to know exactly who Quark was.

"Vincent Quark!" said Uncle Raj, taking one step closer. He stared at Quark and held his gaze until the inevitable happened.

"Aaaarrgh!" Storm appeared on the stairway.

Quark stepped back, fumbling for the door handle. He fled, having rapidly changed his mind and his plans for Oliver after discovering that he was not alone. "Don't think that I've finished with you!" he shouted as he ran into the courtyard.

Uncle Raj gave chase, but Quark hastily got into a black Transit van and drove off.

"V-V-Vincent Quark!" Storm stuttered, now feeling brave enough to descend the stairs.

"The one and only!" said Oliver, taking a deep breath.

"What?" said Uncle Raj, unable to decide which question to ask first.

Oliver sighed, walked towards the stairs, and sat down. "He wanted to know where my father was. He said that I was the only chance he had left to find him."

Storm looked about as confused as a cow in a field of AstroTurf. "But I thought . . ."

"Can we go home?" Oliver asked.

Uncle Raj nodded.

Without looking back, Oliver left. Storm and Uncle Raj followed, Storm ranting and blabbering. Oliver was not listening.

Their walk through the woods and back to the car was a blur. Oliver had lost all concept of time, although he was vaguely aware that it was getting late. The disappointment of failing to find his parents was exhausting. Another day was ending and he was still no closer. In fact, he felt further away than ever.

Oliver walked wearily in front of Storm and Uncle Raj, needing space, time to think, time *not* to think. He just needed to be alone. When they reached the car, his energy was exhausted.

They began their long drive back to Wales. Luckily for Oliver, Storm fell asleep within minutes. Despite the fact that he had to put up with her head flopping on and off his shoulder, it was a small price worth paying for the peace and quiet. Uncle Raj seemed to accept the fact that Oliver needed space.

Oliver's worries weighed him down so heavily that he too closed his eyes and drifted.

Brrrrinng . . . Brrrrinng . . . Brrrrinng . . . went Uncle Raj's phone.

"I'm in Puddingdale!" shouted a very tired and very familiar Welsh accent. It was Uncle Will.

"Oh!" said Uncle Raj.

"Ah!" said Oliver, having completely forgotten about him amid everything that had happened.

"That's good," said Uncle Raj, stalling for time to think of a kind way to tell him that they were not there. "There has been a slight change of plan," he said at last.

"What?" said Uncle Will, his suspicion obvious.

"We are not there *anymore.*"

"Well, where are you then, butt?"

"On our way back to Wales," said Uncle Raj tentatively.

"Hi, Uncle Will," said Oliver, just to remind his relative that he was on a loudspeaker and that there were children in the car.

"You what?" asked Uncle Will. "Oh, hiya, butt!"

"How's Henry?" asked Oliver.

"Fast asleep," said Uncle Will. "And Winston."

"Winston?" asked Uncle Raj.

"Yeah," said Uncle Will. "You said I needed to bring Henry to Puddingdale and not to say anything to Karen about where I was going, so I told her I was taking the dog for a walk."

"Oh," said Uncle Raj sympathetically, but he was smirking, considering the kind of journey that Uncle Will had probably had.

"I don't get it!" said Uncle Will. "Why were you there in the first place? It's in the middle of nowhere."

"I'll explain later," said Uncle Raj. "Meet you back at your mum's. Got . . . go . . . Line . . . break . . . up!"

He ended the call.

"That's mean," said Storm.

"I feel terrible," Uncle Raj said guiltily. "I genuinely forgot all about him."

"He'll be fine," said Oliver. "Take him out for a pint when you get back and he'll forgive you."

Uncle Raj nodded.

Storm was soon snoring, and Oliver closed his eyes.

A Brand New Day

"We're back!" announced Uncle Raj, leading Oliver and Storm into Nan's living room.

Much to their relief, there were far fewer people waiting for them than there had been after their last return. Sat in the living room were Nan, Mrs Minton, PC Sharp, WPC Hughes, and one other lady who looked officious but unfamiliar.

"So you are," said Mrs Minton, looking more annoyed than relieved to see them back again. Nobody even bothered getting up this time. "What on earth has happened to you two?"

Neither of them had given their appearance a second thought. Oliver thought it probably would have looked odd: dirty, torn clothes and his grazed face. Luckily most of their bruises were hidden under their clothing.

Storm smiled apologetically and slumped on the sofa next to her mum and snuggled up. She yawned and once again closed her eyes.

Oliver was not looking forward to the unavoidable barrage of questions and decided to try Storm's tactic.

"Where the heck have you been?" asked Nan. She was only saying what everybody else in the room was thinking. Oliver kept his eyes closed, hoping that somebody else would answer, but Storm was away with the fairies, so it was either him or Uncle Raj.

Luckily, the latter spoke up. "We have been on a quest to find Megan and Paul."

Oliver cringed. He knew that Uncle Raj would not tell anyone anything that they did not need to know, but he still had a sick feeling in the pit of his stomach as he waited to hear what his uncle was going to say next.

Everyone waited for an explanation. Oliver opened one eye and saw Uncle Raj looking tense. He felt it was wrong to allow his uncle to bear everybody's wrath, so he opened both eyes and spoke.

"It was all my fault," he said pathetically. "I begged him to take me there."

"Where?" asked a chorus of voices.

Only then did the thought occur to Oliver that nobody except Uncle Will knew where they had been, and Uncle Will was still miles away. Telling the truth would definitely do more harm than good.

"Cornwall," Oliver announced. He was not sure why he said *Cornwall*. It was only the first place that came into his head, probably because it was at the opposite end of the country to Yorkshire.

Oliver looked at his uncle. His eyes were wide, his lips tight together in a broad, uncomfortable smile that reminded Oliver of a frog's face. Uncle Raj began nodding his head rhythmically to show he was not going to disagree.

"Cornwall?" asked Mrs Minton. "What on earth were you doing in Cornwall?"

"Cornwall," said Uncle Raj, still nodding.

"It's because," Oliver chirped in, rescuing his uncle who was looking increasingly uncomfortable, "I had an idea about where Mum and Dad may have gone. A couple of years ago, we went on holiday to a place called St Ives." He looked around to check that everybody was buying into this, then he continued. "We stayed in a really nice cottage, it was close to a secret cove, high on the cliffs." Oliver did not have to lie about that bit; he had indeed been there on holiday.

There was a general air of confusion.

"It was a special place," said Oliver, "and I remember my mum saying that the next time they fancied getting away from it all, that's where they would go." Oliver paused before finishing his unrehearsed speech. "So I was sure that that's where they had gone . . ."

He sighed. He did not sob; he thought sobbing might be a little over-dramatic.

Every eye was still fixed on him. The air of suspicion and condemnation lifted and was replaced instead by an air of empathy.

"Awwww!" said Nan.

"And had they?" asked WPC Hughes.

Oliver shook his head sadly before pouting his lip; he even made it quiver a bit.

"So you thought that they'd gone on holidays without you?" asked Nan. "They would never do that."

"Well, where else could they be?" Oliver asked. "I had to check it out for myself and that's why I asked Uncle Raj to take me. Please don't be mad with us. I'm really sorry for causing everybody so much trouble."

Oliver knew by the expressions on each of the faces looking at him that victory was his. The disapproving glares had gone, and now he saw kindness, with lashings and lashings of sympathy.

"You poor thing!" said Nan, tears welling in her eyes. "I knew it was all getting too much for you. It's the stress, you know." She turned to look at everyone else in the room. "It's far too much for a little boy to cope with." She moved closer to Oliver, now sitting on the arm of his chair and patting him on his head.

"Henry's just the same. Will took him out for the afternoon with Winston. He phoned a while back to say that Henry was so upset that he's taken him to spend the night at Llewelyn Close."

Oliver hated the gooeyness but he had to put up with it. It was the brave thing to do.

"Everybody has been worried about you," said Nan.

Oliver pouted again. "I wish that everyone was as worried about my mum and dad as they are about me."

Nan ignored that comment and said, "Even Mrs Jones has been on the telephone asking after you."

"Mrs Jones?" Oliver asked.

"Yes, she seemed ever so worried after reading about you in the newspapers. She telephoned to ask if she could come and see you."

Oliver's mind raced back to that fateful Friday when he had been left abandoned in school. Mrs Jones had infuriated him then by not telling him something. Oliver shook his head. "I don't want her sympathy. Or anyone else's, for that matter!"

The lady who Oliver did not know stood up and introduced herself. "My name is Sarah Sidmouth, a Police Family Liaison Officer, and I'm going to help you get through this whilst DCI O'Sullivan is away."

Oliver looked at her as if she had crawled out from under a stone. "Get through this?" he repeated angrily.

"Yes," she added calmly. "I know that it's a difficult time for everyone."

"*Difficult?*"

"I understand," she replied, taking a step closer towards Oliver.

"*Understand!*" said Oliver, his voice getting louder each time this woman spoke. "There is no way you can *possibly* understand!"

He looked around the room and could see frowns of disapproval. He was riled. Frustration seared inside of him and even though he was usually so well-mannered and polite, something made him flip.

"You don't know *anything* about me!" he said. "And I don't know *anything* about you." He turned to look at PC Sharp and WPC Hughes, who were sat on a sofa dunking chocolate Hobnobs into their cup of tea, and said to them, "Or you, or why you are even here!"

"It's my job to offer support to you and your family," said Sarah Sidmouth, clearly attempting to sound sympathetic.

"Then support me by getting your backsides off the sofa, going outside that door, and looking in all the places that you haven't looked yet to see if you can find my mum and dad!"

Oliver knew just how rude that sounded, but he no longer cared. Three police officers were sat on Nan's sofa, doing absolutely nothing, while he was going through hell and back again.

"Mrs Jones is genuinely concerned," explained Sarah Sidmouth, who had partly taken the hint and sat back down, "along with lots of other people. She is bound to be worried about you. I'm sure that DCI O'Sullivan has been keeping her informed about how you are coping. She is a very good friend of the DCI."

"The DCI!" Oliver repeated. He was now shouting. "And Mrs Jones?"

"Getting married in the winter," she smiled.

"Very interesting!" said Oliver feeling angrier than ever. His former head teacher did not care about him; she must have been trying to contact the DCI. "I get it!"

"Maybe it's for the best if you leave for the night," Uncle Raj suggested to Sarah Sidmouth. "I'll stay here." He looked across to Oliver's nan. "Would that be all right with you?"

"Of course," she answered. "I think that Oliver could do with his godfather being around for a little while."

Uncle Raj smiled. It seemed that perhaps Nan was offering an olive branch and sensing the depth of the relationship they had.

All three officers began to leave.

"I doubt that you will see me tomorrow," said Sarah Sidmouth as she opened the front door, "DCI O'Sullivan should be back. It was a mistake me coming in his place. Consistency is always better for the families."

"We'll look forward to seeing him tomorrow," said Uncle Raj as he closed the door behind her. Oliver was convinced that he smirked.

"What should we do about him?" Oliver whispered to his uncle.

"Let's think about him in the morning. No harm will come to him if he keeps still."

Oliver did not disagree. The DCI was one of the last things on his mind.

"Shall I bring some blankets?" Nan asked Mrs Minton. "It's already past midnight and Storm looks so peaceful. After the day she has had, it would be a shame to wake her." Storm had somehow managed to sleep through everything.

"I don't like to impose on you again," said Mrs Minton.

"You're not imposing," said Nan as she went to get some sheets.

The house bustled with activity for a while, and Oliver sloped off to bed.

It was such a relief to lay his head on a soft pillow as his body sank deep, deeper into the bed, and before he could think a single thought, sleep had claimed him.

The moment he woke, he leapt to his feet and headed downstairs, feeling guilty for allowing himself to have wasted precious hours to sleep. He passed Henry's bedroom door, and stopped as he noticed light escaping. Oliver tried the handle and saw Uncle Raj lying awake on Henry's bed.

"Are you OK?" asked Uncle Raj quietly.

Oliver shrugged his shoulders.

"I couldn't sleep either."

"What do we do now?" Oliver asked, sitting on the edge of the bed.

"We start again and we don't give up!"

"But how?" asked Oliver, feeling more despondent than ever before. "We've looked everywhere we can think of" – he shook his head – "and where are we now?"

"Did I hear Oliver Harris admit defeat?" whispered Uncle Raj.

Oliver sighed. "I'm not giving up. I just don't know what to do anymore."

Uncle Raj put his arm on Oliver's shoulder. "Let's not start today with the broken pieces of yesterday. Today is a brand new day."

Oliver nodded.

"We may not know where your parents are, but we do know where they are *not*, and we also know that there will be a few less scientists and corrupt DCIs knocking about the place. So on the scale of things, we're better off. So how about you and me spend an hour or two at your house this morning, and we go back to square one and try a brand new plan?"

"Let's go."

"Now? But it's only just gone five."

"I know," said Oliver. "It's a brand new day."

Uncle Raj smiled, stretched, and followed Oliver downstairs, stopping briefly in the lounge to collect his car keys.

"Hey you!" whispered Storm, from under her blankets.

"Shh!" said Oliver trying not to wake Storm's mum, who was asleep, catching flies in the armchair. "We're on our way back to my house."

Storm immediately got to her feet. "I'm coming too."

Oliver did not argue, and neither did Uncle Raj. Storm was already involved up to her eyebrows, she might come up with some useful ideas, and Oliver needed to conjure inspiration from somewhere. There was also the issue that if he objected, Storm would want to know why, and that would surely end in Storm's mum and everybody else in the house waking and preventing them all from leaving.

Uncle Raj left a note on the kitchen table.

About Time

From the top of the gantry, Oliver's eyes surveyed the labs.

"Where shall we start?" asked Storm.

"I really don't know," said Oliver.

"How about I start in the security room?" suggested Uncle Raj.

"Fine," said Oliver. "I'll start downstairs."

"Where shall I start?" asked Storm.

Oliver was not sure where he should send her. "How about you help me downstairs?"

Storm nodded. "Shall we check out the lab with the arm in?"

"If you want."

Oliver wandered into the electronics lab, walked around, and left, leaving Storm gazing at the robotic arm.

He stepped into the particle physics lab, logged onto the computer, and stared at the screen.

"What are you doing?" asked Storm as she joined him.

"I wish I knew."

"There could be other files. With passwords."

"That's what I was thinking." He began tapping away. "Anything in the electronics lab?" he asked, trying to encourage her back in there and needing to concentrate on what he was doing.

"I don't think so. But that robotic arm . . . It's really cool."

Oliver tried to ignore her.

"What did you say this did again?" asked Storm, running her hand up and down the particle accelerator.

"I didn't."

"But it must do something. It's enormous!"

"It does do something. How about you check out the workshop?"

"OK," said Storm quite cheerfully, leaving Oliver in peace.

He opened document after document, but each time he did he felt even more despondent. The pages and pages of numbers, figures, and grids all meant nothing. Nothing was password-protected. There were reams and reams of data that to anyone other than a professor of physics made no sense at all.

Desperate, he reached up onto the shelf next to the monitor and grabbed a book thicker than the entire works of William Shakespeare that was entitled *The Fundamentals of Relativistic Particle Physics*. He recognised this book as one that his dad often referred to. Perhaps if he understood what he was working on, then he may understand why he is still missing. He opened it on page one and began to read.

"What does this one do?" asked Storm, who had once again returned.

"What?" asked Oliver without taking his eyes off the book. He was still on page one.

"This cylinder thingy?"

"Oh," said Oliver, "it's just the spinning chamber of the particle accelerator." He was not even going to attempt explaining, and he was not in the mood for being courteous. He did not have any patience for Storm's constant questioning. "Why don't you see if you're needed upstairs in the security room?"

"Because I have just been there," said Storm, "and your godfather was also trying to get rid of me and told me that you might need me."

As grateful as Oliver was for Storm's help, he could no longer concentrate.

"What's inside it?" she asked.

"Hydrogen ions," said Oliver, hoping that that would be the end of the questioning for at least another few minutes.

"Why are they so big?"

"The machine?"

"No, the particle thingies?"

"They're not. If you lined up ten quintillion of them, end to end, they would only reach across the diameter of a pea." Oliver laughed then turned to page two.

Storm went quiet. A moment later, she asked, "But what's making the shadow on the inside of the windows?"

"There isn't one. All that's in there are millions of spinning particles."

"Why are they spinning?"

This was the final straw. "Storm!" said Oliver furiously, "Have you ever read a book about relativistic particle physics?"

"No!" Storm shook her head, worried that Oliver's next remark might be a suggestion that she did so.

"Well," Oliver began, "neither have I, so I really need to concentrate."

Storm took the hint. She meandered around the room, stopping every now and then to look at something.

"It's fascinating!" said Storm.

Oliver was close to losing his rag completely. "*Storm!*" he shouted. He had had enough.

Storm instantly took offence. Her eyes welled with tears, and Oliver knew that he had over-stepped the mark, and he was probably right to prepare himself for the imminent lecture on being both ungrateful and rude.

He turned around in his swivel chair and waited for it to land.

It began. "I don't have to be here right now," said Storm. "In fact, I could be at home tucked up in my own bed, watching TV, eating biscuits, and not worrying about you or your parents."

Oliver bowed his head, signifying submission.

"In fact . . ." she continued, swinging her arms around. Oliver was expecting the worse.

"In *fact*," Storm repeated angrily. Her right arm raised and landed painfully on the cylinder with so much force that she cringed. "Ow!" she yelled. It was not enough pain to stop her rant completely, but sufficient to slow her down for a moment. "And I thought that you wanted my help—"

"Shh!" said Oliver, standing up from his chair. "Can you hear that?"

Storm did not answer. She was even more irate about the fact that Oliver had not conceded and had the audacity to interrupt. Her eyebrows simultaneously took a dive. She was all set to continue.

"Look what you've done!" yelled Oliver, pointing to the cylinder behind her. "You've hit the power button!"

The cylinder attached to the particle accelerator lit up like Las Vegas at Christmas. Lights flashed all over it in sequence, then in spurts, before stopping. The sound of a whirring engine started, gradually increasing until there was a deafening roar, as if a jet was preparing to take off in the room where they were standing.

"What have you done?" yelled Oliver, backing out of the room in fear of what was going to happen next.

Storm stepped back, and the cylinder began to shake. "I don't know!" she yelled, following Oliver's cue to leave the room. "I didn't mean to."

The noise intensified. They stood outside the door with hands over their ears. All they could do was watch in frightened expectation.

The noise subsided as the machine appeared to stabilise. It began to emit a steady hum. Oliver felt it was safe enough to return to the lab and assess the damage.

"I told you," he said. "You can't mess about with these machines. They are dangerous!"

"I'm really sorry," said Storm, she looked genuinely regretful. "I didn't mean to do that."

The sound of air escaping turned both their heads. The rear door of the machine slowly lifted. Oliver's eyes were fixed on the far end of the capsule.

What happened next was so remarkable that he feared for his sanity.

As bold as a lion, Oliver's dad stepped outside of the cylinder doorway, clinging tightly to a chunky, old laptop.

Too astonished to do anything but watch, feet rooted to the ground, Oliver watched as his mum followed.

"What are you doing here?" asked Paul Harris, looking concerned.

In the brief moment it took for Oliver's eyes to process the signal to his brain that there, in front of him, were his parents, he stepped forward. He ran towards them faster than he had ever moved before, and threw himself at them, bowling them both over in the process and causing the three of them to land on the floor in a heap.

"Dad!" cried Oliver, tears tumbling down his cheeks. "Mum!" he blubbered, hugging her tightly.

"You should be at school!" said Megan Harris crossly, still on the floor and clambering to her knees. "And what has happened to your face? Are you all right?"

"What?"

"Why aren't you at school?" asked Oliver's dad.

At that moment, Oliver's parents both saw that Storm was standing in the doorway to the lab.

"And what," said Oliver's mum, "do you think you are doing allowing your friends down here?"

Storm looked relieved, but just as confused as Oliver, although she too was very pleased to see them. Instead of explaining, she opened up her arms and came running to join the pile-on on the lab floor. She cried, "Mrs Harris, Mr – I mean *Dr* Harris, I'm so glad that you've come back."

If that was not enough confusion, Uncle Raj appeared at the doorway to see what the hullabaloo was in aid of. "Paul!" he shouted. "Megan!"

He ran into the room, skidded on his knees, and threw open his arms, grabbing hold of the others. They were all in the process of clambering to their feet, but he brought them all back down again. It looked as though Paul and Megan Harris had scored the winning try for Wales against England to win the Grand Slam.

Paul Harris clambered to his feet first and looked down at everyone else. His eyes squinted, his nose curled, and he held his laptop tightly to his chest. "What the Dickens is going on?"

"I've no idea," said Uncle Raj, smiling and still clinging on tightly to everyone else who was left in the heap.

"You're home!" cried Storm, so overwhelmed that she sobbed loudly, holding onto Oliver's mum while she attempted to stand up.

"Dad!" yelled Oliver, who was still clinging to his father's legs. "I'm so glad you're home! I thought I would never see you again."

Paul Harris looked at his watch. "Ever see me again? You've been in school for less than half an hour. How did you get home?"

"What?"

Everyone began firing questions at once: Paul to Oliver, Storm to Megan, and Uncle Raj to anyone who would listen. There was so much noise that nobody could hear themselves think.

"Stop!" shouted Oliver's dad, looking around frantically. "We need to keep quiet!"

"Why?" asked Oliver.

His dad looked reluctant to explain, but then said, "Someone may be upstairs."

"Who?"

"Someone who doesn't know about these labs." Oliver's dad looked around at his son, Storm, and Uncle Raj, and said, "If there's anyone left that doesn't already know."

"Nobody else knows," Oliver reassured him. "Only the people in this room now."

He could see the disappointment in his father's face. The fact that Storm was there in the labs was the evidence that Oliver had broken his promise.

"Where have you been?" Oliver asked frantically. He let go of his dad's legs and got to his feet.

"I haven't been anywhere." His eyes scanned the room. "Let's just keep the noise down until we know that it is safe."

"What are you going on about?" asked Oliver.

"You really had us all very worried," said Uncle Raj.

"Why?" asked Oliver's dad. He looked at the other man. "And what on earth are *you* doing here?"

"I think," Uncle Raj answered, "there are so many crossed wires in this room that soon there are going to be sparks, unless we all sit down and find out exactly what has been going on."

Oliver perched himself against the worktop between his mum and dad, and even though he had no idea about what was going on, he still had a grin fixed to his face. This is what he had been hoping and dreaming of; the end to what had just been the longest few weeks of his entire life. His parents were home. However, this did not stop him being curious.

"So," he began, "where exactly have you been?"

"I dropped Henry off at nursery," said his mum.

"And I dropped you off at school," his dad added. "You know that."

"After that?" asked Oliver.

"Someone was coming," his dad said, "so we came down here."

"So why aren't you in school?" asked his mum again.

"Because school finished almost two weeks ago."

"It didn't!" she replied crossly.

"It *did!*" said Oliver, Storm, and Uncle Raj together.

Paul Harris's expression suddenly changed from confusion to a look of astonished understanding. He looked at his watch, then started to pace. He stopped in front of the computer terminal, pressed a few buttons, threw his arms in the air, and fell upon his knees.

Nobody spoke. They only watched him. His eyes flickered and his lips moved. Oliver thought it was as if he was running through something in his head. He stood up, composed himself, and asked, "What time is it?"

Uncle Raj looked at his watch and said, "Seven thirty."

Oliver's dad's face lit up. "Is it a.m. or p.m.?"

"Definitely a.m.!" said Storm, yawning.

"Then what's the day?"

"It's Thursday."

"Good heavens above!" Oliver's dad looked so excited that he was almost fit to explode. His face beamed. "What's the date?"

"It's the thirtieth of July," said Oliver.

"I don't – it can't – it," said Oliver's dad so frantically that the words for the questions failed to flow.

Oliver tried to read his father's face, wondering what on earth he was thinking. He asked his dad, "After you dropped me at school, did you come straight home?"

"Yes!"

"Did you have a cup of tea in the kitchen?"

"We did," said Oliver's mum, sounding curious.

"Did you see the black vans?" asked Oliver.

"Are they still there?" she asked urgently.

"No, I think that we've got rid of them."

"That's twelve days, twenty-one hours, and sixteen minutes!" said Oliver's dad. He worked through some numbers. "That's more than 309 hours – 18,556 minutes. That's 1,113,360 seconds."

He smiled. "You know," he said, sounding to Oliver like he was ready to tell a long story, "over eighty years ago a Scottish scientist called Alexander Fleming was researching the flu when he noticed that one of his Petri dishes had been spoiled by a blue-green mould that had got into it and killed the

Staphylococcus bacteria. At that moment he knew he had discovered penicillin."

Everyone looked mystified.

"It appears that Mum and I, not unlike Alexander Fleming, have made an accidental discovery." He scratched his head. "It appears that we have taken a journey or, rather, you have taken the journey and we haven't!" He began nodding rhythmically.

"Will you just tell us what is going on," said his wife. "I'm in no mood for riddles."

"I don't get it either," Storm added.

"Well," said Oliver's dad, "if I tell you all" – his voice was excited and quick – "do I have your promise never to tell another living soul? The implications of this getting out are so enormous I can't even begin to explain what could happen!"

Everybody nodded, including Oliver's mum, who had taken – or *not* taken – the journey with her husband but still seemed unaware of how she had or had not been anywhere.

Paul Harris said, "After being followed this morning, or indeed a week last Friday morning, Mum and I came into the labs because we suspected that someone was on their way into the house."

Oliver nodded. Storm and Uncle Raj both raised their eyebrows so high that they almost reached the tops of their foreheads.

"We knew it would be safer to hide out in the labs, because nobody knows how to get into them."

"Did you see the men arriving at the house?" Oliver asked his dad.

"Yes. When I checked the cameras from the kitchen, I saw an army of black suits heading straight for us, so that's when we hid."

"The cup of tea. Did you break a mug?"

"I knocked it over just before we rushed down here."

"That explains that."

"You didn't cut yourself, did you?" asked Oliver's mum, concerned.

"No," said Oliver. "The police bagged it and took it as evidence."

"The police? Evidence?" his dad said. "We really are in trouble, aren't we?"

"Definitely a spot of bother!" said Storm, nodding.

"What happened next?" asked Oliver.

"We came into the labs and hid."

"Were you followed?"

"I don't think so. We'll have to check the security cameras."

"We've already done that," said Oliver, "but the power was cut."

"That's not possible," his dad replied. "If the mains power fails—"

"Then the generator kicks in, then the sluice gates open, and the stored energy from the wind turbine kicks in."

"Exactly!"

"But for some reason the backup power just wasn't there."

Paul Harris scratched his head again. "It is possible, but it would require someone to cut off the mains, trap the sluice gate, block the power for the wind turbine, and detach the generator in the garage."

"Assume that all those things happened," Oliver suggested.

"Then yes, the house could lose power."

"So, why exactly were you in the particle chamber?"

"I figured," his dad began, "that if the worse was to happen and the labs were discovered, then the noise and light within the chamber would put off anybody looking for us. I knew it was dangerous for us to hide in there with all those particles flying around, but it was safer than the alternative."

"I guess so," said Oliver. "But what would happen to the chamber if the power was cut?"

"It would have taken a few minutes for the stored power to be used up. Just enough time for Mum and I to climb inside."

"*Did* the power go off?" asked Oliver.

"It could have flickered, but how long do you think it was off for?"

"A couple of minutes."

"Well, that would explain it. A couple of minutes for you would have been nanoseconds for your mum and me."

"Yeah!" said Oliver. "It will have been long enough to corrupt the experiments, though!"

Oliver's mum, Storm, and Uncle Raj swung their heads back and forth as if they were watching a tennis match at Wimbledon, listening with blank faces.

His dad went on, "I thought the chamber was safe because when the particles spin around, they remain on the outer surface. I don't fully understand what happened, but when the power surged, it would have increased the strength of the magnetic field even further before shutting down. This would have left me and your mother with millions of relativistic particles heading straight for us when the power failed. That is particles moving at speeds close to the speed of light."

He looked at Storm and Raj under the impression that he was helping them along. A combination of blank, confused, and horrified faces stared at him and his wife.

"Wow!" said Oliver.

His dad kept scratching at his head furiously. "Relativity!" he announced. This comment did not seem to help. "Einstein's theory of relativity! I'm guessing that the particles were moving around us at such speeds that they caused a localised disturbance in space-time itself."

"What?" said Oliver. "Keeping you both within a state of greatly decelerated space-time?"

"Good heavens above, it must be!"

"What?" asked Uncle Raj.

"It's the only thing that makes any sense," answered Oliver's dad. "According to Einstein, passing time is experienced at the same rate for all non-accelerating reference frames. My experiment here was to determine whether or not I can slow down the decay of constantly accelerating particles; it seems that we've been caught up in a similar process of delayed ageing."

"I don't get it!" said Storm. "This is weird, too weird."

"It actually makes perfect sense."

"You're trying to tell us that you have been hanging upside down in that thing for nearly two weeks?"

"Ummmm, no. Not upside down. Well, at least I don't think that we were upside down."

"I can tell you what you looked like," said Storm, "I was looking in the chamber window a few minutes ago, and all I could see was dark shadows. I could see right through, so I'm pretty sure I'd have noticed if you two were hanging upside down."

"I can't explain that," said Paul Harris. "Not yet anyway."

"So what made you appear just now?" asked Uncle Raj.

"I don't know."

"I do," said Oliver. "Storm accidentally pressed the *Start* button."

"That would have helped." His dad frowned. "The old particles would have been cycled out before the new particles were introduced, allowing your mum and I back into the chamber in your space-time. That's when I saw you from out of the chamber window" – he gestured to Oliver – "so we thought that we were in the chamber just ten minutes, and my wrist watch confirms this."

He showed everyone how its face said it was still July 17th and the time was not quite eleven in the morning.

There was a period of silence. It was a pause that spoke volumes, representing something so big, something so extraordinarily mind-blowing, that no words seemed appropriate. The explanation somehow seemed to have landed on Oliver's head like a bowler hat, just sitting on the top without sinking in. Understanding about simple particles was one thing, but that did not help him understand how it could work with the more than seven billion, billion, billion hydrogen, oxygen, and carbon molecules that made up his parents. He knew all too well that the sheer implications of what his father had just explained were phenomenal.

"Holy cow!" said Storm dreamily as her hand covered her gaping mouth. She looked at Oliver's mum. "Does that mean that you haven't had a wee for nearly two weeks?"

Megan Harris smiled and shrugged.

"You must be so desperate!"

Oliver smirked. He had a grin fixed upon his face. His parents were home and they had not been kidnapped. They were safe. A million comments floated in and out of his head until suddenly one landed firmly and made him shout, "Henry! We have to tell everyone that you're back!"

He knew that they were not the only people who would be pleased to see his parents.

"Not so quickly," said Uncle Raj. "Before we do that, there are a few loose ends we need to tie up."

Oliver understood why his mum and dad could not just reappear; there would be far too many questions. There was also the matter of another pressing loose end, someone who Oliver had accused of kidnapping his parents, someone who had been hanging around for quite long enough.

A brand new plan was required to bring Paul and Megan Harris back to the real world, back into the world of British Summer Time.

The Cover Story

"So what you're saying is we can't just reappear," said Oliver's mum.

"Exactly," Uncle Raj replied. "If you so much as step one foot outside, you will be spotted, and before you know it the police will arrive, then the press, and everybody else in the whole of Ebbwvenny will start asking questions and wanting to know exactly where you've been."

"So are the police actually out there looking for us?" asked Oliver's dad, wearing the expression of excitement on his face that seemed to have become lodged there.

"Oh yes!" said Storm, sounding to Oliver as if she was trying to reassure his parents that being sought after by the police was not such a big deal. "Don't worry too much; they were looking for us yesterday."

"Why?" Paul Harris's fixed grin had disappeared.

"What have you done?" his wife asked, releasing Oliver from his cuddle and giving him one of her scary glares.

Oliver would have much preferred it if Storm had not felt the need to share this information with his parents just yet. There was no denying the fact that they were going to have to find out about his antics one day, but he was hoping to avoid it, at least for today. He said simply, "I'll explain later."

"You will not!" his mum said. "If you have been in trouble with the police, then I want to know all about it, and I want to know right now!"

"I think," said Uncle Raj, stepping between Oliver and his mum, "that it's going to take a bit of explaining. We must bear in mind that the police are not 'Snow White' innocent in this either. They have also been in trouble with Oliver and Storm."

To Oliver's relief, that comment caused enough confusion to create an interlude before any more questions were fired about his recent conduct. He was especially keen to avoid, by any means necessary, having to explain the unbearably embarrassing part where his parents discovered that he had been headline news and had tried to elope to Gretna Green.

"So the question is," began Uncle Raj, "how do we get you two" – he pointed to Megan and Paul – "to reappear without causing any suspicion about where you have been, and avoid the world finding out that you have actually only been missing for ten minutes and have been hiding in a time machine under April Cottage."

Oliver's mum pouted and shook her head.

"It's not a time machine!" said his dad defensively. "It's a particle acceleration chamber."

"Yes," said Uncle Raj. "The machine that you hid inside, which moved you forward in time quicker than everybody else in the world."

Oliver's dad nodded. "I did it, didn't I?" His expression of exhilaration returned.

"You more than did it," said Storm. "You did it with bells on."

"I did." Oliver's dad smiled while patting the particle accelerator fondly. Still grinning, he turned to Oliver and ruffled his hair, making his already bad hair day even worse.

"We need a cover story," Uncle Raj reminded everyone.

"How about . . ." said Storm, who was good at telling stories, "we wait until dark, drop you off in the Astills's corn field, get some rope, flatten some corn, and make a crop circle, so it looks like a flying saucer shape has landed there, and pretend you have been returned to earth by a UFO?" Her eyes were alight. "Don't you think that that's a fab idea?" she asked with so much enthusiasm she was practically buzzing.

"No!" said Oliver without any hesitation. "That's just stupid."

"I really think it would work," said Storm earnestly.

Everyone else in the room gave Storm a discerning look.

"If that worked," said Oliver, "which it wouldn't in a million years, then think of the press, think of all the attention that would be on Mum and Dad. They would never be left alone. They would either be carted off to be studied in Area 51, or taken away by men in white suits – and I don't mean forensics experts; I mean psychiatric nurses."

"It was just a thought." Storm sounded perturbed. "Do you have a better idea?"

This conversation seemed to focus everyone in the room. The truth was, even though Oliver was relieved that his parents were home again, the reality was that they faced an extremely complex situation that if dealt with in the wrong way could result in the secrets within the lab being discovered.

"Tell me about the police," said Oliver's mum. "Why were they looking for you?"

She had clearly been dwelling on this thought and was not prepared to put it aside, even for the time being.

"They were looking for us looking for you," said Storm.

"But don't worry," said Oliver. "They didn't catch us." He paused, then added, "We caught one of them!"

"What?" asked Oliver's dad, almost choking at the words Oliver had spat out.

"Graeme O'Sullivan," said Oliver. "A good friend of yours, is he?"

"He is, actually."

"Wrong answer!"

Oliver's dad looked confused.

"He kidnapped me!"

"And me!" said Storm.

Oliver's mum was struggling. "Since you left for school this morning, you've been kidnapped. In the past half hour?" She clapped her hand to her mouth.

"Well, actually, we were kidnapped once and then almost kidnapped again," said Oliver, "and that was yesterday, but that's beside the point."

His shook her head in despair. Uncle Raj nodded his.

"Hang on a minute," said Paul Harris. "Can you just explain what you meant when you said, 'We've caught one of them'?"

Oliver very briefly related what had happened, and added, "As far as I know, he should still be there." He looked at Uncle Raj and asked, "Should we let him go now?"

"What?" cried Storm, not giving Uncle Raj a chance to respond. "Are you are actually suggesting that we go back to that place?"

"I think I am," said Oliver.

"Actually," said Uncle Raj, "I think that we all should."

"What if he's not there anymore?" asked Oliver.

"I've got a hunch that says that he will be. I don't think that many people will be out looking for him. I'm guessing that most of his friends will be in hiding, or in a police cell, and his mobile is out of use, so he can't call Mrs Jones for a lift home."

"Mrs Jones?" asked Storm.

"Oh yes," Oliver had forgotten that Storm had slept through the big revelation of the night before. "Sarah Sidmouth announced last night that Mrs Jones is going to marry the DCI."

"What?" asked Storm. "*Our* Mrs Jones, the head teacher?"

"Our *old* head teacher," said Oliver.

"Traitor!"

"That's exactly what I said."

"Who's Sarah Sidmouth anyway?" asked Storm.

"You really were out of it last night, weren't you?" said Oliver.

She shrugged.

"She was the woman acting as the family liaison person, instead of the DCI."

"Oh," said Storm, "but why should *we* bother going back for him?" After the events of the previous day, Oliver thought Storm's apprehension was understandable. "What good could it do?"

"It's called 'just deserts'!" said Uncle Raj smugly.

"How do you figure that out?" asked Oliver.

"Well, technically," Uncle Raj begun, "the DCI has committed kidnap, but, to be practical, we can't report him to the police without framing you two."

"Yep!" Oliver nodded.

"So in order for him to get his comeuppance," continued Uncle Raj, smiling, "then he needs to be framed for a different kidnap."

"I'm sorry," said Oliver's dad, "but I'm really not following."

"Don't worry," said Oliver, "I think I am." He looked at his uncle. "If you're thinking what I'm thinking, then I'm in."

"I think I know what you're both thinking," said Storm, "and even though the whole thing is nuttier than a fruit cake and the barmiest thing that I have ever heard, it's a great idea."

Oliver's parents looked baffled.

"All you'll have to do is stay still," Oliver explained, "we'll tie you up, and you blame it all on DCI O'Sullivan."

Oliver's father looked uncomfortable. "And frame an innocent man?"

"He's not innocent!" Oliver pulled at the neck of his T-shirt showing his dad the bruises on his shoulder that this man had inflicted on him only yesterday.

His mum gasped and went a little queasy. Storm led her to a chair.

The bruises and the words of Oliver, Storm, and Uncle Raj were enough to convince Oliver's dad that his supposed friend deserved all that was coming to him.

"He was the weakest link in your tight chain of security," Uncle Raj added.

"I'm sorry that I've put you all through so much," Paul Harris said. "It sounds as if you've all had such an awful time, all because I trusted Graeme O'Sullivan."

"I trusted him too," said Oliver, sensing how guilty his dad was feeling. "I even told him that we'd been to Yorkshire to Vincent Quark's labs."

"What?" His dad's voice was loud and quivering. His eyes were wide as he asked Oliver, "What do you know about Vincent Quark?"

"Just that he's a nasty piece of work. But don't worry, we had his labs raided."

Paul Harris's face was now dark crimson. "You had his labs raided!" He was shouting. "Where is he now?"

"We don't know the answer to that one," said Uncle Raj. "We certainly knew where he was yesterday."

"Yeah!" Storm agreed.

Oliver's dad steadied himself on the bench behind him.

"What about Silas Tudor?" Oliver asked. "Did he come here to the house?"

"How do you know about Silas Tudor?" his dad bellowed.

"Was Henry at the house when he came?"

"Did you meet him too?"

Oliver nodded.

"Has he been back to the house?" his dad asked, his eyes darting frantically.

"Not as far as we know," Uncle Raj explained. "We saw him in London. He must have been following us."

"London?" Oliver's mum looked up from her chair. "Have you been to London?"

Storm took hold of Megan Harris's hand as she tried to calm her.

"What did he say?" asked Oliver's dad. "What did he tell you?"

"Tell me about what?" asked Oliver, suddenly suspicious.

"He came to the house making demands, dishing out threats, insisting that I share some of my findings with him. I sent him away with a flea in his ear, and I'm afraid that Henry did see him, and he saw us arguing."

"How suspicious!" said Oliver, raising an eyebrow.

"Suspicious indeed," said his dad, gazing admiringly at his son, who had not only found out that Quark was one of his enemies, but had also figured out the password that would lead Oliver to him. "So that's how you knew where the Yorkshire labs were?"

"Yes. So why did you have the job advert password-protected?"

"It's because I have been keeping an eye on them. That's what the DCI has been helping me with. He suggested I record all I can about the labs. That's why I kept it. I was offered a whole load of money to go and run the labs in Puddingdale. I placed the documents under password protection, as I didn't want any of it associated with me. I wasn't interested."

He paused, then took a deep breath and continued, "Until recently, I had no idea where Tudor was, he's only reappeared these last few months. It was because of Tudor that I brought the DCI in to help me. I filled him in on what was going on. At which point, Tudor must have paid him off."

"That would explain a thing or two," said Oliver. "But what about Quark?"

"He seems to have rekindled a relationship with Tudor and they are in it together. So Quark hasn't been arrested, you say?"

"No, but Elwood has been."

"Good," replied Oliver's dad. "One down," he muttered under his breath. "But the raid? What did you tell the police?"

"The police don't know it was us that reported the hostages. The call was anonymous, from a payphone, and Uncle Raj's accent could never be traced back to him."

"I made the gunshot noise," said Storm, smiling.

Oliver's mum began making noises that sounded as if she might hyperventilate. Storm rummaged around the room, then passed her a paper bag and continued to listen.

Oliver's dad now had to sit down too. He was still clinging on tightly to his laptop. "Hostages! What hostages?" He took a deep breath. "I think that these last ten minutes have been the longest of my life!"

Oliver's mum continued breathing into the bag.

"So, were you kidnapped?" Oliver's dad asked.

"We were the first time, by DCI O'Sullivan, but not the second time by Vincent Quark. He threatened he was going to, but left when he saw Uncle Raj."

Oliver's dad scratched his head in much the same way as Oliver did when he was trying to figure out something extremely confusing. "So tell me again, why were you kidnapped by the DCI?"

Uncle Raj stepped in and took over; "The DCI knew that Oliver and Storm knew too much. I suppose he wanted to keep them quiet. That's why he arranged for a secret meeting with them at the old rec. He was covering his own back."

Oliver's dad continued to remould the shape of his hair, scratching it frantically. His hairstyle now matched his son's perfectly.

"The truth is," said Uncle Raj, "the DCI thought that Oliver and Storm would lead him to you. It seems that pretty much everyone has been desperate to find you since a week last Friday."

"What day is it?" asked Oliver's mum.

"Thursday," said Storm. She patted Oliver's mum on her head, then leaned over to give her a cuddle. "So, do you think you can be good victims?"

Oliver's dad shrugged, then added, "What the hell . . ."

"Good boy!" said Storm.

"What about Henry?" said Oliver's mum, picking her head up from between her knees. "Where's Henry?"

"He's with Uncle Will," said Oliver. "Probably heading back to Nan's house this morning."

"Nan's house? Nan's in Holland."

"She is as far as you're concerned," said Oliver. "Actually, she got back a week last Saturday."

"Where does Nan think you have been?"

"She has no idea. She knew that we were in Cornwall yesterday."

"Cornwall?" Oliver's mum took a huge deep breath into the paper bag.

"Don't worry. We're the only ones who know anything about what's really going on."

"Oooohh!" Oliver's mum sighed deeply then placed her head back between her knees.

His dad spoke up. "How did you know about Tudor, Quark, and Elwood?"

"The message."

"You found the message?" his dad gasped. "*Which* message?"

"The video message," said Oliver, confused. "Why, how many messages were there?"

Oliver's dad did not answer that. Instead, he said, "I knew that you'd find them one day. I wasn't expecting it to be just yet though."

"What? You must have suspected something. You knew that people were looking for you, didn't you?"

"I did." His father shook his head, then turned to Storm and Uncle Raj and said, "Thank you both for helping Oliver."

"I just helped my godson when he asked," said Uncle Raj. "Even though I gave him a bit of a hand, he would have found you without me."

"I was coerced into helping," Storm said. "I think it's what you call emotional blackmail. But" – she paused and looked across at Oliver and then his parents – "despite the fact that in less than two weeks, or in your case ten minutes, I've been run over by a van, thrown out of a moving train, forced to sleep in a badger hole, pursued by the mafia, on the front page of the newspapers, *and* kidnapped . . . I wouldn't change a thing."

Oliver's parents looked horrified.

"Don't worry," said Storm, "I've been sworn to secrecy about this place, and I've had the most exciting few days of my life."

Oliver grimaced. Storm had just opened another very large can of worms that he was going to have to start explaining.

"Actually," said Storm, "I *would* change one thing."

"What?" asked Oliver's mum, sitting bolt upright in her chair and still gripping her paper bag.

"I'd change the reaction I am going to face from my mum when we go back home again. She's been acting ever so strange since I hit the black van and eloped to Scotland."

Oliver almost choked. He turned the same red as his father had been several minutes earlier.

His parents' eyes opened as wide as saucers.

"Let's just say," said Oliver, interrupting before Storm dug an even deeper hole for him, "that we will need a good couple of days to fill you in on what we have all gone through to find you."

"It's not over yet," Uncle Raj reminded everyone. "We need to get you to Chepstow, and that's assuming that the DCI is still there."

"I can't see him going anywhere else," said Oliver.

"It *would* be nice to see him again!" said Storm with an evil smile.

"Where is he?" asked Oliver's dad.

"In a deserted warehouse," Uncle Raj explained. "Still dangling!"

"What?"

"On an engine hook, above a pitchfork!" said Storm, rubbing her hands together.

"I think I've heard about all I can take!" Oliver's dad exclaimed.

Megan Harris took another long breath into the paper bag.

"Let's just get this over with," said Oliver.

Storm led Oliver's mum by the arm, while Uncle Raj followed them. Oliver went with his dad into the security room, where Paul Harris placed his old, Dell laptop on the desk. Alongside the sleek and shiny security equipment, it looked about ten years out of place with its metal frame and rubber corners.

"Why did you take that with you?" asked Oliver. It was the first chance he had had to talk to his dad alone. It was a moment he had yearned for constantly over the past two weeks.

"Because . . ." He stopped and looked at Oliver. When he spoke again, Oliver knew he was changing the subject completely. "I can't imagine what would have happened if you hadn't found us. We could have been in there for a very long time."

"I can't believe you were in there without me knowing. I've spent a long time in the labs trying to get to the bottom of who had kidnapped you."

"That's why we hid. I too thought that we may have been kidnapped."

"By Quark?" asked Oliver.

His dad shook his head. "No, not Quark!" His euphoria seemed to have long faded and was now replaced by a sombre look of concern.

"But you're safe now," Oliver reassured him.

"All except for the kidnap!"

"That's just a formality. What I can't believe is that you appear to have found a way to slow time."

"Maybe," said Oliver's dad. He was clearly distracted, looking at his laptop. He dragged a heavy metal desk away from the wall to reveal a safe that Oliver had not known existed. Sinking to his knees, he looked into its recognition pad to let it scan his face, then it opened.

He said, "It's the small observations around the science that lead to the big breakthroughs." He carefully placed the laptop inside.

Oliver stared at the safe, confused. "It's no wonder they were on to you, Dad. I bet every government in the world would want to know how you did that."

"Perhaps! But that's not what they were after." His dad locked the safe and pushed the desk back against the wall.

"Well, what were they after?"

"That's another story for another day."

They left the security room together, walked across the gantry, and emerged back in the kitchen through the larder door.

Just Deserts

Five people in an Aston Martin was not going to happen, so Uncle Raj backed Megan Harris's Mini Cooper as close to the front door as possible.

"Paul and Megan," he whispered, "you'll have to hide in the back."

"Whatever you say, boss," said Oliver's dad, lowering himself behind the driver's seat.

"But isn't it going to be suspicious if we go in Mum's car?" asked Oliver.

"Not really," said Uncle Raj. "If anyone asks, I'll explain that I was taking you and Storm on another one of your wild goose chases, and it was a lot safer to have a car with seat belts for the both of you. I can't see anyone objecting. Can you?"

It seemed reasonable enough.

Uncle Raj returned from the garage carrying a box of tools.

"What are they for?" Oliver's mum asked as she too lowered herself into the back seat.

"It's always best to be prepared." Uncle Raj winked at Oliver.

Their exit from Ebbwvenny went reasonably smoothly. Storm travelled in the front of the car with Uncle Raj, leaving Oliver sitting in the back with his parents either side of him. They may have been crouched down in the footwells with jackets over their heads, but it did not stop him feeling very, very happy. The journey was filled with question upon question. The cover story was finalised and, most importantly, plans were made about what they would do when they arrived at the warehouse in Chepstow.

"So how are we supposed to have got to this warehouse the first time?" asked Oliver's dad as his head popped out from under the layers of coats.

"OK," said Oliver, "you tell them you were home on the Friday morning, you were in the kitchen drinking tea, and then you heard someone coming into the house."

"Was I there too?" asked his mum, sounding a little muffled under the coats.

"Both of you were. Plus, don't forget to mention that you saw a black Transit van parked on the lane when you came back from dropping me and Henry."

"Did I see it too?" asked his mum.

"Yes," said Storm. "And tell them that you both thought you saw black vans following your cars you when you were driving back home."

"So did somebody knock the door?" asked Oliver's dad.

"No," said Oliver. "They are not the type to knock on the door. They crept up to the house, and there was a huge explosion that disorientated you. That's when they grabbed you both from behind. That would be the stun grenade."

Storm took over. "Someone threw a sack that smelt of petrol and oil over your heads, and then tied you up with ropes so tight that you couldn't breathe. You screamed and shouted, but nobody could hear you, then you were dragged across the ground and thrown into the back of a van which was so hot you thought that you would surely suffocate. The next thing you knew, you were in the warehouse."

"That sounds too severe," said Oliver's mum from under her pile of coats, raising her head slightly. "Nobody would believe that."

"That's what he did to us!" said Oliver.

"You poor, poor things," she said, squeezing Oliver's leg.

"That traitor!" said Oliver's dad. "I hope he gets what's coming to him!"

"He will," said Uncle Raj. "But only if this plan of ours goes without a hitch."

"So all of the time I trusted the DCI, he was working for Tudor?" said Oliver's dad angrily. "Surely he wouldn't be rich enough to fund an operation like this one. So Tudor is more than likely working for a Russian billionaire?"

"Ubinon Folovich, owner of Hotel Dubois," said Oliver.

"You really have been doing your homework," his dad said, squeezing Oliver's other leg.

"We'll be there soon," said Uncle Raj. "Everyone stick to the plan."

The car swerved and meandered along the country lanes until it eventually stopped.

Uncle Raj was first to step out. "Let's see if he's still there."

A low, pitiful moan emanated from the underside of the warehouse door. Then they heard a weak and pathetic voice say, "Help!"

Storm was first to wade in, as soon as they had opened the door.

"Ha!" she called out. The DCI was exactly where they had left him.

"Let me down from here," he whimpered.

"You are in no position to be dishing out orders," yelled Storm.

Oliver joined her, and they stood and watched the DCI hanging vulnerably over the pitchfork.

"We've brought your friend," said Storm.

"Who?"

"Someone who once trusted you," said Oliver. Despite the fact that he felt sorry for his prisoner, there was no forgiving the fact that this man had clearly betrayed his family.

Oliver's dad appeared from the doorway.

"Paul!" said the DCI, sounding relieved. "I can explain everything."

"You have deceived me, betrayed me, and kidnapped my son."

"No! The kids . . . They've got it all wrong!"

"They've got it wrong all right!" said Uncle Raj, who had also stepped inside the warehouse. "They got it wrong when they trusted you!"

"Paul, please!" begged the DCI.

Oliver's dad shook his head.

"Let me down!" The DCI looked terrified and exhausted.

"Of course we'll let you down," said Uncle Raj. "But that isn't going to happen yet."

"Stop whining!" Storm barked. "Its pathetic hearing a grown man whine so much." She added, "Missing Mrs Jones, are you?"

"What?" squeaked the DCI, his voice hoarse.

"Was she in on it too?" asked Oliver.

"Just get me down from here, she has nothing to do with this. You've got it all wrong."

"First things first," said Uncle Raj. "We would like to show our appreciation for all the things you have done."

The DCI began to wriggle. Storm grabbed the pitchfork and jabbed it randomly in the air. "First, *coming* down!" she seethed. "Then *going* down!"

"Positions!" said Uncle Raj.

Oliver's mum appeared and climbed into the old metal chest. Her husband followed her. They both stood so that Uncle Raj could bind their arms together behind their backs with some old wires from the toolbox in the car. They stooped into the chest, allowing Uncle Raj to cover them with the same piece of sacking that the DCI had used to bind Storm and Oliver. He closed the lid and secured the chest with a chain.

The DCI watched. "What's going on?"

"It's something to remind you," said Oliver, "that sometimes it's better to do the right thing and stand by your friends."

The DCI might have been about to plead for his release, but Storm stepped closer with the pitchfork. He said nothing.

"I hope that you like prison food," Storm sneered. "You'll be very sorry you ever messed with us!"

Oliver stared at her in disbelief but did not stop her. The way they had been treated by this man was still fresh in both of their minds. Even though Oliver no longer felt as angry and his rage had subsided, the bruises still hurt. Storm, on the other hand, was still basking in it and enjoying every minute. Oliver disliked this man enough to allow her to continue.

"Get me down from here!" yelled the DCI.

"All in good time!" cried Storm. "All in good time!"

"Are you all right in there?" asked Oliver, stepping closer to the metal chest.

"Fine!" came a muffled reply from his dad. "Just hurry up, will you!"

In accordance with their plans, Uncle Raj left the warehouse, holding his mobile phone. Storm jabbed and snarled, and Oliver watched.

Within minutes, Uncle Raj reappeared. He began to unwrap the rope that had been securely tied onto a hinge that took the weight of the hook. Slowly and carefully, he lowered it. The DCI began to descend, arms and legs flapping in all directions.

"Can I do that?" asked Oliver.

Uncle Raj handed him the chain. Storm remained next to the DCI, still snarling and still jabbing towards him with the pitchfork.

Bit by bit, Oliver lowered the chain until their captive hung barely a metre from the ground.

"Drop him!" yelled Storm. "You've been kind enough!"

As she spoke, Oliver turned and the chain slipped. Unintentionally, he did just what Storm had requested. With a thud, the DCI hit the concrete head first.

"Aaaarrgh!" he yelled.

Uncle Raj grabbed the still-bound DCI with both hands. The policeman did not resist. The fall had weakened him and would, Oliver thought, result in a very severe headache. The DCI had become far more compliant, and Uncle Raj hoisted him off the ground and sat him on top of the metal chest.

DCI O'Sullivan did not speak. He only smiled vacantly, with the same expression Oliver had seen on comic-book characters with stars and rabbits whizzing in circles above their heads.

"This is going to be easier than I thought," said Uncle Raj.

Oliver, who felt amazingly calm, continued with the plan. He went to help his uncle.

The DCI began grinning at Oliver, making him feel mightily uncomfortable. "Is he all right?" Oliver asked.

"He will be," said Uncle Raj. "Concussion, I think, or rapid change in blood pressure. He's been hanging upside down for a long time."

"He hasn't been the right way up," snarled Storm, "ever since he thought he could mess with people's lives and get away with it!"

Olive imagined stars continuing to twinkle above the DCI's head, and their plan proceeded.

Uncle Raj nodded towards the door. Oliver and Storm knew this was their cue to leave. "They're on their way," he told them.

Oliver was reluctant to leave his parents with their mad prisoner, but Storm handed him the pitchfork and made her way out of the warehouse. Oliver watched his uncle untie the knot binding the DCI's hands, and then he too downed the weapon and followed Storm. They quickly got into the car and waited for Uncle Raj.

He appeared soon after and, wasting not a single moment, they drove off down the track as fast as the car would allow.

"What did you do with him?" Oliver asked.

"Nothing!" explained Uncle Raj. "He was happy to sit on the metal chest. I just left him there."

Oliver felt increasingly anxious.

"He was so confused," explained Uncle Raj, "I just closed the door tight. I'm pretty confident he won't be able to find his way out. In fact, in the state he's in, I don't think he could find his way out of a paper bag."

"But what about Mum and Dad? Are they safe in there?"

"I don't think he even knows where he is, let alone anybody else. He certainly won't be able to unlock the chest."

"How long will it be until the police arrive?" asked Oliver.

"The average time for a police car to respond to an emergency," said Uncle Raj, "is fifteen minutes."

Both Oliver and Storm ducked down in the back of the car, just in case.

"When you phoned," Storm asked, "what did you tell them?"

"I didn't phone them," said Uncle Raj. "I was afraid they would trace the call back to me, so instead I sent them a text."

"A text?" asked Oliver. "Which phone did you use?" He was worried the phone would automatically be traced.

"Phone number four."

"But you only have three," said Storm.

"I got a new one. It's not registered to me, so there's no tracing it back to us."

"What did you say in the text?" asked Oliver.

"DCI Graeme O'Sullivan holding hostages Paul and Megan Harris Unit 4, Sunnyvale Industrial Park, Chepstow."

"I didn't know that you could text 999," said Storm.

"Only if your phone is registered to someone with speech problems," explained Uncle Raj.

"So how did *you* do that?" asked Oliver.

"It just so happens—"

"You know someone?"

Uncle Raj nodded. "I asked a friend. I met them last night when you were asleep."

"Ben?" Storm asked.

"He knows how it all works." Uncle Raj smiled.

Sirens could be heard in the distance. Oliver and Storm both stooped in the car, but they were still able to see blue lights flashing as a convoy of police vehicles headed in the opposite direction.

"Told you," said Uncle Raj. "Let's get you two delivered back home."

"I wish we could have stayed and watched," said Storm.

"Too risky!" said Oliver.

After a while, Storm nodded. "Where shall I tell my mum we've been this time?" she asked.

"I really don't know," said Oliver. "I'm running out of excuses."

"Let's make it believable, shall we?" said Uncle Raj.

"How about Alton Towers?" suggested Storm.

"As if!" said Oliver. "Remember, I'm still mortally upset and searching desperately for my parents. I'm hardly likely to take a jolly to the theme park."

"Hmm," said Uncle Raj.

"How about just driving around," said Oliver, "looking for them?"

"Is that believable?" asked Storm.

"*I'd* believe you," said Uncle Raj.

"Let's just go back to my nan's house," said Oliver. "We'll explain how I couldn't sleep, so we went out for a ride in the car, but decided to come back home again."

On their return, explanations were complicated. This time Oliver allowed any wrath directed at him to sail over his head before drifting up into the clouds and floating away. All he could do was sit and wait.

Mrs Minton was still there, but increasingly anxious to return home. "We've imposed for long enough," she told Oliver's nan.

Sarah Sidmouth had returned. Oliver thought that might have been because DCI O'Sullivan had not turned up to work again. She sat on the sofa, frowning at him.

Oliver frowned back. Her mobile rang and she left the room.

"But we can't go," Storm was saying. She had been involved in the quest of finding Oliver's parents for almost as long as Oliver. She desperately wanted to stay, to be there, and to know how it all ended.

Sarah Sidmouth returned to the room. "There has been a further development," she explained. "I don't want to build your hopes up too much, but the police have received information this morning that sounds promising. There are officers searching for your parents right now."

"Please," said Storm. "My friend needs me," she told her mum. "Leaving him now would be like a captain deserting his ship, a centurion turning his back on his men—"

"All right!" said Mrs Minton. "We'll stay a bit longer, as long as you promise not to do another vanishing act."

"Cross my heart and hope to die," said Storm. Oliver knew very well that a vanishing act was not on her agenda today.

Everybody sat waiting. Oliver, Storm, and Uncle Raj knew that they were waiting for the police to turn up with Megan and Paul Harris. Nan, Mrs Minton, and Sarah Sidmouth also sat waiting, but they were not as sure what they were waiting for.

"You must stay here now," insisted Sarah Sidmouth as time ticked on. "You give your families a fright every time you go out and don't tell them where you are going."

"That is true," said Storm. "You don't know who you might bump into, and you don't know who you can trust. It's funny—" Storm stopped herself before she asked the liaison officer whether she had heard from the DCI.

However, after a while she could not help but ask, "You still here then?"

"That's not very polite," said her mum, frowning.

"No!" said Storm. "Sorry!" Then even though she tried not to, she asked, "Where is DCI O'Sullivan?"

Nan replied first. "He's a very busy man."

"Yes," said Oliver. "He's probably tied up on another case."

Storm sniggered and Oliver smirked.

The front door opened.

"Oliver!" sang a very friendly and extremely enthusiastic little voice. It was Henry, closely followed by Uncle Will and Winston.

"I've been on a sleepover!" Henry announced. "And so has Winston!" Winston meandered around everybody in the lounge, sniffing for the ones with biscuits.

Oliver smiled. He was very pleased to see his little brother, and Winston too.

"Winston slept with me," said Henry. "And Uncle Will came too."

Uncle Will stared blankly at Uncle Raj. "Yes!" he said. "We were so late coming home from our long, long walk last night that we couldn't wake everyone else up. We went back to *my* house."

"Winston was feeling sad after Auntie Karen told him off!" announced Henry. "That's why he had to sleep in my bed!"

"What did he do this time?" asked Oliver.

"He only brought her a present from the garden last night."

"What was it?"

"A Mickey Mouse!" Henry giggled. "But Auntie Karen was so sad, she jumped up and down and shouted lots!"

"But you're back now," said Oliver. "How about that game of football?"

"Really?" said Henry, his face lighting up with joy. "You've got time to play football with me?"

Oliver felt mightily guilty for breaking his promise and not giving his brother the attention he needed. Deep down, he knew that the ends justified the means and the biggest gifts he could give his brother right now might be on their way home.

"I want to be goalie!" said Henry.

"Anything you want," said Oliver, leading his brother out into the back garden.

"Can I trust you not to leave the garden?" shouted Nan.

"You come with us if you want," said Oliver.

Nan declined, but Storm accepted. So did Sarah Sidmouth, obviously not trusting their word. Probably rightly so, thought Oliver.

He gave his brother a pat on the head and a reassuring smile. "It's all going to be all right," he said.

Nan and Mrs Minton regularly came outside to check on them, but each time they brought supplies: cold drinks and food. The sun shone and the day was bright. Oliver knew that the day was brighter than any other day before, and it was not just because the sun was shining.

The morning drifted into afternoon and soon inside the house came the sound of a commotion that required inspection. Raised voices, doors opening, general confusion, and then, as Oliver walked back into the lounge, he saw his mum and his dad waiting to greet him.

"Mummy! Daddy!" squealed Henry at the top of his voice. Taking off from the kitchen like a jet fighter, he ran to them both and held them as tight as his little arms allowed, tears pouring down his cheeks and his sobs of joy filling the entire house.

Oliver was a little more reserved, but still he was very pleased to see them. He joined in the hug, closely followed by Storm, Nan, Uncle Will, Uncle Raj, and even Mrs Minton. It did not come to an end until Winston joined in, as he decided to greet everyone with a great big sloppy kiss.

In the hallway behind Oliver's mum and dad were PC Sharp and WPC Hughes, as well as several officers who all smiled to see the family reunited.

The next few hours at Nan's were not dissimilar to the occasion when Storm and Oliver were returned by the police after their first trip to Yorkshire. Chaos and relief reigned. There were medical officers, detectives, explanations, and even more explanations.

Fortunately, this time the press had not been allowed into the house. Oliver assumed that this was because the police did not want a story that the whole reason behind the disappearance might be a corrupt DCI.

People arrived and people left, but Oliver had his feet firmly on the ground and his eyes firmly on his parents.

"So what happened?" Uncle Will asked Paul.

"Well, Will," Oliver's dad began to explain. "It all happened while I was drinking tea last Friday morning. There was a loud noise, then the next thing I knew, Megan and I were being hurtled out of the house and into a van. We were taken to an old warehouse, and left there. Occasionally, we were brought some food and water, but from what I gather we were taken hostage."

Gasps echoed from all over the room. Oliver looked over at his dad. He looked comfortable with the storytelling. His mum joined in too.

"One night," she explained, "it was cold and dark and . . ."

Oliver smiled. He knew how wonderful his mum's stories were, and how she revelled in an audience. But Oliver did not need to listen; he felt as though he was the boy at the end of the story who got everything he could ever wish for. He had his mum and dad home again, and his life back to normal, just the way it should be.

Oliver left them to it and found a quiet space in the kitchen where he could be alone with Storm.

"Thank you," he said.

"You're welcome."

"No, you have been a really wonderful friend." Oliver did not know where this emotion was coming from, but he instinctively, unintentionally, hugged her. No sooner had he done it than he quickly withdrew his arms and turned a shade of scarlet.

"Really," he said, "you have been the best friend anyone could ever have. I can't thank you enough."

"Oh yes you can!" said Storm, grinning. "I'll make you a list."

Oliver grinned, knowing that this was not a threat but a promise.

"We make a good team," he said.

"I knew we'd find them. I didn't doubt you for a minute."

Oliver's smile changed to a snigger. "Yeah, right."

He left the kitchen and went in search of someone else he needed to speak to.

Uncle Raj was deeply engrossed in a conversation with PC Sharp. "Have you got a minute?" Oliver asked.

"What's up?" asked Uncle Raj as he and Oliver walked out into the hallway.

"Absolutely nothing!" said Oliver, grinning from ear to ear. "I just wanted to say thank you."

"There's no need. I was merely doing what any godfather would do for their godson, or a friend would do for their friend."

"But you didn't have to do anything, and you did."

"Do you know, Oliver, I feel that I have learned a thing or two about my godson over the past few weeks. Especially what a remarkable young man he has turned out to be."

"Hey," said Oliver, "I just want you to know I'm sorry I ever doubted you, and I will never do that again."

"You had every reason to doubt me. But don't worry, I would help you all over again."

"Even eat the snails?" asked Oliver with a grin, but squirming at the thought of it.

"Now that could be the test of our friendship," smirked Uncle Raj, ruffling Oliver's hair. "Oh yes, you know that friend of mine who works in Scotland Yard?"

"Ben?"

"Yes. I spoke to him on the phone a little earlier, and he told me that they have made six arrests from the siege last night."

"Really?" asked Oliver, keen to hear the fate of his enemies.

"Possession of illegal firearms, and possession of unlicensed human tissue. They were wanted by Revenue and Customs for importation of illegal machinery. *And* two of them were wanted by MI5 for terrorist activity, namely falsifying entry into the government's central research laboratories in London."

"That's great! They'll get their just deserts too, without implicating any of us in the process."

"That's the top and bottom of it."

Oliver gave a sigh of relief. "And the DCI?"

"Well, we won't be seeing him for quite a while either," explained Uncle Raj. "They always throw the book at corrupt policemen. He will not be getting married this winter, that's for sure. *Ten years* next winter, that's a possibility."

"Anything on Quark?"

"No one seems to have anything to say about Vincent Quark. *But,* it looks like the labs in Puddingdale were on the property of Silas Tudor. They'll probably want to lie low for a while. I expect Folovich will help keep them both safe for now. In any case, they won't be in a state to come after your father's work for a good while."

"It all seems to have worked out, doesn't it?"

"Seems that way," smiled Uncle Raj. "Now you make sure you keep in touch, and answer your e-mails!"

"Scout's honour," replied Oliver, saluting with his three fingers.

"Come and stay for a weekend," said Uncle Raj. "You could even bring Storm if you want to."

"Only if you take us to the zoo."

"No chance!" said Uncle Raj, grinning from ear to ear.

"Oliver!" came a voice from the living room. "Come on!" said his mum. "We're going home."

Those very words sang like nightingales in Oliver's head, causing a very dazed but contented smile to spread across his face.

Goodbyes were said, including an extra-special goodbye to Nan and Uncle Will. Then there was a drive in the back of a police van. Oliver, his mum, dad, brother, and Winston were on their way to April Cottage.

This time, walking through the front door truly felt to Oliver like returning home. The sun beamed in and bathed each room with light, and the fact that the Harris family were back where they belonged filled the house with warmth and contentment.

If Oliver had learnt anything over the past few weeks, it was to value his friends and family and not take them for granted. The truth was, he had learnt far more than that, like how to be a detective, how to spot a corrupt DCI, how to become a compulsive liar, how to get his best friend in big trouble, and how to catch an escaped meerkat. Not to mention how time travel is possible in a basement.

Within no time, the police officers had left and suitcases were loaded into Paul Harris's Land Rover. Oliver and Henry were directed into the back seats.

"So?" asked Oliver. "Where are we going?"

"You should know better than to ask that," said his mum.

"Go on," Oliver pleaded. "Give me a clue."

"Well," said his dad. "You are so good at solving mysteries recently, let's try another one. It's south of Mexico, but north of Argentina."

"Ah," said Oliver, geography not being his strongest point. He stepped into the car and smiled. He really did not care *where* he was going. What he cared about was who he was going *with*.

"So what about Winston?" he asked, concerned that he would have to go and stay in the dreaded kennels.

"Don't worry," said his dad. "Your Uncle Will has become very fond of Winston recently and has offered to look after him."

Oliver grinned, wishing he could be a fly on the wall when his uncle broke the news to Auntie Karen.

Almost on cue, Nan's car drove up, with Uncle Will in tow. "We wanted to wave you off on your adventures," said Nan, stepping out of her car. "Make sure you all stay out of mischief!"

Winston saw Uncle Will and headed straight for him, greeting him with much enthusiasm. They had certainly formed a tight bond recently, thought Oliver.

"Have a wonderful time!" cried Nan.

"Be good!" shouted Uncle Will as they stood waving goodbye.

Paul Harris's Land Rover, packed to capacity, hurtled down the driveway. Oliver was first to start the chorus of "Summer Holiday", and did not stop singing all the way to the airport.

Note from the author

I really hope you enjoyed this story. Oliver's and Storm's adventures don't stop here.

Keep your eyes on <u>www.OliverandtheMissingScientist.co.uk</u>

for information about their next adventure.